IT WAS MADNESS...

It was madness of the worst kind because of its facade of logic. It was the worst kind because its creators were as brilliant as they were ruthless. For five years they had taken step after logical step on their way to an act of supreme madness.

They were a force to be feared more than any other because their power came from within the White House itself. And it had the backing of powerful forces within the government's most secret agencies.

Now two people—a desperate man and a re-markable girl—dare to challenge the madness... and stop it before it boldly and lethally destroys the man who holds the highest office of all.

Also by Tedd Thomey

THE BIG LOVE

Published by
WARNER BOOKS

THE PRODIGY PLOT

Tedd Thomey

WARNER BOOKS

A Warner Communications Company

To R.R.,
for his many contributions to this work.

WARNER BOOKS EDITION

Cover design by Peter Thorpe

Warner Books, Inc.
666 Fifth Avenue
New York, N.Y. 10103

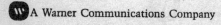 A Warner Communications Company

Printed in the United States of America

First Printing: September, 1987

10 9 8 7 6 5 4 3 2 1

REO (Rawhide's Eyes Only)
Alert Memo No. CL-1
To: Rawhide, White House
From: Saddlebag One
Subject: *Prodigy*

From time to time, incredible subjects arrive on your desk. So this one should not surprise you or seem impossible to accept.

The subject is a young person with rare political/economic/military acumen and intuition. We have been testing her informally for about five weeks. During that time, we asked her hundreds of questions involving obscure but important governmental decisions far beyond the interest or intelligence of most university graduates, even those with doctorates.

I will not bore you with all the details. Instead I will offer you one example of her ability, an example demonstrating that her skills on occasion are superior to those of the most experienced presidential advisers.

Our experts asked: "The year is 1955. Can you devise a plan for the most efficient overseas locations for six hundred of the air force's strategic bombers?"

Her reply: "You have asked the wrong question. You have not factored the vulnerability of overseas bases into your thinking. The correct question is: 'Should the six hundred strategic bombers be based overseas?' The answer is no. The majority of those bombers should be based in the United States where they will be safer from enemy attack, can be maintained better at a lower cost and serve as a war deterrent. They can be refueled in mid-air to reach long-range targets."

The subject is a child who is *thirteen years old*. In recent years, our experts have put that question to hundreds of men and women who applied to the Defense Department for top-grade advisory positions. She is the only one who told us—correctly—that our

1

question was wrong. She was the only one who knew the correct answer, which was worked out years ago by the Rand Corp. of California.

I recommend that steps be taken to add the subject—code name Chicken Little—to your senior staff. For obvious reasons, information about her must be restricted to three or perhaps four of the most devoted members of your White House inner circle.

Very critical point: Chicken Little is scrupulously honest and trustworthy. She can be a tremendous alternative to the intelligence recommendations and planning of the CIA and National Security Agency, both of which often have strong (and sometimes devious) political motives behind their recommendations.

It is essential that you have REO input from a source far outside the normal governmental channels. I hardly need remind you that faulty recommendations from the CIA, NSA, and FBI led in the past to our disgraceful embarrassments in Iran, Lebanon, Vietnam, and elsewhere.

More recently, the CIA itself has been rocked by numerous spy scandals, accusations, and defections involving China, Taiwan, and of course the Soviets. Corruption and scandal have even spread to the heretofore immaculate FBI.

Unfortunately, our arrangements with Chicken Little must be informal, as I will explain in a future memorandum.

REO (Rawhide's Eyes Only)
Alert Memo No. CL-2
To: Rawhide, White House
From: Saddlebag One
Subject: *Prodigy*

I see by the speed of your reply and your questions that you recognize the possibilities—and the problems. The disadvantages are many but are greatly outweighed by the advantages.

The thirteen-year-old girl is Ginger Ingrid Johnssen, nickname Gin, code name *Chicken Little*. Born in California, she is of Danish heritage. She graduated from high school at age twelve. She has been raised by two aunts, both of whom will be security risks but controllable.

Chicken Little uses Radio Shack computer systems for her rather remarkable research into civilian and government data banks. We intend to equip her with a much larger, updated communications laboratory.

Unfortunately, Chicken Little is a sensitive child who cannot perform under pressure. She will not be able to work directly or indirectly with any members of your staff other than myself.

It will be necessary for her to work in her laboratory at home, as she has always done, under the continued guardianship of her aunts. Surveillance will be 100 percent but must be indirect.

In answer to your question, Chicken Little has an astounding ability to analyze vast data bank quantities of political/intelligence/military/economic info and arrive at recommendations that are uniquely effective. We believe this is because as an individual she doesn't suffer from the "committee mentality" or the sanitized "group think" rationality, which so often dilute the recommendations of your usual sources.

You should be delighted by the length of her REOs. They will be the way you like them—short and precise.

We have given her the code name *Chicken Little* because of her age and because many of her REOs must necessarily be from an abrasive devil's advocate viewpoint, warning of troubles ahead, e.g., the sky may fall.

Transmission: We will not risk sending Chicken Little's REOs to you via the normal White House

4 / Tedd Thomey

communication systems, where leaks have occurred in the past. Her REOs will be delivered by supersonic jet couriers.

We learned about Chicken Little in a routine letter from one of her aunts, Mrs. Pamela Astrid Johnssen, who lives in San Cristo, not far from your ranch in Santa Barbara County.

Mrs. Johnssen makes the usual claim of being the friend of a dear friend of yours, in this case one Reggie Ronson.

It was because of her proximity to your ranch that Mrs. Johnssen decided to write to us about her niece.

Naturally, the CIA is investigating to determine if it is merely coincidence that Mrs. Johnssen lives so close to the ranch.

P.S. Please give my fondest regards to Rainbow and tell her we are pleased that she likes our new code name for the First Lady.

☆ ☆ 1 ☆ ☆

To White House insiders, the most fascinating aspect of the presidential crisis was the way the rest of the world overlooked the role of Gin Johnssen.

Her full name was Ginger Ingrid Johnssen. Her code name was Chicken Little.

When the crisis erupted, she had been a presidential adviser for four years.

On the first day, the papers said the murdered man was an El Dorado Park employee, a sprinkler installer.

The day after that, the TV guys said he was a horse trainer.

Then the L.A. *Times* said no, he was a Chinese cook from Taiwan.

But the scat didn't hit the fan until Wednesday when the Santa Barbara paper ran his picture and said he was a CIA guy just in from Nicaragua. And that he'd been found dead near the president's mountaintop ranch.

All those CIA references were a crock.

Rick Moore had better facts. He knew who the dead man was.

Rick also knew the killing was connected with TimTomTon.

TimTomTon is a secret outfit funded by the CIA. It does the same kind of spook work as the CIA but operates separately.

Some say TimTomTon is bigger than the CIA.

On the tube the next night, Dan Rather said it was a big story that was going to get bigger. That was because the murdered man was a Russian who had facial surgery that turned him into a Chinese.

The next day the *Daily News* said it was the other way around. Still harping on the CIA theme, the *News* said the CIA guy had surgery that turned him from a Chinese into a duplicate of Errol Flynn.

The newspapers and TV never did get it straightened out. They never did dig out the fact that much of what happened was a TimTomTon plot created by the U.S. government.

And they missed completely the pivotal role of Gin Johnssen, the president's youthful adviser.

Rick knew part of the truth. That was because he was there in Santa Barbara County's El Dorado Park when the man was killed.

Rick Moore was a thirty-one-year-old loser who, up until that spring, hadn't done much with his life. He was formerly a park employee and half-assed university naturalist. But he lost those jobs when his whole life began to change so drastically.

He loved El Dorado Park. He particularly loved the park early in the morning when all was quiet. That was when dew sparkled on the huge yellow-green catalpa leaves and made the spiderwebs look like elegant chains of tiny diamonds.

So he was deep in his earthen foxhole observation post that morning in May when Gin came jogging by. He'd been absent since March, and during those two months a lot of things in the park had changed.

But Gin's bare legs were just as lovely and enticing as ever when she came jogging by on the path she always took.

She was only seventeen years old, a little more than half Rick's age. Sometimes she looked even younger. Other times there was something about her that made her seem very mature.

Her mass of hair was brass on gold. She was the most

beautiful young woman Rick had ever seen—and he was a connoisseur of beautiful young women.

As Gin's running shoes went tap-tap on the firm clay surface overhead, Rick looked up through one of his observation ports and admired her thighs.

Gin wore pale pink shorts. Very loose. Very short. He glimpsed a lovely shadow.

Then she was gone. Rick sighed and returned to his task of taking notes on the new fox family that had moved in during his eight-week absence.

Over by the base of the biggest catalpa tree, the male fox heard Gin's footsteps and retreated into his earthen den.

In his small notebook, Rick marked down the time: 7:24 A.M. Instead of writing in the usual data, *male fox, gold & red,* he wrote: *pussy, blond, maybe.*

A little naturalist humor there, to give horny Dr. Porterfield a chuckle when and if he read Rick's report. There was a possibility, very slight, that the zoology professor might give Rick back his job at U.C. Santa Barbara.

Rick also jotted down an authentic observation, *sct. rd. myro,* which referred to the fresh scat outside the fox's burrow. The scat was flecked with bits of red because the male had been eating small cherry plums from a myrobalan tree.

A few minutes later, Rick heard Gin scream.

He scrambled up from the deep hole and ran. Never before had he heard anybody scream in such a way.

He found her a couple of hundred yards on the other side of the pond. She was standing on the bridle path near the tall alders and a smaller myrobalan.

Her head was bowed. She covered her face with her hands and wept hysterically, a reaction to what she'd discovered near the path.

Then Rick saw the dead man. At first, just his shiny, black shoes, sticking out from under the myrobalan tree with its purplish leaves and small cherry plums.

Then he saw part of the man's dark blue business suit.

Rick stepped closer and looked at the victim's face. With the greatest shock, he realized he'd met this man only a few days previously.

The man was Chinese. He had a depression in his head the size of a small avocado. It was in the left temple area and the skull looked broken. A lot of blood had oozed out, but now the flow had stopped.

Grazing in the tall grass nearby was a big, beautiful horse.

The horse had no rider.

Rick had seen that grayish white horse once before.

You don't forget a horse like that. Not when the man who usually rides it is the president of the United States.

REO: No. 14
To: Rawhide, White House
From: Chicken Little
Subject: *Andropov*

I regret to state that it is necessary for the U.S. to take the unusual step of joining with the Soviet KGB to cleanse Yury Andropov of guilt.

Andropov headed the KGB when the shooting of Pope John Paul II was planned.

Now that Andropov is the all-powerful leader of the USSR, the United States must use *misinformation* techniques to convince the world that Andropov had nothing to do with the attempt on the pope's life.

If we cannot cleanse Andropov of guilt, public outrage will become so great that it will be almost impossible for America to deal with the Kremlin in any normal way.

☆ ☆ 2 ☆ ☆

It was Aunt Louise who told Rick that Gin was the president's illegitimate daughter.

She mentioned it casually—a little too casually—the first time they met.

The conversation with Aunt Louise occurred in March— two months before the man was slain in El Dorado Park.

That death was the first of a series of murders that occurred near the president's ranch.

Rick met Aunt Louise unexpectedly on the morning that he finally made his move. His big move to get acquainted with Gin. The move that got him involved with Gin's family and did a number on his whole goddamned life. All he wanted was a chance to talk to Gin for a few minutes.

Instead he was stalked by her goddamned Aunt Louise, a strikingly beautiful older woman who fed him all that scat about Gin being the president's daughter out of wedlock.

What a crock.

Aunt Louise had such a straightforward way of talking that at first Rick believed her. It took him part of a week to catch on.

Rick Moore was tall (six feet three) and athletic, with a mass of dark curly hair. If his nose had been a quarter inch shorter, he would have been considered handsome.

He was so stubbornly independent that at times he seemed not too bright. But he wasn't the only one taken in by Aunt Louise's tricks.

Later, after that first meeting with Aunt Louise, he found out from Gin that Aunt Louise was a masterful liar. Since her early childhood, Aunt Louise had been able to tell lies

that were marvels of interwoven logic. Very complicated.
Very realistic.

Aunt Louise was a pathological liar who sometimes told
lies for no purpose other than the joy of being creative.

She'd made a fortune in Santa Barbara real estate. When
Rick got to know the family better, it became obvious that
Louise lied to make many of her real estate deals.

When Rick thought back, he realized it was unusual for
Gin to tell him the truth about her Aunt Louise.

"She's got this little twist," Gin said one day, tapping her
temple. "Up here. For years, she went to an analyst...."

Gin didn't like to talk about herself or her aunts—she had
two of them—and never mentioned anyone else in her
family, such as her father or mother.

After Rick got to know Gin a little better, he decided his
interest in her was far more than lust for her beautiful body.
He decided she was the woman for him, the one woman for
whom he was willing to change his whole life.

Eventually he acquired a few more facts about her. Her
name was Ginger Ingrid Johnssen. Her family had come
originally from Scandinavia, and that explained her fair skin
and blondness.

Her other aunt, Pam, was also a Johnssen. Aunt Pam was
older than Aunt Louise.

Aunt Louise had been married so many times she had a
flock of names. The name she usually used on legal documents was Clara Louise Remington.

The family setup was peculiar. Gin lived with her two
aunts alternately. The aunts lived in side-by-side houses.
One month, Gin lived in Aunt Louise's house. And the next
month she lived in Aunt Pam's house.

Getting acquainted with Gin was one of the most delicate
maneuvers Rick had ever tried to pull off. It was like trying
to catch a butterfly in your hands without breaking its wings.

For weeks, Gin kept avoiding him when she jogged in the
park. She usually jogged very early in the morning, which
was when Rick was down in his foxhole, making his daily
observations.

Whenever he came up from his foxhole, she changed

direction and ran off. She wouldn't look at him or talk to him.

So one morning, hoping to talk with her, he followed her home from the park. It was just a simple decision, made on the spur of the moment. Much later, trying to analyze how he became involved in the series of murders, he asked himself this question: "Would I have followed Gin home that morning if I knew all the agony that was in store for the two of us?"

The answer was always yes.

A man meets a woman like Gin only once in a lifetime. And Rick was glad he didn't blow his one chance.

After they left the park, Gin jogged for awhile on the street leading into her neighborhood. Then she slowed to a walk.

Wearing a grimy gray sweatshirt and wornout Adidas, Rick walked fairly close behind her.

God, the view was beautiful from back there.

Today she wore yellow shorts. They were a warm yellow, almost hot, a different yellow from her abundant hair, which was a mixture of brass and gold. Sometimes she wore pink or lavender shorts, or pale green ones that reminded him of camellia leaves.

All were very short. All fit the same way.

He had always been an ass man. And he was turned on by Gin's to a degree he'd never felt before.

There was nothing deliberate about the way Gin walked. She was just walking in the natural way that she always walked.

Sex was written all over that walk. Wanton sex. But when, much later, Rick finally had the opportunity to look into her eyes—dark brown with incredible gold flecks—he knew at once that she was a virgin.

She knew he was walking right behind her, but she wasn't thinking sexy. When he got to know her better, he discovered with the greatest disappointment that sex was very low on her list of priorities. And she had more priorities in her busy life than any seventeen-year-old should ever have.

After he learned how old she was, he continued to think of her as a woman. A fully mature, absolutely enchanting woman with the equally enchanting qualities and vulnerabilities of a teenager.

Those contrasting qualities didn't clash. They complemented each other. For example, can a woman who wears braces on her teeth be considered sexy? Absolutely, but only if she's as gorgeous as Gin. Gin wore a whole set, uppers and lowers, a mouth full of what looked like polished silver. Of course, Rick didn't know about the braces that morning when he followed her along Arroyo Drive. Much later, as they finally started to get acquainted, he was in for shock after shock and surprise after surprise.

Gin's house was about three blocks from El Dorado Park and less than a mile from the president's ranch. As she and Rick walked along, they passed rows of California rancho homes surrounded by tall eucalyptus trees that gave off a sharp medicinal smell. Half the time they walked in warmish shade. The rest of the time they walked in soft morning sunlight that would have let him shoot her at f-8 or f-11 if he'd had his Konica along.

When they turned onto Rosebay, her street, a car passed them. It moved very slowly. Rick was aware of it but ignored it. He kept his eyes focused on that lovely photo target just ahead.

Less than a minute passed. And then the damnedest thing happened. A strange woman appeared out of nowhere. She ran up to Rick and began blistering his ears with language he hadn't heard since he was a photog in the marines.

The woman had been driving the car that passed them. Now the car—a silver Porsche—was parked awkwardly where she'd abandoned it. It was partway up a nearby driveway beside one of the rancho homes. The driver's door was open and the idling engine was wasting a lot of heavy power.

The woman shrieked at Rick: "You son of a bitch!"

That was the mildest thing she said. Finally she stopped cursing and began demanding answers.

"How dare you follow my niece? We don't need any goddamn sex maniacs around here!"

That was Rick's introduction to Aunt Louise.

3 ☆ ☆

☆ ☆

Rick's first glimpse that morning of Aunt Louise was quick, about one-sixtieth-of-a-second shutter speed.

He saw that except for being taller and much older (probably in her forties) she was almost a carbon copy of Gin. She was just as golden blonde, fair-skinned, and gorgeous, and she was built just as sexy.

Then his vision was blotted out. Before he could duck, Aunt Louise whipped off her hat and raked him across the face with its brim.

It was a wide-brimmed hat, the same shade of warm yellow as Gin's shorts. It was made of some kind of hard, finely woven straw—and it all but took his head off.

She was strong. She swung the hat as she would a baseball bat or a tennis racket. The sharp edge of the brim cut his eyelid.

Blood dripped down into his eye, blinding him and making him feel like a fool. It had been years since he'd been hurt physically by a woman.

With his good eye, he saw the flash of yellow continue in a big sweeping motion. She put the hat back on her head. Somehow, despite her anger, she positioned it exactly as before. It was a very sophisticated hat, the kind models wear at such a smart angle in high fashion magazines.

The blow knocked the sense out of him. For a few moments, he forgot completely about Gin. He stood there like an imbecile, wiping his eye and listening while Aunt Louise raved on, accusing him of being a pervert, and worse.

When she hesitated, trying to think up additional accusations, Rick angrily blasted her back, his voice more forceful and commanding than hers.

"And you, madam, are a crock of scat."

That got her. For a moment, she was perplexed by the word. Then she made an interpretation, and her face turned red.

"Yes, ma'am," he added politely. "We're talking shit here. Fox shit."

He expected more anger, but she was a woman with varied emotional resources. Like an expensive transmission changing gears, she went effortlessly from rage to something surprisingly like respect.

"I see," she said quietly.

He didn't know what she meant. But she made it very clear that her opinion of him was undergoing a drastic change. She looked him up and down, from the filthy toes of his Adidas to his curly black hair.

Then she walked over to the Porsche and shut off its engine. She reached in for its keys and slammed the door shut.

Then she came closer to Rick than before and spoke to him in a pleasant, inviting tone.

"Do you have a minute? I'd like to talk to you. . . ."

She gestured toward the house beside the Porsche, indicating he should follow her.

He looked around for Gin and saw she had disappeared.

He had no interest in Aunt Louise, or what she wanted to talk about. But what the hell. Talking to her might be the way to get introduced to her beautiful niece.

It was a large redwood mansion, with overhanging ranch-style eaves. When they entered the foyer, Aunt Louise locked the front door and took off her broad-brimmed yellow hat.

Then, using only one hand, she took off one of her long, dangling earrings. It was made of polished mahogany in a triangular shape.

She took the earring off slowly, her cold blue eyes looking straight into Rick's, her fingers moving seductively. Her forefinger stuck straight up, giving him a message he could understand even with one eye bleeding.

He wiped his eyelid with the back of his hand and saw

less blood on it. It didn't feel like much of a cut after all.

"My office is upstairs," she said. "This way."

As she started up the steps, she beckoned for him to follow. He noticed that she had a compact, well-shaped ass. By no means as beautiful as Gin's. But for an older woman it was a very sexy ass.

At the top of the steps, a hallway led to several doors, two of which were open. One was an office. The other was a bedroom.

Aunt Louise chose the bedroom. Rick expected it.

"Come on in," she said, "and I'll show you how Ginger got to be the president's illegitimate daughter."

She closed the door behind them, but didn't latch it. Turning around, she moved in close and touched his sleeve.

Then she began to caress the cloth.

"I love your sweatshirt," she said.

Obviously, she was lying. His tattered gray sweat suit hadn't been laundered for weeks. It was old and stinking. It smelled of ripe sweat and ground-in dirt from his foxhole in the park.

That didn't stop her from putting her arms around his waist and drawing him closer.

Then she reached up and stroked the stubble on his jaw. She wasn't turned off by the fact that he needed a shave.

Nothing turned her off. He hadn't washed his face that morning. Nor had he brushed his teeth or combed his hair.

She reached higher and plucked something from his black curls. A leaf fragment. He wasn't surprised. His hair was always picking up sand and trash from the roof and sides of his foxhole.

She dropped the fragment on the floor. Then she smiled at him. It wasn't a warm smile because, as he eventually learned, she was incapable of genuine warmth.

Eventually he also learned that she was a classically selfish woman who would do anything and hurt anyone to get what she wanted.

She removed her arms from around his waist and walked farther into the room.

Looking around, Rick saw it was decorated entirely in yellow. When she tossed her broad-brimmed hat onto the silky bedspread, it almost vanished because both were the same shade of yellow.

They were interrupted by the sound of wheels cracking twigs on the driveway outside. Aunt Louise beckoned for Rick to follow her to the nearest window.

Standing close together, they looked down at a charcoal-colored Cadillac that had just arrived on the driveway. It was a double driveway that also served the redwood house next door. The Cadillac was new and shiny. A middle-aged man got out.

He had an air of knowing exactly what he was about to do. He wore a silk executive suit of cobalt blue and a black snap-brim hat. Attached to his wrist by a small steel chain was a heavy black leather briefcase.

"The president's courier," said Aunt Louise. She pressed her shoulder against Rick so hard that despite the thickness of his sweatshirt he could feel the heat of her upper arm.

He also got a stronger whiff of her scent. Her perfume was good stuff and very sexy.

Suddenly her hand touched his chin, turning his face so he was forced to look into her eyes. She was annoyed.

"You should be *very* impressed," she said in that sophisticated way of hers. "I'm not talking about the president of a soup company. I'm talking about *the* White House."

Rick didn't try to conceal his skepticism. Instantly, her annoyance became open irritation.

Her fingers held his chin more tightly. Her ice blue eyes glared into his.

"I handle very high-level matters for the president," she said. "I am very close to him. Now watch what happens down there."

She took her hand away. As they looked down at the courier, she put her arm around Rick's waist and drew him close.

"At times," she added, "I am even *this* close to the president."

It was such an obvious lie that Rick started to laugh.

"Silence!" She hissed angrily. "Don't let the courier hear us. He'll only stay a minute. . . ."

Briskly, the courier walked to the smaller door at the side

of the double garage. He placed a blue plastic card, similar to a credit card, in the slot beside the door.

The door opened. He retrieved his card and went in.

From their vantage point one story up, Rick and Aunt Louise could see into the garage through a long, triangular upper window. Rick saw the courier spin the dials of a bright metal combination lock and open the briefcase that was chained to his wrist.

Then Gin came into view. Rick saw her slip a small white envelope into the briefcase.

It was the shiny chain on the briefcase that for a moment made the scene seem legitimate. Maybe Aunt Louise was telling the truth. Maybe the man really was some kind of a government agent who had to be locked to his briefcase.

Aunt Louise disrupted Rick's thoughts by pressing the side of her face affectionately against his chest.

The courier relocked the briefcase. Reaching inside his coat pocket, he brought forth another white envelope. He handed it to Gin. Then he left the garage and got into the Cadillac.

As the charcoal car backed down the driveway, glistening in the bright sunlight, Aunt Louise suddenly turned away from the window.

"Believe it or not," she said. "I *am* the president's close friend. And sometimes much, *much* more. . . ."

There was now such a note of seductiveness in her voice that Rick shook his head slowly with disbelief. She was implying that she was involved in presidential hanky-panky.

Trying to make her story believable, she added details. "I *am* a presidential assistant. Very hush hush." She placed her forefinger, with its orange-painted nail, vertically across her lips. "I go on *secret* missions. I go where I must go, even to the boudoir when required . . ."

She paused, then lifted her head back and laughed so heartily that deep lines appeared along both sides of her red mouth. Her laugh was a little too hearty.

"But not necessarily," she added, "into the president's boudoir—"

Suddenly she grabbed the drawstring on Rick's grimy gray sweatpants. With a fast reflex, he stepped back. Her hand followed, tugging at the cord, trying to unfasten the knot.

Having seen Gin again, Rick knew he didn't want to do what Aunt Louise so obviously wanted to do. Gin was the one he wanted. No matter how gorgeous Aunt Louise was, she wasn't Gin. Now that he'd had a closer look at Aunt Louise, he could tell she was at least fourteen or fifteen years older than him. That made her about forty-five.

A few days later, thinking back to Louise's extraordinary behavior, he decided her sexual fantasies were the most incredible he'd ever encountered.

But the guy chained to the briefcase was no fantasy. So maybe there was a small amount of truth after all in her claims about secret missions.

Eventually, he learned with astonishment that she did have a completely legitimate connection with the president. But the rest of her story was a farce.

However, on that morning he first met her there was nothing legitimate about Aunt Louise's advances. She knew what she wanted and didn't care what she had to do to get it.

"You'll like me. . ." she said, but her smile lacked the warmth of her words. "I guarantee it. . . ."

Rick had never liked aggressive women. He much preferred to be the aggressor.

He tried to ease her hand gently away from his sweatpants. It was no go. She closed her fist tightly around the thick cord.

He tried to shove her hand away. Still no go. She held that string in a death grip while her hard blue eyes looked up at him with the most intense desire he'd ever seen.

To get free, he had to swat her wrist. Damn hard. Too hard. He overdid it.

Shaking her reddening wrist, Aunt Louise cried out in pain, anger, and frustration.

Right then and there, Rick got his first important lesson from her. He learned that a man who inflicts pain on Aunt Louise and then, even worse, continues to scorn her, will almost immediately lose all that he holds dearest in life.

She cursed Rick in anger that was terrible to hear. And then she called her goddamned dog.

"Rowdy!" she yelled.

At first nothing happened. So she called the dog's name a lot louder.

Suddenly Rick heard heavy paws scratching hard for a foothold on the polished hardwood floor down below. Then he heard heavy paws pounding a mile a minute up the stairway. And then this ton of mean-as-hell German shepherd banged through the bedroom's unlatched door.

"Kill!" screamed Aunt Louise.

The events which followed were so improbable—but so real—that for a time Rick almost believed he was being set up by a government spy who used a goddamned dog to achieve her goals.

The growling son of a bitch laid back his black lips and grabbed Rick's crotch with teeth that seemed two inches long.

"Freeze!" yelled Louise.

The dog was talented and well-trained. He froze on command. A little more pressure from those jaws and Rick would have been minus his masculinity forever.

For a long moment, the dog didn't move a muscle or a nerve. Nor did Rick. All Rick could see was the white of a crazed eye, full of murder, plus part of a long snout. The rest of the black snout was buried in Rick's crotch.

The pain went beyond anything Rick had ever felt. The German shepherd kept growling in a deep and threatening way. The vibrations from his throat shook Rick's crotch to the bone.

Finally Aunt Louise spoke.

"Release" she said in a matter-of-fact voice. She spoke as if the subject under consideration were of no more consequence than asking the dog to sit up and beg for a cookie.

The big jaws opened and let Rick go.

"Back," said Aunt Louise.

The gray-and-black animal backed up one step and stopped growling. He looked at Rick with great regret.

"Well?" asked Aunt Louise.

Rick touched his crotch as gently as he could. His fingers explored all the vital tender parts.

"Well?" Now she was getting impatient.

His exploration continued. Everything seemed intact. But the ache in his left ball was so great it reached his toes.

Aunt Louise went over to the bed. Rick followed. The dog watched.

There was only one way to find out if his parts were still working. And besides he had no choice. If he didn't do it, the goddamned dog would see to it that he never did it again.

For an older woman, she wasn't bad. In fact, she was damned good. But, of course, she was such a welcome change from the dog's jaws that Rick realized his judgment was probably impaired.

REO: No. 20
To: Rawhide, White House
From: Chicken Little
Subject: *Falklands War*

Sir, I failed badly by *not* filing an REO warning you that Argentina intended to invade the Falkland Islands.

When I decoded the CIA report stating that this bloody and unnecessary invasion was imminent, I assumed you already had the information. I didn't dream that you hadn't read the CIA warning—and thus were unable to act.

If Argentina had known you opposed the invasion, it would never have gone to war against Great Britain.

Henceforth I will file my REOs even when they duplicate CIA reports.

I was unaware that you do not always read the CIA alert memos.

I am very pleased that you feel it necessary to read all my REOs.

☆ ☆ 4 ☆ ☆

While down in his foxhole the next morning around seven fifteen, Rick observed the man who later turned out to be the Sandinista government's top spook in the U.S.

But at the time Rick didn't know it.

Rick's foxhole was a rectangular excavation near the park's northern boundary. It was about seven feet deep and just wide enough for him to move around comfortably without bumping into his two old cameras.

The foxhole's roof was constructed of sweet-smelling new redwood planks concealed under gray earth from which grew small fruitless blackberry plants. The roof was slightly elevated to give him observation ports on all four sides and also vertically.

Using the forward port, he was up on the foxhole's top dirt step observing the vixen identified in his notes as Mrs. F. She was a gray fox, but in name only. Her plush fur was mostly golden with touches of white. No gray. She was a young mother. Usually Mrs. F was followed by Little Otis, the most rambunctious member of her family, plus his orange-colored sister and his little brother whose fur was brick red. Mrs. F's long bushy tail was their favorite plaything.

This morning, however, Mrs. F was by herself, lying in a patch of warm sunlight. She was near a sluggish stream that was only five feet from Rick's forward port.

A brown dove cooed lazily nearby, and the morning breeze tickled the shiny new red leaves of the eugenias. As they flickered in the sunlight, the leaves performed a trick,

21

changing hues from red to brassy gold, and then immediately back again to red.

Rick reflected, as he did almost every day, that he had the best part-time job in town. He was paid to stay outdoors in the clear smogless air and observe nature at her very best. He hoped his prof, Dr. Porterfield, never found out that if Rick had to, he would pay the professor to let him work in the place he loved the most.

As Rick kept the fox under observation, his eye picked up the distant bridle path where equestrians often rode. It was there, a few months previously, that he'd seen the rarest incident of all.

That was the only time the president had ridden into the park from his nearby ranch, accompanied by equestrian friends. The president's horse was a handsome grayish white animal, and the president sat easily in the saddle.

At this time of year, the stream was warmish and almost clear. On its surface floated tiny dandelion seeds carried there by their silvery umbrellas. Under the water, along the edges of the stream, were streaks of undulating brown algae attached to the triangular stems of sedge. Darting here and there were tiny Gambusia fish, searching briskly for their breakfast of mosquito larvae.

Mama fox rose leisurely to her feet. She stretched and yawned. She moved closer to the stream. This time she didn't drink. Instead she turned slowly around and with delicate movements dipped the white tip of her long tail into the water.

Like those of all the park's foxes, her golden tail was remarkably long and full, as long as the rest of her body.

It was an exciting moment and quite rare. Rick had never seen a fox deflea itself. Conditions had to be perfect for both the fox and the observer. He held his breath and tried not to make a sound. He adjusted the tripod very slightly on his no. 2 camera, the ancient Canon with the silent shutter.

The morning light wasn't too bad. If he was lucky and got a photo of Mrs. F unloading her fleas, he might get a bonus from Dr. Porterfield. Rick had never witnessed such a scene and doubted if Dr. Porterfield had ever seen one either.

It was then that Rick noticed the peculiar, man-shaped shadow that had no business being there. It was on the ground beside the biggest eugenia tree. The shadow was on the other side of the stream, maybe twenty-five feet from Rick's forward port.

Rick didn't move. And the shadow didn't move.

Carefully bracing her rear quarters on the grassy bank of the stream, Mrs. F put more of her tail into the water. She was in no hurry.

Rick had been working in that particular foxhole every morning for much of two weeks. He knew the shape of every tree, every shrub, every blade of grass, and every patch of humus visible from all five of his ports. He was certain this particular shadow had never been there previously.

Who the hell else had a reason for squatting amid the eugenias at this early hour of the day? Another naturalist watching Mrs. F? Hardly. A naturalist, amateur, or professional would notify another naturalist before invading his territory. A transient? Maybe. Once in a great while Rick would discover a tramp or a hitchhiker sleeping in the park. But this wasn't a tramp's prostrate, sleeping shadow. This was the shadow of a seated, erect person, and it didn't budge for two ... then three ... then four minutes. ...

Very strange. During that time Rick was equally motionless and silent. He had trained himself to observe from a position that he could hold comfortably for as long as ten minutes, if necessary, or longer.

This shadow seemed to be equally well trained. Was this shadow watching the fox? Or was this shadow watching Rick?

Rick's position enabled him to observe Mrs. F and the shadow simultaneously. Still backing up very slowly and deliberately, Mrs. F had immersed herself in the water up to her underbelly.

She was a particularly lovely animal because her coat was such a shiny pure gold. Where it was wet, her fur had turned to rich brown, but her belly remained mostly white.

Rick couldn't help smiling because she looked like a cartoon. Her position was totally unfoxlike. If she saw her reflection in the water, she would doubtlessly be embarrassed.

Her beautiful head turned lazily. Her dark elliptical eyes looked up at his port. But he was certain she didn't see him.

Now Rick began to move. With such exquisite slowness that he hoped Mrs. F wouldn't be aware that he was lining up the camera on its tripod.

Meanwhile, the shadow still hadn't moved. Very odd.

The time involved had become much too long—perhaps seven minutes. Maybe Rick's suspicions were faulty. Maybe the shadow was simply the result of a branch that had been broken the day before.

Now Mrs. F's body was totally immersed. Slowly she lowered her head into the clear water, covering her eyes, which remained open. Now her pointed black ears and white snout were immersed. Only her black nostrils protruded above the surface.

Rick lined up the shot. He hoped the vixen would remain immersed for a minute or two to get rid of as many fleas as possible.

Very gently he depressed the button. The sound-proofed shutter was almost totally silent.

With her ears under water, there was no way for Mrs. F to be aware of what he had done. But she knew. Instantly, she erupted from the stream. Water exploded everywhere. Droplets came through the port as Rick got off his second shot.

One moment Mrs. F was there. The next second she was gone.

Droplets and fine spray hit his cheek and eye. But he remained motionless. He noticed that the shadow was gone from over by the eugenias. What the hell did that mean?

He continued to watch through the front port. Nothing moved except a glistening droplet of water that deposited a speck of brown algae as it rolled down the back of his hand.

In his journal, he wrote down the time, 7:29 A.M. and v.f., his code for *vixen, fleas*. Later, for Dr. Porterfield's benefit, he would add the animal's Latin designation, *V. fulva*.

Hearing light footsteps overhead, he knew Gin was approaching on the path from his rear. She was right on schedule. Soon she passed directly above his right port.

She was walking, not jogging, because she was on her way to feed the rabbits and was carrying food.

This morning she was wearing iridescent blue shorts, very short. He got his usual glimpse up her bare legs. God, what beauty. God, what a beautiful route up to the Garden of Eden.

Gin knew Rick was down there but gave no sign as she passed.

He watched her walk alongside the stream until she passed from view. Leaving the foxhole, he wriggled through the short tunnel that led to the rear exit. Then he began to walk, following the curving bank of the stream until Gin came back in view.

She was quite far away, kneeling near the wire fence where she liked to leave food for the rabbits. Usually she brought halves of avocado and apple in a small paper bag.

On the previous morning, he'd learned a little about Gin from her Aunt Louise. Gin was extremely shy and so dedicated to her work that she was practically reclusive.

This morning he decided to try a different tactic. Maybe she'd be willing to talk for a moment about the rabbits.

If so, he could give her good advice. She wasn't aware that her pets were in danger. She should leave the food inside the fence instead of outside where the rabbits were vulnerable to the foxes.

Having left the food on the ground, Gin rose, folded the paper bag, and put it in the rear pocket of her shorts.

Then she turned, but she didn't look at Rick. Instead she looked off to the side where a man had just emerged from the trees.

Rick smacked his fist hard against his palm. How about that! By God, he'd been right all along. The son of a bitch had been lurking in the eugenias, spying.

He was a fat man, wearing an army camouflage uniform with a helmet and boots. The irregular blotches of olive green, black, brown, and tan all over his shirt and trousers didn't camouflage the fact that he had a large, overhanging belly.

At first Rick was smart. He stayed back in the shrubs, watching as the fat slob very purposefully approached Gin.

What the hell was he up to?

Rick resented him but had to respect him. The man had shown considerable discipline and skill. For more than ten minutes he'd observed Rick without moving a hair. For your average fat guy, or even your average unfat guy, that kind of discipline was nearly impossible.

At that time, of course, Rick had no way of knowing that the intruder was a spook from Nicaragua, a top operative for the Sandinistas.

Rick also wasn't aware then that much of the time Gin was under surveillance by TimTomTon operatives because of the work she was doing for the president. On that particular morning, however, there was an unavoidable gap in the surveillance, and she was on her own for nearly half an hour.

Rick watched as the fat slob and Gin carried on a brief but intense conversation. Then she shook her head and tried to edge away from the man. Rick moved closer and could see that Gin was badly frightened.

He began to run. He saw the fat slob place a hand on Gin's shoulder, preventing her from escaping.

Rick covered a lot of ground rapidly, but he was still too far away to do Gin any good. The man's hand spun Gin completely around. Then he patted her very familiarly on the ass. She didn't like that at all. She began to struggle. But he held her tightly by the shoulder.

Rick let out a loud yell. "Stop that!"

Trying to run faster, feeling growing rage and frustration, he watched as the fat slob pulled the paper bag from Gin's rear pocket. He unfolded it. He inspected it. Then he folded it flat and put it back in her pocket. His palm stayed in her pocket, touching her ass far longer than necessary.

From that point on, Rick reacted from raw anger instead of intelligence. As he approached them, the fat slob spun Gin around a second time until they were facing each other.

Still grasping her shoulder, he caressed the front of her blouse with his other hand.

Gin screamed and almost wrestled herself free.

Rick bellowed. "Bastard! Get your hands off her!"

Gin shot Rick a grateful glance, but the fat slob didn't even look around.

That made Rick hate his guts all the more. The fat slob had known all along that Rick was there, yet he had the brass to feel her all over. It was almost as if he wanted a witness to see him treat her like some kind of street whore.

After that Rick made mistakes. His first mistake was getting too close to the fat slob. His second mistake was grabbing the collar of the man's camouflage blouse and tying to yank him backward. The man was crafty. He let his considerable weight fall back on Rick.

Rick wasn't ready for that and went badly off balance.

Before Rick could recover, the man made a quick turn. He threw a handful of fine white powder in Rick's eyes. The pain was tremendous.

REO: No. 29
To: Rawhide, White House
From: Chicken Little
Subject: *Vulnerability*

A major study to be released by the Brookings Institution reveals that all-out nuclear war is now more likely because of the vulnerability of the outdated U.S. nuclear communications network.

The $180 billion budget for missiles, planes, bombs, and other nuclear weapons is being wasted for this reason: *The Pentagon hasn't spent the money for communications systems to make the weapons work as intended.*

Most U.S. nuclear communications data is carried on regular commercial phone lines *that can be jammed.*

Such jamming will wipe out U.S. ability to launch

a coordinated retaliatory nuclear strike against the USSR.

☆ ☆ 5 ☆ ☆

Pain and distortions.

Rick is unconscious. But part of his brain insists on parading bits and pieces from his past.

He is not the only one in his family to know pain.

Rick is blind.

But in his mind he can see. Pictures of his past and present life. Some are like Kodachromes in sharp focus. Some are black-and-white negatives, murky and mysterious.

Rick can see himself in a Latin land far away. . . . He is a curly haired, dark-eyed boy who speaks Spanish as well as English. . . . He is oiling the chain of his green bicycle. . . . It is propped up on brown adobe bricks so the rear wheel spins freely. . . . He is turning the pedals . . . making the rear wheel spin faster and faster until the spokes are a blur of bright chromium. . . . The bottom of the oil can makes a pleasant cricket sound—click, click. . . .

In his adult mind Rick senses the danger. He tries to warn the boy not to let his small fingers get too close to the speeding chains. But he fails. The boy catches his little finger between the chain and sprocket. Like a knife, the speeding chain severs the tip of his finger.

Pain. And other memories in clear focus. The boy's mother is a beautiful, brunette French woman living with her husband in Managua. . . . Her name is Janine. . . . Her husband is a gray-haired German man, Gerald Hans Mohr, much older than she. . . . Some say he is a former major in

Hitler's Waffen SS and that he fled Germany in the closing days of the war and went into hiding in Nicaragua.

Two sons are born. . . . The first is Gerald Hans Mohr, Jr., nicknamed Jerry. . . . The second is Richard D. Mohr, nick-named Rick. . . . (Years later, the family name is changed to Moore. . . .)

After the difficult birth of Rick, Janine's health is poor for a very long time. . . . She cannot care for her children and must be hospitalized. . . . Her husband loses his clerical job at the Renault agency in Managua. . . . He is an alcoholic who cannot tolerate poverty. . . . In his misery, he makes a very bad bargain with a conscienceless Nicaraguan businessman. . . .

Did it actually happen? Did Rick's father sell his two small sons for a few cordobas?

Rick knows the answer too well.

New pain. Fire in his eyes.

He can remember the white substance that struck his eyes. . . . But he cannot remember the face of his attacker. . . . There is no Kodachrome or black-and-white negative of the face of the man who threw the white powder. . . .

Rick has cloth wrappings on his eyes. . . . He is in and out of consciousness. . . . Time is a blur. . . .

His mind asks questions that are never answered. "Who was he? Why did he harm me?"

Rick hears medical people talking. Their voices are far away. They say he will regain only part of his vision. They say he will not be able to distinguish colors.

The medical voices imply that he will never again be able to look clearly through the eyepiece of his camera and see the golden foxes of El Dorado Park. He will never achieve his goal of being a Yousuf Karsh or Ansel Adams.

Rick is not a religious man, but he asks for help. *Oh, God, help me. Help me to see again. Help me to find the man who did this to me.*

Much more time passes. His prayers for help are unanswered. He knows this is because he has always been a loser.

He was a loser in Nicaragua when he was taken from his

parents. . . . He was a loser in the U.S. Marine Corps when they kicked him out. . . . He was a loser in marriage when his wife turned out to be a bisexual with unpredictable appetites. . . .

Pain in his eyes. . . . Pain in his memories . . . Then, like the clank of a heavy SLR shutter, he suddenly becomes conscious and aware, to a degree, of where he is.

He realizes he is lying on his back in a queen-sized bed.

The bedsheets have a familiar fragrance . . . a woman's perfume . . . He remembers where he first encountered that sweet, musky fragrance. . . . It's Aunt Louise's fragrance . . . horny Aunt Louise. . . .

Slowly Rick becomes aware that Aunt Louise is in the room with him because he can hear her talking loudly and aggressively nearby.

He also hears a second voice.

Because of the pain, his mind is not working well. . . . Why can't he recognize the second voice? . . . It is a woman's voice . . . whose?

The second woman comes close to the side of his bed and speaks to him.

"Mr. Moore." Her voice is soft and lovely. "Are you awake?"

"Call me Rick," someone replies, and he realizes it's his own voice. But it sounds strange, like an echo trapped deep inside his head. He knows the white powder has affected his eyes, but his hearing as well?

"Oh, thank God!" says the young one. He can hear the rapid intake of her breath. "He's awake!"

Now he can also hear a flurry of activity. People are rustling around in the room.

The young one tells him how glad she is that he's regained consciousness.

A man speaks in a professional tone, probably a doctor. "Very good. Our friend Rick has rejoined the real world. But we mustn't tire him."

"Are you still in great pain?" the young one asks with loving tenderness. "Is there anything we can do for you?"

"Please. . . ." Rick can hardly say the word. His throat is

too dry. Talking makes it hurt, but he must find out if the young one in the room is the person he hopes and prays is here.

"Oh, shit," he says because he's forgotten her name. Stupid. But at least he remembers to apologize. "I meant to say scat," he says.

She forgives him. But the stupidity continues. "Your name," he says finally. "I can't remember—"

"Ginger," she says in that soft and lovely voice. "But please call me Gin."

Gin, of course. How could he ever have forgotten?

"I've been waiting since yesterday," she says, "to thank you for the wonderful thing you did—"

What does she mean? What could he have possibly done to make her sound so grateful?

The pain worsens. He is very tired, and his mind is trying to slip back into the murky black-and-white negatives of unconsciousness. But he wants very much to know what she's grateful for.

She says it again, and this time he understands.

"Thank you," she says, "for saving my life."

It makes no sense. It must be another distortion. Or perhaps it isn't. There is truth here. He is certain this is the first time in his life that he has actually carried on a conversation with Gin.

Other truths: During all those days in the park they hardly spoke. And yet during all those days he was falling in love with her.

Now, for the moment, his thinking processes are clear enough to understand the rest of what Gin is saying. She is telling him a story.

"After the powder hit your eyes," she says, "you were crazy with pain, I knew you couldn't see him at all because your eyes were shut so tight. Yet you managed to put your hands around his throat and fall into the water with him. It was a miracle. . . ." A long pause. She draws in her breath more sharply, a sweet sound. "And that's how you saved my life. When the park ranger came up in his jeep, you still had your hands around the man's throat. . . ."

She continues with her story, saying the investigators decided the powder was designed to kill Rick, not just blind him. It failed because it was partly washed away when he fell into the stream.

Rick tries to turn, hoping to look up at her lovely face. But, of course, he can't see her. Nor can he turn in the bed because he is strapped down.

"Mr. Moore," says the man with the professional voice, "don't try to move. You are tied down to keep you from causing more harm to your eyes."

Aunt Louise tries to butt in. But Rick cuts her off, rudely, and asks Gin to keep talking. Her voice makes him feel warm and pleasant and unafraid of the future.

While he listens to Gin talk about the man he should have killed—and who nearly killed him—another part of Rick's brain is filled with a desire for vengeance. For now, he will let this desire rest. But when the time comes, when his strength returns, he will find the son of a bitch, whoever he is, and do what must be done.

Gin explains that the man who attacked Rick carried forged credentials. His exact motives were unknown, but it was believed he intended to kidnap Gin after killing Rick.

"The powder has not been identified," says Gin. "Only a small amount did the damage. The doctors say that if all of it had stayed in your eyes you would have died in terrible agony."

Her words are filled with tenderness and sympathy. If only he could see her face, he might know if she feels more than pity.

"Your attacker is part of the Nicaragua Connection," says Gin.

Nicaragua Connection. Those words trigger a deep reaction. How could Gin know about Nicaragua? Rick's mind slips away from what Gin is telling him. . . . He is drifting back in time. . . . More memories of his family's pain. . . . Rick's father sells his two small sons to the conscienceless Nicaraguan businessman for an insignificant sum. . . . When he later realizes the enormity of what he has done, their father puts a bullet into his brain but fails to kill himself. . . . He is paralyzed and crippled. . . . From his pain comes determination to undo the wrong he inflicted on his family. . . . At great risk to himself, he comes out of hiding and contacts wealthy, former Nazi relatives in Munich. They send money. . . .

Rick's mother, Janine, has been a charity case in a Catholic hospital, suffering the pain of a near-fatal kidney disease. . . . She is twenty years younger than her husband. . . . Her physical pain is not as great as the pain in her heart from the loss of her children. . . . She will never understand the madness that drove her husband to commit such massive cruelty against her and her children. . . .

One day, a frail old man in a wheelchair is rolled to Janine's bedside in the Sisters of Charity Hospital. . . . He gives her money, a very large sum in American dollars. . . . When she realizes he is Gerald, her husband—punished by God to the extreme—she forgives him. . . .

More images. Details of his boyhood in that hot tropical country with his older brother Jerry . . . the viewfinder of his mind brings it all back. . . .

Fearing arrest by the authorities for child-stealing, the businessman sells Jerry and Rick to a childless couple living in poverty in El Jordon, a village near Managua. . . .

Jerry is two and a half years older than Rick and much wiser. . . . Whenever Rick is sad about the tragedy of their real mother and father, Jerry tells him jokes and funny stories that ease the pain. . . .

"Think of something funny," says Jerry, "especially when things are saddest. Think about a pig that can fly by flapping his eyelashes. . . ."

One day a beautiful woman in an immaculate white uniform comes to their hut in El Jordon. . . . She is their mother, Janine, recovered at last from her illness. She has used some of the money from their father to buy nurse's training at the hospital. . . . She pays a generous sum to their foster parents. . . . Then mother and sons return to Managua to live at the Sisters of Charity Hospital while she completes her training. . . .

"You see," Jerry tells Rick with joy shining in his dark

eyes, "if you can think funny, it's possible for wonderful things to happen. If a pig can fly, a mother may some day find her children. . . ."

Janine teaches her sons English because she intends to take them to America. . . . She does not permit them to speak the French and German they learned previously from her and her husband. They speak only Spanish in school and English at home. . . .

New pain in his eyes. And bad images in the viewfinder.

Where is his brother Jerry now? What happened to Jerry after they grew up in California and their mother became a physician, specializing in children's diseases?

What happened to Jerry after he became a photographer and won a Pulitzer for the *Los Angeles Times*?

What terrible thing happened to their mother after she was awarded the title of California Pediatrician of the Year? Why isn't their mother here with her healing hands?

REO: No. 33
To: Rawhide, White House
From: Chicken Little
Subject: *National Security Council*

Since you first took office two years ago, you have neglected to set down clear guidelines for your National Security staff to follow.

At present, this neglect seems to be only a minor oversight. But it could have crucial significance.

This agency is mushrooming in size. It is my belief that its staff is carrying out bizarre secret operations regarding Iran and Nicaragua.

These people are overzealous in their dedication to the Oval Office.

You must not let them function unchecked.

☆ ☆ 6 ☆ ☆

AUNT LOUISE

I don't care what my sister, Pam, believes. I am the girl's mother.

From the prolonged and insistent way the front door chimes rang, repeating the first notes of "Lara's Theme," I knew Pam was down there and doing her damnedest to come in. And I knew she was drunk on cheap beer.

Drunk or sober, my sister loves to pry. She was dying to come upstairs and see Rick, the young man lying so still in my bed. She knew Gin was up there with me.

I didn't answer her ring. And I gave orders to my household staff that Pam wasn't to be admitted unless I gave permission.

If my sister were to come upstairs, she wouldn't just bother Rick. She would pester the two silent men in dark business suits who were seated patiently on my yellow tapestry love seat waiting to question Rick.

Saddlebag One told me the evening before that the attacker in the park was a threat to Gin. And also to Rawhide.

Saddlebag One tried to minimize what had happened. He refused to admit that Gin's life was in danger. He simply told me that two men would be assigned to protect Gin at all times. And two more would be assigned to watch over Rick.

So, of course, with all that happening it would have been ridiculous to let Pam come upstairs.

My older sister is a blabbermouth and a continual embarrassment to me. For seventeen years she has been telling anyone who will listen that she is the girl's mother.

She always refers to Gin as the baby, even though Gin is seventeen years old. And she goes around telling people the same dreadful story that we've all heard a hundred times:

"Of course, the baby's mine. I gave birth to her at 2:34 in the morning at the Pacific Hospital in Santa Barbara. The doctors nearly lost me . . . and I was so sick afterward that I couldn't nurse her. But she was a healthy baby anyway. And in the afternoon when they brought her in—so I could see her for the first time—they said: 'Look, Pam. Look at your beautiful baby. She's so healthy she's drinking up all the milk in the hospital.' "

The same drivel over and over again. And all lies. My sister Pam is a lying bitch.

Continually, Pam tells lies about me. She gossips about my former husbands. She tells people I had five husbands. Not true.

I had four husbands. Two of them were wonderful naval officers. And all four loved me very much.

Pam claims to have a birth certificate that proves Gin is her daughter. I have seen the so-called document. It is a fraud. Not even a good fraud. It is more of her lies.

I possess the only authentic documentation that will stand up in court. I paid a great sum of money for the birth certificate that proves I am the girl's mother.

I have lawyers on retainer who charged me a fortune to produce the blood test evidence and other legal papers that prove beyond all doubt that I gave birth to this remarkably gifted child.

I try to be a good person. I tell the truth at all times. And I brought my daughter up to always tell the truth.

Of course, sometimes I may tell a fib to keep from hurting someone's feelings.

I always do my best to pay no attention to the fact that my daughter calls me Aunt Louise instead of mother. The poor dear. She is still too young to understand a mother's longings and feelings.

And of course, it is her work for the president that takes

all her time and prevents her from living a normal life and having normal feelings.

If my daughter weren't so occupied with her presidential responsibilities, she would gladly appear in court on my behalf. I know she would gratefully acknowledge the authenticity of the newest evidence. It was produced only two weeks ago by my attorneys.

It proves legally and conclusively that I gave birth to Ginger Ingrid Johnssen seventeen years ago in the bedroom of my very own home. With my good friend, Dr. Malcolm L. McAlice, in attendance.

Today I stood beside my daughter in that very bedroom, sensing her admiration for the way it is decorated in the warm yellows that we both love so much. With a mother's intuition, I also sensed her feelings for the youngish man lying there with the white wrapping around his eyes.

"What do you think, Aunt Louise?" Gin asked with just the slightest tremble in her words. "Will he be able to see again some day?"

"I'm positive of it," I replied, but I really wasn't sure. "He's a very strong man."

His yellow pillow was wet with dark blotches of perspiration. He had lapsed again into unconsciousness. I stroked his hand where it lay on the yellow coverlet. The skin was warm, a good sign.

He wasn't a handsome man because his nose was too long. But there was good strength in his features. He was fairly young, in his midthirties. He had curly black hair and beautiful dark eyes. His complexion, normally ruddy, was now pale and sickly.

"Thank you, Rick," I said. "Thank you a thousand times for saving my daughter's life."

He didn't hear me. I was saddened to see his condition.

Only a few days before, he had been virile and strong. It had been difficult for me to ward off his advances because he was so charming and persuasive. I finally ran him from the house by calling my dog Rowdy.

Seeing this change in Rick was hard to accept. He lay there so blind and weak, all his muscles terribly flaccid, including the one he'd threatened to use on me. I wondered if he would ever be able to use it again.

I kept stroking his hand, hoping the contact would awaken him.

"Stop that," said Gin.

She gave me a sharp glance that I didn't like at all. She took Rick's hand from mine and began stroking it.

"I know what you made him do on Monday." She spoke in almost a whisper so the two men in the dark business suits couldn't overhear. "Couldn't you restrain yourself just once?"

It was very insulting of her to speak to her mother like that. She never spoke to her Aunt Pam like that. She never spoke to anyone else like that.

Why would she continually speak like that to the one person who loved her the most and did the most for her?

She made me so angry I decided not to tell her about the expensive camera I'd bought for Rick. I'd give it to him in good time, to show my appreciation for something he'd done for me. And also to give him encouragement by showing him I believed his vision would improve enough for him to use it.

Gin and I were interrupted by the sound of tires down on the driveway, informing us that the president's courier had returned.

"Oh, dear!" Gin rubbed her nose the way she does whenever she's upset or preoccupied. "I completely forgot to finish the second one on SigInt!" As she hurried from the room, and down the stairs, she called back to me. "Saddlebag One will be terribly upset!"

I went over to the window. Looking down at the driveway, I watched her dash past the black Cadillac and the courier standing beside it. She slipped her coded card into the slot beside the garage's side door, unlocking it.

Going inside, she slammed the door shut behind her. A moment later she passed the garage window en route to her work area, which was hidden from view.

Having been there more than once, I knew her work area consisted of banks of international telecommunication machines, microprocessors, keyboards, a giant monitor screen, several small monitors, and almost enough data processors to equip a laboratory at Cal Tech. She had electronic access to the most minute international historical data, dating from the Dark Ages all the way up to what decisions Rawhide made in the last hour.

Heaven only knew what she did inside there while the courier waited patiently outside. Most of her work was in codes too complicated for her to explain even to her mother.

Because she was still a minor, a guardianship had been established for her, consisting of my sister Pam and me, plus certain White House personnel who operated under many code names. Saddlebag One, an elderly man, was her chief contact.

As one of Gin's guardians, I was given limited access to the least sensitive portions of her work. Even though I provided documentary proof that I was her mother, Saddlebag One kept on referring to me as her aunt.

Even more insulting to me was the fact that Pam was granted guardian status equal to mine, even after I offered proof that she was a drunken blabbermouth.

Saddlebag One arranged for a large mobile laboratory to be connected to the rear of my double garage to accommodate more of Gin's circuitry and data banks. Although I informed them I neither wanted or needed the money, I was paid $5,000 a month, in cash, as rent for the garage and the space occupied by the mobile laboratory.

One day when Gin discovered the amount of the rent I was receiving, she flew into a rage. Usually she was a docile child, not the least bit temperamental.

"No! No!" she shrieked. "I cannot work under such conditions. You must give the money back!"

I didn't believe her. Neither did Saddlebag One. But it was true. For the next six days, not a solitary message was sent from my garage to Rawhide.

I agreed to return all the money, payments that went back for three years. Gin didn't accept my word for it. She insisted that I write the check then and there for the full amount, $180,000, and give it at once to Saddlebag One.

Which I did, of course. And Saddlebag One, the old dear, later tore up my check, as I knew he would.

Gin knew mountains about Star Wars, communication networks, the Afghanistan invasion, and the fact that President Nixon could have prevented the monstrous leap in oil prices if he had heeded the warnings from several senior members of his staff.

But she had no practical sense about her own financial standing or mine. She insisted that the courier hand over an envelope containing a single fifty-dollar bill as payment for each report as she turned it in.

No more. No less.

"If they paid me more," she declared with the quick wisdom of the very young, "they would expect more. And I am doing more now than I really want to."

Thank God no one ever mentioned to her that the government communication equipment in our double garage and the adjacent lab was worth over $1.5 million. If she'd known about that figure, she would have expected me to write a check for it. I could have covered the amount, of course, but I wouldn't have been happy about it.

I don't even want to think about all the other costs involved. Among the most expensive were the flights— sometimes twice daily—by the supersonic courier jets that flew her reports to Washington in less than three hours.

In an emergency, of course, she could transmit almost instantaneously via computer, using a circuit supposedly secure from TimTomTon and CIA snooping. Since the two agencies were capable of many dirty tricks, the president preferred the slower but safer courier routes.

I hardly need explain that the entire White House operation on my property was informal, to say the least. No financial records were kept. No receipts were ever given.

After a while, I turned away from the window because Rick was talking in his sleep again. He muttered something about the Nicaragua Connection.

I went over to the bed and listened. He kept repeating the same two words, *Nicaragua Connection,* the same ones I had heard Gin mention. Quite often when I asked her about her work, she mentioned the Taipei Connection, or the Libyan Connection, or the Lebanon Connection, the Afghanistan Connection or the El Salvador Connection. But never in any specific way. Most of those countries have reasons to hate the U.S. government and its president.

I have my methods. I have my ways of learning things. I am still getting royalties for the electronic grinding tool I invented years ago when I worked for McDonnell Douglas. I know enough about circuitry and telecommunications to get by. Shortly after Gin's equipment was put in, I ran a simple lead to my desk in the library. All I had to do was open the second drawer in my desk. The small screen there let me see part of whatever Gin was currently working on.

Of course, I couldn't fool Saddlebag One, the old dear. He let me do the interception for forty-eight hours. Then he ordered the technicians to black me out, permanently.

He put his warning to me in the most courteous way: "Mrs. Remington, if you ever do that again, you will suffer what is known in computerese as a glitch. You will be glitched into a little grease spot on the floor, and your loving family will step on you every day."

I touched Rick's unmoving hand. With Gin away, I could stroke his hand as long or as much as I pleased.

And if the two silent men in the dark business suits weren't present in the bedroom, I might have stroked something else. A little stroking in the right place at the right time might do wonders for even an unconscious man.

I glanced over at the tallest of the two men. He was a beautiful man. Like his companion, he was probably Latin. Light olive skin. Elegant dark eyes. A cleft in his chin almost as deep as my cleavage.

He was all business. Told me his first name was Ignacio. But wouldn't give his last name. Wouldn't say more than two words at a time. But I knew his type. Those elegant eyes were the giveaway. Smart-ass eyes. Experienced eyes. Give me five minutes alone with him, and he'd be all over me, begging for my goodies.

My thoughts were disturbed by an abrupt commotion on the stairs. Suddenly my damn sister, Pam, burst into the bedroom. Her long platinum hair was a mess, flying around her shoulders like something from a witch's closet.

I didn't know who let her in, but heads would roll when I found out.

I called for my housekeeper. No answer. I called for the cook. No answer.

Pam kept mouthing off, blabbing away at the top of her lungs about some kind of nonsense. As bold as brass, she walked over to the two men who were now standing in front of the window.

I called for Rowdy. The big German shepherd always frightened Pam half to death and chased her away. But even the damn dog didn't show.

"Half-wits!" Pam shook her finger at the two men as if they were naughty schoolboys. "Why aren't you doing something about it?"

They didn't speak. They looked at her as if she was drunk or crazy.

"Don't just stand there like half-wits!" raved Aunt Pam. "Don't you know he's escaped?" Her voice became more shrill. "And you damn well know who, don't you? The maniac who hurt this poor boy here!" With her arm, she made a big sweeping gesture at Rick, lying motionless in the bed.

The two men didn't look at Rick. They gazed at my sister as if she were a garden slug they wished they could step on.

After a long pause, the dark one with the cleft chin sighed. Then he spoke. "We know. . . ." His voice was very bored. "Sooner or later, Dr. Sierra always escapes. . . ."

7

☆ ☆ ☆ ☆

AUNT PAM

I am Gin's mother, of course. And I've got the proof hidden away where my sister, Louise, will never find it.

From the very first day that Rick Moore came into my daughter's life, I could sense the change in her.

Of course, the baby didn't say much about him then. He was about twice her age—and she was very shy. But I could tell by the way she *didn't* talk about him that he was having an effect on her.

On all other subjects, the baby told me everything. She never lied to me. Never.

That's the way I raised her. I didn't want her to be in any way like my sister, Louise.

It's true that the baby didn't always tell me something as soon as it happened. She would be busy with her circuits, her data banks, and her classwork at U.C. Santa Barbara. And I would be very busy with my job at the nursing home.

But later she *always* told me. She loved to tell me things, loved to tell me her secret thoughts the way any good daughter likes to talk to her mother.

She told me these things because she loved me. We always had a wonderful relationship. The way the baby and I were so close drove Louise crazy.

After the baby got so involved in her terribly secret computer work, I was amazed that she even told me a lot of those details. She told me because she trusted me.

Of course, I didn't understand what it all meant. I just let her talk to her heart's content about whatever was bothering her at the time.

She told me more than I ever wanted to hear. I heard about the closed-loop system, character-oriented protocol, circular mil, high-level data link control, and a thousand more.

I didn't give a damn about what they added up to. But I remembered every detail she told me.

I didn't want to remember. I just couldn't help it. I happen to have one of those minds that can remember everything. Sometimes it's a curse.

So it was through the baby that I first learned about the escape of the Nicaraguan agent, the S.O.B. who damaged Rick's eyes so badly. The TV news, radio, and newspapers never did mention that slippery character . . . or even anything he did.

But the baby mentioned him only minutes after he got loose. She called him Dr. Sierra, one of his code names.

When she came in from the garage lab to take a short break, I could see she was troubled.

"I picked it up," she said, "from TimTomTon, circuit 2 . . ."

She rubbed her nose in that cute way she has when she's really concentrating. I wanted to tell her she shouldn't frown when she does that because she'll get wrinkles, but I decided for once to keep my mouth shut.

"It's fantastic," she said.

She poured herself a glass of cold milk from the fridge. "The TimTomTon report said it only took Dr. Sierra forty-five minutes to break through four security gates and motion detectors in the federal blockhouse in L.A. The one they said was totally escape proof."

She often mentioned all the mumbo-jumbo goings-on of TimTomTon. That's the name of the separate security system that watches over the baby and all the rest of us.

TimTomTon isn't directly CIA. It isn't FBI or Secret Service. It isn't National Security Agency. It's a sort of subsidiary of the CIA and a gigantic system in its own right. It's so elite that it answers only to Rawhide, Saddlebag One, and their inner circle.

Most of the time TimTomTon does good work. But when some of its half-wits screw up, which is oftener than you might think, they really make a mess of things.

"I'm worried," said the baby. "What if Dr. Sierra decides to come back and finish what he started with Rick?"

Whenever the baby worried, I worried. I knew that if I could get her to talk about the problem, her mind would be eased.

"I don't think I know that name," I said. "Have you mentioned him before?"

"No. Because Dr. Sierra's name only came up this afternoon."

She told me Dr. Sierra was believed to be the number one man in charge of the Sandinistas' entire apparatus in the United States.

From what the baby had told me before, I knew the sole purpose of the Nicaragua/Sandinista apparatus was to assassinate Rawhide.

"Gotta run—" The baby put the empty glass down on the sink drain board. "I was so busy with Dr. Sierra, I kept putting off my afternoon check on SigInt. See you later, sweetie."

As she went out the back door, I wished she'd call me mom or mother. But what the hell, a mother can't have everything. And "Sweetie" was very nice.

Even nicer was the fact that she still let me refer to her as the baby after all these years.

She'd always handled the business of having two aunts very diplomatically. She always knew I was her mother. But she called me Aunt Pam because it was my father's wish.

When the baby was born, my father thought she was a disgrace because I wasn't married. I went along with the two aunts idea to keep peace in the family.

After father died and the baby was growing up, she continued to call me Aunt Pam. She did it to pacify Louise, who was always so damned jealous of my being a mother.

As I dried the last of the dishes and put them away, I thought about how casually the baby had mentioned SigInt. I knew what the word meant because she'd explained it to me. I still found it impossible to believe that my baby could go into the garage and communicate with that thing. SigInt is a U.S. satellite with an antenna as big as a football field. From an altitude of 22,000 miles above Russia, it can pick up an electric discharge as small as that of a flashlight battery.

If some half-wit Russian in Leningrad hits any letter or number on his keyboard, SigInt can intercept the discharge and read whatever he's punching in.

I glanced at my pendant watch, the one the baby gave me for my birthday. Nearly five fifteen. Still plenty of time to get to my night job at the nursing home.

I drank a nice cold can of Coors. Then I decided to make another attempt to see Rick and find out if his condition had changed.

For most of the week, my half-wit sister had managed to keep me away. But I knew that on Thursdays her housekeeper sometimes left at five. So I might have a chance.

I was feeling good that evening. Like everyone else, I have my good days and bad days.

But in some ways I'm different from other people. Many years ago, while riding on a bus in Hollywood, I met a Rosicrucian lady. She was a Hindu, wearing a lovely orange sari. She understood religious law, the meaning of illuminated consciousness, and all that.

She told me wonderful and terrible things about myself and my baby daughter Gin, who was riding on my lap.

The woman said everything in my life and my baby's life was preordained. She said that all the good and bad things that would happen in our lives were meant to happen and could not be stopped.

The Rosicrucian lady told me that on good days I would have the power to do good things for my baby. She said I shouldn't worry about what would happen to us on the bad days because there was nothing I could do about it.

As the years passed, I never forgot what the Rosicrucian lady told me. That was why I had such a strong positive feeling as I prepared to go over to Louise's house.

I felt sure I could get in and see if Rick's eyes were any better. I knew he badly needed cheering up. And I knew, from my work at the nursing home, that he would welcome having his back rubbed and his pillows fluffed up.

Our two redwood houses, mine and Louise's, are side by side, separated by the double asphalt driveway. When we inherited the two houses many years ago from our parents, they were identical tract homes. They are built in a California rancho style with open beam ceilings and gravel roofs with a gentle slant.

When the houses were built, they were fairly small, with two bedrooms. My house, sort of a dirt brown color, is still small and badly in need of paint and fixing up. Louise's house, however, is a beautiful rancho mansion, white with yellow trim. It's nearly three times as large as mine and worth a fortune. She added a big upstairs section, extra baths and rooms downstairs.

In addition to the big wad she made in real estate, Louise has income from three of her four ex-husbands. One was an admiral, now deceased, who left her a big pension. Another one was a naval commander, a flier who was shot down in Vietnam.

I went out through the back door of my house and along the driveway to the front door of Louise's house. I rang the door bell. I rang it a long time without getting an answer.

As I listened to the damn thing play a few notes of "Lara's Theme"—for about the thirteenth sickening time—I couldn't help thinking about what a terrible showoff Louise was. She'd buy anything that was trendy or show-offy just to prove she could afford it.

Fairly certain that the housekeeper wasn't in, I went around to Louise's side door. Now came the tricky part. I unlocked the door with the key Gin had given me and which I'd sworn practically in blood never to reveal.

I knew I was under surveillance, because TimTomTon had viewing and listening devices planted all over my property and Louise's. But I didn't care. TimTomTon continually made surveillance reports on my activities, but nothing was ever mentioned to me about them.

Very quietly, I opened the door a few inches, but I didn't go in. Just inside was a hallway where Louise's goddamn dog usually slept. So I had to be very careful. One mistake and he'd chew me to shreds.

When I heard Rowdy breathing and scratching, I eased the door shut and went back to my house. I took about a half pound of ground chuck from the fridge. It pained me to waste such good meat on the son of a bitch. I simply couldn't afford it, which was why I only did this once in a while.

I left my kitchen door open, then I went back to Louise's house and unlocked the side door a second time.

I knew I was taking a terrible risk because that German shepherd is a killer. But whenever I'm having a really good day, I feel I have the confidence and power to do impossible things.

After I met the Rosicrucian lady on the bus, I wrote away for lessons. I studied the Rosicrucian method for many years and learned more about what my good and bad days meant. That's why I felt so certain I could gain power over that big dog. Not for very long. But long enough to get to that upstairs bedroom and see what was happening.

Holding the saucer of raw ground chuck in one hand and the smallest of Louise's plastic trash cans in the other, I whispered to the beast very seductively through the partly opened door. I told him about the juicy treasure awaiting him.

He came almost at once, sniffing and snorting. On things like food, my half-wit sister is a pinchpenny, feeding him cheap dry stuff from the large economy bags. So he went for my burger surprise in a big way.

Fortunately, he's a smart S.O.B. He knew why I was holding Louise's trash can, because I'd used it on him before.

If he misbehaved in any way, I would pop the ground chuck into the can, put the lid on, and he would miss his big treat.

Even so it was a dangerous business. If I made one mistake, he would blow his top and go for my leg. I've got a three-inch scratch on my artificial foot as a reminder of a minor mistake I made last year with the furry bastard. I've worn the plastic foot for years, ever since I lost my foot in a traffic accident.

Growling in his throat, but quietly, the black and gray beast followed me back to my house. I put the dish of meat down on my kitchen floor. Rowdy went in and chomped away like he hadn't eaten since April Fool's Day.

I closed my door to keep him in there.

My success with the German shepherd made me feel so wonderful that I was sure I could handle Louise and anything she tried to do.

Returning to her side door, I went in very quietly. For a few moments, I paused in the dim hallway to rearrange my hair.

I used to be an actress, and after that a beautician. So I know how to keep my long platinum hair immaculate, shiny, and in a neat coil.

But for Louise's benefit, I mussed my hair and let it hang down the side like the tail of a horse badly in need of brushing.

Sometimes my drunk act doesn't work on Louise. Other times it helps me pick up info about her that I wouldn't get otherwise. By no means is Louise a genius. But neither is she an imbecile.

As I went up the carpeted stairway to her bedroom, I stamped my red wedgies hard on the steps. I made a lot of noise, especially with my artificial foot. I also cursed loudly about nothing in particular.

I knew the Coors I'd just drunk would heighten my fair complexion, as it always does, making me look overheated, pink-cheeked, and blowsy. After I entered the bedroom, with all its sickly yellow furnishings, I sucked my breath in hard. Then I blew it out a few times to make sure the odor of Coors accompanied me.

Louise was sitting by the bed, holding Rick's hand. The two men in the dark business suits were standing together over by the window. They stopped talking when I came blowing in.

I babbled some nonsense and wobbled around a little. I made it look like I stumbled accidentally against the foot of the bed.

In her sharpest, meanest tone, Louise said exactly what I expected. "Damn old fool!"

Right away I noticed that Rick was awake. Wearing white

hospital-style pajamas, he was sitting up partway against two yellow pillows. It was a good sign, even though the white wrappings around his eyes looked so grim.

Turning, I shook my finger at the two men. "Half-wits!" I raved. "Don't you know he's escaped? What're you goin' t'do 'bout it?"

First they looked at me with disgust. Then with mild curiosity, as if they wondered how I'd acquired such supposedly secret info. Then they went back to looking bored.

Louise pretended not to care about what I'd said about Dr. Sierra escaping. But Rick was interested and turned his curly head toward me.

"You old fool!" Louise gave me her best stabbing look, aimed directly at my heart. "You've got to take better care of yourself. You look awful!"

She paused so her next remark would have a more deadly impact. "For a woman of fifty-five, you look more like sixty-five!"

Another one of her stupid, unnecessary lies. And less original than usual. The lying bitch. I'm fifty-two, and she'll never see forty-six again.

But it didn't matter. I was interested in Rick, not her. And I'd already accomplished much of what I came for.

I'd seen with my own eyes that Rick was getting better. And I'd reminded the two half-wit security men about what they were supposed to be doing. Maybe now they'd do a better job of protecting Rick in case that Dr. Sierra character came back to finish him off.

I have to admit that because of her facelift Louise is a good-looking woman. That's one of the reasons she usually gets her way with men. In no way does she look her age. In bad light, she could pass for about thirty-five. But I'll never tell her that.

She gave the nearest security man a loving look and spoke in a loving tone.

"Ignacio, would you mind escorting my dear sister downstairs?" She paused for effect. "And then *out*!"

Ignacio was a handsome devil, very Latin and very quiet. His dark bright eyes didn't miss a thing. He didn't make any move toward me. Instead, his dark eyes studied what Louise was doing with Rick's hand. She was rubbing the tip of her little finger against the tip of Rick's little finger.

I knew she was doing it deliberately, to irritate me. And to remind me how she had lost the tip of her pinkie. When we were kids, I accidentally cut her fingertip with the lawnmower while we were playing a game in the grass. Years later, she claimed the scar got infected and her doctor was forced to amputate the tip of her finger.

She rubbed the scarred stub of her pinkie slowly against Rick's finger. I suppose she was giving him some kind of a sex hint. But it looked ridiculous.

Ignacio thought so, too. I don't think he liked the way Louise was trying to work both sides of the street like a two-bit hooker. All the time she was giving Ignacio that loving look, she was rubbing Rick's pinkie in a half-wit loving way as if trying to turn it into something else.

Stupid. Why his littlest finger?

Then I noticed something strange. The tip of Rick's little finger was exactly like hers. The tip was missing from both their fingers. How do you like that for something weird? A coincidence? Maybe yes, maybe no.

Ignacio finally took a few steps toward me. I pretended to sway drunkenly in his direction. Then I lost my balance and fell against him. He was quite tall.

Bracing me with his arm, he started walking me toward the bedroom exit. I liked his arm. It was hard as stone. Obviously, here was a man who kept in shape.

As we went out, I mumbled and blew some Coors up toward his face. "Hey, good lookin'," I said, "wanna come over to my place an' fuck?"

From Ignacio there was no reaction at all. He kept walking me through the doorway. From the bed came a laugh that had to be Rick's. It wasn't a big laugh. But it was another good sign about his condition.

From Louise came the anticipated remark dripping with scorn. "Drunken slut." Long pause. "Thank you, Ignacio. Be sure to tell me if she gives you trouble."

He walked me down the stairs and out of Louise's

mansion. I kept up my wobbly act all the way. When we reached my back door, I stopped and untangled my arm from his. I stood there and waited for him to leave.

But he wouldn't leave.

My God, I thought, the handsome young devil likes me and wants me. And me with only twenty minutes to get to work. My god, what a shame.

Later I realized I was wrong. It wasn't sex that he wanted. He just stood there, looking down at me. But he still didn't say anything. For some reason I couldn't think of anything to say either. Which was not at all like me.

I think I was tongue-tied because he was so dark, so virile, and so handsome. And because his dark shiny eyes looked down at me in such a compelling, hard way.

That's when I had the premonition that what he wanted to tell me was of extreme importance. I knew it would have a direct bearing on my life, and, more important, on the baby's life.

My Rosicrucian premonition didn't go far enough. It gave me no warning that someone would suddenly dart around the corner of my house and attack Ignacio from the rear.

The attacker was a tall man holding a piece of steel wire. Before Ignacio could react, the man brought the wire loop down over Ignacio's head and tightened it around his neck. I couldn't believe what I was seeing. Dressed in white pajamas, the attacker was Rick! The white wrapping was shoved up on his forehead, freeing his eyes.

Rick was even taller than Ignacio and stronger. Twisting the wire hard around Ignacio's neck, he yanked Ignacio one way and then the other. Ignacio tried to tear the wire away from his throat, but it was too tight, cutting so deeply that bright blood was welling up.

As Ignacio fell to his knees, the sounds that came from his throat were the most terrible sounds I've ever heard. They were the strangled cries of a man who knew he was being killed.

"Rick!" I cried. "Stop, stop!"

I couldn't understand this sudden, terrible change in him.

Why had Rick changed from a nice, average man into this terrible murderer?

It was obvious that he'd gone berserk, probably from the effects of the poisonous stuff tossed in his eyes.

Somehow I had to stop him before he threw his life away with such an act of madness. I got behind him and tried to pull him away from Ignacio. I'm strong, from lifting those bedridden patients at the nursing home, but I couldn't budge him from Ignacio. They were locked together like welded metal.

The crazy scene went on and on like a videotape that was out of sync. I knew the surveillance cameras were picking us up, but why didn't anyone come?

"Help!" I cried. "Oh, God, help me!"

I kept pulling at Rick's head, bending his head back. He didn't like that. He lashed out backward with his foot. He kicked me so viciously that I fell hard against the driveway. My artificial foot came off, and I scraped the side of my face on the rough asphalt. My jaw felt like it was broken.

Then, despite the pain, I got smart. I heard Rowdy barking like mad behind my kitchen door, reacting to all the ruckus we were making.

I crawled over to the door and opened it. The German shepherd shot forth like black lightning.

"Kill!" I shrieked. "Kill!"

I knew Rick would be no match for that beast. Rowdy was full of growling fury. His ears were laid back, his jaws were open, and his fangs were exposed like knives.

But I was wrong about Rick. As Rowdy leaped, Rick turned and delivered a perfectly time soccer kick. His boot came up under Rowdy's jaw with terrific force. There was the ugly snap of breaking bone. The dog was catapulted into the air. He came down on his side with a crunch. After that, he didn't move or make a sound.

For a moment, Rick looked at the dog. Then he looked down at Ignacio, who was half-lying on the asphalt, his upper body supported by the wire that Rick was still holding with both hands.

Ignacio was silent. His neck was twisted and broken.

Rick let go of the bloody wire. Ignacio's upper body dropped to the driveway as if it were a sack.

As Rick came toward me, I saw the blood on his hands and screamed. There was even blood on his little finger that was so short and scarred.

Even after Rick struck me with his fist, I kept screaming. It was an enormous blow on the same aching side of my face that had struck the asphalt.

But it didn't stop my screaming. By then I should've been unconscious, but I wasn't. I had no strength. I couldn't get up. I couldn't even pick up my artificial foot.

I lay partway through my kitchen doorway and watched Rick walk calmly away toward Louise's garage where the baby was at work.

Despite the shock and incredible pain, I was fully aware of everything that had happened. And afraid of what else would happen.

Once again I knew the Rosicrucian lady was right. Even though I had the premonition, I couldn't stop what happened.

I knew the baby was in terrible danger. It was up to me to save her. Or to summon someone to save her. But I was too weak. I couldn't do a thing to save her.

REO (Rawhide's Eyes Only)
Alert memo No. CL-9
To: Rawhide, White House
From: Saddlebag One
Subject: *Assassination plot*

Herewith are the rest of the facts—as we know them now—about the events at Stirrup. Chicken Little was in far greater danger than anticipated. She escaped execution by going down to the impregnable bomb shelter beneath her communications lab.

If you had gone to the ranch as planned, you would also have been in grave danger. When we recommended that you remain in Washington, we were acting on intelligence which, though incomplete then, proved later to be accurate.

In Memo No. CL-8, I indicated that the conspiracy was devised by the two brothers and that Richard D. Mohr, a.k.a. Richard Donald Moore, the younger brother, was in it from the beginning. Our sources in Managua have since made this revision: The younger brother didn't join the Sandinistas conspiracy until early last month.

His older brother is Gerald H. Mohr, Jr., a.k.a. Gerald Hans Moore, Jr.

The two brothers changed their names to Moore when they came to the U.S. from Nicaragua as teenagers.

There is no question about the primary objective of the Mohr-Moore brothers; *Chicken Little, whom they realize is a national resource.* Their plan was to kidnap her and extract from her, through the usual methods, all the data and counsel she has worked up for Rawhide.

If unable to kidnap Chicken Little, they were under orders from their Sandinista leaders to kill her. After destroying her base at Stirrup, they were then to move north to your ranch, a distance of less than a mile.

Their goals at the ranch would parallel those of the three other strongly negative terrorist forces, which we know are working separately against your administration. They are *Wing* (Taipei), *Claw* (Libya), and *Beak* (Lebanon). Their goals: *Assassination of Rawhide, followed by economic/political turmoil throughout the Western world.*

Regarding the cleanup at Stirrup: Only two members of the TimTomTon unit were deleted. One was deleted on the driveway. The other was deleted in the master bedroom. They were known by the code names Ignacio and Luis. They were placed in body bags and lifted out by 'copter to Disposal Site 3 in the desert. Their absence will require no explanation. There is no record of their ever having been in this country. They have already been replaced by two of the many contras from Nicaragua who have been trained by TimTomTon.

Please inform Rainbow that we have taken her suggestion. A reprimand has been placed in the file of the TimTomTon executive director. No further action against him is planned at this time.

Question: Do you wish to continue the employment of Chicken Little now that the risks and security matters are so complicated?

REO (Rawhide's Eyes Only)
Alert memo No. CL-10
To: Rawhide, White House
From: Saddlebag One
Subject: *Assassination plot update*

I was delighted by your reaction. We will continue the Chicken Little and Stirrup operation in a new location.

I agree that Chicken Little's value is now greater than ever because of critically escalating events in Lebanon, Libya, Nicaragua, Afghanistan, Taiwan, West Germany, and Eastern Europe.

It is vital that Chicken Little's analyses of those areas continue unabated as a source of input separate from the CIA, NSA, and their political motivations.

During the more than four years of our association with Chicken Little, she has acquired data bank expertise that verges on genius. Without detection, she is able to tap into CIA, FBI, and NSA data banks that are otherwise invulnerable.

Through such techniques, she acquires the data that enables her to be so useful to you across a broad spectrum of major crises.

In answer to your question about how Chicken Little first became interested in government research;

on her thirteenth birthday, she received a simple Radio Shack computer from her Aunt Louise.

She used it to win the grand prize in a national contest—a large, elaborate system. Its telecommunication accessories enabled her to do geneology research on her family. From that she graduated to extensive research into history, then politics, military intelligence, and related subjects.

I beg to correct you on one point. I did not originate use of the term *national resource*. If you will recall, sir, you first referred to Chicken Little as a *national resource* in one of the informal chats we had during the Falkland Islands invasion. Even the Secretary of State agreed that if it had not been for Chicken Little's belated but still vital counsel, the damage to America's prestige would have been far greater.

The rest of this memo concerns our continuing investigation into the security matters at Stirrup. You may decide to skip reading this portion of this memo because it is routine. I agree with your assessment that the Stirrup fiasco was not the worst of the fiascos involving TimTomTon this year. We are all aware that by its very nature security is an imperfect business.

TimTomTon's imperfections are no worse than those of the Soviet R&R penetration operations that control the activities of Dr. Sierra out of Managua. R&R, as you know, is a subdivision of the KGB. Dr. Sierra is a brilliant agent assigned to the Sandinistas. If the R&R higher-ups hadn't meddled, his operation at Stirrup would have been very simple and undoubtedly successful.

Dr. Sierra wanted to kill the younger Mohr/Moore brother and kidnap Chicken Little from the park while she was jogging. Dr. Sierra knew that TimTomTon's park security was imperfect. Our contact within the Sandinista government tells us the Soviet R&R people stupidly ordered Dr.

Sierra to blind young Mohr/Moore, a tactic which led to a series of fiascoes.

At first, we believed the thrown powder was designed to kill Mohr/Moore, but now our experts theorize it was intended to immobilize him by damaging his vision.

After Dr. Sierra was arrested (and subsequently escaped), the R&R made matters worse by ordering him to go into hiding. This left the older brother, Gerald, in charge of the next step in the Chicken Little kidnap operation. Gerald Mohr/Moore is also a brilliant agent but comparatively new and lacking in field experience.

Instead of a simple plan, Mohr/Moore went for the too elaborate idea of taking his younger brother's place. This was approved by the R&R completely against the advice of Dr. Sierra.

The plan failed only because Chicken Little noted the danger on one of her monitors and went down immediately into the bomb shelter. This shelter was installed on orders of TimTomTon's executive director. *Its success is the only reason he received a reprimand instead of removal from his position.*

Please inform Rainbow that we will change the reprim and to dismissal if she recommends it.

Further revision: Our Managua network advises us now that young Mohr/Moore was in no way part of the conspiracy. TimTomTon has confirmed this. We will therefore employ young Mohr/Moore at the new operation, *Stirrup B,* enlisting him under the name he prefers, Richard D. Moore, a.k.a. Rick Moore.

Mohr/Moore by no means knows the whole picture, but he knows too much to be left on his own. We will therefore convince him that to prevent further harm to himself he will have to cooperate fully with us.

Unfortunately, young Mohr/Moore has no intelligence/security expertise whatsoever.

Nevertheless, he will be used as one of several decoys. This is because we are certain that Dr. Sierra and the older Mohr/Moore brother will renew their efforts.

We are reasonably certain that both are in the Southern California/Arizona area.

TimTomTon assures us that the decoys will aid the recapture of Dr. Sierra, Gerald H. Mohr/Moore, Jr., and their associates.

I cannot share TimTomTon's optimism.

☆ ☆ 8 ☆ ☆

When Rick shut his eyes in pain, he was in California. When he opened them a month later, he was in central Montana. Meanwhile, a whole lifetime of events fell on him.

Worse than being blinded was the knowledge that his brother Jerry was some kind of a Sandinista agent, and very probably a murderer.

The damage to Rick's eyes was supposed to be temporary, except for the cornea of his left eye which was permanently scarred. He was told that for the first time in his life he would have to wear glasses.

For days after the two Latino TimTomTon agents were slain, Rick refused to believe that his brother was responsible.

His interrogators also accused Rick of assisting his brother Jerry in murdering the two security agents. Relentlessly, they questioned Rick for two days and nights about his relationship with his brother. Most of the interrogation sessions were directed personally by Saddlebag One.

Rick never saw their faces because he still had the wrapping on his eyes. They sat around his hospital bed in

Santa Barbara—maybe half a dozen grim-voiced government men—and asked question after question.

Then, suddenly, their tone changed. They must've discovered evidence that cleared him, but they didn't say so.

They didn't apologize. They didn't admit they were wrong. It was just that black became white as the whole line of their questioning changed.

Gradually, because of the way they pieced it together, he began to accept their theory that Jerry had killed two men—and had tried to kill Gin.

Rick was revolted by the evidence that Jerry had come within inches of breaking into the bomb shelter under Aunt Louise's house and gunning Gin down.

They brought some very expensive government doctors to Santa Barbara to do the cornea transplant on Rick's left eye. He sensed from things that were said—and from rolling motions he felt—that the surgery was done in a mobile clinic, a large government trailer.

While his eyes were still bandaged, they put him on a small government jet and flew him to a military base in Montana.

He should have guessed that they were cooking up a special assignment for him. But he was so out of touch with their real goals that he thought their primary concern was for his eyes.

Whenever Rick asked about Gin, Saddlebag One told him not to worry.

"You'll see her soon," Saddlebag One explained in that careful, old man's voice of his.

Two of the government doctors flew with Rick to the military base in Montana. Also on the plane were several of Saddlebag One's staff men.

When Dr. Shadduck, the government ophthamologist, took the last of the wrappings off Rick's eyes, he found himself sitting on a cold metal stool in an old, drab clinic.

The room was dimly lighted, but even that small amount of illumination hurt his eyes. Squinting, he saw several people standing nearby in the shadows. He didn't recognize any of them.

The vision in his left eye was blurry, but he could see pretty well with his other eye. He expected the long-awaited unveiling of his eyes to be a big and very pleasant event. It wasn't. Because Gin wasn't there. And that made him angry and distrustful.

Shoving the doctor's hand aside, he got up from the stool and headed for the nearest door.

Very abruptly, three men in dark business suits came out of the shadows and stood close together in front of him. They barred him from the door. One was middle-aged, the other two were young.

"Where's Saddlebag One?" Rick demanded of the closest man, a dark-skinned Latino. "Damn it, I want Saddlebag One."

They ignored his protests. They ignored his questions about Gin. They didn't touch him. But by walking very close to him the three grim-faced men herded him back to the doctor and his assistant.

Rick hated the way these people did things. These men, especially Saddlebag One, were very tricky.

He had been on the military base for over twenty-four hours without seeing Gin, the most important person in his life, the woman he was ready to change his whole life for. Obviously, something had gone wrong, but they wouldn't say so.

They had screwed everything up in California and had nearly gotten her killed. Had something else been bungled as badly?

The three Latinos forced him to sit. Then they stood silently behind Dr. Shadduck and his assistant.

Dr. Shadduck raised his mirror scope and spoke professionally but softly. "A little patience, please, Mr. Moore. The more anxious and uptight you are, the worse it is for your good eye. How many times must we remind you?"

When the exam was over, Dr. Shadduck handed Rick a pair of glasses and told him to put them on. The lenses were tinted to light smoky gray. Even after the doctor adjusted them, the nosepiece and ear bands were very uncomfortable.

The glasses improved the vision in his left eye, but not as

much as he hoped. Once again Rick got up from the stool and headed for the door. And once again the three grim-faced Latinos blocked his way. The one with the darkest olive skin spoke in a respectful way. "Mr. Moore, where do you think you're going?"

"Out, of course. I am going to find Miss Ginger Johnssen."

"Sorry, sir."

One man took Rick's right arm and held it tightly. The other two grasped his left arm, pinching the flesh viciously enough to make him wince.

They escorted him from the doctor's examining room along a short hallway and then into an almost bare conference room.

They locked both of the room's doors. They indicated Rick was to sit on one of the four flimsy, gray metal chairs placed around a flimsy table topped with scratched gray plastic.

Removing the uncomfortable glasses, he looked around the room. His vision was really lousy.

He put the glasses back on and was able to see the objects on top of the table—a dirty brown pottery ashtray, a crystal vase with dusty artificial pink rosebuds, a ballpoint pen, and a pad of yellow notepaper with ruled blue lines.

"My name is Teodoro," said the oldest and darkest of the three men. "I am sorry that Miss Johnssen has been delayed. But you will see her shortly. Meanwhile—"

"When will she get here?" Rick demanded.

Teodoro didn't like being interrupted. His face darkened. "Soon. Meanwhile, we have much work to do. Let us be pleasant to each other and see what we can accomplish."

He spoke in Spanish to the other two, telling them to join Rick at the table. As they pulled out their chairs, Rick decided to see what he could gain by being friendly.

He greeted the pair politely in Spanish. "*Encantado.*"

It was obvious by the change of expression in their dark eyes that they understood. But the did not return his courtesy.

He tried again. "*Quiubo?*"

They stared at Rick coldly. He stared back just as coldly,

letting them know that if they wanted it friendly the next move would be up to them.

"Why am I here?" Rick demanded. "Why Montana for Christ's sake?"

Teodoro didn't give him a direct answer. "I will be your chief instructor," he said, "and these others will assist me with the class.'

He didn't bother introducing the two young ones by name.

"What class?" Rick asked.

"Indoctrination," said Teodoro. "This is going to be the quickest one-man indoctrination course anybody ever attended. We've got eighteen hours to turn you into an operative for TimTomTon."

Leaning down over the table, Teodoro shoved the yellow pad and pen over to Rick.

"Moore, you *will* take notes."

Five minutes ago, Rick had been Mr. Moore. Now he was plain Moore and losing more status rapidly.

"Hold on," he said. "What makes you think I want to join your outfit? Does Saddlebag One know about this?"

"He does, Moore. *He* ordered this indoctrination for you. He is fully aware of your eye problem and other problems."

Teodoro scowled and gave Rick an unnecessary display of strength. He raised his hands chest-high, close to Rick's face. He clasped them together so tightly that the almost black veins stood out against the dark olive skin. Like the rest of him, his hands were extremely muscular.

"Pay attention, Moore. You should understand the chief reasons for bringing you into TimTomTon."

"Must I?"

It was a dumb thing to say, but Rick was tired and didn't like the man's attitude.

Reacting to the sarcasm, Teodoro drew back his clasped hands as if to bash in Rick's jaw. His face was full of black fury.

Just as quickly the moment passed and the fury vanished. Teodoro put his hands carefully on the table.

"You are stupid," he said. "One reason we need you is

because of your brother. But the chief reason is Ginger Johnssen. She is a national resource—and we will teach you how to protect her."

Suddenly his attitude changed totally. The mere mention of Gin's name seemed to have an effect on him.

The attitude of his two silent assistants also changed. All three gazed at Rick as if they were the guardians of the world and he was an extremely important part of their plans.

The next question was almost on Rick's lips: "Why me?" But he didn't have to say it. Teodoro had given him the hint. And finally Rick began to understand it more clearly.

They needed him because of his close resemblance to his brother Jerry.

If Jerry and Rick were to stand close together, slight differences in their appearances were apparent. But viewed singly and apart, they seemed like twins.

At any rate because of that resemblance, Rick realized he might be able to protect Gin in a way that he never dreamed possible.

He nodded curtly, letting them know he was willing to hear their proposition.

"Good," said Teodoro, almost smiling.

The glare from the overhead blue-white fluorescent light irritated Rick's eyes.

He shielded them with his hand. The gesture made him feel like a wimp.

It also brought back his anger and strong desire for revenge against the man who had weakened him like this.

"Teodoro," he said. "Will I have a chance to get back at him, the man you call Dr. Sierra?"

"Certainly. That's another reason for your training."

Teodoro warned that Rick would never be a match for Dr. Sierra if they were to meet one on one. Teodoro didn't spare Rick's feelings.

"Moore," he added. "You are a raw recruit in our kind of work. You are nothing. *Nada. Mierda.* But Dr. Sierra is a sorcerer. He is ten thousand times more efficient than you can ever hope to be." That was enough of a put-down. But

Teodoro wanted to make his point even stronger. "Moore, describe Dr. Sierra as you remember him."

That part was easy. The image of Dr. Sierra was burned permanently into Rick's memory. He described exactly what he had seen—a fat slob in an Army camouflage uniform, carrying a deadly powder in his fist.

Teodoro shook his finger at Rick as if he were a kindergarten pupil unable to tell time or tie his shoelaces.

"Wrong, Moore. Dr. Sierra is not—repeat *NOT*—a fat slob. He was able to give you that illusion. He is, in fact, about your height and weight. He is very tall, muscular, and trim."

Properly impressed, Rick kept silent as Teodoro described Dr. Sierra as a man of thirty-five, a neurosurgeon trained at the University of Moscow, a jet pilot, an electrical engineer, and an attorney who practiced before the highest courts in the USSR and Nicaragua.

"But he is neither Russian or Nicaraguan . . ." Teodoro permitted himself a wry smile. "We do not know where he was born. We know nothing of his family. We have only two photographs of him: one taken when he was a medical student. . . ."

From an inside pocket in his business suit, Teodoro brought forth a thin, shiny black leather billfold. He took out a photo encased in plastic and handed it to Rick.

It was a black-and-white photograph, a head and shoulders shot of a young man. He was fair-skinned with short dark hair. His chin was strong, his lips were full, and his eyes, probably blue, reflected supreme confidence.

"He is a witch," said Teodoro. "He can change his physical appearance at will."

Teodoro reached down to two large rectangles of white cardboard that were propped against a leg of the table. He placed the first one face up on the tabletop and told Rick to examine it.

Although Rick had never seen it before, he recognized the huge blowup as one of his own photos. It was the head of Mrs. F, the golden vixen he'd photographed a month ago defleaing herself in the stream in El Dorado Park.

This was his second shot, showing her erupting in a frenzy of action from the water. It was a beautiful color photo. Surrounded by a halo of spraying droplets, the fox's head was slightly out of focus, emphasizing her blurring motion in a rather artistic way.

Teodoro placed his finger on something in the photo's background.

"Moore, what's this?"

Rick examined the spot, which was about the size of a dime. It was a man's face. It was surprisingly clear, because during the instant it was taken the man had moved into a patch of sunlight in the eugenia trees.

"By God!" Rick said. "That could be Dr. Sierra!"

"It *is*." Teodoro placed the second photo blowup on the table. "We had this enhanced by space computer technology at Cal Tech."

Measuring about ten by fifteen inches, it was an enlargement of Dr. Sierra's face, including part of his camouflage helmet. Its green, black, and brown colors were too intense because of the enhancement techniques.

The pink and beige hues of his face were also too intense Nevertheless, it was a very remarkable enlargement, unlike any Rick had ever seen before. Dr. Sierra's eyes were iceberg blue, eyes that could intimidate, frighten, or terrorize.

Teodoro tapped the photo with his forefinger. "This achievement indicates that you may eventually be of value to us in photographic surveillance techniques. It is only the second photo we have of Dr. Sierra—and the *only* color photo."

For comparison, Teodoro placed the small black-and-white photo on the table beside the enlargement. He pointed out the difference. Plastic surgery had given Dr. Sierra a smaller, thinner nose and slightly fuller lips. His strong chin lines were unchanged.

Perhaps because of the surgery, Dr. Sierra's face had aged very little in the dozen or so years since he was a medical student. He looked very youthful.

"Thanks to your photo," said Teodoro, "we will know

what facial basics to look for the next time Dr. Sierra changes his appearance.''

Teodoro leaned closer to Rick. To emphasize his next words, he lowered his voice.

"Moore, some years ago Dr. Sierra was hospitalized in Denver under another name after being in a plane crash. After his discharge, he disappeared. After we belatedly learned his identity, we studied his hospital records and learned that he had another injury, dating back probably to his childhood.''

For emphasis, Teodoro spoke more slowly and deliberately. "A strange injury to *el miembro viril*. The *pene*. You understand?''

Rick nodded. Teodoro's words were Castilian, not the colloquialisims Rick had known in Nicaragua. But the meaning was the same.

"His injuries were typical of an abused child," added Teodoro. "Most of the penis was severed and there were scars on the testicles. The man's sex drive remains, but he cannot perform the act. Can you guess what this has done to his personality?''

"*Hecho una desgracia*," said Rick. "Misery.''

"Absolute misery," said Teodoro. "And tragedy for others. The man is a beast. His cruelty knows no boundaries. He takes his repression, his neurosis, and frustration out on others by being unspeakably cruel. . . .''

The room became silent. The two younger Latinos shifted uncomfortably in their chairs, as if embarrassed by what Teodoro had found it necessary to explain.

"Now then, Moore." Teodoro's tone became crisp and businesslike. "Now that you know all this, answer this question. If called upon, could you *kill* Dr. Sierra?''

Rick didn't hesitate. "Absolutely.''

"Revenge? Because of what he did to your eyes?''

"Yes.''

"Could you kill someone *else* to protect Ginger Johnssen?''

The other two Latino men looked at Rick with intense dark eyes, awaiting his reply, watching for a sign of weakness.

"I think so . . ." Rick said. "If there was no other way. . . ."

The other two looked at him with disgust, but Teodoro seemed satisfied.

"Moore," he said, "when we finish with you, you will no longer have doubts. You will be able to kill anybody!"

REO: No. 36
To: Rawhide, White House
From: Chicken Little
Subject: *Adversary*

In some of my reports to you, I must perform as a devil's advocate, as ordered by Saddlebag One.

If my reports are unfriendly and overly critical, that's because I am trying to illuminate certain significant facts that you may not have.

Example: Last march the X-ray laser space weapon was given its first test in Nevada. Code-named "Cottage," the secret atomic blast was proclaimed a success by Star Wars supporters.

My data reveals that you were not told that the weapon will fail in space because the Soviets have devised a countermeasure. Their missiles now utilize "fast burn," making them virtually invulnerable to the X-ray laser.

☆ ☆ **9** ☆ ☆

Rick never saw Gin at the military base in central Montana.

After his quickie indoctrination, which was extended to

twenty-eight hours, he was put back on the small, silver government jet. Along with Teodoro and his two sidemen, he was flown to a small air force base. It was an old, antiquated base in western Montana, in high mountain and blue sky country near the Idaho border.

They told Rick that Gin was in the vicinity. But at first they wouldn't let him see her.

As he learned more about how he would be part of Gin's TimTomTon security, he could scarcely believe his good luck. He had the feeling then that he'd turned the corner and the bad days and nights were behind him.

He felt good. His eyes felt better. Just thinking abut being closer to Gin made him fell relaxed, the way Dr. Shadduck wanted him to feel.

He'd brought along the new Konica-1 camera Louise had given him in California. It was the best camera he'd ever owned. But he didn't look forward to shooting pictures with the handicap of glasses.

True, some of the most artistic of all photographers wore glasses, But he knew he'd have trouble. He'd always looked through the viewfinder with his left eye, which was now really lousy.

Soon after Rick's arrival on the air force base, Teodoro continued his lectures and classwork on TimTomTon security and intelligence-gathering techniques.

On the first morning, Teodoro insisted that Rick read a written order from Saddlebag One. It was brief. It authorized Teodoro to continue Rick's indoctrination for as long as necessary, "but not to exceed seven days."

Rick was never told the significance of the seven days. Each day at 7:30 A.M., he reported to Teodoro's classroom in Quonset Hut 3B. Rick was the only student.

Dealing with the use of weapons, codes, other communication methods and related topics, the class went for five hours straight. It broke for a thirty-minute lunch in the base cafeteria and then continued for five more hours.

The afternoon sessions included basic instructions on computers and their use in telecommunications.

Wherever Rick went, he was accompanied by Teodoro

and his pair of so-called assistant instructors. The two young Latinos maintained their silence. They did no instructing.

Rick became certain they were security men, stationed there to keep him from going AWOL.

He was told his pay would be more than two hundred dollars a day and less than three hundred. He was told he would be paid in cash at the end of each week. Teodoro refused to tell him how long his pay would continue.

Rick liked the sound of the money arrangement. If they actually paid him that much it would be a fortune by his standards. It would be at least ten times what he'd earned as a part-time park ditch digger. And twenty times what Dr. Porterfield squeezed out of his naturalist budget for him at the University of California, Santa Barbara.

Nevertheless, on the fourth day, when he still hadn't seen Gin, Rick balked. He stayed on his cot in his bleak, stale-smelling, unfurnished room and refused to leave.

He told them his eyes were bothering him from all the classwork, which was true. But mainly he told them he wouldn't budge until he saw Gin.

They didn't force him to get up. They didn't threaten or make loud noises. They had other ways. After a few phone calls, one of which undoubtedly involved Saddlebag One, they promised Rick that he would meet Gin that evening, after class.

That day the class really dragged. Rick couldn't wait for dismissal at six o'clock.

The morning's proceedings began with Teodoro ordering Rick to sign a secrecy agreement. It was a long, printed form, which he didn't bother to read all the way through. By signing it, he agreed to keep secret every detail, large or small, that he learned about TimTomTon.

Under the heading, Penalty, there was a paragraph in large black type stating that any violation of the agreement terms would result in federal imprisonment for up to twenty years and a fine not to exceed $50,000.

There was no mention of death or execution. Rick assumed that was spelled out somewhere else in the form in very small print.

Next he was required to sign a shorter form, certifying that when necessary TimTomTon was authorized to store his personal possessions. Included were the old camera, clothing, and other stuff Rick had left in his one-room apartment in California. The apartment rent would be paid by TimTomTon for "as long as necessary."

After he signed the forms, a wimp arrived, pulling a small cart that turned out to be a portable lie detector. The red-headed wimp was a tall skinny man, middle-aged and extremely stooped with arthritis.

As Rick watched the man slowly and methodically set up the dark green machine, moving with exquisite care, he could almost feel the pain in his own spine.

He never learned the wimp's name. The man operated the machine's dials and switches without saying a word, doing exactly what Teodoro told him to do.

Teodoro gave Rick the impression that it was an extraordinary machine, more sophisticated than the average polygraph, and that it could evaluate more than just yes and no answers.

He spent much of the morning attached to the machine. Teodoro had an unusual knack for asking the same question in at least three different ways, with three different shadings of meaning.

While the interrogation continued, Teodoro's assistants sat in their usual silence at the other side of the room. All Rick knew about them were their names—Percy and Eduardo. They took no part in the questioning but listened to everything.

Many of the questions were about Rick's early life in Nicaragua plus the two years he spent with his family in Mexico City. Teodoro asked the questions while thumbing through a thick packet of papers, which Rick assumed was the dossier they were assembling on him.

The info was thorough. They had the correct names of Rick's parents, Janine Marie DuBois and Gerald Hans Mohr, Sr. They knew his mother was French and his father was a German who served in Hitler's Waffen SS. They had his correct birth date and the correct birthdays for his older brother Jerry and their parents.

Teodoro's questions also indicated that they knew Rick's father had sold him and his brother to a Nicaraguan man and then later, in remorse, had fired a bullet into his brain.

"What became of your father?" Teodoro asked.

"He died in a home for the aged and senile in Managua."

"How old were you when you last saw him?"

"About twelve, going on thirteen."

"How old was your brother at that time? Be as accurate as you can."

"About fifteen and a half."

"Do you remember when you and your brother joined the *niños exploradores* . . . and went to camp?"

Rick nodded, impressed again with how much detail Teodoro had acquired. Rick and Jerry had spent only a week with other Nicaraguan boys at the youth camp. That was when they were in their earlier teens, before their mother took them to Mexico City and later to America.

"Did you know who sponsored that youth camp?" asked Teodoro.

"Our church, I believe."

"Wrong. It was sponsored by the Sandinistas. That was back when they were still Communist rebels running around in the back country."

Teodoro paused. He looked at Rick rather grimly. "This means, of course, that you were a Sandinista back in their early days."

"Hell, no," said Rick. "I went to their camp for a week—and that was it."

"But you later attended their Monday night meetings?"

"Hell no. I had too many odd jobs to do."

"But your brother went?"

"Yes, I believe he did."

"Of course, he did. That was when he became thoroughly indoctrinated into the Sandinistas and swore to uphold their credo."

Teodoro nodded. Then he held up his hand with the little finger extended.

"Another thing about your brother. Did you know he had surgery on his left hand?"

"No."

"The tip of his little finger was removed to make him resemble you as closely as possible. The shortened finger was observed when your brother murdered those two contras back in California."

Rick made no comment.

Teodoro rustled through the packet of papers. Then he nodded very slowly, as if something he'd encountered was very significant.

"When was the last time you saw your mother?"

Rick knew that question was coming and dreaded it. Many years had passed, but the memories were still painful.

"The last time—" Rick said. "It was the day she received her award. I attended the ceremony with Jerry."

"That was the California Pediatrician of the Year Award? And it was awarded in Los Angeles?"

"Yes."

"About how old were you then?"

"Twenty-six."

"That was when you were in the Marine Corps?"

"Yes."

"And soon after that you were dishonorably discharged from the marines?"

"Yes."

"And all those events occurred about five years ago?"

"Yes."

"Will you tell me what happened the day after your mother received her award?"

"Yes. There was an accident."

Rick's mouth and tongue suddenly felt very dry. When he tried to swallow, his throat felt tight, and he coughed.

"I have the details," said Teodoro, reading from one of the reports. "She was in Sacramento to receive another medical award, a citation for her work with mentally handicapped children. While walking to the convention hall, she was killed by a hit-and-run driver—"

Teodoro stopped reading. The red-headed wimp gave Rick a sympathetic glance and then turned quickly back to his dials and graphs.

Rick stared down at the gray wires attached to his bare forearm and upper arm. He waited for the questions to resume. Instead, Teodoro changed the topic to Jerry and began a brief monologue.

"I can see by the other interrogation reports that you were questioned in detail many times about your relationship with your brother for the past few years."

He placed the dossier down on the table and closed the manila folder.

"All those reports jibe pretty much with several others. Where necessary, revisions have been made. We are now reasonably certain that at no time were you aware of your brother's part in the conspiracy to kill the president and Miss Johnssen."

Teodoro walked around the table and sat in the chair beside Rick's. There was no change in his attitude. He was still the professional instructor and agent, impersonal and unfriendly.

But Rick sensed that their relationship might be about to change. Teodoro gazed at him in an almost fatherly way.

Rick judged Teodoro to be in his late forties. His face was relatively unlined, a condition Rick had observed before in certain thick-skinned Central American men of plump middle age.

Nevertheless, Teodoro's age and years of job stress were clearly evident in other ways: The whites of his eyes were a brownish yellow with the most prominent red veins Rick had ever seen. Teodoro's habit of constantly grinding his teeth had worn some of them down to brown stubs.

Teodoro's breath was terrible, probably befouled by stomach trouble, too many cigarettes, too much tequila, and the bottles of pills he took constantly to help his digestion. He reminded Rick of a male fox who was getting well on in years, a survivor of many battles who could usually outthink his younger rivals.

During the remainder of Teodoro's monologue, while he talked about Rick's brother Jerry, his voice softened noticeably. Rick was surprised. He had always believed that veteran operatives who worked for the CIA and its affiliates, such as

TimTomTon, were towers of ice who never showed human warmth.

"I know you and your older brother were very close," Teodoro said. "I know that at times he was a father and mother to you. Now I'm authorized to tell you things about your brother which at first you won't accept. I want you to listen carefully and be ready for questions. We can argue later."

Then Teodoro dropped the bomb.

He told Rick that TimTomTon was 100 percent certain Jerry had killed their mother.

"That's a lie!" Rick shouted.

When he started to rise in protest, Teodoro put a heavy hand on Rick's shoulder and pushed him down. His stubby fingers dug painfully into the muscles of Rick's bare upper arm where the wire sensors were attached. For a man of his years, Teodoro's strength was unbelievable.

"Be quiet!" he ordered. "Answer the questions."

He glanced at the operator of the lie detector. "Everything OK?"

The wimp said yes.

Teodoro turned back to Rick, his dark eyes glittering and intense. "Were you aware your brother was in Sacramento the day your mother was killed?"

"Yes."

"Were you aware that the rental car that killed your mother, a yellow Honda wagon, was traced to your brother?"

"No. Do you have any proof?"

"Be quiet," said Teodoro angrily. "I ask the questions, not you."

He told Rick there were written records—Jerry's signature and driver's license number—which proved that he'd rented the Honda. It was later recovered by the Sacramento police who found evidence in its damaged front end linking the car to the victim.

"Strands of your mother's hair were caught in the broken headlight," said Teodoro. "Fibers from your mother's skirt—Fortrel polyester—were embedded in the twisted front bumper—"

"That's not proof," Rick said. "What proof do you have that my brother was driving?"

Teodoro's face darkened with renewed anger. He turned to the wimp and told him to disconnect Rick from the machine.

"Well?" Rick asked after the wires were removed. "What's the proof?"

Teodoro didn't answer. He turned his back on Rick. Then he ordered Percy and Eduardo to take Rick to lunch.

When Rick returned to the classroom at 1:00 P.M., the wimp was gone and so was his machine. Teodoro continued one of his security lectures and ordered Rick to take notes. His voice was chilled and aloof.

During the rest of the afternoon, no reference was made to Rick's brother or mother. Looking into Rick's file, Teodoro read selected portions from the results of his personality and intelligence test a few days previously. He told Rick it was unfortunate that he didn't have the exact kind of ERA personality that TimTomTon required for its PMs.

"That's why there's an E/I designation on your file," Teodoro said. "Normally, you would be rejected as not fit for TimTomTon service."

Seeing that Rick was annoyed by all the gobbledygook letter designations, Teodoro offered brief explanations.

ERA stood for externalized, regulated, adaptive individual, which was the kind of man or woman TimTomTon normally recruited.

PM was the designation for paramilitary officer, the job Rick had been picked for. PMs were the lowest classification of TimTomTon agents.

E/I on Rick's file indicated that he was even lower in classification that the others on the low list. E/I stood for externalizer/internalizer. An externalizer was the preferred personality, sort of an aggressive extrovert who was a doer, not a thinker, a person who followed orders without questioning them. An internalizer was sort of an introvert, a person who might do a lot of thinking and question his orders. An internalizer might be too flexible and take a too-imaginative approach to solving problems of security and intelligence-gathering.

Because Rick was a combination of externalizer and internalizer, it was anticipated that he would be difficult to work with. It was also anticipated that he would rely more on his own ideas than those of TimTomTon, a negative variation that was considered close to disloyalty.

Despite Rick's many shortcomings, he would be sworn in with the rank of paramilitary officer. He would be highly paid. He would not be permitted to resign. His term of service would be indefinite and subject to cancellation without advance notice.

At five o'clock Teodoro concluded his lecture and said the class would be dismissed an hour early that evening so Rick could meet someone very important.

As he walked out the Quonset hut's front door, Rick felt his heart begin to thump.

A beautiful blond young woman was standing on the wooden porch, waiting for him.

Gin.

She smiled at Rick. Not a big smile, because she was shy about showing her silver braces.

God, she was beautiful. She was the crème de la crème, the choicest of the classic blonds, the truest of the natural blonds.

And there she stood at last, waiting for Rick—and no one else.

☆ ☆ **10** ☆ ☆

Rick took off the tinted glasses. He closed his left eye. And then with his good eye he could see the true color of her hair and the light pinks of her incredible complexion.

God, she was beautiful. And sexy, without even trying.

In his fantasies she was so young and sexy that every time he thought about photographing her in the buff he nearly had an orgasm.

Now that he was finally close to her again, it was obvious that his fantasies hadn't done her justice. It had been over a month since he'd seen her. He discovered at once that he hadn't correctly remembered all the details of her treasures.

Her abundance of hair was the color of newly polished brass, not the dull gold of his fantasies. Her eyes were larger and darker than he'd remembered, the loveliest dark smoldering brown, with tiny gold flecks that made them deeply luminous.

If he'd had his new Konica along, he would've immediately taken pictures of her to make sure he never forgot those details again. As quickly as possible, he would've shot thirty-six Kodachromes because the backlight was so perfect.

The late afternoon sun was off to the side behind her, slightly filtered by clouds. It outlined her great mass of hair and the curving line of her cheek with a thin rim of gold, the kind of highlight sometimes used in paintings by the old masters.

Where it met her shoulder, the curving line of her throat was another perfect picture.

But, of course, there wouldn't have been any photos, even if he'd had the camera. He could sense that she was too lens shy and too self-conscious about her braces.

Even though she was shy, she was still very sexy in that natural way that was hers alone. It was one of her contradictions. Her youth and innocence made her all the more desirable and charismatic. Some day he would find out if he were good enough with a lens to capture that charisma and innocence on film.

He put the tinted glasses back on and smiled at her.

She looked down at her blue-striped running shoes, then at his shoulder, and then at the Quonset hut behind him

"Do you mind . . ." she gave him a fleeting glance from beneath dark gold lashes, ". . . if we jog?"

"Great!" His voice sounded too stupidly enthusiastic, but maybe she didn't notice.

She wore pink shorts and a matching pink blouse. The shorts emphasized the long, slim lines of her legs. Although the blouse was a bit loose, it couldn't conceal the proportions of her breasts. She wasn't large. She was just right. She wore a runner's bra that kept her from jiggling.

As they slowly jogged side by side along the dirt shoulder of the military road, she spoke a few more words. She explained that she tried to jog each evening just before dinner.

"I'm on my way home . . . ." she said. "Would you like to join Aunt Pam and me for dinner?"

That really amazed him. He accepted at once and hoped he'd managed to keep from sounding too eager and juvenile.

After that, she was silent for a long time. They ran past many ancient Quonset huts of different sizes, all painted a drab beige. Some looked like command centers and offices. Others were barracks, rec centers, and enlisted men's clubs. Everything looked old and weatherbeaten.

In the parking lots they passed, there were very few air force vehicles and civilian cars, indicating that perhaps the base wasn't being used too much.

When they turned onto a dirt side road, Rick noticed they were being followed by a blue air force van. It stayed about fifty yards behind and kept pace, moving slowly.

Glancing back, Rick saw that Teodoro's two security men, Eduardo and Percy, were on the van's front seat. Percy was driving. Their van was followed by a blue air force sedan. Probably more security people. Both vehicles were equipped with tall radio antennas.

The dirt road climbed a hill that was covered with tall ponderosa pines and a few tired old balsam firs. In the distance were ranges of dark blue, snow-streaked mountains, part of the Rockies.

The hill was steeper than it looked. Gin was still running without effort, but Rick soon noticed he was out of shape, breathing too hard.

His feet began to hurt because he wasn't wearing running

shoes. Everything he wore—soft leather lowcuts, tight dark brown slacks, and a white Nike sport shirt—had been supplied by TimTomTon.

The shoes had thick spongy soles. As the hill grew steeper, they felt like lumps of concrete.

Finally they began jogging downhill toward a broad valley with a green meadow. A small, silvery stream wandered down the valley's center.

Breathing more easily, Rick stole an occasional glance at Gin. He found it impossible to believe that these few minutes were the longest time they'd ever shared alone. She had been constantly on his mind for an eon. But actually they'd had very little close contact from the time he'd first met her weeks before in El Dorado Park.

The longest contact had been during the long darkness of his convalescence in Aunt Louise's bedroom. During that period of less than a week, Gin and he had occasionally talked, but never alone. Louise, or someone from TimTomTon was always nearby.

There was so much he wanted to talk to Gin about. Not just questions about her strange work for the president. He'd let her tell him about that in her own good time.

There were so many little personal facts about her that he wanted to know. What movies did she like, what kind of rock—Springsteen, Madonna, Manilow, Prince, or Ronstadt? What did she like on her burgers and hot dogs—onions or pickles or both?

Now that they were together at last, Rick realized how tremendously his attitude toward her had changed. True, he still lusted for her body, as any red-blooded, normal male would. But now he was also aware that along with the lust was love for this shy person, genuine love that made him think very seriously about taking another chance at marriage.

As they jogged to where the road curved across the meadow, he wondered if she'd like to stop for a minute or two to catch her breath. It would be wonderful to lie on their backs in the tall cool meadow grass, look up at the deep blue Montana sky . . . and just talk.

It wouldn't hurt to ask.

"Gin," he began. "How about—"

Suddenly the dark green meadow directly ahead of them erupted with twin explosions and violent red flames.

As dust, smoke, shooting sparks, and chunks of earth swirled high in the air, Rick heard the roar of a jet plane directly behind them.

He knew what was happening because he'd undergone rocket attacks like this while training with the marines in the Southern California desert.

It was insane! Someone was making a crazy mistake!

The first two rocket explosions were about a hundred yards ahead of them, much too close. The next two blasts were a lot closer, shaking the earth violently beneath their feet.

As the jet thundered directly overhead, very low, Rick threw himself at Gin. He bowled her over.

Only seconds had passed since the first rockets hit, but his reflexes were slow. He knew he should've knocked her down a hell of a lot quicker.

As they rolled together on the hard-packed dirt of the road, he tried to cover her body with his own. But he was clumsy and off the mark. She rolled out from under him.

At last they stopped rolling. Rick pinned her down. She lay on her back, and he could feel her softness even though most of her was rigid with fear.

He caught a glimpse of terribly frightened brown eyes, and then he squashed her as flat as possible while all kinds of junk rained down on them.

The second pair of rockets struck less than fifty yards from them. Murderously close. The stuff that fell on them—and all around them—included smoking clumps of dirt, some with grass attached, rocks large and small, and a shattered section of rotted pine branch.

The heavy junk that thumped down on Rick's back didn't worry him half as much as their exposed position on the road. They had no protection whatsoever. This part of the green meadow was flat as a billiard table.

Rick lifted his head just high enough to look around. He smelled the strong stink of sulphur and other chemicals from the rockets. He saw the plane a long way off, starting to climb. Then it turned to come back. It looked like an air force fighter bomber or attack jet.

He knew he had to get Gin somewhere else, fast. Wasn't there a crooked little stream nearby? But where? On their left? No. So it had to be to the right.

He grabbed Gin's forearm and yanked her upright as hard as he could. Thank God, she didn't resist. If she had, he would've dislocated her arm.

He bellowed for her to follow, a waste of breath because he gave her no choice. As he plunged into the knee-high grass, he dragged her along behind, holding her forearm in a death grip.

The stream had to be close, concealed by the grass. But where the hell was it?

As they sped along, Gin became less of a burden because she'd found her feet and was almost keeping up. Smart woman. She knew what they had to do.

Abruptly there was another roaring sound in the air. A second silvery attack jet whooshed low over them, its thunder echoing across the valley. This one Rick could positively identify. It had air force markings and was an F-16 fighter.

As they ran, he saw the second jet pursue the first one, which also had air force identification. Then he heard the boom-boom-boom of heavy machine guns.

Now he was totally bewildered. The planes were twins. Why would one Air Force jet attack another?

Gin and he stopped running. He put his arm protectively around her shoulders. As they watched the battle in the nearby sky, he felt her whole body shuddering against him. She was frightened to death but hadn't panicked.

Everything was happening so fast he wasn't sure what he was seeing. A trail of greasy black smoke poured out behind the first jet. Then it made a broad diving turn and vanished behind a high, pine-covered hill.

Rick heard an explosion, muffled by the hill. Then a huge cloud of black smoke erupted above the trees.

"It crashed!" Gin screamed. "How awful!"

The second plane circled in the sky, like a vulture eager for its next meal. Then it abruptly flew away. After that the sky was silent. But not for long.

Hearing a different sound behind them, Gin and Rick turned quickly. A third plane was low in the sky and slanting down directly toward them.

A third plane? Impossible!

It was a slow, propeller plane of small and light construction. It had air force markings. From under each wing, a light machine gun was firing. Snap-snap-snap. Rick could see green tufts of grass flying in the meadow as the bullets came toward them.

Jesus H. Christ, was there no end to this? And where was the stream?

He dragged Gin through the tall grass, looking for a depression, any kind of hollow in the ground that might give protection.

Then he saw the stream. It wasn't very wide, but it was deep, and that's what they needed more than anything else in the world.

They flopped into the chill water seconds before the little plane passed overhead. The stream was at least three feet deep, more than enough to cover their bodies.

Rick pushed Gin's head under. Then he plunged deeper and pulled her down until they struck the sandy bottom. He got on top and stayed there, holding her down. They stayed immersed a long time. The water was very cold and so clear that Rick saw a tiny brown trout dart past.

At first, Gin didn't fight. But then she began to kick and

flail her arms, knocking off his glasses. She probably hadn't taken in enough air. He let her up, just enough to gasp and splash for air. Then he heard the plane start another pass. Again he shoved her face deep into the stream. He felt vibrations in the water that might have been bullets.

This time they stayed down so long that Rick ran out of air. Gin was squirming so violently he knew she was in trouble.

He let her up. He raised his dripping head out of the water and sucked air. He wanted to suck a lot more, but held his breath in order to listen for the sound of the propeller. He heard an engine. But it wasn't the plane. It was the van, the blue air force van, bouncing toward them through the grass. It slid to a stop, with its front wheels in the water. Percy and Eduardo threw open the doors and jumped out.

Rick had forgotten all about them and the van. Now it occurred to him, very belatedly, that he'd made a mistake. He should've taken Gin back to the van for protection instead of wasting all that time hunting for the water. Then he saw all the bullet holes in the van and decided he hadn't been so dumb after all.

Percy and Eduardo ran over to the stream. Percy helped Rick pull Gin from the water. Eduardo tried to help, but wasn't much good because he suddenly discovered he'd taken a bullet through his upper chest. He sat down on the grassy stream bank and began cursing in almost hysterical Spanish. As a vast quantity of blood soaked the upper part of his business suit, he slid into the stream and sat there up to his waist.

Reacting to the shock of his wound and the cold water, he began to stutter, "D-Dios! D-Dios!"

Percy and Rick helped Gin over to the van. She was dripping wet, coughing up water, and shivering. She looked more appealing than ever because of the deep way she was breathing and because of how the wet pink blouse clung to her breasts. Her wet pink shorts were almost transparent, revealing scanty white bikini panties underneath. Percy located the dark jacket of his business suit in the van and draped it over her shoulders.

"Thank ... you ..." Gin looked at Percy and then at Rick. "Thank you both ... very much."

She was still shaking, coughing, and breathing very deeply. But her words were almost calm. Rick was amazed at how calm she was. She looked a hell of a lot calmer than he felt. With one hand she held the lapels of the dark coat together just below her chin. With the palm of her other hand she squeegeed the water from her brass-yellow hair, flattening the long shining strands against her temple, her cheek, and the shoulder of the coat.

Hearing the crackling sound of a two-way radio, Rick turned and saw that the other air force vehicle, the sedan, was parked nearby. It had approached with such stealth that none of those near the stream were aware of its presence.

The two blue-uniformed security men on its front seat were in no hurry to get out. They were busy receiving instructions on their radio.

"Will do ..." the man beside the driver spoke into a hand mike. "Will deliver them to the dispensary ..."

An hour later, Gin and Rick were still seated in the dispensary exam room, wearing matching robes. Each was white terry cloth with a blue air force symbol above the breast pocket.

A young air force physician and his elderly nurse were in the process of completing the exams. By his questions, the doctor seemed more interested in Rick and Gin's mental state than anything else.

Teodoro sat on a nearby sofa, listening to everything they told the doctor. Teodoro was silent and impassive, but the way he chain-smoked Winstons indicated he was feeling plenty of inner turmoil.

It had not been one of TimTomTon's better days.

Percy and Eduardo were in the emergency room having their wounds repaired. A bullet had broken Eduardo's collarbone, necessitating surgery. Another surgeon had removed pieces of glass from several deep cuts in Percy's back. His wounds were caused by a bullet that had shattered one of the van's windows.

When the doctor and nurse stepped out of the room, Rick tried once more to ask Teodoro the questions that had been bugging him much of the evening.

"Weren't those our own planes? Didn't they have—"

"Shut your mouth!" barked Teodoro. *"Security!"*

He placed his forefinger vertically across his tightly closed lips and glared at Rick. Then he made a vicious slashing gesture across his throat, a warning Rick decided not to ignore.

They sat in silence until the young doctor returned. He brought Gin's and Rick's clothes, which had been laundered and dried. He also returned Rick's glasses, which air force personnel had recovered from the stream.

The doctor gave them a friendly nod. "You may both go. So far as I can tell, you are each as fit as can be—and very lucky."

Rick and Gin dressed in separate rooms. Then Teodoro drove them to the base's administration complex.

He took them into an interrogation room. But there was no interrogation. Teodoro warned them not to talk, either to him or each other.

It was another bleak military room, almost bare of furniture. Gin and Rick sat on wooden folding chairs so old and rickety they looked like veterans of World War I. Teodoro sat behind an antique rolltop desk and waited for its phone to ring.

For a long time, the room was silent except for an undersized yellow jacket that buzzed in frustration at the room's single window.

At last the phone rang. Teodoro said yes, then no, then hung up.

After that, the phone rang incessantly. Rick could tell by tinny, metallic sounds that escaped from the earpiece that most of the calls were from different men and women. All of Teodoro's replies were short barks, a yes or no followed by a code word.

Some of the voices on the line were agitated. But the man

who called the most frequently seemed at ease and very sure of himself. Rick suspected he was Saddlebag One.

A little after eight o'clock—about three hours after the attack—Teodoro gave Rick and Gin a dinner break.

"I want you back here in seventy-five minutes," he ordered. "No more, no less. At that time, you will receive a briefing that will—by necessity—be somewhat incomplete."

Gin phoned Aunt Pam and was told that their dinner had been kept warm in the oven. A sergeant armed with a holstered .45 pistol drove them to Aunt Pam's in an air force minibus. It was about a fifteen-minute drive in the dusk along the hilly dirt road on which Gin and he had jogged.

When they passed the meadow where the planes had attacked, they saw a dozen parked vehicles, several armed sentries, and a lot of men with portable lights who seemed to be examining the areas where the rockets struck.

As the minibus left the valley, Rick's mind wrestled with the stupidities and improbabilities of the air attack. If security was so lax, why did TimTomTon take the risk of allowing someone as valuable as Gin to jog where she could be killed with such ease?

Were those genuine air force fighter planes? Or was the one that was supposedly shot down a phony? And what the hell was a Mickey Mouse propeller plane doing on a jet fighter base?

It was dark when they arrived at Aunt Pam's Quonset hut on the side of steep mountain. The hut, and a smaller one nearby, were concealed beneath a dense growth of ponderosa pines.

Rick noticed that several air force police, armed with rifles, were stationed around the two Quonset huts. Recalling the color slide he'd seen during his indoctrination, he recognized their weapons as fast-firing 7.62mm Galil NATO rifles. Each man also carried a hand radio and extra ammunition.

Additional armed guards were stationed beside the big trailer that contained part of Gin's communications lab. The security arrangements looked much tighter than they'd been around Aunt Louise's and Aunt Pam's houses in California.

The minibus driver declined Gin's invitation to come inside. He said he'd wait in the bus.

Aunt Pam's Quonset hut was immense and expensively furnished. As Gin and Rick passed through the music room, TV room, and library, Gin explained that it had formerly been a four-star general's residence. The smaller hut next door had housed the general's adjutant.

Aunt Pam was waiting for them in the dining groom. Her long platinum hair was in a neat bun, but her face was flushed. She sat at the head of the dining table and was very drunk.

The long narrow table was set with an elegant lace cloth, gleaming goblets, silverware, tall unlighted red candles in silver holders, and fresh lilacs in crystal vases.

Everything was immaculate, except where Aunt Pam sat. There the lace tablecloth was in disarray. Three empty beer bottles lay on their sides on her dinner plate.

Holding a fourth bottle of Coors, she poured beer and foam into a wine goblet. Most of the foam surged over the rim and onto her hand.

"Hi, Rickie!" she chirped. "Welcome to Montanie!"

Licking the foam from her fingers, she rose to her feet and headed on a wobbly course toward the kitchen.

"Sit rightie down," she called back over her shoulder. "Dinner's 'bout four hours late and completely ruined . . . but that's all rightie right."

Embarrassed by her aunt's condition, Gin apologized for what appeared to be a social disaster in the making. In a voice too low to be overheard, she explained that Pam's drinking problem had become worse ever since the evening in California when she'd witnessed the violent strangling of the TimTomTon agent.

"Poor thing," whispered Gin. "She has terrible nightmares."

Soon Pam returned carrying platters heaped high with roast pork and scalloped potatoes. She spooned great quantities onto their plates, ignoring their protests that they weren't that hungry.

Four hours earlier, the pork was undoubtedly tender and juicy. Now it was dry and tough. The potatoes were dry and crusty.

"We won't have time to finish all this," Gin said. "We have to get back . . ."

While they tried to eat, Aunt Pam finished her goblet of beer and sang happily to herself.

Suddenly she came around the table, put her arm around Rick's neck, and spoke loudly into his ear. Her breath was strong enough to power a truck.

"Hey, half-wit," she said, "know why I'm so happy?"

"We don't have time," said Gin.

Ignoring her, Pam rubbed her cheek affectionately against Rick's and began a rambling discussion of queen bees. It took Rick a while to catch on. In California, Aunt Louise had been the queen bee, living in a big fine house and lording it over her sister Pam who had little money and no social status.

But now the tables were turned.

"I called heads," said Pam. "That made me the queen bee."

Gin explained that there had been a coin toss to see which of the sisters would occupy the general's big, lovely house. Pam won. As a result, Aunt Louise was stuck in the adjutant's humble little house and had no luxuries.

Pam removed her arm from Rick's neck and poured more suds into her goblet.

"My half-wit sister can't take it," she said joyfully. "Sits around all day crying her half-wit eyes out."

The more Pam talked, the more uncomfortable Gin became. She put her fork down, moved away from the table, and gave Rick a meaningful look.

Glancing at his watch, he pushed his chair back and stood up.

"We've got to get back," he said.

"We're late," added Gin.

"Oh, no, you don't!" said Pam. "We're goin' to start

partyin' rightie now. . . ." She paused as inspiration struck. "Let's all go over to half-wit Louise's and drink beer. We'll all sit aroun' like half-wits . . . an' cry our eyes out."

"Sorry, Aunt Pam." Gin took Rick's arm and guided him toward the door. "See you later."

They hurried outside to the minibus and got in. As they drove away, Aunt Pam watched from the lighted doorway. Her face was sad.

REO: No. 41
To: Rawhide, White House
From: Chicken Little
Subject: *Soviet Safety*

The full-scale, city-defense version of Star Wars (SDI) will cost trillions. *It will not be perfect.*

Since only perfection is acceptable in a nuclear space defense system, this means Star Wars won't work.

Nevertheless, you must offer the Star Wars technology to the Soviets. If we Americans are ever to know safety again, it will be because the Soviets feel safe.

If the Soviets don't feel safe, they will give a higher priority to the first-strike premise. If that strike is launched, the sky will indeed fall.

☆ ☆ **12** ☆ ☆

Gin and Rick arrived back at the administration complex at nine o'clock, fifteen minutes early. Teodoro wasn't ready and made them wait.

When they were admitted to the briefing room, they found Teodoro standing before a large wall map, holding a slender pointer stick. He introduced the other two men in the room, an air force bird colonel and a civilian whom he called Lariat, a code name.

"No need to go into all the preliminaries," Teodoro said. "This is approximately the flight path of the two F-16s."

Using the stick, he pointed to the bottom section of the map, which Rick now recognized as a blowup of part of the base. The meadow was tinted dark green, the meandering stream was blue, and the mountains to the west were outlined in light green.

Teodoro's tone was so matter-of-fact—and his explanation so vague in places—that many minutes passed before Rick realized the significance of what was being discussed.

The rocket attack had been only a test. The rockets were real enough, but everything else had been a simulation. The first F-16 hadn't been shot down. Its pilot had pretended to be disabled by emitting black smoke and then had faked the crash behind the mountains. The whole scam was a test to see how well Rick would do when called upon to protect Gin under the extreme pressure of combatlike conditions.

As the full realization hit Rick, his blood boiled. These fools had *deliberately* endangered Gin's life in some cockamamy exercise!

Rick couldn't keep silent. He butted into Teodoro's measured discussion with words he intended to be biting but restrained. But the whole thing was so outrageous that it was impossible for him to keep the lid on his wrath.

"Bastards!" he shouted. "How could you run such a risk with her? You must—"

"Silence!" ordered Teodoro.

"No! No way! I want you to—"

Suddenly the slender stick came down with vicious force diagonally across Rick's neck. The pain was bad enough. But much worse was the humiliation of being whipped like a child in front of others.

As Teodoro drew his arm back for another blow, Rick seized the stick and twisted it from his grasp. He broke it in half and hurled the pieces to the other end of the room where they clattered against a metal filing cabinet.

No one said anything. The bird colonel cleared his throat as if to speak but realized it was wiser not to.

Lariat, the civilian, wore a thin, smart-ass smile. Rick decided he liked him even less than Teodoro.

Teodoro's anger was as great, or probably greater, than Rick's, but he didn't let it erupt. He brought his face so close to Rick's that the dark enlarged pores beside his nose looked like miniature craters. The fury in his brown-black eyes was hot enough to scorch skin.

But when he spoke, his words were cool and perfectly controlled. "Moore, you are close to washing out. You did very badly on this evening's simulated rocket test. And at the moment you are on the thin edge of insubordination. If you don't—"

Rick didn't let him finish. "Shove your fucking job!" he shouted. "I resign! And Gin resigns with me!"

Turning his back on Teodoro, Rick grabbed Gin's arm and started toward the door.

But Gin refused to move more than a few feet.

"No, Rick! You can't—"

"She's right," said Teodoro. "Nobody *resigns* from TimTomTon. You are expendable. And *she* is expendable."

For emphasis, he jabbed his forefinger in Gin's direction. "If we want you *out,* you simply *disappear*—and that's it!"

He made no effort to soften the threat in his words. The effect on Gin was chilling. She looked so frightened Rick could see there was no way to take her out of there. At least not then. She clutched his arm with both hands, as if afraid that he might try to do something violent to Teodoro.

"Rick," she said, "you must do exactly what he says." Her hot brown eyes looked up at him imploringly. "He can't personally *delete* you. But he can arrange for others to make the *deletion.*" Although she spoke in a whisper, it was obvious she wanted Teodoro to hear how hard she was trying to make Rick cooperate. "Listen to me, Rick. They're *everything.* You're *nothing.* And *deletion* means a body bag buried in the desert. Is *that* what you want?"

It was Rick's turn to feel the chill. His mind couldn't accept what he'd heard. Such a thing couldn't happen in America. Or could it? Could they possibly consider destroying someone as important as Gin?

As reality sank in he had to face the fact that some of the hardest words were Gin's, not Teodoro's. And that made a difference. He doubted that Gin would lie. Or would she, under great pressure?

"Please," she said. "You have no choice."

She was right, of course. Rick was no match for Teodoro. Not then. He was beaten. It was so hard to admit but so undeniably true.

As he spoke the words of surrender, he looked defiantly at Teodoro to let him know that what was happening was only temporary. "All right," Rick said. "I'm cooperating."

Gin gave him a glance of gratitude.

Pointing at the map with his stubby forefinger, Teodoro continued his briefing about the two jet planes. He explained that the test had two goals.

Goal A: To see how Gin and Rick would handle the stress of being under combat attack. Gin received a passing grade. Rick received a failing grade, for reasons Teodoro said would be explained at another time.

Goal B: To lure Dr. Sierra out into the open. This effort was very successful, up to a point. Dr. Sierra was presumed to have been the pilot of the small plane that machine-gunned Gin and Rick.

Teodoro explained that TimTomTon had learned in advance—from its Managua connection—that Dr. Sierra was planning the air assault. No details had been obtained beforehand. Data processed after the attack indicated that the plane, equipped with folding wings, had been hidden aboard a large grocery trailer towed by a truck. At a point ten miles from the air base, the plane had taken off from the highway. It flew too low to be picked up by radar. But its final approach to the meadow had been observed.

The F-16s were ordered to shoot it down. The jets had returned in less than a minute, but by then the light plane had disappeared.

Teodoro pointed to an area of the map not too far from the meadow. "It landed here," he said. "On this dirt road beneath a stand of very dense and tall pines. The pilot was extremely skilled, which is why we're sure he was Dr. Sierra."

He explained that the plane's wings were slashed off by tree trunks, but the fuselage remained almost intact. Within minutes, a TimTomTon copter landed at the site, but by then the pilot had disappeared.

Teodoro didn't appear to be embarrassed by the fact that once again Dr. Sierra had escaped when escape seemed highly unlikely. His forced landing had been on the base itself, with TimTomTon and air force personnel only moments away. Yet no one had seen him. And his present whereabouts were unknown.

"He had inside help," said Teodoro. "We believe he was helped by base personnel. He—"

"Hold on!" interrupted the bird colonel with a display of anger. "Why us? Why drape your shit all over us?"

To emphasize his displeasure, the colonel moved closer to Teodoro. As he strode past, Rick saw that the back of his neck was glowing bright red.

Teodoro let him come very close. Leaning forward, he whispered something in the colonel's ear. The message had an immediate effect. The colonel backed away and didn't say another word. Now his face was redder than his neck.

That concluded the briefing. At a signal from Teodoro, the man called Lariat snapped open a small metal briefcase. He removed a white business envelope and handed it to Rick.

"Your first assignment," said Teodoro. "Prepared by Lariat with recommendations from Saddlebag One and myself. You will memorize every word. Tomorrow morning you will return it to me for disposal."

He shot Rick a glance of utter disgust, making it clear that he had opposed giving him the assignment.

"That's it," he said. "Moore, you are dismissed."

As Rick left the room, he saw Gin approach Teodoro and

begin a conversation. Their voices were too hushed for him to hear.

Holding the white envelope, he waited in the corridor. In a few moments, the bird colonel and Lariat came out. They walked past Rick without a word or glance. Half a minute later, Gin came out. She was very pleased as she made her announcement.

"Guess what, Rick. He won't say it to you, but he thought you did very well when the rockets hit." She smiled so happily her braces flashed like silver. "Not only that. He gave permission for you to spend the night at Aunt Pam's!"

Rick was so flabbergasted he didn't know what to say.

"It's partly because of Dr. Sierra," Gin said. "And because Aunt Pam and I don't want to be alone in the house—" Shyly she looked down at the floor. "Do you mind, Rick?"

Did he mind? God, what a question. For weeks he'd waited for some kind of a move from her, anything that showed more than a polite interest.

And then, Jesus H. Christ, suddenly here it was. Or was it? She was so complicated and unpredictable that Rick couldn't be sure. What was on her mind, really? Nothing? Or everything?

The same buck sergeant drove them to Aunt Pam's in the same air force minibus.

During the ride, Gin sat close to Rick, her arm touching his. He switched on the dome light, opened his envelope, and they read his assignment together.

The orders were brief and unsigned:

Paramilitary officer Richard D. Moore will be given documents identifying him as his brother, GERALD HANS MOORE, JR. He will go to Iverness, Idaho. He will make contact with a man, code name ST. PAUL. He will determine if ST. PAUL is an authentic associate of DR. SIERRA'S. He will receive verbal orders on how this will be accomplished.

Folding the envelope, Rick placed the assignment in the pocket of his sport shirt.

Gin whispered so the driver couldn't overhear. "I don't

like it. It's dangerous. I'm frightened for both of us. I want out—''

"Let's talk about it tomorrow," Rick said

Suddenly he was as excited as a kid on his first date. He put his arm tentatively across her shoulder. She didn't draw away. He held her close. He could feel her trembling through the thin cloth of her pink blouse.

When they arrived back at Aunt Pam's luxurious Quonset, it was close to eleven. All the inside and outside lights were on, and the armed guards were on duty.

The sergeant said he would return at seven in the morning to pick Rick up. Then he drove off.

When Rick and Gin went inside, they found Aunt Pam in the TV room. She was sitting in an oversized easy chair, with her head tilted back, an empty Coors bottle on the floor near her feet. She was dead drunk and snoring lightly. Her shiny platinum hair was mussed and hanging in front of her eyes.

An old black-and-white Humphrey Bogart movie was flickering on the TV screen, probably *To Have and Have Not,* because Lauren Bacall and Walter Brennan were in it. The sound level was thunderous. Gin turned the set off. They eased Aunt Pam up from the chair and walked her to her bedroom. She did not resist.

After putting Aunt Pam to bed, Gin returned to the TV room. She opened its closet and took out two sheets and a dark blue air force blanket.

The large sofa converted into a double bed with a good mattress. Rick helped her put on the sheets and blanket.

They didn't talk, and Gin didn't look directly at him. She was very nervous. So was he.

After she placed the single pillow on the bed, Rick moved closer and stood beside her.

"Shall I get another pillow?" she asked.

For the first time since reentering the room, she looked directly at him. In her eyes he saw a mixture of deep feelings.

He saw confusion. He also saw love. Or was it something closer to desire?

Rick put his arms around her and drew her small body close to his. He put his face into her great soft mass of brass-on-gold hair and breathed in its light fragrance. He could feel her breasts pressing against him.

"Oh, God," she whispered. "I'm so frightened—"

"Of me?"

"No. Of them."

She drew her face back and looked up at him strangely. "Oh, God, I want out—"

"Out of TimTomTon?"

"Yes! But I'm afraid!"

She was being unpredictable again and going too fast for him. She was also doing something else. Her lower body was pressing against him and starting to move in a way that he never expected.

Not from her.

"No more words. . . ." Her voice was warm and whispery. "I want you to love me. Please love me, Rick!"

☆ ☆ 13 ☆ ☆

Gin put both hands behind his head and pulled his mouth down to hers. Her mouth was hot and wet, and her tongue quickly touched his.

He was dumbfounded. All this time he had considered her shy and virginal and unreachable. God, how little did he know.

Laughing joyfully, she suddenly broke away from him. She put her fingers into her mouth and removed the silver retainer.

"Oh, God," she said, "how I hate this damn thing!"

She placed the retainer atop a small end table. Then she

turned and quickly kissed him again on the mouth, deeply. Just as quickly, she broke away once more. "Not yet, Rick."

Now what? Blood was pounding in his temples and rising in his crotch, and all she was doing was being elusive and playing games that bewildered him.

She returned to the end table and opened its top drawer. She took out a roll of nontransparent Scotch tape on a plastic dispenser. Cutting off a small piece, she moved to the closest wall and stuck the tape on the head of a brass tack that supported a landscape painting. Then she stuck other small pieces of tape on what appeared to be tiny nail heads in two other walls.

"Microminiature wide-angle lenses," she whispered. "TV surveillance."

She tossed the tape back into the drawer. Then she locked both of the room's doors.

Returning to Rick, she unbuttoned her pink blouse and took it off. She gave him a bewitching smile that was totally unlike the Gin he thought he knew. She unhooked her jogging bra at the back and dropped it and her blouse to the floor.

"Now!" she said. "Now you're really going to get kissed!"

She leaped against him. She wrapped her legs around his and gave him a kiss that seared him to his roots. She sucked his lower lip. Then she drove her juicy tongue in and out like a stiletto.

Rick brushed the tips of her breasts lightly with both hands. Then he lifted her off the floor and held her tight. Their mouths remained together as he carried her to the bed.

For a few moments, he left her alone on the bed while he removed his shoes and clothes. She slipped quickly out of her pink running shorts and white bikini panties. Then she lay on her back and let him gaze at all her beauty.

She was far lovelier than his fantasies. Her legs were long and perfect. Where they met, the hair was soft brass on gold, the same shining hue as the mass of hair that streamed from her head across the dark blue blanket.

He leaned down and kissed her skin just above the shining pubic hair. The skin was satin smooth and hot to the touch of his tongue.

"Oh, God," she whispered.

He eased down on top of her. Entering her was like nothing he'd ever felt before. She was soft yet firm. She was more than moist. She was overflowing. She was burning hot.

God, what a revelation.

She was a very experienced woman. She was a loving woman who wanted him as much as he wanted her. She was a loving woman who needed it and reveled in it, a loving woman whose hunger matched his with each strong stroke.

God, she was alive! She reached orgasm immediately and cried with the joy of it. She was such a miracle that he held himself back to feel the miracles continue. She cried with the joy of each contraction and each orgasm. As he moved in and out, her loving pressure around him was extraordinary.

When he released at last, her grasp became stronger and more loving, urging him on to spasm after spasm, each achieving more than the one before.

At last he stopped. But it was only a pause, because her loving pressure continued, inspiring him to continue. More great spasms. More miracles. And more.

Then they lay together silently for a long time without moving, neither wanting these moments to end.

When they did move, the mystique was still there. Rick gazed at her with wonder. Never in a thousand years would he have believed that within this shy young person he would find such a woman.

She broke the mood with a smile, a beautiful smile, because the silver braces were gone.

"Rick, my sweet, you were absolutely the best!" She sighed deeply. "But why are you staring at me like that?"

"Because of—"

"Of what?"

"Well—" Suddenly he felt foolish. "I don't think I can explain it."

"Did I surprise you?"

"God, yes!"

She laughed mysteriously. "You missed them, didn't you?"

"Missed what?"

"My hints. Or do you still believe I'm only seventeen?"

"God, no!"

They laughed together and held each other tightly. Legs entwined, they rolled back and forth on the bed, touching and loving, still under the joyful influence of what they had discovered in each other.

Then she moved away. She sat up and gave Rick the same strange look that he'd seen earlier in the evening.

"Rick, I've got to tell you! I must!"

She bent down. She placed her face close to the pillow. With a quick movement of her fingers, she separated her eyelids.

A shiny brown contact lens dropped onto the pillow.

When she raised her face, he saw that she had one blue eye . . . and one brown eye. She placed her finger across her lips, warning him not to speak.

But he had to because he was in such a state of shock. "*Jesus H. Christ!*"

Quickly she placed her hand across his mouth. It wasn't necessary, because at the moment he couldn't think of anything else to say.

"Come with me," she whispered.

She led him across the room. She unlocked the door to the bathroom. They went in. Leaning over the washbowl, she removed her other brown contact lens. Then she turned on the spray in the green tile stall shower and adjusted the temperature.

They stepped in together under the warm spray. He closed the shower door.

"Now we can talk," she said. "They can't overhear. You understand?"

He nodded. Some of the shock was wearing off. Although she had taped over the surveillance lenses in the TV room, it was very probable that listening devices were still functioning in there and throughout the building. If there were bugs in the bathroom, the sound of the shower would drown out their words.

"I think you understand now," she said. "I'm *not* Gin."

Rick nodded. His mind was beginning to sort it out. All the bewildering events of the evening—from the sham rocket attack to the miracles of the bed—were coming into focus.

"I'm a substitute for Gin," she added. "A decoy."

She put her arms around his waist and pressed her skin against his. Her body was wet and very warm . . . and her touch was still wonderful.

"Oh, my God," he said. "Who the hell are you?"

"Agnes. Isn't that a god-awful name?"

He had to agree. But it didn't matter. As she pressed her wetness against him, the effect was the same as it had been on the bed. Whoever she was, she was one hell of a woman.

"I've got to get out of TimTomTon," she said. "Will you help me?"

"Of course."

He wasn't sure how. But he knew he would help her in any way he could.

God, what a woman. There was no way he'd want to let down a woman who could do what she was doing to him in that shower.

REO: No. 44
To: Rawhide, White House
From: Chicken Little
Subject: *Key State*

If you were Walter Mondale, where would you search for crucial electoral votes? He must have—absolutely—the northeastern industrial states.

If you focus all your strategy and energy on winning just *one* of those states, you will win a great reelection victory.

The key state: *Ohio.*

If the polls show you winning Ohio, you can be sure you will win nearly *all* the states in November.

This strategy was used in 1972 by America's most astute political tactician: *Richard Nixon*.

☆ ☆ **14** ☆ ☆

AUNT LOUISE

I knew all along that she wasn't Gin. My lovely daughter Gin.

But I didn't know until lots later that her name was Agnes Steinberg. She sure didn't look Jewish. Except for her blue eyes, she was an almost perfect replica of my daughter.

Agnes supposedly was born in Russia. But I had my doubts. She was more like those smart, fast-talking ones that you find all over New York and in the Third and Fairfax section of L.A.

She probably looked Jewish before the TimTomTon people fixed her up. They did surgery on her nose and jaw. Saddlebag One once told me it took them two years to find a suitable replacement for Gin and another two years to train Agnes to act and talk like my daughter.

I watched from my window that night when Agnes and Rick made those two visits to Pam's Quonset house next door. I knew the first visit was short because my sister was drunk and spoiled their dinner with all her silly antics.

Those Quonset buildings have thin walls. I paid the sentry $50 to look the other way while I stood close to the wall and listened to what was being said inside by the three of them.

It was nothing important.

But I got a real earful later that night when Rick and

Agnes came back. You wouldn't believe what those two did together. Disgusting. I never would've guessed that Agnes was such a slut.

That stupid Rick is putty in a scheming woman's hands. Why he would waste it on Agnes is more than I can understand.

All he had to do was walk a few short steps to my place, and I would've reminded him of the difference between a young slut and a woman who has more wonderful gifts to give.

Early the next morning, I phoned Saddlebag One at his restricted number. He gave me permission to use it in emergencies. He was fascinated when I told him what those two were up to.

"Agnes wants out," I said. "She's scared and wants Rick to help her. I think they're planning to run off together."

"Any idea when?"

"Today. They left together a few minutes ago in that little air force bus."

"Thank you very much, Louise. Anything else?"

"Yes, of course. *Where* is Gin?"

His tone changed immediately from warm and friendly to cool and businesslike.

"Mrs. Remington, you know that's classified information. And you must excuse me now—"

Suddenly there was a loud whining noise on the line. I'd heard it during other calls. It was his voice scrambler, and he made it whine like that whenever he wanted to cut me off.

I hate that man, although I would never let him know it. He has the power of life and death over my daughter.

It's all Pam's fault. If she hadn't written that letter to the White House four years ago—when Gin was only thirteen— my daughter wouldn't be in the terrible danger she is today.

I only went along with the arrangement because I thought it would be great for Gin's career to work for the president.

I have always enjoyed high social standing. For years my late husband, George L. Remington, was the ranking rear admiral assigned to sensitive work abroad with the consular corps.

Because of Gin's work, I thought we'd be invited to Washington. I thought we'd have cocktails with the president and Nancy. I thought we'd go to parties and meet royalty and some of the big names of Washington.

Instead, it's all been kept a dark secret. Saddlebag One treats us like rag pickers who shouldn't be seen in public.

Most of the time, I think the president is a wonderful man who has done wonders for America. But some of the men close to him, like Sadlebag One, are stinkers.

I was forbidden to tell my friends about what Gin was doing day after day in her communications lab. It was ridiculous for me to keep silent when I knew that damn Pam was blabbing it to her friends all the time.

So I managed to drop a hint or two to Dr. McAlice and some of my other millionaire Santa Barbara friends. Oh, how they envied me for having such a brainy daughter.

Of course, I didn't lie to Saddlebag One when he asked me about those conversations. I told him the leaks were all Pam's fault.

All he had to do was check out a few things to discover what a filthy liar my sister is. Her biggest lie, of course, is her claim that she's Gin's mother.

At least fifteen times, I told Saddlebag One to check with my attorneys to see my birth certificate evidence. It proves beyond any doubt that I am Gin's mother.

And every time, he answered: "I'll be glad to, Mrs. Remington, the next time I come to town."

He thinks he's such a crafty old devil. But I can see through him. I know that when he calls me Mrs. Remington instead of Louise, that he's mulling over something I just said.

I'll never forgive him for the way he continually jeopardized the life of my daughter. All those guards. All those secret agents. And all the terrible mistakes they made. I hate to think of the many times my daughter was in terrible danger—and I didn't even know it.

Saddlebag One paid me a bonus to keep up the charade

that Agnes was my daughter. It was a lousy little bonus. What burned me up even more was the way he and his young assistant, Saddlebag Two, gave more facts about the charade to Pam than they did to me.

That damn Pam. God, how she loved to drop little hints that she knew where Gin was. Lies. All lies. Never in a millennium would Saddlebag One allow Pam to have such sensitive information.

And, of course, there couldn't have been a grain of truth in Pam's story that Saddlebag One had made the charade even more elaborate by adding two more actresses. Can you believe that somewhere a woman was going around pretending to be me?

And would you believe another woman was pretending to be my sister? What a laugh!

But when I phoned Saddlebag One and asked him about that, his answer was odd. "Louise," he said, "there are stranger things on heaven and earth than you can suppose ... and that's not an exact quote. But I will tell you this much: you'll be seeing Gin sooner than you think."

I suppose what it all amounted to was this: To keep Gin out of danger, TimTomTon set up the decoy arrangement in Montana, making it look almost identical to our setup in Santa Barbara. Agnes pretended to be Gin, but of course she had no ability to send advisory messages to the president.

Pam and I were there in the Quonset huts to make the setup look authentic. Rick was also there as a decoy. The setup was successful enough to bring Dr. Sierra out of hiding in that small plane. His machine-gun attack on Agnes and Rick almost got them killed.

Meanwhile, Gin was working in secret somewhere else in still another communications lab, a replica of our Santa Barbara setup.

If, as Pam claimed, a couple of actresses were there pretending to be me and Pam, I knew it would never work because Gin would be too uncomfortable in such a setting.

When I tried to extract a little more information from Saddlebag One, the scrambler phone whined like a siren, and I had to hang up.

A day or so later, Pam invited me over for a drink and said she had some news about Rick and Agnes. But, of course, I wouldn't set foot in that big place of hers and have her lord it over me.

So she gave in and came over to my stinking little place. I never could understand how Saddlebag One could allow the widow of a rear admiral to live in such squalor.

Pam and I sat in the kitchen because it was cooler and also because I didn't have a dining room. I set three bottles of cold beer out on the table.

I must admit she looked nice that afternoon. She had on red slacks and a blouse with a design of abstract red and green lilies. Of course, my genuine silk blouse was in better taste, tailored yellow without any print.

I set out a glass for her. But she insisted on drinking from the bottle.

What a guzzler. She said she didn't like my cheap brand of beer, but she chugalugged two bottles before I'd sipped half my little glass of Chivas Regal.

"Guess I might as well tell you," she said.

But, of course, she made me wait while she started on the third bottle. She was disgusting.

I knew she didn't have anything important to tell me. I also knew she was deliberately making me wait, keeping me in suspense, hoping she could get me mad enough to lose my temper.

But I was too smart for her. So she finally got around to saying her little say.

"TimTomTon's madder than hell!" she bleated. "Rick was supposed to go on a solo mission—but he sneaked Agnes out with him. They're hiding out together!"

I sipped my drink, and then I gave her a blast. "That's not news! I knew *that* the morning they left."

"So?" She pretended not to be surprised that I knew. "Bet you didn't know TimTomTon has lost them . . . and is ripping up half of Idaho trying to find them!"

I never lie, but sometimes a fib is allowable.

"I heard that too," I said. "From Saddlebag One. Why are you wasting my time with all this drivel?" I was glad to see I got under her skin with that remark. Her eyes got squinty and wrinkly as she tried to think of something to come back with.

"Well, did you know Rick foolishly ran off before he even collected his first paycheck—about $1,500 for a week's work?"

I wasn't surprised and said so.

"Well, did you know they're living off Agnes's savings? She gets $2,000 a week, because she's a more experienced intelligence agent than Rick."

"I know all that. When are you going to tell me something worth hearing?"

Her brown eyes grew very wise. "Ok. I'll bet you didn't know this. Saddlebag One only wants Rick arrested. But there's a secret bunch in TimTomTon that wants him shot on sight!"

If true, that was definitely news. But I didn't give Pam any satisfaction on that subject either.

"Garbage! Rick's too valuable!"

That got her. Angrily, she jumped up from her chair. She began pacing up and down in front of me, slapping the sole of her brown wedgie noisily against the hardwood floor. She did that on purpose, trying to start an argument about how she lost her foot. That was old history and I didn't fall for it.

"Garbage?" she scolded, very sarcastically. "If anybody puts out garbage, it's you, Louise!"

So then she went even further back into our family history. She dragged out that old skeleton about how I supposedly gypped her out of her ownership of *my* beautiful big house.

"Take a look at this!" she declared, her eyes lighting up like fifty cents worth of fireworks at a county fair. She opened that filthy white plastic purse of hers, the one with all the broken stitching. She brought out a snapshot. It was a Polaroid, and the colors weren't very good. She shoved it in front of my face. "Ever see this before?"

It was a picture of an old black leather wallet. I recognized it at once. It was the soft, wornout wallet that my dear father carried for years.

"Where did you get it?" I asked.

She tried to look superior and clever. "I didn't bring Daddy's wallet itself . . ." She paused for dramatic effect. "Because I knew you'd make a grab for it."

That was a lie, of course, but I let her ramble on. She told me she'd found the wallet the week before in an old suitcase while packing her stuff to leave Santa Barbara.

"You'll never guess what was folded in with Daddy's driver license and car insurance papers . . ." She held up a second snapshot. "This . . ."

It was badly out of focus. But I could see it was some kind of handwritten letter.

"Daddy wrote this," she said. "Years ago. Wrote it to Litton and Litton, his lawyers . . ." As she explained what was supposedly in the letter, she became excited and breathless, and her cheeks turned bright pink. She raved on and on.

She said the letter was authorization for Daddy's lawyers to draw up a deed turning ownership of both our houses over to her. He also wanted his will changed the same way.

I was proud of how I didn't lose my temper. I didn't even let myself get angry, even though her raving made me more and more nervous.

"For years," Pam said, "I knew about this letter. For years I kept searching for it, because Daddy told me he was going to write it. . . ."

Then she added the big lie that I just knew she'd get around to: how Daddy always hated me and never trusted me. And that was why he intended for Pam to have title to both houses.

"But he wouldn't have put you out," she said. "He always wanted you to have a place to live . . . ."

Her soft chin wrinkled up and began to quiver. She was on the verge of tears, and I knew she was remembering how terribly the old man changed when his kidneys went bad. During the last weeks of his life, his skin turned yellow, and there wasn't a thing the doctors could do for him.

She lowered her head. The tears began to fall, dampening the lap of her red slacks. I kept silent. I didn't have the heart to tell her that Father's letter was worthless and would never stand up in court. When he fell ill, he left many personal matters unattended to.

I went over to her and touched her shoulder. Suddenly I felt my own tears start. Pam stood up. She put her arms around me. I held her tight. We cried together, the way we did when we were children and something had gone wrong. It was the first time in years that we embraced and wept like that. I couldn't remember the last time it had happened.

It was Father who always wanted us to be closer instead of squabbling all the time. But after he died we drew even further apart.

During those moments of closeness, we didn't speak. I knew she was remembering Father and what a wonderful loving man he was. Pam always thought she took after Father. But she was wrong. I was the one that took after him the most.

After a while, Pam and I drew apart. We dried our tears and sat down. We looked at one another, still remembering. I didn't tell her that I'd known for years about Father's letter. I'd never been able to find it among his things.

Pam smiled at me, a little sadly. "Do you remember the scrapes we always got into when we were little?"

I smiled back.

But then she had to spoil everything.

"You told the lies," she said, "and I always caught hell from Daddy because of them."

If she'd just kept her moth shut, we could have had a pleasant afternoon together. But she could never let well enough alone. In a few seconds, we went from being friends right back to being blood enemies. She raised hell about the title to the two houses. She insisted she would use Father's letter to regain the ownership.

By that time she'd finished her third beer. She was looking around for another bottle, but I refused to get one for her. She'd had enough. She wasn't drunk, but she was getting there. And I wanted her as sober as possible to hear what I had to say.

I told her Father's letter wouldn't do her a bit of good. I

told her the courts would laugh at it. She knew I was right. I know more about real estate law than she could learn in a thousand years. But she had to argue and curse. She went back to all the old accusations. She was wrong about everything.

It was all perfectly legal. I inherited my house from Father, just as she'd inherited hers. It wasn't my fault that she'd gone broke and couldn't pay the taxes and upkeep on hers.

It wasn't my fault that the bank wouldn't give her a loan. It wasn't my fault that she'd come begging to me for money.

It wasn't my fault that I could take away her house anytime I wished. All I had to do was call in my note, and her place would be mine. The only reason I didn't do it was because of my memory of my loving father. I knew he wouldn't approve.

I tried to explain it all in language she could understand.

"Please, Pam. Listen to me—"

She wouldn't, of course. She called me a bitch, and worse. Then she threw one of the beer bottles down on the floor. It broke into a shower of sharp brown glass.

Then she rushed out my door, limping in that exaggerated way just to make me mad. But I didn't get mad. I enjoyed watching her leave in such an angry and miserable state.

☆ ☆ **15** ☆ ☆

AUNT PAM

I knew all the time that the baby was in Texas. But I can keep a secret.

I sure as hell wouldn't let my half-wit sister, Louise, know where my daughter was doing her thing.

Of course, I didn't know the exact location in Texas. Probably up around Lubbock, where there's a military base.

All I knew about the place was that the baby hated it. Saddlebag One had hired a couple of Hollywood actresses to replace Louise and me.

One old bag pretended to be me. The other old bag acted like Louise. They even lived in separate houses, close together.

A few days after we were reunited, the baby told me how bad it was. Those old actresses drove her crazy. She just couldn't put her mind to her work.

It was the first time in her life that she ran into such a mental block. All the time she was in Texas she wasn't able to write even one advisory memo.

She told me Saddlebag One just about had a stroke worrying about her. And even Rawhide, the president, sent down a message telling how concerned he was about her.

That half-wit Saddlebag One should've known better. He should have know it was the first time the baby had ever been away from her family.

She dragged and drooped because she missed me so much. And I suppose she missed that half-wit Louise a little, too.

I'm also pretty sure she missed Rick. A lot.

Weeks later, when we were together again and talking about so many things, she very carefully kept from mentioning her feelings about Rick. That was always the baby's way. If something was bothering her, she kept it deep inside.

She knew about Agnes, of course. And she knew Agnes ran off with Rick, to Idaho. I know that bothered the baby terribly. But she never mentioned it.

I was sorry Rick took Agnes with him. But I didn't blame him. I liked Agnes very much because she never lost her sense of humor no matter how bad things got.

I liked Rick even more, even though he was a half-wit at times. And I could understand his physical needs.

Rick is a virile man. He's very masculine and headstrong. He was under tremendous strain from TimTomTon, and he needed all the companionship and release from tension that Agnes could give him.

A lot later, after so much had happened, the baby told me about some of the secret things that Rick tried to do in Idaho. He made a terrific blunder.

The trouble was, of course, that Rick was so inexperienced. They didn't give him enough spy training. So when he got out there on his own he kept screwing up.

I didn't exaggerate when I told my half-wit sister that Rick was in danger of being shot by TimTomTon. Teodoro gave the order. He wanted Rick killed to keep him from lousing up the whole Idaho operation.

Those people are unbelievable. They kill one another without even blinking. That's why I worry all the time and have those nightmares about the baby.

At first, Rick and Agnes decided to sever all connections with TimTomTon. They wanted to get as far away from the danger as they could.

But then Rick changed his mind. He tried to make the contact with St. Paul as ordered.

The baby told me he did it because of all the pain he felt whenever he thought about his family. He wanted so desperately to know the truth about his brother, Jerry. I don't think Rick ever accepted the theory that Jerry killed their mother.

He hoped St. Paul would be able to tell him certain things about his family. Things that happened in Nicaragua when Rick was a child. St. Paul was supposed to know a lot about Rick's family, as well as everything that had gone on for generations in Nicaragua.

The baby told me that St. Paul had worked for the contras in Nicaragua before swinging over to the Sandinistas. The contras were the link between St. Paul and Dr. Sierra.

No, that's wrong. It's easy for me to get mixed up on who's who in Nicaragua because they're all such a bunch of killers.

On second thought, this is more likely what the baby told me: Years before, St. Paul had worked for the Somoza regime before swinging over to the Sandinistas. So it was the Sandinistas—those bloody Communists—who were the link between St. Paul and Dr. Sierra.

For a long time when he was very young, Dr. Sierra had directed the murder machine of General Somoza, killing scores of innocent men and women.

Then he switched his allegiance to the Sandinistas and continued doing the same kind of murders for them.

Rick's orders from TimTomTon were very specific. *He was told to keep his presence absolutely secret from St. Paul. He was to make no direct contact.* All he was supposed to do was to snap a telephoto picture of St. Paul. And he was supposed to confirm—through certain other identification processes—that the man in Idaho was indeed St. Paul and not an impostor.

If the man turned out to be legitimate, then he could perhaps unknowingly lead TimTomTon to the man they really wanted—Dr. Sierra.

It was from Idaho that Dr. Sierra launched his airplane attack on Rick and Agnes. TimTomTon had reason to believe Dr. Sierra had returned to Idaho after the attack.

I think the baby told me so many details about Rick and Agnes because she was struggling to clear up their relationship in her mind.

The baby was probably jealous of Agnes. It was a feeling she'd never had before, and I don't think she understood it.

Rick and Agnes thought all along that they had given TimTomTon the slip. They went first to some little half-wit town in Wyoming and stayed there quite a while.

They thought they were in hiding. But they never were. Wherever they went, they were on a short leash. TimTomTon knew where they were every minute.

The baby told me that eventually Rick and Agnes quietly made their way to the mountain town of Inverness in Idaho.

They had a terrible time locating St. Paul because he lived in kind of an old penthouse on top of the town's ancient fire station.

The location was a smart move for St. Paul. The fire station was the tallest building in the neighborhood. There was no place high enough nearby to provide a decent vantage point to keep the penthouse under observation.

The best Agnes and Rick could do was rent a room in a nearby ramshackle little one-story hotel. From their window they could watch the fire station across an alley.

They took turns using binoculars. They spent a long, boring week watching the alley doorway that led to the penthouse. During the entire time, they didn't see one person go in or out that doorway.

Naturally, the baby didn't have all the details about what Rick and Agnes did to pass the time. But I could guess.

If Agnes hadn't been there, and in a loving mood, Rick would've gone bananas because of all the waiting and fidgeting.

Finally, on the sixth or seventh day, they saw a fireman walk down the alley and go in the doorway. He was too far away to be identified.

But Rick noticed something that seemed amiss. The fireman's shirt that the man wore was much too large, and he was wearing blue jeans instead of the black trousers that other firemen wore.

Rick and Agnes watched the doorway for half a day. In the afternoon, the man came out. He was still dressed the same, but now he was carrying two plastic pails.

Rick decided to follow him. But first he told Agnes to stay in the bedroom and keep the doorway under observation in case the man with the pails wasn't St. Paul.

That was the only smart thing Rick did during the whole episode. Agnes stayed put, a decision that may have saved her life.

She waited two days for Rick to come back. But he never did. Fortunately, they'd made emergency plans in advance to meet somewhere else.

It turned out that the man with the two buckets was

actually the contact, St. Paul. He walked about half a mile to a small cherry orchard on the outskirts of town. Rick followed. The cherry orchard was one of the clues he'd been told to watch for.

The man went into the orchard and began picking a certain kind of pie cherry; that was the second clue, which indicated he was St. Paul.

Rick made a couple of half-wit blunders. He'd forgotten his camera, so he couldn't snap St. Paul's photo. Even worse, he went into the orchard and made the mistake of talking to the man.

The baby didn't know exactly how everything happened after that. She did know that St. Paul had a small pistol hidden in one of his cherry pails.

He didn't shoot Rick. Instead he shot and killed one of Teodoro's men, Percy. The baby decoded all the data about the shooting and other stuff from TimTomTon reports. Percy had followed Rick into the cherry orchard to keep an eye on him. When he saw Rick violate his orders by talking to St. Paul, he opened fire.

Rick escaped from the orchard only because St. Paul allowed him to.

Much, much later Rick learned that St. Paul was a friend of the Moore family many years before in Nicaragua. When Rick and his brother were small boys, St. Paul had helped reunite them with their mother after a long and strange separation.

Afterward I wished the baby hadn't told me all that terrifying stuff. It gave me more nightmares about the danger the baby was in.

And I had to worry all the time about goofing up and accidentally mentioning more than I should to Louise. The baby told me repeatedly to keep all the Rick and Agnes stuff secret.

After the fight my half-wit sister and I had in her Quonset hut, we didn't talk for a day or so. We'd had worse fights in the past, so before long we patched it up.

One morning, she came over to my elegant big place, and

we had coffee. I was amazed that she came. It was the first time she ever set foot inside.

She looked very lovely that day, wearing an expensive yellow housecoat. I had to admit she got her money's worth from that face-lift.

At first, I thought she wanted to talk some more about Santa Barbara and Daddy's letter. But she didn't. She talked about a lot of trivial things. Although she pretended to be totally disinterested in how magnificent the general's house was, I could tell she was terribly envious. Then she sprang her deal.

"Pam, dear." Whenever she called me dear, I knew she was cooking up something rotten and devious. "Pam, dear, I've been thinking. Would you trade Quonset houses with me for $5,000?"

At first I was dumbfounded. I needed the money badly, and it all sounded so simple and easy.

"Would you really?" I said.

As soon as the words came out, I knew how dumb they were. I can read my half-wit sister like a cheap paperback book. For a split second, I saw the left side of her mouth twist the way it always does when she's lying about money.

It meant, of course, that I would never see the $5,000—or even $5.

She would manipulate.

She would lie.

She would connive.

She would be the queen bee in the general's great big house and I wouldn't get a dime. That was how those deals of hers always worked out. So I said, "No, thanks, Louise." I said it so sweetly that the taste of the words lingered in my mouth.

She didn't give up. Handling it like one of her real estate deals, she offered to set it up for me in half a dozen different ways. And each time I said no.

She got madder by the second. But she kept control of herself.

For a long time she glared at me. Then, without another

word, she got up and went back to her lousy little dump.

In a way, I felt sorry for her. She's had that sickness about lying since we were youngsters.

She knows the full extent of her lies. She claims that people don't listen carefully to what she says. But that's a lot of b.s.

I was glad she left. If we'd had another one of our wingdings, I might have gotten upset and revealed something about the baby, Rick, or Agnes that was supposed to be secret.

My half-wit sister has a hundred ways of making me mad. Like the way she drinks her coffee or Chivas Regal with her little pinkie sticking out. She does that to remind me that it's my fault her finger is disfigured, which is a lie, of course.

Years ago, I used to get back at my sister by reminding her how I lost my foot. But I had to stop doing that because it made her so crazy.

It was her fault that I lost my foot. It happened many years ago when she was sixteen and I was about twenty-two. She'd just obtained her learner's permit. She insisted on driving me to the supermart in my old Dodge convertible. She had to be smart and show me how good she was. She was a very good driver, but not good enough to take the Nipomo Road curve at that much speed.

The car hit a giant eucalyptus that was solid iron. We turned over and I flew out. The edge of the open car door came down like a hatchet and cut off my foot just above the ankle.

I used to have nightmares about that accident. But not any more. Now I have nightmares about the baby. The only way I can get back to sleep is by having a Coors or two.

Right after the baby was born, Louise became jealous of me because I was a mother and she wasn't. But she didn't give a rap about the baby until Gin became an important person working for the president. It was then that Louise developed this terrible compulsion to claim the baby for her own.

I wish Louise would worry more about the baby's safety,

instead of trying all the time to prove that Gin is her child.

In my nightmares, I always pray about the first letter I had written to the White House. I pray that it didn't exist. I pray that I had never written it.

And always when I wake up I remember with such a terrible feeling that I *had* written it. The letter was preordained and so was everything that followed. And I couldn't change it. I wrote letter after letter to that half-wit in the White House. All I asked was that the baby be given back her normal life. All I wanted was for her to be safe again and separated from those idiots who ran her life.

The White House never replied to those letters. Or even acknowledged that they had been received.

REO: No. 45
To: Rawhide, White House
From: Chicken Little
Subject: *Apology*

Sir, I cannot work under the present conditions. That's why I have not sent you any REOs for many days.

I apologize for my behavior.

REO (Rawhide's Eyes Only)
Alert Memo: No. CL-16
To: Rawhide, White House
From: Saddlebag One
Subject: *Advisories*

Knowing how vital Chicken Little's REO advisories are to the Oval office, I can assure you that we are moving heaven and earth to reestablish her communications with you.

Because of the way this matter has been mishandled, I hearby submit my resignation, effective now.

REO (Rawhide's Eyes Only)
Alert Memo No. CL-17
To: Rawhide, White House
From: Saddlebag One
Subject: *Debacle*

Thank you for not accepting my resignation at this time. I am aware that it will remain on your desk to be acted upon when you deem it necessary.

I accept full responsibility for the Chicken Little debacle. My staff and I underestimated her sensitivities.

We predicted that the separation from her aunts would affect her work, but we never expected the interruption to be so prolonged.

We failed to anticipate that the absence of young Richard D. Moore (a.k.a. Mohr) would have such an effect on her. For this failure, I have dismissed six members of my staff, including the two psychiatrists specializing in problems of the teenage psyche.

I know you are aware that this is the first significant interruption *in four years* in Chicken Little's extremely intense work schedule, a very impressive record.

You will recall, of course, that she was thirteen years old when our association began. She is now seventeen and is somewhat belatedly experiencing the yearnings and frustrations that plague most teenagers.

In matters of the heart, Chicken Little is woefully immature. She is confused about her affection for Moore, who is fourteen years older than she is. Moore, you will recall, suffered permanent eye damage at the hands of Dr. Sierra.

It is indeed unfortunate that Chicken Little's indisposition coincides with the newest crisis in Lebanon. I can assure you that when you receive her next REO you will see that she has regained her unique political/economical maturity and perceptions.

That advisory, of course, will be concerned with the plight of the thirty-nine hostages held captive on Flight 847.

I know how important Chicken Little's evaluation is and that you need it at once. I believe she can telecommunicate with sources in Iran who know that Rafsanjani, speaker of the Parliament, is a moderate and the key to secretly obtaining the hostages' release.

Be assured that her REO will be on your desk as soon as is humanly possible.

REO (Rawhide's Eyes Only)
Alert Memo No. CL-18
To: Rawhide, White House
From: Saddlebag One
Subject: *Delay*

Please accept my deepest apology for the continuing delay regarding Chicken Little's REO on the Flight 847 hostages. It should be on your desk first thing tomorrow morning.

I understand your great concern about the delay. I also understand fully why Rainbow suggested my demotion to acting director with appropriate reduction in remuneration.

As you know, the security problem for Chicken Little has become massive. It was our attempt to solve this problem that resulted in the interruption in Chicken Little's work.

We know that many international terrorist groups have the goal of kidnapping her to gain access to her unique knowledge and analysis of U.S. and world affairs. If they can't do that, they will attempt to kill her—or maim her mentally.

The groups most dedicated to harming Chicken Little—and yourself—come from Nicaragua, Lebanon,

Libya, Taiwan, El Salvador, Iran, Cuba, Afghanistan, Western Europe, and, of course the USSR. All have operatives in the U.S. who are under close surveillance.

The security of the original Stirrup—and also at Stirrup B in Montana—was so inadequate that I have ousted TimTomTon's director. Please inform Rainbow that the new director is the man she suggested.

Shortly, we will complete work on base Stirrup C, which will have the finest security in the world.

Chicken Little and her aunts have already been moved to Stirrup C. Chicken Little is at work in her new and greatly improved communications lab.

Her work regarding Flight 847's hostages is going well because she received an affectionate letter from young Moore.

When the timing is appropriate, we will have Moore explain to Chicken Little why it was necessary for us to have someone on our staff write that particular love letter.

Stirrup C is in a desert location in the Southwest. See accompanying map for exact site. Because of the base's remoteness, I am confident that there will be no recurrence of the disgraceful security lapses at bases Stirrup and Stirrup B.

P.S. I am pleased to inform you that we have had enormous success with our Nicaragua source code-named Lopez/Mendez. He is also know as St. Paul. I regret to reveal that he deleted one of our TimTomTon paramilitary officers, Percy Castillo, a step that was absolutely necessary, I assure you.

I am confident that through Lopez/Mendez and others we will capture or delete Dr. Sierra, thus ending the greatest threat to Chicken Little and Stirrup C.

In a previous alert memo, I noted that Dr. Sierra is a man of such stature that he is a personal friend of USSR leader Gorbachev and Cuba's Fidel Castro.

Because of his intellect, skills, and connections
in high places, Dr. Sierra unquestionably is the most
dangerous and powerful terrorist at large in the world
today.

May I remind you once again that until Dr. Sierra
is eliminated you must accept all precautions
prescribed for the personal safety of yourself and
Rainbow.

I realize that at times these precautions are irksome
for you and the First Lady.

My staff and I are grateful for your continuing
cooperation.

Please give my warmest regards to Rainbow.

REO: No. 46
To: Rawhide, White House
From: Chicken Little
Subject: *Flight 847 Hostages*

Thirty-nine American lives are at stake in that
hijacked TWA airliner in Beirut.

Do not repeat the mistakes President Carter made
in dealing publicly with the captors of hostages.

Stay personally out of the negotiations. Have no
contacts with the media. Make no threats at this
time against any terrorists anywhere.

Send a team secretly to negotiate with Rafsanjani,
the moderate who is speaker of Iran's Parliament.
He will go in secret to Syria and deal directly with
the leaders of Hezbollah—the militant Party of God—
telling them it will be in their interest to free these
hostages.

Be patient.

☆ ☆ **16** ☆ ☆

After twenty-four hours of patiently observing hundreds of people traveling across the river, Rick finally did it.

He spotted Dr. Sierra.

Dr. Sierra was a passenger on one of the many small casino boats that shuttled day and night across the rushing Colorado River at the Nevada-Arizona boundary.

The key to Dr. Sierra's identity had been revealed to Rick by St. Paul in the cherry orchard. It was a strange ID: "Watch for a man with no hair on his left forearm."

In this barren region, the rushing Colorado bisected one of the hottest parts of desert. The temperature that afternoon on the blue-green river was a fiery 121.

The rectangular-shaped shuttle boats weren't air conditioned. Each boat had a powerful outboard motor to overcome the swift currents. Each boat took two minutes to cross the river from Bullhead City, Arizona, to Laughlin, Nevada. All the people who rode the shuttle boats to the Laughlin gambling casions were lightly dressed and perspiring in the heat.

Because the desert air was very dry, the heat, though awesome, was quite bearable. Most of the people who disembarked were in high spirits, partly because the ride was free, but mostly because they were eager to try their luck at the tables and slots.

Rick stood in a crowd on the loading dock at the Edgewater casino and watched two dozen men and women get off one of the boats. Because of the heat, most of the men passengers wore short-sleeve sport shirts.

Behind the tinted glasses, Rick's vision was far from

123

perfect. But the afternoon light was very good. He was close enough to observe the arms of almost all the men who walked single file through the boat's narrow doorway.

A few of the men had little or no hair on their arms. Dr. Sierra had a light growth of black hair on his right forearm. But there was none on his left forearm. St. Paul had informed Rick that the skin of Dr. Sierra's arm was burned years before in a plane crash.

When at last Rick saw Dr. Sierra, he reacted instinctively. It had been nearly six weeks since the white powder had been thrown into Rick's eyes, and his hatred for the man had intensified every day.

Rick felt a flicker of loathing—and also fear—as Dr. Sierra walked slowly past in the moving throng, less than fifteen feet away.

The man's iceberg blue eyes showed no sign of recognition. He looked straight ahead. His face was much different—rounder and fuller—than in the photos Teodora had shown Rick back in Montana. In his left hand, Dr. Sierra carried a small blue travel bag.

Had he noticed Rick? Perhaps not, because Rick was off to the side, concealed in a second throng of people waiting to board the white-and-blue boat.

But, remembering the training Teodora had given him, Rick knew that Dr. Sierra was a master of self-control in this kind of situation. If he'd spotted Rick, he would never indicate it outwardly.

Instinctively, Rick violated one of Teodora's most rigid rules of surveillance. The moment he spotted Dr. Sierra, he'd reacted externally. For a millisecond, Rick's mouth had tightened and his eyes had flickered. To an amateur like Rick, those reactions were nothing. To a pro like Dr. Sierra, Rick might as well have fired off a gun.

According to Teodora, Dr. Sierra had exceptional side vision. He might well have studied Rick while staring straight ahead.

Rick was careful not to watch Dr. Sierra walk from the unloading platform. Nor did he follow the man, though he badly wanted to.

As soon as the two dozen passengers debarked, Rick went aboard with two dozen new passengers. He sat down on a white, plastic-covered bench beside a woman and two middle-aged men. In a shrill voice, the woman talked excitedly about the money she had just won at the Edgewater casino.

Most of the boat's large windows were open, permitting dry, hot breezes to blow in from the river. Rick stared at the greenish water rushing by so powerfully. By refusing to turn his eyes to Dr. Sierra's direction, he hoped to be inconspicuous.

He formed a hasty plan. His seat was close to the front. Just before the boat left, he would quickly get off and follow Dr. Sierra to the casino.

The plan failed. As the driver revved the engine to leave, Dr. Sierra suddenly appeared in the boat's open doorway.

God Almighty. He'd not only spotted Rick but was in pursuit! But the driver held up his hand to keep Dr. Sierra from boarding.

"Sorry, mister. No more seats."

"How about that one?" Dr. Sierra pointed to an empty place on the seat directly behind the driver.

Swiveling his chair, the driver determined that he was correct and waved him aboard.

As he went to the seat, one row ahead of Rick's, Dr. Sierra glanced down, avoiding contact with Rick's eyes. He wore a tailored white sport shirt with a small blue biplane emblem over his heart. He also wore trim white shorts. He was well-muscled. Rick saw no bulge in his pockets that might have been a weapon.

After sitting down, Dr. Sierra placed the small travel bag on his lap.

As the boat roared away from the dock, Rick knew he had two minutes to form a new plan of action. And this one better not fail.

In two minutes, the boat would cross the river. It would dock on the Arizona side where there were several parking lots, large and small. In those parking lots, Rick would be more vulnerable than he was on the boat. This man who had executed hundreds of innocent people wouldn't find one more much of a challenge.

Rick had no weapon. If Dr. Sierra had one, it would be in the bag. As soon as that thought crossed Rick's mind, he acted. He leaned over the backrest of Dr. Sierra's seat and snatched the blue bag off his lap.

Before Dr. Sierra could react, Rick turned and dived through the boat's open window. He was in the air perhaps a second, just long enough to hear a small but very loud siren go off.

Jesus H. Christ! There was an antitheft device in the bag.

The water was cold, a tremendous contrast to the 121-degree heat of the air. Rick knew the current would be fast, but it was beyond belief. As he dived in headfirst against the rushing green water, it almost tore the bag from his grasp and nearly ripped the collar off his shirt. Rick quickly turned his body and swam straight down, going with the current. He went as deep as possible and swam as fast as he could. He stayed down to the limit of his lungs, a strategy he hoped would carry him as far downstream from the boat as possible. He didn't doubt that Dr. Sierra would follow him into the river. Everything Teodora had told him about the man indicated he was fearless when pursuing a victim.

Finally Rick was forced to the surface for air. He was very impressed by the distance the current had carried him. The rectangular boat was so far upstream that it looked about the size of a shoebox.

Rick's vision was poor because he'd lost his glasses. For a few moments he stayed at the surface, sucking in the superhot air and searching the waves for another swimmer. When he saw what looked like a head in the water, he felt a small glow of accomplishment. Dr. Sierra was a long way upstream, probably because he hadn't swam as hard as Rick had.

Obviously he was a strong swimmer or he wouldn't have dared to dive in. But Rick was confident that he could do as well or better. For six months in the marines, Rick had been attached to a Navy SEALS unit. He'd learned 101 techniques of aggressive swimming.

Again he dived and swam underwater with all his strength. Despite the handicap of the small bag and his shoes, he moved well.

When he resurfaced, he had put a lot more distance

between himself and the other swimmer. They were both in the middle of the river. Turning, Rick scanned the rolling green waves in all directions. He didn't doubt that a rescue boat would be sent to pick them up.

His eyesight was blurry but good enough to see that two possible rescue boats were coming upstream. They were speedboats, churning the waves white. They were maybe a quarter of a mile away.

Rick had to avoid them. If they picked him up, the authorities would ask questions. They would have witnesses who saw him steal the bag. They would take the bag away, and he would lose whatever advantage it might contain. Undoubtedly Dr. Sierra would also be picked up—and would try to reclaim the bag.

Rick changed direction. Each time he dived, he swam toward the Nevada shore. It was very hard work. His progress was slow because the current tried to draw him back toward midstream.

Many minutes passed. When he came up for the umpteenth time, he saw that he had succeeded in avoiding the rescue boats.

Then, without warning, he was exhausted.

He couldn't believe it was happening. While training with the navy swimmers, he'd swam much farther than this. But that was ocean swimming. The racing Colorado River currents were in a different league.

He lay on his back, floating, panting, and swallowing water. He was too exhausted to see where he was. The bag felt like a hundred pounds of bricks. He knew it was one of the reasons he was exhausted. But he refused to get rid of it.

When the back of his head suddenly bumped into something, he was afraid one of the rescue boats had come up behind him. Then he saw that he'd struck the end of a small fishing pier. He grabbed one of the slippery perpendicular log supports. Turning slowly, he braced his body so the current held him tight against the slimy green log.

As his strength returned, he realized how lucky he was. This was the only fishing pier on this side of the river. The others were all on the Arizona side. If he'd been a bit farther out in the river, he would've missed the pier completely.

Moving slowly along the log supports, he worked his way to the shore under the pier. It was in a small inlet where the current was almost leisurely.

For a few minutes, he rested in the warm mud under the pier, his tired legs floating in the water. The mud was brown with a yellowish tinge. He experimented with the blue travel bag, slowly raising it from the water. The goddamned antitheft device screamed like a teenager on a roller coaster.

He shoved the bag back under. He opened the zipper and felt each of the objects in the bag until he found a small rectangular thing that vibrated. Removing it from the bag, but keeping it beneath the surface, he waded out into deeper water and released it. The current tore it from his hand and carried it away, soundlessly.

He looked around to see if he had attracted any attention. He saw no one. He estimated he was at least five or six miles downstream from where he'd dived in.

Leaving the river, he walked slowly and awkwardly toward some thick brush. Because of the swimming overexertion his legs felt like thick sticks. Dropping onto his belly, he wriggled deep into the wiry green brush until he was sure he couldn't be spotted by a boat or copter.

After a while, he sat up and examined the muddy travel bag. It was a blue and white Pan American Airways carry-on bag with a canvas strap. His left hand held the strap in such a death grip that for a strangely long time he had to struggle to open his fingers.

He poured out at least half a gallon of river. Then he dumped all the objects onto the hard yellowish ground. The stuff included a pistol, a very wet U.S. passport, an equally wet and very thick packet of currency, a clip of ammunition, and a long, very damp white envelope containing some kind of papers.

The bag also contained a mysterious object that Rick couldn't figure out. It was hard black plastic, flat and square. It was some kind of an electronic device with two switches.

The pistol was smaller than a 9-mm. It was fully loaded.

It was dark metal and foreign-made, probably Russian because of the backward R in the lettering on the barrel.

The thick packet of U.S. currency was tied with white string. He flipped through the bills and saw that they were mostly hundreds plus a lot of five hundreds. He estimated the total at more than $10,000. It was far more than he'd hoped for and was badly needed because he'd nearly used up the cash Agnes had loaned him back in Idaho.

He looked at his mud-streaked wrist watch, a $27 Timex. The hands said 3:12, indicating that a little over half an hour had passed since he dived off the boat. The watch wasn't waterproof but was still ticking. After the long bath it just had, he hated to trust it. But he had no choice. Before Rick left Montana, Teodora had failed in his promise to supply him with a watertight, shockproof Camats Swiss stunt watch.

According to the Timex, Rick had about forty-five minutes to get to the Gold Dust Club. If he was late, Agnes would raise hell.

But he couldn't leave yet. During Teodora's quickie indoctrination, Rick was instructed always to search equipment for enemy silent beepers. So far one hadn't turned up in the bag. He turned the blue and white bag inside out. He squeezed all its seams and the cloth strap. He found nothing. He re-examined the two mysterious objects—the flashlightlike thing and the flat device with two switches. He was tempted to leave them behind because one or both might contain a silent beeper.

Picking up the pistol that seemed to have Soviet markings, he released the clip. One by one, he pushed out the brass cartridges and let them fall onto his palm. The seventh cartridge was definitely lighter than the others. He tugged at the round-nosed slug until it broke free. It was hollow.

Inside were tiny electronic components that matched information Teodora had given him. It was a silent beeper. Undoubtedly, it was sending a signal back to Dr. Sierra so he could trace the whereabouts of the bag.

Rick put everything except the beeper back in the bag and closed the zipper. Slowly, he eased himself to a standing position in the scratchy blue-green brush. The branches were stiff, dry, and had a strong bitter odor similar to sagebrush.

He looked around, trying to locate anyone nearby who might have followed the beeper. Teodoro had mentioned that most of the time Dr. Sierra worked alone. But occasionally he used one or more backup people.

He walked down to the muddy shore. He threw the beeper as far as he could and watched it make a small splash in the speeding waves.

But he still had the bad feeling that the damn thing had done its job.

The fierce heat had nearly dried his lime green sport shirt and beige trousers. His pants were a mess, caked with ugly yellow-brown mud that looked like he'd lost a battle with diarrhea.

He removed his lowcuts and socks. He waded into the river, bent down and let the rushing water launder his clothes.

Ten minutes later, he looked fairly presentable as he walked along the asphalt highway toward the Nevada town of Laughlin. His shoes and socks were dry, and the hot breezes were rapidly drying his Jockey shorts as well as his outer clothes.

Soon the intense heat made him sweat so much that his clothes became damp.

Cars, ponderous recreational vehicles, buses, and trucks whipped by at high speed. The traffic was much too thick, making it easy for someone to spot him.

Leaving the highway, Rick cut across a bed of alkali so white that the blast of reflected sunlight hurt his eyes. Then he climbed a small hill and went down the other side.

After that he was shielded from the highway by a series of low rolling hills. The desert ground was lousy for walking. In some places, he sank into soft yellow-white sand. Farther on, the ground was hard but covered with loose and treacherous red-brown gravel the size of dried peas.

After he'd covered possibly two miles of desert, the sun got to him. He wrapped his shirt around his head, but it didn't help. Woozy from the heat, he was now sweating water by the quart. A short time ago, his problem had been too much water. Now he was thirsty as hell and daydreaming about tall tumblers of ice water, cans of cold beer, and giant bottles of Coke.

He recalled a line from his geology textbook at the university: "Never underestimate the desert. If it's 120 in the shade, it will be 140 or more out in the open." Right now it felt more like 150. Rick needed shade. And needed it fast.

REO: No. 49
To: Rawhide, White House
From: Chicken Little
Subject: *Stealth*

There is a secret move within the air force to divert funds from the proposed Stealth bomber to an extension of the B-1 bomber production beyond the one hundred authorized by Congress.

Technology for the Stealth bomber is progressing more rapidly than anticipated. Its flying wing design (no fuselage) and radar-absorbent structure will reduce its radar signature dramatically.

In a nuclear war, one undetected Stealth bomber will be more valuable than a fleet of B-1 bombers.

The fund diversion project is spearheaded by Wingman, code name for General Eldon James Fostoria.

☆ ☆ 17 ☆ ☆

Rick stumbled up a small burning-hot hill. Then another. And another.

At the bottom of one of the hills, he discovered a dead tree. It was a pine, its sparse branches covered with dry red needles and small globules of sap resembling dried clear glue.

Nature quiz: *What the hell was a pine tree doing in this furnace madness?*

Forget it. Rick flopped into its meager shade and prayed for his brain to cool off.

After a while, he sat against the rough red bark of the tree's trunk and watched a tiny hummingbird hover in the air nearby.

Instead of working on his survival problem, his brain insisted on worrying about another of nature's quirks. *What the hell was a hummingbird doing in a furnace where there were no flowers?*

The hummingbird's tiny body changed colors instantly as it darted about, going from brilliantly translucent green to drab brown and back to green.

Suddenly it darted lower, almost disappearing in the shadow of a large reddish orange boulder. Rich watched with amazement at its long quick needle of a bill attacked a giant spider.

Turning over, he rested his chin on his hand and discovered his good eye was giving him a good picture of desert warfare. He watched a battle that defied every law of nature.

Hummingbirds were nectar lovers, not fighters. The spider, three times as large as the bird, was a wolf spider with thick hairy legs, a species that supposedly came forth only at night.

The bird darted in, touched the spider, and darted back. Rick moved closer for a better look.

Extraordinary. The hummingbird was giving the spider a haircut. Each time it darted in, it clipped off one of the spider's hairs. Was it possible that the hummingbird had discovered a minute source of moisture? Or was it building a nest?

Rick didn't find out because abruptly a man's voice spoke close behind him.

"Afternoon, fella. What's going on?"

He'd crept up so silently that if he'd been Dr. Sierra he could've deleted Rick in an instant. The stranger squatted down beside Rick and gazed at the oversized spider. As they watched, the hummingbird darted in again and clipped off one of the spider's stiff leg hairs.

"Fancy that," said the stranger. "Look what that rascal's doin' to my kin'folk."

Rick sat up and looked him over. He was as old as the desert. As he unfolded his long body and stood up, Rick understood why the man regarded the spider as practically a blood relative.

He was at least six feet eight inches tall and bore a striking resemblance to the spider. The arms and legs that stuck out of his grimy white T-shirt and khaki walking shorts were amazingly thin. They were covered with sparse white hairs that matched the few straggly ones on his weatherbeaten chin.

"M'name's Elijah. Yours?"

"Rick."

He seemed pleased with Rick's name. He extended a hand with long, bony fingers. They shook.

Elijah wore an antique red baseball cap with the bill in back. Reaching up, he turned it around so Rick could read the two words stitched in large, once-white letters across the front: GOD FIRST.

As soon as Rick read the message, the old man launched onto a monologue about his likes, dislikes, and other matters. He talked so fast that it was hard to keep up with the rapid change of topics.

Elijah wasn't his real name . . . He'd adopted it in order to do God's work . . . He liked Rick because he was interested in desert wildlife . . . He hoped Rick was a God-fearing man . . . He despised the people in the Laughlin gambling casinos because they put God last, instead of first . . . He disliked women because they talked too much . . . He liked spiders, prairie dogs, armadillos, lizards, and other desert creatures because they understood the secrets of life and could survive in killing heat . . . He hated the cities of the world because they were godless and would soon be destroyed . . . He lived in the desert because it cured his arthritis, hay fever, and hives . . . He was eighty-six years old and hadn't collected any Social Security because it violated the laws of God . . .

When Elijah finally paused for breath, Rick asked if he had any water. Immediately the old man dropped to his knees. He said a hurried prayer, which included a blessing for Rick.

"Please forgive me," he said. "I should've known." Taking Rick's hand, he helped him rise. But he didn't release Rick's hand. "You really must forgive me," he added. "I should've known you were thirsty."

Leaning down, he kissed Rick's palm. Then he kissed the skin on the inside of Rick's forearm. When he tried to kiss Rick on the mouth, Rick realized he was dealing with a rare species of queer. One who was eighty-six years old, nearly as tall as Kareem Abdul-Jabbar and built like a spider. Rick slammed his fist against the skinny chest and drove Elijah back. One blow was sufficient.

"You must forgive me," the old man said with downcast eyes. "It will not happen again." He was as good as his promise. He didn't touch Rick again.

Gesturing for Rick to follow, Elijah led the way up a slight incline and then down into a dry gully where a vehicle was parked. It was an ancient dune buggy with its rusty engine mounted in the rear. It had a tattered canvas top, no windshield, giant doughnut tires in back, and small motorcycle wheels in front.

In place of its rear seat, the buggy was equpped with a battered once-white, household hot water tank lying on its side. Turning the spigot, Elijah filled a cracked, pink coffee mug with water and handed it to Rick.

The water was almost boiling hot from the sun, but Rick gulped it down. Elijah filled the cup twice more before Rick's thirst diminished.

Turning his baseball cap around so the bill was in back, Elijah climbed behind the buggy's steering wheel and told Rick to take the adjacent bucket seat.

"I owe you a favor," Elijah said. "Where to?"

"A favor? Why?"

Elijah gave him a flirtatious wink. "For this—" He gave the palm of his hand a big noisy smooch.

"OK," Rick said hastily. "OK."

"So where to?"

"The Gold Dust Club. But stay off the highway."

"You got it. Fasten your belt."

Rick put his green shirt back on. After they were belted in, the old man started the engine and they took off in a cloud of yellow dust.

Elijah was a terrible driver who managed to find every rock on every hill and in every gulch. As they bounced along, he explained that the buggy was equipped with a powerful '69 Cadillac engine.

"Only hits on 'bout three cylinders," he apologized. "Otherwise we'd be flyin'."

They flew anyway because of the rocks. In less than fifteen minutes, they left the open desert and bounded onto a service road that led to the Gold Dust Club's parking lot.

The large lot was jammed with out-of-state cars, mostly from California. Without telling him why, Rick asked Elijah to let him off at the far end, away from the busy entrance where Dr. Sierra's people or the authorities might have lookouts posted.

As Rick stepped out, Elijah's long, spidery arm reached out. But his hand didn't quite touch Rick.

He opened his palm. "A contribution, Rick? A dollar for the work of the Lord?"

Rick didn't have a dollar. But what the hell—easy come, easy go. Unzipping the blue bag, he reached in and extracted one of the hundreds from Dr. Sierra's damp packet. When he handed it to Elijah, Rick expected him to be surprised or at least impressed. He was neither.

"Thank you, Rick. The Lord do work in very decent ways." He gunned the big engine in neutral, causing it to backfire and to sound like a string of firecrackers going off. Passersby gave them sharp looks, attention Rick could do without.

"Remember, Rick," the old man warned gravely. "If the Lord sees you gambling in there, he will loose his terribly swift sword . . . ."

Rick assured him that he would avoid the temptation. Satisfied, Elijah clashed his gears, and the dune buggy roared away.

Rick waited until a red Sunshine Tours bus unloaded at the casino's main entrance. Then he joined its group of tourists as they went in.

Inside the noisy casino, it was forty degrees cooler. The place was filled wall to wall with hundreds of intense people who weren't having any fun. All Rick saw were bright lights and glum faces. The slots weren't paying off. The dice were cold. The blackjack cards might as well have been blanks.

Rick let the slowly milling crowd push him toward the monstrous slot machine where he was supposed to meet Agnes. Twice as big as a Volkswagen, the brilliantly lighted machine was surrounded by a mob of people watching a punk rocker try to make a fortune.

She was bizarre. Her hair stuck out in black spikes, her eyelids were bright red, and her cheeks were painted yellow. She wore black hightop tennis shoes and immensely oversized white coveralls with side pockets big enough to hold basketballs.

It was a dollar machine, and she was playing five coins at a time. She had to use both hands to pull the gigantic handle. When two rows of sevens came up, she let out a delirious cry of joy. It wasn't a major jackpot but it was a big payoff. Scores of coins clanked down into the machine's metal pan, where there was already a big pile of dollars. The machine hesitated. Then it dumped more dollars onto the pile. Hundreds of heavy coins. The clatter as they fell was deafening.

The punk rocker screamed. Raising her arms, she leaped high in the air. When she came down, her head turned for a moment, and Rick realized there was something familiar about her profile.

Oh, God. The punk rocker was Agnes in a bewildering disguise!

Pushing through the crowd, Rick went to her side. She gave him a big happy smile and immediately wiped it off when she saw how griped he was.

He cursed under his breath. "Jesus H. Christ! Is this a low profile?"

"Sorry, Rick. I thought I'd lose—"

"Why didn't you just shoot off rockets?"

"Next time I will! Don't just stand there. Help me!"

They each scooped hundreds and hundreds of dollars from the pan and the carpet below. They dumped the coins into her enormous pockets and dumped the rest into Dr. Sierra's blue travel bag.

"What room are we in?" he asked.

"Two zero two."

"Give me the key."

"No!"

"Give it to me!"

"No! Rick, don't leave me!" There was near-panic in her voice. "I can't walk!"

It was true. Because of the vast, bulging amounts of metal in her pockets, she was so heavy she could scarcely move.

Rick couldn't help her. He had to get out of there. The mob around them had grown larger and was attracting attention.

People were laughing and pointing out the dilemma of the woman who'd won so much money she was about to keel over.

Finally Agnes opened her purse and angrily gave him the room key. He melted into the crowd. As he climbed the stairway, he looked back over the sea of hundreds of heads until he found her.

Slowly and ponderously, leaning for support against one of the casino cash girls, Agnes was making her way to the cashier's window.

Then Rick saw someone who made his blood freeze.

Eduardo. He was at the base of the stairway and starting up.

Jesus H. Christ.

Rick had been so concerned about Dr. Sierra that he'd forgotten about TimTomTon. If Eduardo had him spotted, he could be damned sure that others from TimTomTon were nearby.

One of Eduardo's arms was in a black-cloth sling, probably because of the wound he'd received back in Montana. His other hand was tucked inside his coat.

Rick knew what that meant. A weapon.

He put his hand into the travel bag. But he couldn't get to the gun because it was buried in coins.

Then he was inspired. He threw a handful of dollars down the steps. Then he threw another handful. And another. People on the steps dropped to their knees to intercept the bouncing shower of shiny metallic discs. They were joined by a shrieking mob from the main floor who ran up the steps and fell to their knees, picking up coins.

Pandemonium. Within moments, Eduardo was surrounded by shouting men and women fighting for dollars.

He couldn't move.

Rick ran up the rest of the steps to the second floor. He was in luck. Room 202 was only a few steps from the stairway. He went in and locked the door behind him. For the moment, he felt safe. But it couldn't last.

Since he'd been spotted by Eduardo, he could assume that others from TimTomTon—and perhaps some of Dr. Sierra's people as well—very likely had Agnes under observation.

Suddenly someone pounded on the door.

Eduardo?

Not yet.

Agnes was out there, yelling to come in. As soon as the lock clicked, she burst in and slammed the door shut behind herself. She was a ridiculous sight. All she had on were black hightop tennis shoes, blue bikini briefs and a matching blue bra. Smart woman. She explained that she'd slipped out of the oversize coveralls and let them fall—clunk—to the floor. Instantly a mob began fighting over the loot.

"Where's Eduardo?"

"Still on the steps. They knocked him down."

"Jesus H. Christ."

Rick wrapped his arms around her and held her close. She felt warm and wonderful.

They were in trouble. Deep trouble. But for the moment, at least, they were safe.

REO: No. 52
To: Rawhide, White House
From: Chicken Little
Subject: *Aroma*

At first, Mondale's selection of Geraldine Ferraro as his running mate seemed to be a masterstroke.

Now the public perceives her as a liability and disaster in the making.

This is because of the roundabout way she has dealt with the problems of her campaign financing and her husband's real estate manipulations.

No matter how skillfully she explains those matters, the voters know that something *smells*.

☆ ☆ **18** ☆ ☆

Agnes and Rick didn't have a lot going for them. He estimated they would be safe for a half hour to forty-five minutes.

It might take that long for TimTomTon—or Dr. Sierra—to locate their room.

Or it might take a lot less.

And then what?

He looked the room over. It was a typical hotel cell for lower middle-class tourists, offering no protection for whatever Rick and Agnes were up against. Painted foam green, the door wasn't even wood. It was some kind of flimsy composition that would break at the first impact.

He asked Agnes how she was registered.

"Mr. and Mrs. Elliott L. Taft," she said. "From L.A."

That might help. TimTomTon—or Dr. Sierra and his people—would lose time checking out all the single women who'd registered as man and wife.

Agnes read his thoughts.

"This is a hooker town," she said. "I'll bet a bunch are registered as Mr. and Mrs."

"How come you know so much about hookers?"

Instead of an explanation, she gave him an exaggerated clown smile. She brushed her hand over the black spikes of her punk-rocker wig. Then she removed it and let her shining blonde hair fall loose to her shoulders.

God, she was beautiful. Even the red and yellow punk rocker makeup on her face didn't detract from her beauty. The almost transparent blue bra and bikini briefs made her body look sinfully voluptuous.

There was only one woman who was more beautiful. Gin. Rick wondered if he would ever see her again.

"Well?" he demanded. "How come you know so much about hookers?"

Rubbing her soft cheek against his, she informed him that he needed a shave, badly.

"For your information," she said brightly. "I played a hooker on TV in 'Night Run.' And I was a hooker's horny daughter in 'Child's Play.' Satisfied?"

Rick assured her he was. He also assured her that they were wasting time.

They moved more quickly. With brisk strokes of a towel, Agnes wiped the paint off her face. He went through her things on the bed and found his camera bag. It contained his spare pair of glasses. He put them on.

Drawing Dr. Sierra's old, worn pistol from the Pan-Am travel bag, Rick extracted the clip. The cartridges were oily and free of moisture. Satisfied, he inserted the clip back into the grip.

He went rapidly around the room one more time, hoping it would provide some kind of plan. The furnishings were Nevada Moderne: a double bed with an iridescent green spread that needed laundering; twin green lamps beside a headboard of cracked brown plastic; dark green drapes that were starting to fray; a small armchair upholsered in shiny brown plastic; a phone, nineteen-inch TV, air conditioner, and a small windowless bathroom.

"Hey," he said. "What's that?"

Agnes joined him at the room's single window where his attention was drawn to a long narrow piece of perpendicular metal pipe. It was just beyond the edge of the window, almost out of sight.

The window was designed not to open. By pressing his face flat against the pane, Rick could see that the slender pipe was part of construction scaffolding made of a lot more pipe. The scaffolding was attached to the exterior wall of the adjacent room.

"Do you smell fresh paint?" he asked.

"Yes. Look."

Agnes pointed overhead to two panels that didn't match the rest of the ceiling. They had been freshly painted a slightly different shade of light green.

The mismatched panels were on the ceiling adjacent to the room with the scaffolding.

"A bit of luck," Rick said. "Maybe."

He put the pistol in his pants pocket. Then he placed the small brown armchair on the bed, close to the wall.

While Agnes steadied the wobbly chair, Rick clambered up onto it. By bracing his feet on its wooden arms, he was able to climb high enough to reach the ceiling panels.

Sinking under the pressure of his weight, the chair's legs went deep into the blankets and soft mattress. Suddenly both the chair and bed began to wobble like crazy.

Agnes couldn't hold the chair. It flipped over and launched Rick into the air. He missed the bed and crashed heavily to the floor.

The thump of his butt against the rug was loud enough to be heard across the river.

Agnes tried to apologize, but he told her to shut up.

For a long part of a minute, neither of them moved. They listened for sounds indicating they'd blown it and were about to be discovered.

Nothing happened. Except for the loud hum of the air conditioner, the room was silent.

"This time you go up," Rick said. "I'll steady the chair."

She was willing, but first she had to pull on a pair of shorts striped red and white like a stick of peppermint candy.

"I have to be decent," she explained.

"Jesus H. Christ. Hurry!"

"Otherwise," she added in that funny way of hers, "we'll lose time while you rape me."

She was right. When she was up in the air, legs apart and braced on the chair's arms, her perfumed crotch and its Garden of Eden were a lovely temptation an inch from his face. She was high enough to put her hands on the freshly painted ciling panels.

"Push straight up," Rick said. "See if they move."

Made of some kind of light composition, the first panel moved slightly. She gave a little leap and shoved harder. The panel moved up and sideways, opening a crevice several inches wide between itself and the adjacent panel.

With a little cry of surprise, she lost her balance and fell. Rick caught her and braced himself against the chair, keeping it from falling. She was game to try again. Another leap and she shoved the second panel off to the side. Again she fell and Rick caught her. But she'd done the job. Now the two panels were dislodged far enough to indicate that the opening in the ceiling was going to be about two feet wide by five feet long.

After that things moved faster. Rick climbed the chair, jumped to the opening, and clung to the solid edge. He knocked both panels aside, clearing the opening. Then he pulled himself up through it. He found himself in a room similar to the one he'd just left. But there was one big difference. A lot of this room had been damaged by fire.

Daylight from the window revealed badly charred walls and flooring. The room had been stripped of its furnishings and reconstruction was under way.

A new interior wall was partly built with raw pine two-by-fours. When Rick glanced through the skeleton construction, he saw that the fire had damaged additional rooms. All were in various stages of reconstruction.

A handsaw, claw hammer, and other tools were placed neatly in an open toolbox atop a wooden sawhorse. According to the damp dial of his Timex, it was 4:40 P.M. Very likely the workmen were finished for the day.

Returning to the opening in the floor, he knelt and looked down at Agnes's upturned face.

"We're moving," he said. "Start tossing up the stuff."

Standing on the bed, she tossed the objects up to him one by one. First, Dr. Sierra's Pan Am travel bag. Next came her purse, Rick's camera bag, a pair of white leather sandals, and a small suitcase. The final object was a big black cloth bag stuffed with old clothes. It was light in weight but too large for the opening.

"Forget it," he said.

"No, Rick! We need it. It's got all kinds of costumes."

There wasn't time to argue. She removed enough of the clothes so the bag slid through. Then she balled up the rest—two pairs of heavy trousers and a greasy mechanic's shirt—and hurled them high enough for him to catch.

"Hurry!" he said.

"OK!"

Using the bed like a trampoline, she made a couple of practice jumps. Then she extended her arms above her head and gave a mighty leap.

Rick caught her wrists and yanked her up into the opening.

She cried out with mock pain. "Ow! You're stretching me. I'm not a rubber duck!"

"You are now! Quack!"

For a moment, she clung to the edge of the opening. He reached down, grabbed the waist of her red and white shorts, and pulled her up the rest of the way.

After helping her to stand, he replaced the two panels and covered them with heavy new timbers from the reconstruction project.

"Do you realize!" he asked, "the risks we're taking?"

He explained it was possible that someone had left the panels loose to lure them up into a trap.

"Either side could have us staked out," he said. "Dr. Sierra's people. Or TimTomTon people—"

Agnes swore in violent Russian. Then she gave him one of her quicksilver smiles. That was another of her qualities that he found intriguing—her ability to go in mere seconds from darkest anger to the height of comic optimism.

"If they get us," she said, "I'm to blame because of my dumb costume. Will you boil me in chicken fat . . . or Chanel No. 5?"

"Is hokay," he replied in fractured Russian. "Maybe in vodka."

"Thank you, Rick." Again the quicksilver smile. "When I'm around you, I feel lucky. How do you feel about me?"

"Lucky. Now hurry."

She put on the greasy black mechanic's shirt. Then they quickly gathered up the rest of the stuff and moved into the next damaged room, ducking through openings in the interior wall reconstruction.

Soon they began to perspire heavily because the burned rooms lacked operating air-conditioning. Rick didn't doubt that the outside temperature was still around a fiery 121. It seemed hotter in here.

They moved to still another damaged room. It was almost completely filled with stacks of fresh-smelling new lumber, wall paneling, and other construction materials.

The next room was less heavily damaged but lacked furnishings. The fourth room looked like one they could use. When they squeezed through the burned hole in its interior wall, they discovered it was otherwise undamaged. Its orange-accented furnishings smelled smoky and dank but were intact. Best of all, the air-conditioning was working.

They dumped their stuff on the floor and on the satin,

synthetic, orange bedspread. Then Rick opened the bathroom door and discovered a man standing there in the dimness.

"Hi, little brother," the man said. "Been waiting for you."

Jerry. His brother Jerry.

His brother, the murderer.

☆ ☆ 19 ☆ ☆

It wasn't possible. For a moment, Rick felt as if his eyes were betraying him again, distorting his vision.

But the tall, slim man was definitely his brother Jerry.

As Jerry walked toward him into the stronger light, Rick saw that he was holding a gun. An old, worn pistol. Identical to the Russian-type weapon in Rick's pocket.

Jerry aimed at Rick's heart.

He was extremely calm and knew exactly what he planned to do.

"Move very slowly," he said. "Sit on the bed."

Rick did as ordered.

When Jerry spoke to Agnes, his gaze remained fixed on Rick's eyes.

"On the bed, Agnes. Sit close to Rick."

She said nothing. Slowly, she followed his commands.

She was amazingly in control of herself. No emotional reaction. No unexpected movements.

Jerry told them to fold their arms across their chests.

"Do *not* talk," he said. "Do *not* look at each other. Keep looking at me."

He took one step to the rear and carefully placed his back against the wall.

"You have been condemned to death," he said. "*Both* of you."

His eyes were so ruthless and cruel that Rick couldn't believe this man was his brother. Certainly not the funny cutup of a brother he had known when they were small boys. Certainly not the older brother who had inspired him to go into photography and had also inspired him in so many other ways.

"But," Jerry added grimly, "I will not carry out your death sentence *unless*—"

Quickly he stepped closer and placed the black barrel of the pistol hard against the side of Rick's head. *"Unless you force me."*

Then he stepped back. From his pocket, he drew a short, squat silencer. Rick knew from photos he'd seen in his indocrination manuals that it was a Soviet silencer because of its short length. With slow, practiced movements, Jerry screwed the silencer onto the pistol barrel. He didn't look at the pistol. His eyes remained locked with Rick's.

"Excuse me," said Agnes. "May I ask a question?"

"No."

Rick wondered if Jerry had noticed the bulge of the pistol in Rick's trouser pocket. Probably. If so, why hadn't he taken possession of it? Rick decided his gun made no difference. Jerry knew very well that Rick could never kill him.

Jerry's blunt answer didn't deter Agnes from asking her question.

"Aren't you Rick's brother?"

"Shut up!"

"Well, aren't you?"

Jerry's reply was a quick, angry movement of the pistol. He slapped it very hard against the side of her face.

She cried out with pain. Despite the blow, she insisted on speaking out again.

"I'm disappointed. I expected you two to look more alike—" She drew in her breath sharply and nervously. "That's all. I'm finished."

Jerry tried to hit her again with the pistol. But Rick

managed to intervene and caught the blow on his forearm. The pistol knocked his arm hard against Agnes's face.

"Do that again, Rick. And I kill you!"

Jerry's words were like steel striking steel, and his expression was brutal.

Rick decided Agnes was right. He and Jerry no longer resembled each other as closely as when they were younger. Their similarities included their height, over six feet; slim, muscular builds, small ears, blue-gray eyes, ruddy complexions, and curly coal black hair. No beards. No mustaches.

But after that the resemblance ended. Jerry looked far more than two and a half years older than Rick. There were unmistakeable signs of great stress and possible alcoholism in the lines around his eyes and tight mouth. His face was blotchy—bright red on one cheek and part of his nose, sickly pale white elsewhere.

Suddenly Jerry kicked his brother's foot. "Listen to me!"

He thought Rick wasn't paying attention. He was wrong. Rick had heard every word Jerry spoke.

"This is the way we play it," Jerry said. "You shove off. *Right now. Right this minute.* Leave Nevada. Don't go back to California. Go somewhere far away and disappear. Do you know the reason?"

"No."

"If you don't go, then I've got to kill you."

"Why?" It was a stupid question. But Rick had to say something.

Jerry rubbed his mouth with the back of his hand and Rick noticed that the tip was missing from his little finger.

"Rick, *hermanito*, it's more complicated than you'll ever understand. It goes a long way back..."

Jerry explained that he had been recruited by Dr. Sierra while working as a photographer for the *Los Angeles Times*. Unknown to Rick, Jerry and Dr. Sierra had made the arrangements two years previously to set Rick up close to Gin and her aunts in Santa Barbara.

"I arranged for your park job," Jerry said. "And also your nature job for the university. Do you know why?"

Rick had a hunch but kept his mouth shut.

"A reasonable strategy," Jerry added. "Eventually, I would take your place. Then I could get to know Gin ... and through her I could get to the president. Do you know why it failed?"

Rick shook his head.

"Because I couldn't kill you *then*. And because—"

Abruptly, there was almost a cry in Jerry's voice, as if he were protesting the terrible things he was required to do. Then he finished it. "And because I *still* can't kill you."

For a moment, Jerry's pale face seemed to soften. Rick saw a trace of the brother he had once known so well. A trace of family affection? A memory of something they'd shared?

Then the moment was gone. As if to cover up his lapse, Jerry began to speak more quickly and aggressively. He spoke in short sentences and covered a lot of topics. He denied being responsible for their mother's murder. He insisted that was a TimTomTon project designed to force Jerry to flee the U.S. and confuse Dr. Sierra's plans.

Jerry knew Rick had been in contact with St. Paul back in the cherry orchard in Idaho. For that crime against Nicaragua, St. Paul would be hunted down and executed.

Then Jerry told Rick why St. Paul—also known as Lopez-Mendez—had risked helping him. The reason was a blockbuster.

It went all the way back to when the brothers had been kids in Nicaragua. St. Paul had helped their mother find Jerry and Rick after the family was broken up. During their father's long hospitalization, she and St. Paul had been lovers. If true, it was a hell of a revelation. Rick would never have guessed that his mother was capable of such a thing.

Jerry stopped talking. He gave Rick a moment to think about all the disclosures he had just made.

"So we're back to *numero uno*, square one," Jerry said. "You promise to disappear ... and I promise *not* to kill you."

Rick made no comment. He was still thinking.

"What about Agnes?" Rick asked.

Jerry had his answer prepared: "She stays with me. We have plans for her. Because of her resemblance to Gin."

Rick said no. He barked it loudly so there could be no mistake about his feelings.

Then Agnes spoke up equally loud and clear. "Absolutely not! I stay with Rick!"

Immediately, they realized they'd made a blunder. They should have negotiated instead of refusing so flatly. Jerry lost his temper just as he had one day when he and Rick were boys and arguing in Managua. The conflict then had involved Jerry's new Peugeot bike. Rick wanted to borrow it because his bike had a flat tire. Jerry said no and blew his stack when Rick persisted.

It was the worst and most memorable argument of their boyhood, a big blowout about nothing, but the effects lasted for days. And now Jerry was being just as unreasonable.

"She comes with me!" he raged. "Because I say so!" That was the same kind of big brother argument he'd used when they were kids. No other explanation was offered. Because he was the older one made it right and gave him an excuse to lose his temper.

Now Jerry repeated himself. *"Because I say so!"*

Jerry released a firecracker string of curses in Nicaraguan Spanish and English. It was an unnecessary overreaction because Rick and Agnes hadn't pushed him that far. He raised his pistol as if to shoot. His manner was so threatening that Agnes gasped.

Never before had Rick seen that dark, intense look on his brother's face. It was authority mingled with irrationality. He looked so tired and strung out that he might do anything to get his way.

When Rick heard the air-pressure sound of the silencer, he thought Jerry had fired.

He was wrong. The shot was fired from overhead.

Instantly Jerry reacted by angling his pistol upward and pulling the trigger twice. The weapon sounded like something in a bad spy movie, like two spurts of air escaping from a bicycle tire.

Suddenly there were fumbling and scratching noises overhead, on the ceiling behind Rick and Agnes. Rick turned in time to see someone fall through an opening in the ceiling into the room. It was a man with an elongated body and very thin, spidery arms. He crashed to the floor and lay still. Something red followed him down and landed on his white T-shirt. The red object was a dirty baseball cap bearing the phrase GOD FIRST. Both words were blood-stained.

He was Rick's benefactor from the desert, old Elijah. He'd been watching through a large opening in the ceiling. It was identical to the one in the other burned room.

With great accuracy, Jerry's bullets had struck Elijah in the forehead. The two holes were close together just above the bushy white eyebrows. In Elijah's hand, held tightly in the brown spidery fingers, was a gun with a long, narrow silencer.

Hearing a grunt, Rick turned back to Jerry and saw that Elijah had shot him in the side of the rib cage. There was a growing red stain in the light blue cloth of Jerry's sport shirt.

"He's hurt!" cried Agnes.

"Forget it," said Jerry. "It all but missed me."

Jerry walked slowly backward toward the room's exit. He kept the pistol aimed at Rick and Agnes.

"Don't look at me," he grunted with pain. "Look at the old man. And try to get the message."

He put his hand on the doorknob and slowly turned it.

"Rick," he said. "Are you too dumb to get the message?"

Rick didn't reply. All he wanted was for his brother to open the door and get the hell out.

"You always were the dumb little kid," Jerry said.

Why was he so slow about leaving? Rick wanted to shove him out the door. But he made no move.

"The message is there on the floor," Jerry went on. "TimTomTon blew it again." Finally he opened the door and started out. But he still didn't leave. "Remember, Rick. Next time it'll be *you* laid out on the floor."

The door closed behind him.

Rick went over and made sure it was locked.

Agnes remained seated on the satiny orange-colored bed-spread Her face was pale with shock.

Rick knelt beside old Elijah. He touched the thin, leathery wrist to make sure. No pulse. Nor had he expected any.

Slowly Rick's mind began to accept some of what was now so obvious.

It wasn't by chance that the old man had found him out in the desert. He'd been sent on his mission by TimTomTon.

Rick couldn't understand why they'd selected an eighty-six-year-old man for such an assignment. Surely he wasn't supposed to work alone. But where was his backup?

Elijah had failed. But he'd come within a few inches of succeeding. If his bullet had been a little more accurate, Jerry would be dead.

And if that had happened Rick would be free of Jerry's deal. But Jerry wasn't dead.

Part of Rick was glad his brother wasn't dead. But another part wished he *was* dead.

Agnes rose from the bed. Her soft warm hand touched Rick's cheek. Then she placed her arms comfortingly around him. She didn't speak. She didn't have to. Rick knew she was thinking the same thing he was.

He had to face it. Jerry was a bloody Sandinista murderer. And Rick needed Jerry dead.

REO: No. 58
To: Rawhide, White House
From: Chicken Little
Subject: *Pony*

One of your favorite stories is about the boy who wakes up on Christmas morning to find his room piled high with horse manure. He starts digging, convinced that somewhere in all that mess there has to be a pony.

That's similar to the situation in the Philippines where we are guilty of negligent optimism. Manure is piled everywhere. If the U.S. continues to support

President Marcos, we will dig, dig, dig *ad nauseam*. But we will find no pony.

Our National Security Agency and CIA insist on bolstering Marcos at all costs. They are wrong.

☆ ☆ 20 ☆ ☆

They were in critical need of Gin's help, as quickly as possible, to break the codes.

But first Rick and Agnes had to find her.

St. Paul had told Rick she was in Bullhead City, Arizona. But where?

Despite its name, Bullhead wasn't a city. It was a small, dried-out desert town bisected by State Highway 95, its only main street. Its population of maybe a couple of thousand was just big enough to make the search for Gin complicated.

For the time being, Rick and Agnes decided they'd be safer staying on the Nevada side of the Colorado River, where there were more tourists.

If and when they were able to come up with a decent search plan, they could be in Bullhead within minutes by driving over the Davis Dam bridge.

After leaving the Gold Dust Club, they took a cab to the giant recreational vehicle park spread over terraced slopes just west of the Riverside Hotel and casino. For $550 a week, plus a $500 deposit, they rented a motor home that was nearly as long as a Greyhound bus.

Their wheeled mansion was located on a new, asphalt-paved terrace in the middle of the park. It was surrounded by scores of other parked recreational vehicles, from small Toyota camper trucks to monster Winnebagos and Southwinds.

Rick and Agnes found it comforting to be in the midst of

so many people and to hear familiar family sounds: TVs turned to high volume, the hum of a hundred rooftop air conditioners, toilets flushing, garbage disposals grinding, and men and women out for an evening stroll, chatting about the desert's ceaseless heat and how it wasn't doing a thing for Uncle Ed's arthritis.

Knowing all those people were nearby gave Rick a sense of security. But that was offset by a stronger sense of insecurity.

They might be free of surveillance by Jerry and Dr. Sierra. But it was more likely that they were being watched around the clock. If not by Jerry and Dr. Sierra, then certainly by TimTomTon's people, possibly set up as close as the adjacent Winnebago.

They decided not to waste time worrying. Their most immediate problem was evaluating the stuff in Dr. Sierra's bag. They had to use its documents to figure out what Dr. Sierra's next move would be. Very likely he was here to harm Gin and had been given her Bullhead City address by the traitor—or traitors—in TimTomTon.

There was a possibility, very slight, that something in the bag would tell them where Gin's new communications lab was located. If they could find her, Gin might be able to solve whatever codes were hidden in the blue bag's documents.

If they were lucky, the process of finding Gin might be quick. But if the documents were complicated, or useless, they could be delayed for hours or a day . . . or longer. And any delay put them at greater risk.

On top of all that, Agnes and Rick had a hell of an argument to settle. Agnes wanted them to get out of there immediately and disappear . . . for good.

Rick refused.

She used her sweetest persuasive powers.

"Rick, you darling idiot. You've got to do what your damn brother said. You've absolutely got to get out!"

"No."

Whenever Agnes was upset like this, her eyes turned a deep smoky blue and she continually chewed the pink lipstick off her plump lower lip.

No matter what arguments she used, Rick kept saying no.

Among other things, he wanted one more crack at the son of a bitch who had blinded him. He knew he was being stubborn and not too logical about it. But he had to do it.

Finally, Agnes blew higher than Mt. St. Helens. To break through his stupidity, or at least get his full attention, she began calling him obscene names, including such originals as "imbecile-rectumhead" and "jerk-shitbrain."

That strategy didn't work. So she switched to logic, stated slowly and precisely in university English.

She mentioned the murder of Ignacio, strangled by Jerry with a wire. She mentioned the murder of Ignacio's assistant, shot through the heart by Jerry. She mentioned the death of old Elijah, shot twice in the forehead by Jerry.

She reminded Rick of the murder of his mother. Also by Jerry.

"These people . . ." she said, "Jerry and his friends. They deal in death every day. They are professionals. So what chance does an amateur have?"

Every word she spoke strengthened the steel links of her logic. But Rick knew that this time logic wasn't the answer, not for him.

He couldn't run away. He had to make one more all-out effort.

If he was lucky—luckier than he'd ever been in his whole life—he just might be able to protect Gin from Jerry and Dr. Sierra in a way no one else could. Probably because of his resemblance to his brother.

He couldn't put it into words. But deep inside he had the unshakable feeling that he was the only one who could save Gin when the time came.

But first he had to find her.

After a while, Agnes cooled off, and they put the argument on hold. She wouldn't speak to Rick, or look at him. But, using the motor home's microwave oven, she cooked them a supper of molasses baked beans and juicy franks. She was also willing to keep working on evaluating Dr. Sierra's many documents.

They sat at the white, plastic-topped table in the dinette,

eating, drinking Bud, and silently poring over everything from the blue and white travel bag.

The document that interested Rick the most was a water-stained, partly wrinkled page of stock quotations from the *Los Angeles Times* of the previous Tuesday. Before their noisy squabble, Agnes had offered the opinion that some kind of message was buried in the stock listings.

Looking for tiny pencil or ink marks, he scanned both sides of the newspaper page, including the American composite and the commodities lists. He found nothing meaningful. He wondered if any special markings might have been washed off when the paper was under water.

Agnes's studies of the other papers also produced nothing.

Bored and frustrated, she snapped on the TV. A Pink Panther movie appeared on the screen, showing Peter Sellers as Inspector Clouseau, riding in a tiny foreign car with Elke Sommer. Both were nude and making funny remarks.

Agnes laughed. Now she was in a better mood and willing to be friends again. Returning to the table, she handed Rick a small ruled sheet with perforations indicating it had been torn from a spiral notebook, possibly by Dr. Sierra.

"Look it over," she suggested. "It might tie in with your stock pages."

He was very willing to accept input from her. Her TimTomTon training far exceeded his. During the two years that she was being groomed as a Gin substitute, her paramilitary officer training had included a series of TimTomTon classes that focused entirely on document analysis and related technology.

The small sheet of notebook paper was wrinkled but dry. It contained many blurry markings in red ink—letters and numerals written in a strong masculine hand.

Rick checked the numbers and letters forward and backward, up and down. Nothing worked out. When he repeated the sequences, the results were the same. He began to feel very out of it.

It had been more than thirty-six hours since he'd slept.

The combination of food, beer, and rows of meaningless red ink numerals made his eyelids heavy.

Resting his cheek atop his folded arms on the table, he dozed off.

Agnes's shouted words awakened him. "Hey, Rick! You want to go beddie-bye!"

Reluctantly, he sat up. He opened his eyes. Then he came wide awake. She had taken all her clothes off. She was lying on her back on the plush soft sofa. She undulated her pink and white hips slowly in rhythm with the Pink Panther theme on the TV. God, did she know how to rejuvenate a weary man.

Rick stripped off his clothes. In a moment, he was on her and in her.

With Agnes, each time was better than the one before. She knew exactly what he wanted and needed. And since she had the same needs, they flew to the heights together.

It ended quickly. But she didn't mind. She wriggled away from him and got off the sofa.

"Good night, Rick. Happy dreams...."

He slept. He had no dreams. He enjoyed a total blackout that brought blessed relief and relaxation.

When he awoke, two hours had passed. The TV was silent. The air conditioner was humming. And there had been no interference—not even a hint of a threat—from Dr. Sierra, Jerry, or TimTomTon.

Agnes sat beside Rick on the sofa, holding his hand. She had dressed in one of the costumes from the clothes bag. It was part of a very old and faded white lace wedding dress with long sleeves and a long skirt. The costume made her look virginal, a role she adopted with high spirits. She rubbed Rick's fingers lovingly against her smooth cheek and murmured, "Rick, that was the best ten-second one I ever had. You were marvelous."

"So were you. Are you sure I lasted a whole ten seconds?"

"Don't be sarcastic. Anyway, who's counting?"

While Rick put on his trousers and lime green sport shirt,

she returned to the white dinette table and cheerfully shuffled through all the stuff laid out there.

She insisted that they examine it again, piece by piece, paper by paper:

1. A U.S. passport made out in the name of Martin Jessup Hunter and containing an icy-eyed photo of Dr. Sierra.

2. A current but undoubtedly forged California driver's license, also made out to Martin Jessup Hunter and containing a color photo of Dr. Sierra. This one showed him wearing gold-rimmed glasses and a well-fitted, gray wig. The waves in the wig had shiny highlights. He looked twenty years older than when Rick had seen him that afternoon on the shuttle boat. The lines of his mouth were different, as if he were wearing badly made dentures.

3. The Soviet pistol and an extra clip of ammo.

4. A large white envelope that had contained all the documents. The envelope was approximately nine by twelve. It wasn't paper. It was some kind of paperlike composition that resisted water.

5. A flat electronic device with two switches. It was some kind of a mechanical puzzle that defied solution.

6. The thick packet of one hundred and five hundred dollar bills. A recount had produced the good news that the currency totalled nearly $16,000, considerably more than Rick's quick estimate earlier in the day.

Agnes was so animated, and her eyes so lighted with happiness, that Rick knew she was up to something. She was mysterious about it in an affectionate sort of a way. He knew she would tell him eventually, so he asked no questions.

Suddenly she suggested that they give the documents a rest for a few minutes.

"Rick, dearest, I've got things I must tell you . . ."

Her mood became more talkative and expansive. The subject surprised him, as it usually did whenever Agnes was in this kind of a loving emotional state.

For the first time, she wanted to talk about herself. She talked about how she was born in Leningrad but left the

USSR as a child when her parents managed to immigrate to Canada.

"When I was five," she said, "we moved from Ottawa to Detroit. My parents began the process of becoming U.S. citizens, I took ballet lessons and loved being a little American. But then one day it all ended..."

She told the rest of the story in a matter-of-fact way. She sought no sympathy. She explained that she no longer shed tears over what had happened.

"I cried for years," she said. "No one can cry like a little girl with a broken heart..."

Her mother and father were both lawyers. They were summoned back to the USSR to represent their large family in complicated legal proceedings. Involved was a substantial piece of state land on which the family operated small but lucrative private farms.

Reluctant to make the trip, but having no choice, they left little Agnes with foster parents in Detroit. She never saw her mother and father again. They were either executed or died in prison. Their land was confiscated.

"Were they Jewish?" Rick asked.

"No. Latvian."

"But your name... isn't it Jewish?"

"Steinberg? Of course." She gave him the quicksilver smile that made her face light up so beautifully. "But it's not my real name."

She explained that she adopted the name to help her acting career in New York. "Sometimes it worked like sorcery. All those Jewish TV writers and producers... sometimes they liked to give a poor Jewish kid a break."

She took a deep breath. Then her mood darkened. "I want to tell you one more thing about my parents. My mother was afraid to go back. She absolutely didn't want to go. But she went... and it cost her life."

Returning to the sofa, Rick sat beside her. He put his arm around her and drew her very close. Her small fingers tightened around his. They held him so tightly that her fingernails turned from pink to white.

"Do you know *why* she went back?"

Rick could read the answer in her eyes. But he knew she wanted to tell him, so he remained silent.

"Because she loved my father. She loved him so much she gave her life for him."

After that they didn't talk for a while. They remained on the soft, deep sofa, holding each other close. He could tell by her rapid breathing that she was agitated by the memories of her family and had much more that she wanted to say.

"Thirsty?" she asked suddenly.

Rick nodded, but he knew that wasn't the subject pressing down on her. Whatever it was, she was stalling and needed time to think.

She went to the fridge and opened a cold can of Bud. She poured it into one glass and returned to the sofa. They sat together cheek to cheek, each holding the glass and taking turns sipping from it. The two of them—each with separate thoughts—gazed at the small bubbles, rising in geometrically straight lines to the layer of foam.

Impulsively, she kissed him on the mouth. He could taste the yeasty beer on her lips and also on her tongue. It was a very pleasant intimacy.

Laughing, she broke off the kiss. "Rick, this is ridiculous! Beer isn't sexy. So why do I feel horny?"

They laughed together, sipped more beer, and kissed again and again, gently, until the beer was gone.

Then Rick kissed her harder and stroked her breast, sending her the signal that he was ready. And letting her know that for her benefit he had more than a ten-second dalliance in mind.

"No, Rick."

She broke away and slid over to the end of the sofa. She turned, lifted her legs onto the cushions, and used her folded knees as a barrier to keep him away. She pulled down the faded lace skirt of her wedding costume and covered her knees in an exaggerated display of modesty.

"Listen to me, Rick. Please."

He listened. At first, she hesitated, unable to find the

right words. Then she found them and they came forth rapidly.

"Rick, I have always fallen in love easily. And just as easily I have fallen out, with no pain afterward. But with you it's not the same—"

He tried to speak, but she shushed him.

"Listen, Rick. I think I'm like my mother. I'm going to go on with you, even though I know you're wrong and stubborn . . . and it's very dangerous. No more arguing with you. No more fighting—"

Rick tried to move closer to her, but she shoved her knees at him.

"Listen, Rick. You're bright, but you're not the brightest man in the world. Nor the most handsome. And certainly not the richest. But to me you're the dearest—and that's much more important."

She stopped talking. But she still wouldn't let him speak. She put her finger across her lips.

Then she came quickly across the sofa to him and placed her finger across his lips. Just as quickly she went over to the TV and jabbed its buttons. It came on with a blast of noise. The Pink Panther movie was over, replaced by a screen full of vibrating, zigzag white lines and tremendous static.

She put her lips against his ear and whispered. Her voice was so faint that he doubted if any surveillance device could pick it up. He could scarcely hear her.

"Rick, dearest. I know you're in love with another woman. But I can handle it. Yes, I really can. And to prove it I'll take you to her. I know where she is."

She went back to the table and beckoned for him to follow. She picked up the flat black plastic object with the two switches, one on either side.

She put her lips to his ear. "Simple as one, two, three—" She operated one switch once and the other one twice. A slot opened up. A white plastic card slid soundlessly into view.

"The code key to Gin's lab," she whispered. "While you were sleeping, I took a cab to Bullhead and cruised the streets. It's a small town, so I was able to find Gin's new lab. Aunt Louise's Porsche was parked out front.''

He was very impressed. And also angry.

"Damn you, damn you—" He seized her shoulders and gave her an affectionate shaking.

"Think of all the damn time we've wasted," he said, impatiently. "Why the hell didn't you tell me sooner?"

Her reply was still another link in her steel chain of logic.

"Because I wanted to keep you alive as long as possible.''

He kissed her on the forehead. She was a unique woman. She was warm and loving. She was always responsive, and she was smart.

She was exactly the kind of woman he was sure Gin would turn out to be.

REO: No. 62
To: Rawhide, White House
From: Chicken Little
Subject: *Magic*

Since you began your political career, you have lambasted the evils of deficit.

However, your administration will add more than $2 trillion in red ink during your White House years.

Amazingly, this monstrous deficit has been fueling high economic growth and creating new jobs.

This is known as Rawhide Magic. (And luck— because of falling oil prices and interest rates!)

One of the blessings of the presidential system is that someone else will be occupying the Oval Office when the trillions in IOUs come due.

Is this the way you want history to remember you?

☆ ☆ 21 ☆ ☆

It was 9:40 P.M. but still blistering hot outside. The desert sky was blue-black and endless, dusted with a zillion stars.

Rick and Agnes stood on a rundown residential street in Bullhead City and inspected the two small houses. They were about fifteen feet apart, with a heavy growth of tired old cactus between them.

As their eyes became accustomed to the darkness, they could see that the houses were very old. They were dusty wood frame houses, similar but not identical.

Each house probably had one small bedroom. Each had a peaked, slanting roof. Each roof sagged in the middle from old age. One roof was made of corrugated metal sheets warped by the desert sun.

The other roof had once been covered with small white rocks. But winds had blown away most of the rocks. Both houses were badly in need of paint.

For many minutes, Rick and Agnes stood across the street, observing. Dim lights were on in each house. Each had an operating air conditioner in a front window, but there were no other signs of activity.

If the pattern were the same as in Santa Barbara, Montana, and Texas, Aunt Louise lived in one house and Aunt Pam in the other. Which was which? And in which one would they find Gin?

Rick carried a thin plastic shopping bag into which he and Agnes had transferred most of the documents and other stuff from Dr. Sierra's travel bag. The loaded pistol was in the waistband of Rick's trousers, concealed by the lower part of his sport shirt.

Their first survey revealed no hard evidence of exterior security on either house—no fences, no closed-circuit TV scanners, no floodlights that could be turned on in an emergency.

They decided to circle the block and check the rear of both houses.

It was a very small city block containing a single row of seven small houses. All the houses were old and ramshackle. All were dark except Aunt Pam's and Aunt Louise's.

There were no sidewalks or street lights. In almost total darkness, they walked down a side street. Then they made a left turn and went a short distance until they were on the street directly behind the two dimly lighted houses.

Now they saw the first evidence of security. The other backyards had no fences. But the backyards of the aunts' houses were surrounded by new galvanized steel wire fencing about six feet high. There were no rear gates.

The chain-link fence looked ordinary. But it wasn't.

Rick stepped closer to Agnes and spoke in a whisper. "Notice those two strands?"

She nodded but made no comment. None was needed. They both had seen examples of that type of sensor wire in their TimTomTon instruction classes.

One black strand ran near the top of the fence, the other near the bottom. They were made of practically indestructible material. If anything passed over or under the fence, the sensors would send a silent alert to a central alarm system.

Nevertheless, it was a strangely incomplete security system. Why were the fronts of the houses unprotected? Rick began to wonder if Gin was really here.

Would TimTomTon risk placing someone as valuable as Gin in such a flimsy-looking setup?

Rick and Agnes continued their slow walk around the block, passing within a hundred yards of where they had parked the long motor home.

When they were about half a block from the front of the aunts' houses, they met a man who was out walking his dog on a leash. Because of the darkness, they couldn't see the finer details of his face. But they could smell the stench of his cigar. It resembled burning plastic. His dog was old, fat and slow.

When Agnes and Rick drew closer, the middle-aged man greeted them in a friendly manner and then stopped to chat. Because of the heat, he was shirtless. An enormous bare belly, pale white in the darkness, hung over the belt of his walking shorts.

"Noticed you lookin' at the houses," he said.

"Interesting, aren't they?" replied Agnes, very carefully.

The man was eager to talk about the houses. If he was a TimTomTon agent, he was a very skilled one because he talked like a small town person with little education. He used a lot of "ain'ts" and "he don'ts" and laughed continually in the wrong places.

He explained that he had lived in one of the nearby houses until two months previously. Then it was purchased by a corporation from Chicago.

"Big *mo*-tel outfit," he said. "Loaded with cash. Offered so much that me an' the wife couldn't turn it down. Bought all the houses on the block. Moved ever'body out. Changed the zoning. Gonna put in a whopper of a *mo*-tel."

Lowering his voice to a confidential tone, he admitted he was puzzled by some of the goings-on.

"Did a big job on them two." With his cigar, he gestured down the street at the pair of occupied houses. "Dug up the back yards. Hauled a lot of heavy construction stuff into each house. And then they moved in some women . . ."

He paused to let the significance of his last remark sink in.

"That's the funny part," he added. "*Mo*-tel. And strange, sexy-lookin' women. Kinda makes you wonder, don't it?"

Impatient to leave, his dog kept grunting and pulling at the leash. There was a faint odor of skunk in the hot night air, and it was probably having an effect on the dog. The man gave Agnes and Rick a cheerful "good night" and strolled on down the dark street. They waited in the shadows until he disappeared.

"He could be trouble," said Agnes. "Do you still want me to do it?"

Rick could sense from the reluctance in her voice that she

was ready to renew the big argument they'd had back in the r.v. park.

He didn't blame her. This setup had too many missing pieces. The wisest thing by far would be to leave now and try to get as far away as possible from the dangers of TimTomTon and Dr. Sierra.

Agnes guessed what he was thinking. But she didn't chicken out or renege on her promise to go into one of the houses and search for Gin.

"I'm ready," she said. "It's crazy, but if it has to be done . . ."

They stayed on the side of the street opposite to the two houses. As they came closer, they saw that while they'd been circling the block they'd lucked out. A dusty silver Porsche was now parked in front of one of the houses.

It was Louise's car. And it meant that the other house was Aunt Pam's.

Now they knew which one to choose. They didn't want to contact Aunt Louise because she might mean more trouble. But Aunt Pam liked Agnes and might help them.

"Well," said Agnes, "if I'm going to look like Gin, I guess I better complete the package."

From her white leather handbag she drew out the wire retainer to which were attached her silvery braces.

Rick held her handbag while she inserted the device into her mouth.

When it was in place, she made a sour face. "God, I hate this thing. Tastes like rusty nails."

Rick turned the shopping bag over to her. She put her handbag in on top of Dr. Sierra's documents. Then she kissed him on the cheek and departed.

He stayed in the shadows across the street and watched her walk briskly up to the front door of Aunt Pam's house.

Suddenly he felt a rush of guilt. He remembered what had happened to his mother. He remembered how Ignacio had been strangled with the wire. And how old Elijah had been shot twice in the head.

Something inside warned him to call Agnes back. She was taking a far greater risk than he was. The moment she stepped through the door she might be killed. But he made no move to help her. What she was doing had to be done.

He watched her knock on the door. She waited a long minute. Then the door opened a crack.

Another lengthy wait. Then the door opened wider and she went in.

The next period of time was hellish. He fidgeted. He wished he was a smoker so he could light up. But, as a test of willpower, he'd given up on cigarettes and whisky while in the marines. He wished he had gum to chew or some hard candy to suck on. Anything to make the dragging minutes easier to accept.

The man with the fat dog returned, walking very slowly. He paused midway between the two houses and stared at them.

He touched a flame to the stub of his cigar. He cleared his throat. He spat on the ground. Finally he and the dog moved slowly on down the street and disappeared in the gloom.

More waiting in the shadows. Rick wished his old Timex had a luminous dial so he could tell how long she'd been in there.

He put the watch to his ear. He heard nothing. He wound it and pressed it again to his ear. The damn thing had quit. That long bath in the Colorado had finally jammed the works.

More waiting.

Then the front door opened. Agnes stepped out. Yellowish light from inside the house outlined her as she beckoned for Rick to join her.

Quickly he crossed the street and approached her on the low concrete stoop. She was nervous but otherwise looked all right.

When Rick followed her through the doorway, a buzzer went off inside. He took another step, and the buzzer got much louder. Abruptly, Aunt Pam pushed past Agnes, waving her arms and yelling at Rick.

"Out! Get out!"

Her outstretched small hands hit his chest. For an old woman, she packed a good wallop. Rick retreated and went out the door.

The buzzer stopped.

"Metal detector!" yelled Pam. "You half-wit! What are you doing?"

God, she was mad. Her face was red. She kept brushing her hand angrily and unsuccessfully at long strands of platinum hair that hung in front of her eyes.

Rick removed the old pistol from his waistband. He placed it in a shadow on the concrete stoop. He took one step through the doorway. The buzzer remained silent.

But Pam kept her hands up, ready to shove him out again. She was so agitated he was sure he and Agnes didn't have a prayer of staying inside. He was wrong. In a moment, Pam calmed down. She closed the door and invited him into her living room.

The little house was amazing. Outside it was flimsy. Inside it was a fortress. The walls and low ceiling were constructed of concrete blocks. They weren't rough, cheap cinder blocks. These were hard, smooth blocks. They looked solid enough to resist a rocket or a shell from a 105mm howitzer.

The work had been done with great skill. Very probably the blocks had been installed without disturbing the ramshackle exterior shell of the house.

To add more space, most of the interior walls had been eliminated, creating one large room that served as a combination bedroom, kitchen, and living room. All the windows had been eliminated, except for the front one that contained the air conditioner.

Rick noticed heavy steel shutters installed on either side of the window. They appeared to be operated by hydraulic levers controlled by automatic electronic sensors. Similar shutters were installed beside the front door.

Installed in the ceiling were several closed-circuit TV eyes, which moved soundlessly and continually, monitoring everything in the room.

No armed men were present, because Gin couldn't abide that kind of activity. They were probably stationed nearby in one or more of the other houses. Other security personnel could be on duty there, too, manning the remotes that kept the house under total surveillance.

Obviously, Saddlebag One and his associates didn't intend to repeat the security mistakes they'd made in Santa Barbara. Gin would be as safe here as in the gold vault at Fort Knox.

The room's furnishings were contemporary and deluxe. Included were a combination refrigerator and freezer, pale green with chrome trim, a matching electric stove and dishwasher, a Scandinavian-style pale wood dining table with curved-back chairs, a double bed with a warm pink spread, and a large, comfortable-looking sofa covered with the same shade of pink fabric.

An open door revealed that the bathroom was also reinforced with concrete blocks. It was an unusually large bathroom.

Agnes and Aunt Pam stood together near the bathroom door. Each gave Rick the same warning gesture, finger pressed across lips, reminding him to keep silent. Beckoning for him to follow, they went into the bathroom. When he entered, he saw why it was so large. Half the bathroom's space was required for the opening to a well-lighted stairway that led down to a locked steel door. It was a very long stairway, made of concrete painted white. The door, also white, was about two stories below.

On the door was a large sign that read Brain Box.

At the top of the stairway was a computer with a screen, keyboard, and an identification monitor.

The monitor resembled a pair of binoculars. Rick knew what it was for, because Teodoro had shown him a picture of one.

Agnes pointed to her eyes. Then she pointed to the monitor and nodded confidently. During the long time that they'd been together back in Idaho, she had mentioned one day that her brown contact lenses were designed to defeat this type of identification machine.

They were about to find out if that was true. She pulled out the white plastic card from Dr. Sierra's stuff in the shopping bag. She inserted it in the computer slot. Then she punched in Gin's code, using the keyboard.

After the code—M-21, M-3, MX-4—appeared on the green screen, Agnes leaned over. She looked into the binocularlike device.

For what seemed like half a minute, the computer whirred and beeped while it studied the retina patterns in Agnes's contact lenses. Her lenses were designed to duplicate the retinas of Gin's eyes.

Retinas were supposed to be like fingerprints. No two alike.

Colored lights—red and blue—lit up on the computer keyboard. Then there was a loud metallic click at the bottom of the stairway as the white door unlocked. It swung open.

Agnes gave Rick a triumphant smile. Then she picked up the shopping bag and went down the stairs.

After she passed through the doorway, the steel door closed behind her. Rick heard a click indicating that it was relocked.

He and Aunt Pam went out into the main room and sat together on the foam-rubber pink sofa. They didn't speak.

She handed him a cold can of Coors from the six-pack on the coffee table. She opened another can and they drank. The beer was exactly what Rick's parched throat needed on a hot, uncomfortable night. As he sipped, he glanced up at the ceiling and the nearest TV eye.

Pam joined him in looking at the ceiling. She shrugged and sipped more beer. They both knew there was no way for them to fool TimTomTon. The men who were operating all this surveillance gear had a very good idea of what Gin and Agnes were trying to do.

They knew that Agnes had gone down to the underground lab to contact Gin. Even if the two women didn't talk, it would be obvious that Agnes was turning over Dr. Sierra's documents to Gin so she could interpret the information they contained.

Rick decided Gin would choose one of two alternatives. If she stayed down in the lab, that would indicate she'd found nothing terrific in the documents. But if she left the lab, that would indicate she was on the verge of finding something terrific—something she didn't want the traitor in TimTomTon to know about.

In that case, she would need another place to work, such as the mobile home. But would TimTomTon let her leave?

Rick and Aunt Pam stayed on the sofa for a long time. They drank more beer. They made small talk. They fidgeted. They stared at the front door, hoping it wouldn't open. If it did, TimTomTon people would come in and demand to see exactly what Gin was up to.

"That damn door makes me nervous," said Aunt Pam.

Rising from the sofa, she walked into the bathroom, beckoning for Rick to follow. They stared down the long white stairway at the white door.

At last, it opened.

Gin passed through and came up the steps. She was in a hurry.

At first Rick was positive she was Gin, because she was dressed differently from Agnes. Then he had his doubts because the two were so identical.

But when Gin approached the top of the stairs, he knew for sure that she was the genuine Gin. Agnes was lovely and sexy. But Gin was more so. She wore tangerine-colored shorts and a modest white blouse.

God, what a figure. Every movement she made on the stairs was provocative. But what set her apart from other women, and Agnes, was her innocence. She didn't think sexy, but it was written all over her, every step of the way.

She hurried past Aunt Pam and Rick, gesturing for them to follow. When they joined her in the main room, Rick paid closer attention to what Gin was carrying.

In one hand, she held the thin plastic shopping bag filled with Dr. Sierra's stuff. Slung on a broad strap over her shoulder was a fairly large and heavy camera case.

She stepped very close to Rick and whispered urgently, close to his ear.

"Where's the gun? Hurry!"

He led her to the front stoop outside. As she passed through the doorway, the metal detector buzzed loudly. Probably a reaction to her camera case.

The old pistol was still on the concrete stoop where Rick had left it. He picked it up.

"Keep it," said Gin. "Whatever you do, *don't* shoot it!"

☆ ☆ **22** ☆ ☆

Together Rick and Gin hurried off into the darkness. He put the heavy pistol back into the waistband of his trousers.

"How far is it?" Gin's words were low and tense. "The motor home—"

"Less than a block."

They walked a dozen steps in the hot night air. Then she spoke again.

"Watch for the man with the dog. There's a faction within TimTomTon that wants us dead. He's one of their lookouts."

Walking more rapidly down the street, they searched through the gloom for the pot-bellied figure of the man and the smaller shadow of his dog.

As they strode along, Rick felt again the effect she had on him. It was total attraction. Each time it happened, he marveled at the power she had over him. Strangely, he couldn't remember the exact feeling whenever they were separated, no matter how hard he tried.

He made up his mind that this time they wouldn't be separated. No matter what happened, he would see to it that she was protected and they stayed together. There was so much for them to talk about. So much for them to share, so many things to do together.

"Much farther?" she asked.

"No."

"After we get in," she said, anxiously, "don't wait. We've got to drive off immediately."

Within a few moments, they saw the long, high shadow

of the motor home, parked near a growth of fat cactus. At
almost the same time, they saw the man and his dog nearby,
heading toward the motor home. The man and dog were so
close that Rick could see the rounded outline of the big bare
belly. He could also see the dim glow of the man's cigar,
but this time he didn't smell it. That was because there was
such a fresh odor of skunk in the hot night air.

The dog began to bark. Very loudly. Suddenly something
small and black skittered past Rick in the darkness. The
stench of fresh, pungent skunk became a hundred times
stronger. It was overwhelming. The dog went crazy. He may
have been fat and old, but for a few moments he became a
young hellion of an animal. Chasing the skunk, he went
past Rick and Gin at full speed, dragging his owner on the
leash.

The man bellowed and cursed. He leaned backward. He
tried to drag his feet. But nothing he did slowed the dog's
juggernaut pursuit.

Then the skunk turned and came back. The dog went
berserk. He turned one way, then another.

The leash became tangled around the man's legs. The dog
gave a mighty yank, and the man dropped like a felled tree.

At the same instant, the motor home erupted in flame and
smoke.

The blast was so enormous that for a millisecond it turned
the black night sky into daylight. The flash illuminated
everything for hundreds of feet in all directions—old wooden
houses . . . TV antennas . . . unpaved street . . . a red-and-white
stop sign . . . long needles on a barrel cactus . . . a telephone
pole . . . sagging electric wires . . . a low shrub with scarlet
blossoms . . . an abandoned, overturned, dented metal trash
can.

Reacting instinctively, Rick dived at Gin and bowled her
over before the first pieces of debris began to hit them. They
were much too close to the motor home, less than fifty feet
away. The noise and concussion were devastating.

As the darkness closed in again, a huge chunk of something whirled close by. It rammed against the air like a giant

boomerang, creating a pressure wave with sucking noises that hurt Rick's eardrums.

He covered Gin's body with his own and for a split second recalled that this was exactly how he had protected Agnes during the rocket attack on the meadow.

He pinned Gin to the ground as more junk whirred, whistled, and rocketed past.

The ground vibrated as the heavy stuff banged down around them. Rick felt tiny stinging fragments strike his exposed neck and hands. They felt like hot needles but didn't pierce the skin.

A large flat piece of what might have been thin sheet metal clanged down across his legs. It was so big and lightweight that he was able to reach back and pull it over them.

After that, most of what came down was light stuff that rattled like hail against their protective cover.

The odor of cordite and burned fuel was heavy in the air.

The noise stopped.

Once more the darkness began to be illuminated, this time by flames. Rick raised his head and looked around. The huge motor home was gone. All that remained were the dark profiles of the heaviest pieces—the bent steel chassis and the engine.

The wreckage burned with roaring flames fueled by gasoline. The fire lit up all the scattered debris around them. It also lit up the bodies of the bare-bellied man and the dog. The man was headless. The leash was still tangled around his legs. The dog's body—split like a frankfurter—was jammed between his legs.

Rick shoved the piece of sheet metal away. He and Gin sat up.

The fire was so bright that he could see her very clearly. Her face and white blouse were splotched with soot, but otherwise there wasn't a mark on her.

The firelight made her blonde hair appear to be flaming red. Her eyes were huge. She was frightened out of her wits, but she could still talk.

"Look," she said.

Because of the ringing in his ears from the concussion, her voice sounded hollow and weird.

"Look..." She pointed to the ground near the man's head. "A remote..."

Jesus H. Christ. It was a rectangular metal switch box, about the size of a paperback book. A remote detonator.

There wasn't time to dwell on the significance of it. It was a catastrophe that warned of bigger catstrophes to come.

Somebody in TimTomTon had intended for the bomb to destroy Gin and Rick after they reached the motor home. But it had gone off prematurely because the man who held the detonator tripped and fell.

It was beyond Rick's comprehension. Who in TimTomTon was the traitor willing to murder the president's advisor with such an involved plot? Or was it a giant mistake? Was the blast intended for someone else?

He shoved such questions from his mind. They had to get out of there before someone made another attempt to kill Gin. They couldn't go back to Pam's house or Louise's. But they had to go somewhere.

Rick grabbed Gin's hand and yanked her to her feet.

"Wait!" she cried.

She bent over and struggled with something. It was the strap of her large camera case, tangled around her arm. She slid the strap up onto her shoulder. Then she picked up the plastic shopping bag containing Dr. Sierra's stuff. Rick tugged on her arm, trying to make her move, but she refused to run.

"Wait!" This time her cry was even sharper.

For a moment she stood unmoving on the street. In the reflected firelight her face was bright orange. She was a picture of concentration. Her eyes were closed. Her small jaw was set. She was making a decision. She made it fast. Then she pointed down the street.

"Louise's car!" she cried. "Have you still got the gun?"

Rick felt his waistband. The pistol was hanging more than halfway out. If he'd started to run, he would've lost it.

"Keep it safe!" she cried. "It's the key to everything!"

Side by side, they ran down the dirt street. When they reached Louise's dusty Porsche, doors were starting to open on some of the nearest houses, even the unlighted ones where the surveillance crews were stationed.

Curious people were peering out, wondering about the blast. One of them was Pam, standing in her partly open doorway.

"You drive," said Gin.

After they got in, she reached up to the sunshade above the windshield and found the key. Rick jabbed it into the ignition. The engine was still warm and caught at once.

They purred slowly down the street. When they reached the next block, he switched on the headlights. Then he tromped the pedal. It was the first time he'd driven a car with so much under the hood. The drive train was smooth as whipped butter, and the acceleration was out of this world.

He turned left, then right, and they shot onto Bullhead's main street, Highway 95.

The narrow strip of paving was nearly deserted. He drove south toward Needles. Within seconds, they were racing through the hot night at more than 90 miles per hour.

Because of the darkness, his fatigue, and the gray tint in his glasses, his vision wasn't good. He knew he should drive slower, but they couldn't risk being caught.

Gin began to sniffle as if coming down with a heavy cold. In a few moments, Rick realized it wasn't the sniffles. She was crying.

"Stop!" she cried. "Stop the car!"

Rick couldn't believe she was serious. He kept his foot heavy on the pedal.

She seized his arm. "Stop! We have to go back!" She pulled so hard on his elbow that the car swerved.

He roared at her. "Are you insane? They tried to kill you back there!"

"I don't care! I have to go back!"

He lifted his foot. Turning toward the dirt shoulder, he braked the heavy car to a sliding halt.

Angrily he snapped off the headlights. But he left the greenish dash lights on and the engine idling.

Then he turned to her impatiently. "What the hell is it?"

"I'm . . . terribly sorry!" She wouldn't look at him. Shoulders shaking, she sobbed into a white tissue, drawing deep breaths.

"Sorry doesn't do it! Jesus H. Christ, we're parked here like sitting ducks!"

The snarl in his words upset her further. In her anguish, she tore the tissue to shreds. She wept as if her heart were breaking.

Then she seemed to get a grip on herself.

"Look—" she cried. "Look at this—!"

In the green light from the dash, he saw that she had removed a fairly heavy rectangular object from what he'd thought was a cloth camera case. She held it up so he could see it.

It wasn't a camera.

It was a portable computer. One corner of its plastic exterior was crushed, and its small viewing screen was shattered.

Rick realized from her words and actions that the damn thing was very important to her, and that he'd probably broken it when he knocked her flat just as the bomb went off.

He was amazed that the mishap had such an emotional effect on her. In the light from the dash, the biggest of the tears running down her cheeks were a glistening green.

She seemed to have no understanding of why he'd done what had to be done. If he hadn't knocked her down, she would've been killed.

She also didn't understand their need to drive like hell to get ahead of the pursuit that doubtlessly was already under way. She continued to cry, drying her eyes with a new tissue from her pocket.

"It's no big deal," Rick said. "We'll get you another."

"No, we can't . . ." The tears began to flow twice as fast as she held the computer up with both hands and gazed at its damage. "This is the ASD analyzer," she said sadly. "A special issue. The government has only *two* of them!" Her tears splashed down onto the broken plastic screen. "And the other one is thousands of miles from here. With the CIA bigwigs at Langley!''

☆ ☆ 23 ☆ ☆

Rick didn't know what to say to her.

He began to see that Gin had every right to fall apart. The events of the last half hour would've wrecked anybody's nerves, and she was under more pressure than any of them.

According to her Aunt Pam, Gin had the brain of an Einstein, which was why she could do special work for the president. But her body and nerves were those of an extremely sensitive and shy seventeen-year-old.

No wonder she cried her eyes out. Tonight she'd done something she'd probably never done before. She'd put herself on what amounted to a combat front line.

She'd taken an unauthorized leave of absence from her fortress.

She'd nearly gotten killed.

And now, after all the risks, the whole thing was going down the tubes.

"Still want to go back?" Rick asked.

She nodded and dabbed at her eyes. She was totally miserable.

He eased the Porsche into gear but kept his foot on the brake. He tried to think of a quick remark that would get her mind off her troubles. Anything would do, as long as it switched the subject.

"Have you ever thought of changing your name?"

She didn't take the bait. She kept trying unsuccessfully to dry her eyes.

"Your name reminds me of booze. At the moment you're a Gin Sour."

She gave him a sharp sidelong glance, then fastened her gaze on the floor.

"That's awful. What do you mean?"

It was progress of a kind. At least she was talking.

"It's a cocktail. Gin, lemon, and orange."

"I don't drink."

"Neither do I. Used to. Not any more. That's why I'd like to call you something besides booze."

Her tears and sniffles were definitely decreasing.

"Such as?"

"Well, how about Ginny? Don't some of your friends call you Ginny?"

She shook her long golden hair. "Sometimes. But I don't have many friends. Not since I was thirteen and started this job—"

"Well, *I'm* your friend. Can't I call you Ginny? Maybe just some of the time?"

"I suppose . . ."

"Thanks." He took his foot off the brake and the car moved slowly forward. "Still want to go back, Ginny?"

"Yes. I'm sorry, but—"

Suddenly she grabbed his elbow. "Wait! Stop! How utterly dumb!"

He stopped the car.

"Utterly dumb!" she cried. "I forgot about Louise's!"

She opened the glove compartment. It was unusually oversized, probably custom-made. It contained a computer screen and keyboard.

Rick stared at it. "What the hell is *that* for?"

"You know Louise. Has to have every new gadget. She uses this one to compute her real estate deals away from the office."

From a pocket in the cloth case, Ginny drew out a slender interface cable.

"Maybe I can . . ."

She plugged one end into the portable ASD analyzer on her lap. She plugged the other end into Louise's larger computer. She punched keys on both computers. Then she turned and smiled at Rick. It was a happy, radiant smile that showed the silvery braces on her teeth and made her look like a child.

"It's OK!" Her words remained joyful, and the tears were still on hold. "It's technically possible!"

In this kind of a youthful mood, she was certainly a Ginny, not a Gin. From now on, whether she liked it or not, he would call her Ginny. At least some of the time. Maybe it would help lift her morale when things got rough.

She needed time to work with the two computers, an hour, maybe more.

But they couldn't stay exposed like this on the highway. They needed a place to hide the Porsche and themselves.

Rick remembered passing a dark gas station about half a mile back. It might be the answer.

He made a U-turn. Soon their tires crunched over the gravel of the Chevron station's rutted and bumpy parking lot. A dim night bulb burned in the office, but all the other lights were off.

Sweeping across the parking lot, their headlights picked out two dusty, derelict cars with flat tires. Beside them was a third car under a piece of dusty blue canvas. Getting out, Rick inspected the canvas. It was some kind of a boat cover, big enough to hide the Porsche.

He parked beside the abandoned vehicle, shutting off the engine and headlights. As he threw the cover over the Porsche, a cloud of yellow dust erupted, making him cough.

The blue cover wasn't a good fit, but it was good enough to conceal the Porsche from highway snoopers. He climbed under the cover and got back in beside her.

The dome light gave her enough illumination to work with. She began punching keys. When she had the pattern she wanted on the car's screen, she asked Rick for the cartridges from the pistol. He released the clip, shook out the six brass cartridges and handed them to her.

She held each one to the light and inspected it. When she found the one she wanted, she handed the rest back to Rick. He returned them to the pistol. She placed the cartridge in a deep slot in the battery-driven analyzer on her lap. With a tiny tool from the cloth case, she made adjustments on the slot until the cartridge fit snugly.

Then she began punching numbers and letters onto the car's computer keyboard. She repeated the sequences, changing each code in succession by one numeral.

Time passed. The car grew uncomfortably hot and close. Outside the desert temperature was still past 100. Inside the Porsche it was much hotter.

"Ginny, do you mind if I turn the motor on?"

She nodded indifferently and kept on punching keys.

Rick switched the engine on and let it purr. Soon the air conditioner reduced the temperature to a cooler level.

After a while, she finished punching the keyboard. She placed a small notebook on her lap and began copying part of the data off the screen.

She gave Rick another smile. "We've almost got it."

Then, realizing he had no notion of what she was doing, she gave him a brief explanation in nontechnical language he could understand.

It was high tech of the highest order. The technology had been invented by the Soviets and stolen by American agents. The Soviet cartridge was composed of hundreds of layers of thin brass. If it were accidentally fired in the pistol, only a few of the layers would be damaged and a small amount of data would be lost. In the thin layers of brass—permeating the molecules of the metal—were coded instructions.

The cartridge was the successor to the microdot, but it was more secret. Tens of thousands of words and numbers could be inscribed onto one cartridge.

"The words are Russian," she explained, "but the analyzer can translate them into English or Spanish—or whatever."

"And the instructions—" Rick said. "I presume they are for my favorite son of a bitch? Please excuse my language, Ginny."

She laughed very cheerfully. "You know, I sort of like Ginny after all. And, yes, the instructions are for Dr. Sierra."

He laughed with her until struck by a sudden thought.

"My God, this afternoon I came within a whisker of throwing your high tech into the river."

He explained how he'd hurled the beeper cartridge into the Colorado. If he'd chosen the wrong cartridge, they would've lost Dr. Sierra's instructions, probably for good.

Digging deeper into the plastic shopping bag, Ginny brought forth several of Dr. Sierra's documents, including the page of newspaper stock listings over which Rick had labored so unsuccessfully back in the motor home with Agnes.

Ginny copied decoded data from the stock lists and other documents into her notebook. She wrote swiftly, using abbreviations for nearly every word. Her concentration was the most intense he'd ever seen.

More than an hour passed.

When she lifted her head for a moment to rub the fatigue from her eyes, he decided it was time for an interruption.

"Would you ever consider quitting?"

"Quitting what?"

"Your work for the president—"

"Of course not."

"Even if it gets more dangerous?"

She didn't reply. "No more questions. Please. Or I'll turn back into that Gin Sour you hate so much."

She gave him a short, bitter laugh. Then her face became grim as she wrote even faster in the notebook.

Watching her in the rays from the dome light, he was struck as always by the lovely line of her profile. Even her grim expression couldn't detract from her beauty. And the soot in her great mass of hair couldn't diminish its brass on gold luminescence.

There were dry tear tracks in the smudges on her cheeks. They made him wish he had along his new Konica, which had probably been destroyed with the motor home. A picture of this kind of concentration, including the tear tracks, would make a special page in anybody's professional album.

More time passed. About once every ten minutes, a vehicle roared past on the nearby highway. The heavier vehicles, probably motor homes, caused the Porsche to rock slightly.

Sitting there with nothing but thoughts of impending troubles was very boring. Rick wondered what she'd do if he suddenly kissed her. Just a quick one, maybe only on the cheek, hardly enough to interrupt her work.

He didn't get the chance.

"I'm finished," she said. "Head for Needles."

He threw off the canvas cover, got back in, and headed south again on Highway 95. He shoved the speedometer past 100 miles per hour.

"It's all here," she said, "and Dr. Sierra's instructions are now *your* instructions—"

"Mine? Get out of here!"

She wasn't joking. "A very important assignment . . . and it's all yours . . ."

She explained that the big boss himself, Saddlebag One, had originated the plans.

"There's a *maggot* in TimTomTon," she added. "That's Saddlebag One's preferred term for mole. No one knows the maggot's identity, but there's plenty of evidence—"

"Such as tonight's blast?"

"Yes. Saddlebag One authorized me to contact you . . . and to help you. But I'm sure he never dreamed the maggot would go to *that* extreme —"

She shuddered from the memory of how close they had come to being in the motor home when the bomb went off.

Then she shook it off. Rick was impressed with how confident she seemed now. The work with the two computers had restored her totally.

"Don't drive so fast," she cautioned. "I've got a lot to say about your assignment . . . and Needles isn't very far."

He kept the speed at 100 and figured she wouldn't notice.

Fact by fact, she revealed the details of the Soviet R&R's instructions to Dr. Sierra. Funded by the KGB, R&R was the Soviet equivalent of TimTomTon and a subdivision of the KGB.

Dr. Sierra's original mission—scheduled to start the next

day—included a long journey to the Orient. First to China, then Mongolia, and from there to Taiwan.

The information was so stunning that Rick clenched his fingers on the wheel, and the car swerved dangerously.

"Hold everything!" he said. "Are you telling me that *I'm* going to China?"

"Yes."

"Why me?"

"Because there's a coded amendment to Dr. Sierra's instructions. Your brother Jerry is under orders to make the China trip instead."

"And that's why Saddlebag One wants me?"

"Yes."

"When do I go?"

"Tonight."

"You're out of your mind!"

"Definitely not. And while you're there you'll try to locate one of their personnel. His code name is..." She turned back the pages of the notebook until she found the name. "Lamma. A very important agent who works with Dr. Sierra."

As they sped along the dark highway, she spent a lot of time and talk convincing him that Saddlebag One had strong reasons for wanting Rick to make the trip instead of a more experienced paramilitary officer.

One of the reasons was trust. Until Saddlebag One identified and eliminated the maggot or maggots in Tim-TomTon, he had to be extremely cautious about those he worked with. He trusted Rick because he was so new he hadn't had time to become entangled in TimTomTon's political and ideological undercurrents. He also trusted Rick because Ginny had strongly recommended him.

But, of course, the chief reason was Rick's resemblance to Jerry. His brother had made at least two undercover trips to the Orient on Dr. Sierra's behalf. If Rick was lucky, Dr. Sierra's Oriental associates would work with him instead.

It was after midnight when they reached the lighted outskirts of the desert city of Needles, California. For the last five minutes, Ginny had kept silent as she rapidly wrote more data into her small spiral notebook.

The idea of traveling on a spook mission to China was such a blockbuster that at first Rick failed to understand all the implications of Ginny's words.

But as they drove into the heart of the city the biggest missing part of the plan began to plague Rick's thoughts.

He didn't like it. And he wasn't about to accept it without an argument.

"I go alone," he said. "Is that what you've been telling me?"

She stopped writing. "Yes. Of course."

"You won't come with me?"

"No. Of course not."

She gave him such a strange look that he knew the idea hadn't occurred to her.

"But I'll need you," he said. "You know all the little details and everything. You'll know who to contact over there and how to do it. I don't know a damn thing."

For a moment, Rick thought she was about to change her mind. She sat there unmoving, holding the red ballpoint pen in midair, staring out the windwhield into the dark night.

Then she shook her head. "Of course not. There's no way I can go. Absolutely none . . ."

But the way she said it made him think he still had a chance. He decided to try another tactic.

"What about Agnes? Can't she go with me instead?"

Ginny gave him such a frown that for a moment he thought he might have broken through her reserve.

Her next words were spoken with so much care that it was obvious she had strong feelings about Agnes.

"You must go alone. Agnes would be helpful. But it's out of the question."

Rick didn't mention Agnes again. He tended to his driving. But he hadn't given up on Ginny. There was still time to persuade her.

If he could change her name—and even get her to like it—he certainly ought to be able to make other changes.

At any rate, he intended to give her one hell of an argument.

☆ ☆　**24**　☆ ☆

Rick lost the argument. He never had a chance to bring the subject up again. The China Connection strategy was so elaborate—and so carefully worked out by Saddlebag One—that there was no way to take Ginny with him.

Near the center of Needles was a safe house where she would stay until all was secure back in Bullhead City. The safe house was an ordinary desert residence on a side street near the business center. It was not a fortress. It was a safe house only because supposedly no one else knew about it.

Saddlebag One himself had gone there and leased it. Ginny knew about it. And now Rick knew about it.

Saddlebag One had sworn on the sacred memory of his mother that his national resource would be safe there indefinitely.

Rick wished he could be as certain.

It was an old weathered and sunbeaten wood frame house similar to those in nearby Bullhead City but somewhat larger. In the rear was a double garage.

Rick ran the Porsche into one half of the garage. Then he backed out the sleek dark blue Jaguar XJ6 that was parked in the other half. He closed the garage door.

He never saw the inside of the safe house. There wasn't time. He had to be in Barstow before dawn to catch a plane.

For a few minutes, Ginny and he stood beside the Jag's open door while she finished giving him instructions, plus special equipment, from Saddlebag One.

She gave him a U.S. passport with his photo and a fake name, Roger George Van Buren. She gave him Chinese, Taiwanese, and Mongolian visas with the same name. She also gave him an American Express Gold Card in that name.

Then she gave him a second U.S. passport with his photo and a different name—James Kenneth Minton, his brother's alias. She also gave him three visas in the same name.

She gave him $5,000 in twenties, fifties, and hundreds. He counted the money and signed a receipt. She emphasized that he was to use the credit card for as many purchases as possible. His roundtrip airline ticket via Pan Am was pre-paid, having been billed to a bank account Saddlebag One had arranged in an East Coast city.

"What about the $16,000 cash?" Rick asked. "The money in Dr. Sierra's bag."

"No problem. It stays in the Brain Box until the government picks it up."

"What about Agnes? Will she stay in the Brain Box, pretending to be you?"

"No. She is being moved to another place."

"Where?"

"Sorry. Top secret."

"Will she be safe?"

This time Ginny's answer wasn't as prompt, indicating she was uncomfortable in some way about Agnes's new setup.

"Agnes will be safe," she said, "as long as she does exactly what she's told."

Ginny unlocked the Jag's trunk and took out a brown synthetic leather travel bag. She handed it over to him. It contained a spare black sport shirt, black Polyester trousers, heavy black all-wool sweater, underwear, and toilet articles, including an Atra razor. If he needed more clothes or supplies, he would buy them on the way.

"Now here's the most important part," Ginny said.

She handed him her little spiral notebook, the one into which she'd copied all the decoded data from the computers. She'd removed the pages with the code translations. All that remained were nearly a dozen pages with instructions she'd written down for Rick.

"They're not in code," she said. "I wrote in abbreviations. They won't mean anything to the casual reader."

To make sure Rick understood the abbreviation, she asked him to read them aloud.

He sat on the Jag's front seat and read quickly through most of the pages. Then he stopped.

"What the hell is this? What's *5.2 mil Ulan Bator*?"

She explained that Ulan Bator was the capital city of Soviet Mongolia and that he would go there and possibly pick up a letter of credit for 5.2 million dollars.

"Jesus H. Christ! Whose letter?"

"It will be made out to your brother. Under this name." She pointed to the abbreviation *Jas. K. Min.* on a page in the notebook. "James K. Minton."

"What's the money for?"

"Part of the financing for Dr. Sierra's plot to assassinate the president. We know it's a very elaborate plan, with connections all over the world. But we know none of the details. We hope you'll dig them out."

"What do I do with them?"

"Everything's in your instructions. Skim them quickly to see if you understand."

Rick gave the rest of the pages a run-through. The instructions were complex, but they were in sequence and made pretty good sense.

"All right. Take the clip out of Dr. Sierra's gun. Give it to me."

As he drew the pistol from his waistband, he smiled. Less than two hours ago, she'd been sniffling and crying like a first-grader on the first day of school. Now she was giving crisp commands like a Marine Corps captain.

He gave her the clip. She took the coded cartridge from the pocket of her tangerine-colored shorts. For a moment she held it in the light coming from the car's interior.

"I think you should know," she said, "that the computer analysis showed that data on this *hadn't* been previously decoded—" She drew in her breath sharply. "This means

Dr. Sierra *didn't* get his instructions. It also means you'll be safe on your trip until—''

She asked Rick to put the cartridge into the clip, and the clip back into the pistol. Then she placed the pistol in the white plastic shopping bag.

"You'll be safe on your trip," she repeated, "*until* Dr. Sierra gets his replacement instructions for Jerry. So you may need this."

From the bag she withdrew another weapon, a sturdy blue steel pistol, and gave it to him. It had no serial number or manufacturer's name, indicating it was a special issue for TimTomTon.

The pistol was compact but heavy, a 9-mm with polished walnut grips. He released the clip and discovered the gun had a great advantage over other pistols. The clip held sixteen cartridges, meaning it could be fired many more times than an ordinary pistol without reloading. Ginny also gave him an unmarked box of ammunition for it.

Then she gave him another unmarked box. The second box was larger, about nine by six inches and made of thick, heavy, high-gloss black plastic. She opened the side clasp revealing the box was empty.

"In the airports," she explained, "you must put the gun and ammunition in here. They will pass through the metal detectors with no problems. Under X-ray, the gun will resemble an electric shaver."

Rick put the pistol in his waistband.

"I think that does it," Ginny said, "except for one more thing. As soon as you can, memorize the instructions. Then destroy my written ones."

"OK. But before I go, how about a few more answers?"

"I'd rather not. Time is short."

"Do you trust Saddlebag One?"

"Not quite completely."

"Teodoro?"

"I've had little contact with him. But there's someone else who's definitely on my doubtful list."

"Who?"

"Saddlebag One's top assistant. Code name Saddlebag *Two*."

"Can you tell me why he's doubtful?"

"No. It's just a feeling I have."

She stepped away from the Jag and closed the driver's door. Her large brown eyes softened. "Thanks for calling me Ginny. And good luck, Rick."

It was the first time she'd ever called him Rick.

He opened the door and got out. He took a step toward her. She didn't back away.

She gazed at him with an expression he'd never seen before. Was it concern for his safety? Or was it something else?

Was it yearning for something she'd never had?

As he moved toward her, he was aware for the very first time of why she would be so beautifully photogenic. It was because her deep brown eyes with the gold flecks were wider apart than any other woman's.

Her expression changed suddenly to misgiving and then alarm. But by then Rick had her in his arms. He kissed her.

He made it quick because she was trembling and because intuition told him it was the first time she'd been kissed by a man.

She kissed him back, but with closed lips.

He released her and stepped away. Then he returned and embraced her again.

This time he kissed her longer and with authority. Her mouth softened but remained closed. Even so it was a terrific kiss, accompanied by a hell of an erotic feeling that made him reluctant to leave.

The most amazing aspect of the kiss was how totally provocative she was . . . without knowing it. God, what a waste. But some day, God willing, he would change his whole life for her. Yes, he would marry her, gladly, for a million reasons. And one of those reasons would be the joy of teaching her how to be more provocative.

Again he released her. He got into the Jag. As he put it into reverse, their eyes met. She looked shaken, but pleased. Thank God for that. It was a good beginning.

As he drove away, she stayed there, watching him.

The Jag's tank was full. He drove fast across the desert, climbing long grades, then racing downhill. Interstate 40 was thronged with the headlights and taillights of trucks and cars traveling at night because it was cooler. Most sped along far in excess of the 65 miles per hour limit.

In a couple of hours, he turned off to the Barstow-Daggett Airport. The runway lights were lit. But the rest of the airport, including the small terminal building, was shut down for the night.

He parked and got out Ginny's notebook. Written in carefully rounded abbreviations, her notes said a private plane would pick him up between 2:30 and 3:00 A.M.

His watch was running again but was hours behind. He walked over to the nearest dark building, Aero Repair, and looked into its grease-smeared front window.

A dimly illuminated wall clock reported that the time was 2:40. He wound his Timex, reset it, and waited.

The small propeller plane arrived late. It taxied to a stop far down the runway. Its wing lights winked out, but its cabin lights remained on, and the two engines continued to idle.

He was damned glad he was wearing the glasses. The plane remained a long way off, but he could make out movements. Someone got out and stood in the darkness near the wing.

Rick glanced again at Ginny's notes and did as ordered. *Lv. key on flr. Lok car. Cour. pks. up car ltr.*

The plane was about two city blocks away. As Rick walked toward it, carrying his travel bag, he felt an overpowering sensation that something was wrong.

Why hadn't the pilot brought the plane closer? What was he afraid of? Negative thoughts began to besiege his mind. Dr. Sierra had been out of the picture far too long. Rick and Ginny had assumed that the motor home was blown up by someone connected with TimTomTon.

But they could be wrong. Dr. Sierra and his people could have been involved all along, staying out of sight, manipulating from the sidelines.

As Rick drew closer to the plane, he remembered with a sinking feeling that he hadn't had time to memorize the instructions. The small notebook was in his hip pocket.

The person standing near the wing was a man of about Dr. Sierra's height and weight. His hands couldn't be seen.

Rick made sure the pistol would slip freely from his waistband.

The man took a step forward and spoke. "You Van Buren?" That was a good sign. Only Ginny and Saddlebag One were supposed to know that name.

"Yes."

"Sorry I couldn't taxi closer." The tone was casual and friendly. "Airport rule."

The man ducked under the wing and went to the plane's open door. "Hop in. Let's get out of this stinking desert heat." Minutes later, the lights of Barstow passed beneath them as the plane turned for Los Angeles.

It was a six-passenger Piper. No one else was aboard. Rick chose the second seat behind the pilot. From there he could watch the pilot, but the pilot couldn't watch him without turning in his seat.

The pilot was a well-built man of about forty, wearing a lightweight tan sport shirt, slacks, and oversized glasses with thin gold rims. He seemed like a pro.

He tried some small talk and saw that Rick was disinterested. After that, they flew on in silence except for the droning of the engines.

Rick got out Ginny's small notebook and switched on the overhead reading spotlight. He stared at the first page of instructions but couldn't concentrate.

Closing the notebook, he returned it to his pocket. Every minute he delayed destroying it extended the risk. But at the moment he didn't care.

This was no time for memory work. He was extremely tired. Too much had happened in the last twenty-four hours. Too many bad decisions had been made. Lives had been lost and others threatened. His head was a clutter of aborted ideas and disconnected thoughts. Looming over everything was the immense mental picture of Dr. Sierra on the shuttle boat.

Because of all that Ginny had told him, Rick now viewed Dr. Sierra from an entirely different perspective. The triggering element was anger. By now the doctor was as angry as a green mamba—and twice as venomous—because his priceless Soviet codes had been ripped off and his whole operation screwed up.

To a man of Dr. Sierra's skills, the insult must have been supreme. Ripped off by a lousy amateur! What a disgrace!

Rick grinned with the sweet memory of how the travel bag had felt in his hand as he dived off the boat. He, Rick Moore, nonentity in the spook biz, had bested one of the world's masters of the game. Now he could assume that Dr. Sierra regarded the amateur Rick Moore as a lucky son of a bitch to be destroyed on sight. Only total destruction of the amateur would erase the disgrace.

The sweet feeling was accompanied by a sharper sense of danger. The competition was hardly under way. The amateur had won the second confrontation, by luck, but it might turn out to be a giant among mistakes. Dr. Sierra had been a hell of a threat before. Now that threat was doubled—or quadrupled—because of the disgrace factor. The pro would not rest until his revenge was complete. But, by God, the amateur would give him a run for it, because so many lives depended on him.

God what a responsibility for a beginner, a raw beginner: Agnes's life. . . the lives of Gin's aunts. . . even the lives of the president and his wife. . . and, above all, Ginny's life . . . .

The sound of the plane's engines changed to a lower r.p.m., and there was a noticeable reduction of speed. Rick glanced out the window and saw so many broad rectangles of lights spread out below that they had to be over Los Angeles.

According to his watch, the flight had taken hardly twenty-five minutes. His damn Timex must have quit again.

He looked at the large digital clock above the pilot's many luminous dials and instruments. The fluorescent orange numerals said 3:42, the same as Rick's watch. The flight had been fast. Too fast. He'd given it a good shot but hadn't had enough time to get mentally toughened for what was to come.

As the Piper descended toward the many runways of LAX, he wondered what awaited him down there.

TimTomTon's people?

Dr. Sierra's people?

His doubts about Saddlebag One's plans were beginning to feel overwhelming.

The psyching-up process wasn't working. His resolve and toughness were under attack by brutal facts:

A little over a month ago, he was merely a part-time fox watcher, ditchdigger, and amateur photographer in El Dorado Park. His only problem was getting enough money for laundromats, Big Macs, and university tuition.

Now, after perhaps the world's quickest, rinkydink spy course, he was supposed to be a highly paid paramilitary officer on an undecover mission to the Orient.

Jesus. H. Christ. Supposedly he was going to China so that—in some roundabout way—he would help prevent the assassination of the president.

Why was he being sent to far off China, when the biggest assassination threat to the President supposedly came from a closer source—Nicaragua?

Everything was getting more ridiculous by the minute. Why would they choose an inexperienced misfit and perpetual loser instead of an expert among experts for what seemed to be such a high-level job?

Was Rick's resemblance to his brother the real reason? It hardly seemed enough. There was no avoiding the most likely possibility: *he was being set up*.

He was live bait. He was a rabbit surrounded and outnumbered by foxes.

And he couldn't escape. Even if he decided to run off and abandon the mission, the foxes would track him down and tear him to pieces.

Worst of all was the feeling that Ginny had changed. She wasn't just in some remote place giving advice to the president. She was now in the business end of intelligence, out in the field, giving direct orders, taking dangerous risks, manipulating people.

Jesus H. Christ and Holy Mother of God. There was an ever-growing possibility that Ginny was one of the foxes.

Goddamn. If she was as deadly as the rest of them, would he want to go on calling her Ginny? Was he stupid to think of planning a whole new life with her?

REO: Report No. 69
To: Rawhide, White House
From: Chicken Little
Subject: *Weapon of Terror*

Before you order the battleship USS *New Jersey*
to open fire on bases in Lebanon, be advised
that you will be unleashing one of mankind's
unique weapons of terror.

The sound of each incoming sixteen-inch shell
(weighing as much as a Volkswagen) will terrorize
the populace for miles around.

The Lebanon terrorists will be unable to strike
back at the USS *New Jersey*.

They will therefore go after a closer, easier
target: hundreds of U.S. Marines.

Has the Pentagon informed you that the marines
beachhead cannot be adequately defended?

☆ ☆ **25** ☆ ☆

The rabbit decided to think like the foxes.

Rick decided not to make the Pan Am flight to China.

THE PRODIGY PLOT / 195

Instead he rented a bronze Chevy Cavalier at LAX. He rented it under a fake name by counting out a bribe of four $100 bills to the woman at the rental counter.

In the airport gift shop, he bought a new Pulsar chronograph watch and dropped his old watch in a trash can.

Then he headed for Santa Barbara. He needed more time to develop and think through his alternative strategy.

He decided the best place to do that was back in El Dorado Park where the serenity was conducive to creative thinking. Hell, he might even go back and sit in his beloved foxhole for a few hours. What better way was there to study the deviousness of foxes? Foxes knew the art of patience. Foxes knew how to wait until the rabbit made a mistake.

By God, he would sit there in that damp foxhole, smell the good earth, and patiently figure it all out.

By God, he would devise ways to bypass every Goddamn one of the foxes—from Saddlebag One to Dr. Sierra, from Teodoro and Eduardo to Saddlebag Two, from his lousy brother Jerry, even to Ginny.

And, yes, he would also have to include Agnes as possibly one of the foxes. And Pam, too. And, of course, that goddamn lying bitch of an Aunt Louise.

In Culver City, he pulled off the 405 Freeway and found a phone booth.

During their week together in Idaho, Rick and Agnes had shared more than the joys of being bed buddies. While cooped up in that miserable motel room—waiting for St. Paul to identify himself—they had entertained each other and passed the time by trading personal secrets.

Agnes was one smart-ass woman. Soon after her Tim-TomTon training, she had set up her own message center and phone machine.

"A backup," she explained. "Just in case they try to do me dirt."

She had given Rick her secret phone number, listed—as a joke—under the fictitious name of Agnes Ronni Reagan.

She'd also revealed another secret: her chief goal in life wasn't to be only a Tony-winning actress. She wanted to marry a man she could love and trust. She wanted to have five children—no more, no less.

As he'd listened, it occurred to him that being married to a woman like Agnes could be very good for a man. She wasn't Gin, of course. But she had a lot going for her, and her personality sure as hell lacked the flaws that made Ginny so maddeningly different and unpredictable.

Standing in the phone booth, Rick opened his fat billfold. From the center of many greenbacks, he drew out the $100 bill on which he had written Agnes's phone number. A paperclip segregated it from the others.

It was a 201 number, meaning it was somewhere in the Newark area. Exactly where didn't matter, because she wouldn't be there anyway.

If he was lucky, she would be somewhere in a TimTomTon data center with access to the kind of high-priority SigInt satellite feedback he needed.

He dialed. As he waited for her answering machine to come on, he remembered the personal secret he'd traded her for this number. She'd insisted on knowing why he'd received a dishonorable discharge from the marines.

The phone rang and rang. As he waited, he recalled that finally, and reluctantly, he'd revealed that he'd gotten the colonel's horny young wife pregnant. One morning at five o'clock, the colonel had caught his wife and Rick drunk and passed out in the colonel's bathtub. It made no difference that they were decently dressed. Within thirty-six hours, Rick was off the base and out of the corps.

The answering machine clicked on and he heard Agnes's recorded voice. She was in an upbeat mood. First she gave the time and date. Then the message:

"Rick. Don't take the Pan Am flight. Dangerous. TimTomTon wants to arrest you at the terminal. Take another flight. The good news is that, for some obscure reason, Dr. Sierra has failed to inform the Soviet R&R that you intercepted his orders from Moscow. 'Bye, dearest. I love you and your bod.''

As he left the phone booth, Rick smacked his fist joyfully

against his palm. By God, his intuition had finally been on the ball. Or at least it seemed so, if Agnes could be trusted.

And if she was right about Dr. Sierra's failure to communicate with the Soviets regarding his loss of the codes, then Rick would be stupid to waste time mooning around in his Santa Barbara foxhole.

Seven hours later, he parked the Chevy rental at San Francisco International Airport. His luck was still holding.

While on Interstate 5, he'd heard a news report on the car radio. Pan Am Flight 222 to Beijing had been delayed at LAX by a search for a bomb. No bomb had been found, and the 747 left for China two hours behind schedule. If he'd been one of the passengers, the foxes would have nailed him like fresh meat.

Even luckier was his airline connection in San Francisco. CAAC, the China airline, only made one flight a week to Beijing, and today was the chosen day.

The plane was completely booked. But at the last minute there were four cancellations, and Rick got one of them.

As he boarded, he discovered that the clever Communist Chinese had bought an ancient U.S. airliner and repainted it brightly in the colors of America's flag, probably to sell more tickets. It was a white Boeing 747 jumbo jet trimmed in red and blue.

As soon as he found his seat, he sat down, took off his glasses, and went to sleep. His exhaustion was so total that he didn't feel the heavy jumbo take off.

After a three-hour nap, he awoke and put on his glasses. He found himself in a Chinese nut house. It flew at 35,000 feet. In the seats surrounding him, and also in the aisles, were masses of hyperactive Oriental kids. Some shrieked. Some laughed and jumped like crazy characters on Saturday morning cartoon shows. Some threw M&M candies at each other. Some scurried on all fours like mice on the floor. A small hot hand pushed its way up Rick's trouser leg and pinched his bare calf.

Before he could stop her, one of the little rascals climbed onto his lap. She was a lovely moppet. She looked up at Rick with dark eyes so serious they seemed filled with a thousand years of Chinese history and mystery. Then she coughed and spit up. A small amount of undigested egg flower soup sprayed his blue-and-white striped sport shirt.

"Oh, my goodness," said the tiny middle-aged Chinese woman in the adjacent seat.

After apologizing for the mishap, the woman reached over and took the child off Rick's lap.

Rick decided to abandon his seat. He picked up his brown travel bag from the floor. He had a lot of memorizing to do—at least a couple of hours worth—a task that would be impossible in this juvenile bedlam.

When he stood up, it wasn't necessary to unfasten his seat belt because the buckle was broken. Walking down the crowded aisle, he discovered that other equipment aboard the old jumbo jet was in equally bad shape.

Overhead spotlights were broken and dangled on wires from open sockets. Gray stuffing protruded from torn seat cushions. A yellow oxygen mask hung from the ceiling like an exotic Oriental blossom.

Rick jostled his way through the thronged aisle until he was all the way forward. All the seats were occupied, so he was forced to sit on what appeared to be an obvious safety violation—a heavy wooden crate parked in front of one of the emergency doors.

From his hip pocket, he drew out Ginny's small notebook. Its thin cardboard covers were warped from being sat on for so many hours.

He studied the first page and tried to memorize a few lines. It was no go. His concentration was blotto.

He was too uptight and nervous. He was also hungry. Although the flight time was seventeen hours, the only food served on the plane were small, dry sandwiches—all of which had been eaten during the first few hours. This was why the passengers brought along their own food in baskets, boxes, or paper sacks.

He gave a $20 bill to an elderly Chinese gentleman in exchange for two pieces of chicken. They turned out to be fried duck and mostly bone.

Again he tried to memorize, but failed. Again he dealt

with the elderly gentleman, who wore a dark business suit and a black necktie. For another twenty he was willing to sell Rick a small cup of a clear Chinese liquor that smelled like roses.

It had been years since Rick had tasted anything stronger than beer. He hated to break his Marine Corps promise to himself about the hard stuff. But this was no time to quibble. He needed something strong enough to ease his hypertension and help him get on with the task.

He took a small sip—and suffered an explosive reaction. The liquor was fantastically powerful, tasted like gasoline, and set his throat ablaze.

For many minutes, he coughed. The liquor cleared his sinuses but did nothing for his brain.

Nevertheless, he hung onto the cup. From time to time, he dipped the tip of his tongue into the fiery brew, a process that brought approving nods from the old gentleman.

Rick's position on the crate had one advantage. It gave him a clear view of the passengers in both directions. None seemed interested in why he chose to sit in such an uncomfortable place and why he was doing such a restless, piss-poor job of concentrating on the small notebook.

Finally the rose-flavored gasoline began to have a tranquilizing effect. One by one, he began to commit Ginny's red-inked abbreviations to memory.

Txi. Grt. W1. meant *Take Taxi to Great Wall*. But what the hell did *B.D.L. 2d. tow.* mean? She'd scribbled down a translation of B.D.L.: *Ba Da Ling*.

But for the life of him he couldn't remember what those three Chinese words meant. *Ba Da Ling?* Was it the name of someone who'd meet him on the wall?

At least he remembered that *2d. tow.* referred to the second tower on the Great Wall. And, of course, *Wt. 30 min.* meant *Wait 30 minutes*.

One by one he memorized the other abbreviations in sequence. At the wall he was to pay $100 for a toy tiger. Then he was to take a taxi to his hotel, the Youyi, which meant friendship.

As soon as it could be arranged, he would go by train

from Beijing to Soviet Mongolia. At Hotel B., whatever that was, he would exchange the toy tiger for the $5.2 million letter of credit.

The next day, he would board a Soviet airliner for the return trip to Beijing. Then he would fly to Tokyo where he would board a Republic of China plane for the flight to Taiwan.

It took him over three hours to commit the ten pages of notes to memory. Even then, he didn't trust himself. Writing on the back of a slick paper napkin, he recorded a series of numerals and capital letters in his own code. If he forgot any of Ginny's abbreviations, his own code would help him remember. Maybe.

He had to stand in line for nearly an hour to use one of the only two toilets on the plane that were still working. Then he tore Ginny's notes to tiny shreds and flushed them. He had to press the metal handle a dozen times before the last fragment of paper disappeared.

Shortly after dawn, the 747 landed at Beijing International Airport. The flight was over ninety minutes late. Thousands of relatives and friends jammed the terminal to greet the six hundred passengers who slowly came down the ramp.

Rick was impressed with how large the airport was. The facilities included an observation deck; comfortable lounges; a crowded currency exchange; a brightly lit, duty-free store; dozens of other shops; a theater showing a John Wayne movie; a recreational hall with ping-pong tables, and several restaurants, European as well as Chinese.

Rick went straight to the Parisienne Café. He downed a bowl of decent French onion soup; a cheese omelette; fried potatoes; a small veal steak, quite tough; and two cups of strong cold tea. The cashier accepted his American Express Gold Card with no argument.

Almost too late, Rick realized he'd made a stupid, amateur mistake. Use of the Gold Card would reveal his whereabouts to TimTomTon and Dr. Sierra.

Fortunately, the café manager spoke passable English and wasn't above doing a little capitalistic business on the side.

He wasn't subtle about it. "Dollars for me, you pay?"

Rick paid him an extra $20 to tear up the Gold Card receipts and carbons and to accept payment for the meal in dollars.

After that, Rick discovered there were no taxis available anywhere at the airport. It would be necessary for him to rent a car and driver. And before he could do that he was required to change some of his American currency into Chinese yuans.

The negotiations went quicker than he expected. The car was a Chinese-manufactured four-door sedan that resembled a black Ford Fairlane. Its woman driver spoke no English but seemed bright enough to understand the instructions in Chinese written down for her by her boss at the rental desk.

Before they left the airport, the driver sprayed the rear section of the car with a strong disinfectant that smelled faintly of orange blossoms. She also sprayed Rick's trousers, below the knees, and drenched his shoes. Then, as if to apologize for such disgraceful behavior, she bowed low and gestured for Rick to get in.

The drive along the broadest boulevards of Beijing was disappointing. Rick expected to see hordes of bell-ringing bicyclists competing for pedaling space, the way such streets looked on TV back home. Instead only a trickle of two-wheelers was in motion.

Shortly after ten that morning, when the car approached the Great Wall, he was relieved to discover that the code phrase *Ba Da Ling* was no great mystery after all. It was simply the name of the town near the section of the wall where he was to meet his contact.

He left the car and driver on a gravel lot near dozens of parked tour buses. Carrying his travel bag, he joined a huge crowd of Chinese tourists as they climbed slowly up three flights of stone steps.

When he stepped out onto the top of the wall, he immediately encountered one hell of a problem. His instructions said *2nd. tow.*, referring to the second observation tower on the wall. But there was no clue about the direction he should take. Was it the second tower on the north wall? Or the second tower on the south wall?

He was certain his memory wasn't faulty. Maybe Dr. Sierra's instructions hadn't included the proper direction. Or maybe the damage to Ginny's analyzer had caused it to skip important data.

He decided to tackle the north wall and see what developed. The stone wall, thirty feet high, was a magnificent sight, angling up a series of steep mountains, stretching miles into the distance as far as the eye could see.

As he studied the wall's unique zigzag pattern, he cursed his bad luck. He'd traveled two thirds of the way around the world. Now he stood atop one of the photo wonders of the world, and he didn't even have a camera.

He joined hundreds of Chinese sightseers who were making the climb in the bright morning sunlight. Because it was warm, the men, women, and children wore lightweight shirts of various hues, and dark thin trousers. A few wore Mao caps, or straw hats, but most were bareheaded.

Their progress was extremely slow because the incline was so steep and slippery. The flat stones of the walkway were as smooth as glass, polished by the shoes of millions of tourists for hundreds of years.

In the steepest places, a handrail of ancient iron pipe was fastened to the stone parapet on either side of the walkway. Hundreds of people clung to the pipe as they inched their way up.

Rick stayed away from the handrail, hoping to climb faster in the center of the walkway where it was less crowded. He gained very little time because his leather soles were treacherous and slipped repeatedly.

His progress was also impeded by dozens of Chinese who halted on the walkway to take pictures of their friends and families. Most wore soft tennis shoes, which enabled them to cling safely to the incline.

Each family photographer carried the same kind of black camera; an inexpensive Chinese copy of the Rollei twin-lens reflex that was popular in the United States in the 1950s. Each photographer squatted on the incline and clutched his camera to his stomach. Then he spent an interminable amount of time patiently staring down into his ground glass to line up the shot.

Whenever Rick tried to walk around one of the posed groups, the Chinese shouted at him in great anger. Some held up their hands like traffic cops, warning him to halt. Others stepped in front of him so he couldn't move through and possibly spoil the picture.

At last, sweating heavily and breathing hard, Rick reached the second observation tower. It wasn't original construction. It was a restoration, two stories high, built with large blue-gray bricks and white mortar.

He followed his instructions. *Wt. ins. stps.* Entering the tower through an arched stone doorway, he took up a position beside two side-by-side wooden stairways that led to the top of the tower.

It took a while for his eyes to become accustomed to the gloom inside the tower. A continual stream of slow-moving humanity climbed up one flight of stairs. Another stream of humanity climbed down the other stairway.

Squatting in the darkness beside the stairway was a Chinese man of indeterminate age. Hung on a cord around his neck was the inevitable twin-reflex camera. For a long time the man remained motionless, his eyes carefully averted. He seemed unaware of Rick's presence.

Rick leaned patiently against the cool dry stones of the wall. He said nothing.

When exactly thirty minutes had passed, the man stood up. He put his arms over his head and stretched.

Then he removed something from his pocket and came over to Rick. In the darkness, the object in the man's hand resembled a handgun. Rick placed his hand near his waistband but did not touch his pistol.

The man handed him a toy animal. Rick held it in a beam of sunlight that came down from above. It was a snarling saber-toothed tiger, carved from wood and about seven inches long.

Rick drew a $100 bill from his billfold. He gave it to the man.

The man put it in the pocket of his shirt. He raised his camera and snapped a quick picture of Rick.

Then, without saying a word, he walked from the tower and disappeared into the throng.

REO: No. 73
To: Rawhide, White House
From: Chicken Little
Subject: *Mistake*

I am aware of your fury regarding accusations that you are reneging on your promise not to cut Social Security.

When I recommended holding the cost of living increase to 2 percent, I did not expect it to result in such a furor.

I made a critical mistake.

Because of my age, I am obviously not competent on matters involving the elderly.

Because of the damage to my credibility, I can no longer continue my work.

Therefore I am tendering my resignation, effective at once.

REO: No. 74
To: Rawhide, White House
From: Chicken Little
Subject: *Resignation*

I withdraw my resignation.

I was not aware that you are more angry with your White House staff than you are with me in regard to recent Social Security flubs and mistruths.

It never occurred to me that mistakes are made in such numbers by your chief of staff and his assistants.

Yes, it's true that I am less naive than when I

began this work. I am very impressed with the amount of nonsense that is generally believed by the public because the government offers it as truth.

You should remind some of your advisers that eventually all political parties die from swallowing their own lies.

☆ ☆ 26 ☆ ☆

AUNT LOUISE

I never said Gin was the president's illegitimate daughter.

Nor did I say my daughter was the president's *legitimate* daughter.

People are forever twisting my words around. They extract meanings I never gave or intended. They take a truthful statement and turn it into a lie.

My sister, Pam, is the worst word twister. Continually she spreads the lie that she is the girl's mother.

And then she has to add the ridiculous line that she had an affair with the president back when he was a Hollywood leading man and she was a bit player.

The truth is that Pam never even rose as high as bit player. The best she ever did was work as a lousy forty-dollar-a-day extra at Warner Brothers.

Pam may have spoken to Mr. Reagan once or twice when they were together on the same set. They were never alone together. There were always dozens of actors and stage-hands around.

Mr. Reagan was well known for how pleasant he was to the little people on the set. He always had a smile or a kind word for the no-name actresses and all the other nobodies who hung around.

Thinking about those past manipulations of Pam's helps put the present into focus and helps me plan my future moves concerning her and my daughter.

It's true, of course, that my sister, Pam, did get pretty friendly for a while with one of Mr. Reagan's stand-ins. His name was Reggie Colombia. But he later changed it to Reggie Ronson in an effort to identify himself even more with the man who some day would be president.

Reggie Ronson was a simply dreadful actor but a gorgeous-looking male. He was taller than Mr. Reagan with big shoulders and a very macho outlook on life. His coloring was only slightly Latino. He was so handsome he could have any woman he wanted.

Like Mr. Reagan, Reggie was also friendly to the little people on the set. He met Pam when she was just another face in a crowd scene in *King's Row*, the movie that proved Ronald Reagan was an unusually gifted actor after all. Reggie and Pam went out together a couple of times. There was never anything serious between them.

At that time, Pam had a miserably dark one-room apartment out on Melrose Avenue near RKO studios. I happened to be there visiting one evening when Reggie came around to pick her up.

I often drove down from Santa Barbara to handle escrows or to find financing for my clients. As soon as Reggie saw me, something electric passed between us.

I could tell by his hungry look how badly he wanted me.

He made some kind of an excuse to Pam to break their date. And thirty minutes later he met me in front of the Wax Museum on Hollywood Boulevard.

I looked like a million that night. I was already doing well in real estate and had spent plenty on my cute outfit. As soon as I got into Reggie's car, he swarmed all over me, going for my goodies.

I can remember that it was an Olds convertible. It was a rental, because Reggie had hardly a penny to his name.

I can remember how he hugged me that first time in those

big powerful arms. He was so enthusiastic he lifted me high off the front seat, so high my head touched the soft canvas roof.

Then he kissed my nipples. I was amazed. My peasant blouse was low cut in front, but not that low cut. To this day, I don't know how he got to my breasts so quickly.

That man had the most remarkable mouth and tongue. Never before or since, has a man stirred me like that and made me feel so desirable and attractive.

Of course, if you talk to Pam about Reggie Ronson you'll get an entirely different set of facts. All wrong. And all lies.

She makes the most outrageous claims. She insists that she and Reggie lived together all those years she was wasting her time in Hollywood, working as a beautician and movie extra.

She insists that they continued to see each other after she quit being a lousy extra and moved back to San Cristo near Santa Barbara. That's one of her biggest lies.

Sometimes she insists that Reggie is the father of Gin. But most of the time, whenever she wants to impress someone, she says the president is Gin's father.

The only truthful thing in her stories is that Reggie became a director after he quit being Mr. Reagan's stand-in. Amazingly, he became an absolutely marvelous director of westerns.

Reggie's best film, the one that won four Oscars, was *Green Arroyo*, shot in Colorado. On the final day of shooting, Reggie himself got into the saddle to demonstrate how he wanted the rider to sit in the saddle.

The horse slipped on loose shale and plunged into the canyon. Reggie never had a chance. He and the horse were both killed. Reggie died without ever knowing that he would become the father of a rarely gifted and beautiful daughter.

Gin was born eight months after Reggie was killed. Because Reggie and I couldn't be wed (he was still married to his third wife), I never told Gin who her father was. I didn't want to put her through the ordeal of facing all those questions.

But, of course, that stupid Pam had to go around claiming she was Gin's mother . . . and having a damn-fool birth certificate. She made the whole thing worse by claiming Gin's father was Mr. Reagan. She started those fantasies back when he was the governor.

In her wretched little mind, she magnified the father image completely out of proportion. Reggie Ronson, the former stand-in, became the father figure, Ronald Reagan. Absolutely outrageous, of course. But she has kept that lie going for seventeen years.

Not once during that long, long time has Pam said she was in love with Reggie, the way I was. Not once has she said they had a beautiful relationship.

That's because she never knew the truth. She never bothered to learn that Reggie worshipped me and that our love for each other, and our needs for each other, were so beautiful.

Pam never cared that my love for Reggie had such a tragic ending. She ignored the fact that shortly before his death Reggie had finally started divorce proceedings so he and I could be married.

Not too many women have known the excitement of being intimate with a man who makes love in Spanish. Reggie was born in El Salvador. Some years ago I lived there with my husband, the commodore who was ranking naval attaché at the U.S. consulate. I wish I'd known Reggie then.

My husband George helped me learn Spanish. But he was dull as dishwater and never spoke any of the Spanish love phrases that Reggie knew so well. Making love with George was like kissing your refrigerator.

In some ways, Rick Moore reminds me of my darling Reggie. Although he's not as darkly handsome, he's just as tall and strong . . . and has those same bedroom eyes.

I know Rick speaks Spanish. One of these days I'll manage to invite him back up to my queen-sized bed upstairs. I bet he knows some words in Nicaraguan that will turn me on like a Christmas tree. And I'll have a few surprises for him.

When George was promoted to rear admiral and we were stationed in Taipei, I learned a lot of unusual Chinese from our two houseboys. The Chinese words aren't as expressive as the Spanish Reggie taught me. But the Chinese can be just as sexy and just as innovative. Making love with one is the answer to a bored navy wife's prayer.

When we were later transferred back to the Eleventh Naval District in California, poor George had his heart attack. He died without ever bothering to find out how I spent my time during the two years we were in Taiwan.

Poor old George lived by strict navy regulations and thought everybody else did too. He even leased me a little Ford so I could make my weekly trips to the Taoist temple in the green hills up behind Taipei.

He thought I went there to study Taoism with the monks in their long saffron robes. But that wasn't all I did. I was the only woman ever invited to wear a saffron robe and to study philosophy and politics with the temple's Master of Heaven in his secret room high above the administration offices.

I never told that blabbermouth Pam or anyone else about my adventure into that strange offshoot of Taoism. She would've been amazed. Most religions, especially the stupid Rosicrucian nonsense that Pam's always bragging about, expect you to subsidize them.

The kind of Taoism I studied was exactly opposite. The Master of Heaven *paid* me to visit him once a week.

It's true that Taoist monks renounce all carnal pleasures. But you'd be surprised at how wealthy they are . . . and also at the things their religion allows them to do.

The Master of Heaven had weekly assignments for me that would've driven poor old dull George completely mad if he'd found out. But, of course, he never did.

Being back in California has been a tonic for Gin. She's happier than I've seen her for months.

I think her new attitude is connected with Rick. It must have been something he did, or said, that night when they drove my car from Bullhead to Needles.

That was the night they both nearly were killed by the

bomb. An experience like that tends to bring people closer together.

I don't care if Gin thinks she's in love with Rick. Or even if Rick thinks he's in love with her. I don't think they will live together, or even become engaged, because Gin isn't ready for any commitment like that.

She's too sensitive and too confused about her feelings. And, of course, she's so devoted to her advisory work. Anyway, I think I know Rick a lot better than she ever will. Even if they began dating, I know Rick would keep me uppermost in his mind. He would find ways to spend time with me upstairs.

Holding hands with a shy teenage girl is one thing. Holding an experienced woman in a special position is something else entirely. Especially if they're on a lovely yellow satin sheet and she's embracing his face with her legs, the way the Chinese often like it.

I am perfectly aware that Rick has had many women in his life. I have had access to the dossier on Rick prepared for Saddlebag One.

I know that Rick was kicked out of the marines for his peccadilloes. I know that he was forced to leave Ventura City College because he got one of his teachers pregnant.

I know everything he did with that trampy Agnes while they were together in Idaho and later in Nevada and Arizona. I'm not the least bit worried about any temporary attraction Agnes may have for him.

When the time comes, I'll take care of Agnes. I'll get rid of her myself. Or I have friends who will get rid of her.

Getting rid of Agnes will be simple. After all, she's merely a synthetic, a replica who'll hardly be missed.

Getting rid of Gin won't be as simple. But, of course, I don't intend to get rid of Gin the way I'll be rid of Agnes.

All I want Gin to do is stay busy with her computer circuitry and mainframe devices while Rick and I keep busy with our own variety of linkups.

And if Rick ever changes his mind about me, my friends in high places will certainly take care of him.

Whenever I say so.

☆ ☆ 27 ☆ ☆

AUNT PAM

She makes me so mad. Sometimes I think I could just kill her . . . and laugh about it afterward.

I've just gotten back to my kitchen after another one of those terrible scenes with Louise. And I'm still shaking.

She gets to me every time. First she sugars me with the invitation. Then she pisses all over me.

This time she wanted to give me the latest dirt from Saddlebag One about the baby and Rick. At first, I thought there might be something to it.

"They went to that motel," she said, "the one in Needles that's a cesspool. And you'll never believe what Rick tried to do to her. Absolutely shocking!"

What was shocking was the way Louise could sit there in that elegant yellow silk housecoat and make up such a ludicrous story. And all the time she was telling it, her icicle eyes gave me a look of such honesty that even God would've believed her.

She insisted that Saddlebag One's record of the incident had been placed in Rick's dossier. She claimed she'd even read the exact statement. "Attempted rape of young woman with pistol. Medical examination discovered lacerations and bleeding around *labia majora*."

What outrageous nonsense. It never happened. I knew the real reason the baby was so upset during her stay in that safe house in Needles . . . and it certainly had nothing to do with rape.

211

Soon after we returned to Santa Barbara County, the baby told me that Rawhide wanted to honor her with a medal for bravery and courage under enemy fire. Even though the bomb blast frightened her half to death, she very coolly and bravely gave Rick the instructions he needed for his mission to the Orient.

The importance of that mission has never been explained to me by the baby. But it must be really something because of all the official and secret goings-on that surround it.

Through Saddlebag One, the baby was informed that the president wanted to award her the medal during a secret ceremony in the White House.

That upset the baby almost as much as the bomb that nearly killed her. She told me many times previously that she would *never ever* go to Washington—or even to Rawhide's ranch—to meet the president in person.

She was very outspoken about why.

"Auntie Pam," her lovely big brown eyes were downcast and the lashes wet with tears—"I know how foolish it sounds. But I couldn't handle it emotionally..."

Of course, she couldn't. Repeatedly the baby had proclaimed the guidelines under which she was able to work.

She was to be paid no more than fifty dollars a day.

And, except for Saddlebag One, she was never to have any personal contact with the president or other members of the White House staff.

The baby knows her emotional weaknesses. And she is continually troubled by them. She tries so hard to overcome them.

Her problem is that God cheated her. He gave her the gift of genius, but neglected to give her the maturity to cope with that gift.

The baby's emotional clock stopped at age thirteen when she first went to work for the president. She is unbelievably complicated. She has a mind that can deal with presidents and prime ministers at their highest levels. She has the sweetest, shyest personality in the world. Sometimes she can be strong, but usually she is too vulnerable in her relationships.

She despises her body. She thinks it's a curse. She wishes

it belonged to someone else. She can't understand why God gave her the body of such a gorgeously attractive woman.

I know there are times when she wants so much to experience the feelings of that woman. But she absolutely can't, no matter how she tries.

And the more she tries, the more bewildered she becomes about herself.

Although she never talks about it, she knows she needs psychiatric counseling. But she's deathly afraid of it. And, of course, there's no time for it because of her presidential duties.

Many times that half-wit Saddlebag One has explained all this to the president. So the secret ceremony backstairs at the White House was cancelled. The Distinguished Service Cross was delivered to the baby by special courier.

Imagine that. The nation's second highest combat medal, awarded usually to men in battle for conspicuous bravery. And no one will ever know about it.

Not even Louise. That surprised me, because in the past Saddlebag One gave her access to quite a bit of secret information about the baby's work.

After the bomb explosion, everything about the baby's communications setup changed drastically. Our houses in the San Cristo suburb of Santa Barbara were turned into side-by-side fortresses almost impregnable to attack.

The baby worked behind underground concrete walls and ceilings so thick an atomic bomb couldn't reach her.

Louise and I were cut off from all knowledge of what her new duties were. So when Louise came up with that half-wit rape story, I knew at once what she was trying to do. She was dying for information about the new assignment the baby and Rick were working on for Rawhide.

I knew a lot because the baby always trusted me *not* to tell her secrets to anyone. She loved to tell me things, the way a devoted daughter loves to tell her secret thoughts to her mother.

After the terrible events at Bullhead City, the baby held back the heavyweight info. But she let me have a hint or two about some of the little things she was involved in.

I even let Louise in on one of them, figuring it couldn't do any harm. And I knew how Louise would erupt when she realized Saddlebag One was giving her the freeze on everything, even the tidbits. It blows her mind whenever I reveal I know something she doesn't know.

"Louise," I told her, "the only rape that happened is in your stinking mind."

Her response was to get all breathless and worked up about it, adding fantasy details about what the sharp pistol sight did to the baby's tender skin.

I shut her off with one word.

"Punishment."

She stared at me, wondering what I meant and hoping I'd tell her.

"Well . . . ," she demanded. "What punishment?"

I let her antsy around for another minute.

"The baby's punishment," I said. "Saddlebag One took away her favorite toy—her new Pilot-M."

"Her new what?"

"Supercomputer. She's forbidden to use it for two weeks. And she's also forbidden to jog in the park."

"For God's sake . . . why?"

"Because she violated security at Bullhead. When she ran out with Rick, she nearly got herself killed, and the government nearly lost what Saddlebag calls its terrific natural resource."

"Oh, that." Louise pretended to yawn. "I know all about that."

She didn't, of course. So she abruptly switched topics to something she loves to harangue me about—the original of the baby's birth certificate.

This time she had a new angle. She warned me that she was in the process of getting a court order to make me produce it.

"If you don't produce it," she added sweetly, "the court will hold you in contempt. And the next step will be jail!"

That's when I realized she'd done it to me again. She'd brought me over to her stately mansion simply to piss all over me about the certificate.

And her half-wit pretext had worked. I knew there was something about Rick that the baby hadn't told me. Something else that Rick had done at Bullhead or Needles.

Probably something emotional. Maybe even romantic.

I found out later that all it amounted to was a single kiss. Rick kissed the baby goodbye before going on his mission to the Orient.

In my stupidity, I thought Louise might have a genuine notion about something less innocent. God, how dumb could I get!

So I stormed out of there, trying not to let Louise see that I was jelly inside and starting to feel all nauseated and ill.

Whenever she hits back at me with that birth certificate stuff, she frightens the bejesus out of me. It's a war of nerves that we've been waging for seventeen years.

She knows I haven't got the money to battle her in court. She hasn't just got lawyers on retainer. I swear she's got the half-wit judge on retainer, too. If I ever bring that original into court, I'll never see it again. No one will ever see it again. Then, all neatly legal, they'll declare Louise is the baby's mother. And I'll be out in the cold.

Louise will call in the note she's held on my house for seventeen years. And that will make her victory complete.

"Never!" I screamed at her. "I'll die before I'll ever show you that certificate!"

As I stormed out of there, she screamed filthy names at me. She was like a woman having a nightmare or a brain hemorrhage or a miscarriage.

Then she started screaming other names at me. She called down the wrath of all her dead husbands on me, everyone from the admiral and lieutenant commander down to the poor apprentice seaman who was her first husband. Somehow she even worked in the names of Reggie Ronson and Ronald Reagan.

"And when you're in jail," she screamed, "Reggie will spit on you. And Ronald will sign your death certificate!"

When I got back to my kitchen, I was shaking so badly I messed up the brown sugar and spices for the ginger cookies I was baking for the baby.

So I poured a cold bottle of Coors, sat down with it, and tried calmly to examine my chances. Because of all her money, Louise's remarks about the birth certificate weren't her usual half-wit blustering and posturing.

This time she had an expensive big city lawyer from L.A. who might be smart enough to make her phony accusations stick.

The only hope I had was the baby. In the past, she'd never taken sides. Although the baby has never said so, I'm sure she knows *I'm* her mother. Not Louise.

And I *think* she would speak up if I'm held in contempt and ordered to jail.

I wish I could be more positive. But I can't. The baby is a deep well with hidden thoughts so far from the surface that I can't even guess why she does some of the things she does.

While I was finishing my beer, the baby came into the kitchen and went to the fridge. She sat at the table and ate a few spoonfuls of cottage cheese from the blue-and-white plastic carton.

We didn't speak. At times like that we're closer when we don't talk. She had sort of a faraway look in her eye, and I could tell she weas daydreaming about something pleasant.

She looked very beautiful and almost happy, her cheeks pink and healthy. Ever since we'd left Bullhead, these changes in her for the better were quite apparent.

Suddenly she wanted to talk.

"Auntie Pam, did I ever tell you how much I like the name Ginger?"

I kept silent but let her know I was listening. She put a spoonful of cottage cheese in her mouth but didn't swallow it. When she spoke, her words were slightly muffled by the cottage cheese.

"Did I ever tell you I don't especially care for my nickname?"

"Why not?"

"Because it's really not a girl's name. It's liquor. And I hate even the thought of liquor. . . ."

She swallowed. She dug another spoonful from the carton and held it in midair.

"Auntie Pam, would you tell me again why you and Louise decided to call me Ginger?"

I'd told her many times that I originated the name and that Louise merely agreed to it after a long hassle. But there was nothing to be gained by bringing that up again.

Rarely did the baby talk about herself in such a personal way. I didn't want to say anything that would slow her down. Once again, I gave her the facts. When she was born, she had an abundance of the most beautiful ginger-colored hair. So it was logical to call her Ginger and have that name entered on her birth certificate.

When she was four months old, she became deathly ill with a fever. All her beautiful ginger hair fell out.

"For over a month," I said, "I worried about how bald you were. And then when your hair finally grew back, it was a miracle. The most beautiful shining gold anyone had ever seen!"

I smiled at her. And she smiled back, showing a hint of her braces. From the time she could talk, she'd always loved to hear the story about the miracle of her hair.

For a moment, we were silent with our separate thoughts. I remembered how her hair changed color again when she was two years old. Many of the strands grew more yellow. Brassy, actually. And that was why her hair was always more shining than other blonds.

She put the lid back on the cottage cheese and returned it to the fridge. Then she turned and looked at me. Her brown eyes were very serious.

"Auntie Pam, can I ask you a favor? A really big favor?"

"Of course."

"Do you mind if I change my name?"

"To what?"

"Ginny."

I nodded. I liked the sound of it.

"Auntie Pam, are you sure you don't mind?"

"Of course not. It's a lovely name. And more feminine than Gin."

Once more she lapsed into silence. I knew there was more on her mind. And very likely she wouldn't tell me what it was.

But she did.

"I really love the name," she said. "Would you mind awfully if we made it official?"

Oh, my God. It was the last thing I expected, and the last thing I wanted. But I didn't let her know.

"Of course, not," I said.

My mind raced ahead. Perhaps I could stall her along and pretend I'd forgotten about changing the certificate.

I might get away with it for a few months. But sooner or later I would have to change it.

When the baby made up her mind about something, she could be relentless. She'd keep after me, very politely, until I did it.

She opened the outside kitchen door, but she didn't go out right away. She had something to add, and it turned out to be a little shocker.

"Do you know who suggested Ginny?" she asked.

"No. Who?"

"Rick. And I guess that's why I like it so much."

For her, that was an astounding revelation, telling far more than the words themselves. Furthermore, she knew the effect it would have on me. And I could tell it was important to her that I should fully understand what lay behind that effect.

I had sense enough not to push her. There were a hundred questions on my mind about her and Rick, but this wasn't the time.

"Got to go now," she said, opening the kitchen door. "The concrete men are nearly finished. Next come the painters, but they say I can start using the new data processing chamber this evening."

Without another word, she closed the door and went back to her labs.

I took another beer from the fridge and drank it slowly from the bottle. I had a lot to think about.

I liked thinking about the baby and Rick. He wasn't the man I'd choose for her. He was twice her age and had been around too much. And until recently he was a loser.

But I was pleased to see that she was able to think about the possibility of having a future with him.

My other thoughts weren't as nice. In fact, they were rotten. Could Louise be behind the name change that the baby wanted? Could it be another strategy to make me bring the original birth certificate out of its hiding place?

I began to think the answers were no. The change to Ginny was too straightforward for Louise to be involved. Furthermore, the baby was always truthful. If Louise had anything to do with it, the baby would've told me.

That damn Louise. Always there was some kind of a new complication in my life caused by that damn Louise. Maneuvering and more maneuvering. Half-wit lies and more lies.

What bothered me was how Louise so seldom made the mistake of falling into the traps of her own lies. Like those about her fourth husband.

She always claimed he was Rear Admiral Remington. Well, he was. And he wasn't.

The navy retired him as a rear admiral, but the highest rank he'd held on active duty was commodore.

And he didn't die suddenly from a heart attack, the way Louise always claimed. He killed himself in their upstairs bedroom. With a handgun pressed to his head. The housekeeper told me about it.

The navy held a secret investigation into his suicide. The findings were never revealed. Louise never mentioned the investigation. But I was able to put two and two together. Her husband killed himself shortly after they returned from his last diplomatic tour of duty in the Orient. I always felt it was something Louise did in China that drove him to it.

Years later, I asked the baby to uncover what Louise might have done. But even her most penetrating computer search couldn't find the answer in the Pentagon's records.

The baby did, however, turn up the testimony Louise gave at the navy inquiry. It was a lot of harmless babbling.

Her damn lies should've done her in. But they didn't.

The only conclusion I could reach was that Louise was a hundred times smarter than I ever gave her credit for. No one else could manipulate that many lies at one time and get away with it.

If I'd ever juggled that many, I would've messed up. But Louise was a genius at mixing the truth with her lies and keeping the whole complicated mess straight in her head.

She did the same thing with her lies about Reggie Ronson. But that series of fabrications wasn't nearly as complicated as some of the other masterpieces she concocted. Where Reggie was concerned, she simply traded places (in her mind, of course) with me.

My life with Reggie became hers. She pretended that the heavenly three years I spent with him were hers.

God knows how hard she tried to get him to fall for her. Even offered him money to sleep with her.

As a stand-in, he never earned the big bucks he made later as a director. God knows he needed the money she offered.

But, bless him, he loved me more than money.

If only Reggie hadn't climbed into that saddle on that goddamn skittish horse. Everything was going so perfectly for us with his divorce case and all. He was so eager to marry again.

When I told him I was pregnant, he immediately set our wedding date. It was to be the day after the premiere of *Green Arroyo*, his masterpiece. And his friend Ronald Reagan was going to be best man. Then came the tragedy. Why does it always happen to the straight shooters instead of the stinkers?

I'm so proud that it's Reggie's name that's on the baby's birth certificate. Not Reggie Ronson, because that was just his stage name.

He was honest with me all the way. That's why he had them put his real name down, the Latino one—Reginald Carlos Colombia.

So, if the truth were to come out, the baby is really Ginger Ingrid Colombia, because that's the name on the certificate.

My maiden name is there, because I never married. Pamela Astrid Johnssen. My last name is Scandinavian.

It's true that the baby was born out of wedlock. But only because of the accident that killed her father. Some day I'll tell her all about that wonderful man. I'll tell her what she inherited from him—her exceptional mind, her truthfulness, and her kindness.

Reggie had the IQ of a near genius. Maybe that's why he never became the usual Hollywood stinker. As a stand-in and actor, his mind was wasted.

But when he became a director, everything fell together. His intelligence, his intuition, his honesty, his humor, all his sensitivities—well, that's why *Green Arroyo* to this day is a classic among classics.

And it will remain so forever.

After I finished my beer, I walked outdoors for a breath of fresh air. I tried to organize my thoughts. But I couldn't. Technicians from TimTomTon—half a dozen of them in white coveralls—were still swarming around my house and Louise's mansion.

The double security fortress they'd constructed was a miniature Fort Knox. When it was finished in a few days, nothing could harm the baby—not an attack by a jet fighter, the heaviest war tank, or even a single individual dressed like a walking bomb.

But I had my doubts about our safety. In my heart I knew the danger to the baby was greater than ever.

I knew Rawhide was scheduled to visit his ranch the following week. Nothing his security people told him could prevent him from coming for a few day's rest.

He'd been warned that so many factions, from the Nicaraguans to the Libyans, were sending in terror squads to assassinate him.

How could he be such a stubborn half-wit? Only that morning, on a back page of the *Los Angeles Times*, was another warning of danger ahead. The little two-paragraph article reported the death of Emilio Lopez-Mendez in Inverness, Idaho. Strangled with a steel wire, his body had been found in a cherry orchard.

I hoped the baby hadn't read it. Weeks before, she'd told me that a man named Lopez-Mendez had saved Rick's life. Lopez-Mendez was better known as St. Paul. And he'd been a devoted friend of Rick's mother. There was no doubt in my mind that St. Paul had been executed by one of Dr. Sierra's terror squads.

As I walked in the warm afternoon sunshine streaming down between my tall sycamore trees, I felt a chill.

I tried not to think about the worst of my nightmares, the one in which I always lift the sheet . . . and find the baby pale and dead in her bed, a shining steel wire twisted around her throat.

Once again, I remembered the words of the Rosicrucian lady I'd met on the Hollywood bus. She'd told me I could never avoid the dark forces rushing toward my life and the baby's.

I stood there in bright sunshine, but I felt a shadow over me.

With the president coming, the baby was in the greatest danger of her life.

And there was nothing I could do to keep that danger away from her.

REO: No. 83
To: Rawhide, White House
From: Chicken Little
Subject: *4 million bytes*

In answer to your question about where my data comes from:

I am linked by computer codes to 99 percent of the U.S. government's data banks, with the exception of two White House channels, two CIA channels, and one Pentagon channel. I am linked to government data banks in England, Japan, France, Germany, the USSR, and those of many other foreign nations.

I am also linked with worldwide data banks of major universities, major newspapers, TV and radio networks, and all the major industries.

Saddlebag One tells me that in two weeks my equipment will be updated with the Pilot-M supercomputer. It has the world's largest memory capacity—4 million bytes.

Data that required a year to process in 1952 will be processed by the Pilot-M in one second.

☆ ☆ **28** ☆ ☆

Rick spent a long, miserable night on the Mongolian train, traveling northwest from Beijing to Soviet Mongolia.

It was a deluxe train in name only. His upper berth had a firm mattress, but the sheets and single brown blanket were grimy from previous use. There was no drinking water and not enough light to read by.

He'd been warned not to drink the tap water in the nearby lavatory compartment. The toilet was burnished stainless steel manufactured in Russia. It looked fairly clean, but the stench rising from it was overpowering. The same stench of old urine came from the water faucet, leading him to believe there was some kind of diabolical plumbing union between the two water systems.

The other three berths were occupied by three aged Oriental men wearing soiled black business suits. During the many hours of their trip together, Rick never learned whether they were Mongolian, Chinese, or inhabitants from an Asian-like planet beyond Mars.

All three had yellow faces, which were marvels of withering and wrinkling. Their ears were pointed like Dr. Spock's. They smoked, drank, and giggled the whole night through.

For the first hour of their association, Rick tried to join in their jokes and fun-making. It was difficult because he didn't know their language and suspected most of their jokes were about him.

Trying to be sociable, he'd broken his Marine Corps vow and was willing to join in their bad habits.

First, he tried one of the brown, limp cigarettes. It tasted damp and stank as if the tobacco had been dipped only moments before in strong horse piss. He couldn't keep it lit.

Next he tried drinking from one of their brown liquor bottles. He quickly discovered it contained the horse piss that had contaminated the cigarette.

It wasn't whiskey. It was some kind of powerful ale. He did his best to chugalug it but failed after the first strong, sour swallow. Giggling at his discomfort, the others passed the bottle around and drank deeply.

As he watched their joyful performance, he had one consoling thought. He couldn't catch anything from them, not even AIDS. Even plutonium 239 couldn't survive contact with that reeking bottle.

Returning to his upper berth, Rick removed his glasses and closed his eyes. But sleep was impossible. The partying, giggles, and hissing sounds of rapid sucking on damp cigarettes continued throughout the night.

The train traveled slowly through the darkness and made many jarring stops. The engineer's touch on the brakes was chaotic.

Shortly after one in the morning, the compartment's lights became very bright. Dressed in soldier's uniforms, Chinese border inspectors opened the compartment door with a bang and came in to check passports and visas. They were grim-faced but polite.

Thirty minutes later, the train entered a gigantic dark railway barn. Each of the twenty cars was elevated by hydraulic lifts while its heavy wheels were removed.

Peering through the compartment window, Rick couldn't believe his ears and eyes. An enormous clanging of steel upon steel echoed through the black caverns of the barn.

He watched in wonder as teams of slender Chinese women in blue Mao uniforms replaced all the train's wheels with larger ones.

Each woman carried a hammer, which she clanged against the wheels. Each crew gave hand signals to the operators of overhead cranes. Huge hooks attached to cables lifted away the trucks of small wheels and returned carrying trucks of larger wheels. The wheel change required nearly two hours of clanging and banging. At last the train began to move again.

Rick walked the length of the train twice before he could find someone who spoke English and was willing to explain the mystery of the wheels.

That someone was a middle-aged Chinese physician who had taken part of his medical training at UCLA.

"In Soviet Mongolia," he explained, "and also in the USSR, the tracks are wider and require larger wheels."

"Why?" asked Rick.

"No one knows..." The doctor waggled his slender forefinger as if issuing a warning. "And no one asks. But it has been said that the Russians use wider tracks to prevent an enemy from invading their motherland by train." The doctor opened his thick medical book and began to read, signaling that the conversation had ended.

Rick began the long walk back to his compartment through the dimly lit and narrow corridors of a dozen other rail cars. Only a few had sleeping compartments. The others were chair cars. Their stiff seats with high backs of slick brown plastic were occupied by Oriental men, women, and a few sleeping children.

In one of the chair cars, Rick came to an abrupt halt in order to peer intently at a seat directly ahead. He removed his glasses, cleaned the lenses, and made sure his weak eye wasn't doing tricks.

Seen from the rear, the man occupying the seat looked exactly like his brother, Jerry. He sat much taller than the Orientals. He wore a dark business suit and carried his left shoulder slightly lower, the way Jerry did.

The man seemed to be asleep, head tilted forward, chin resting on his chest.

Rick felt an attack of acute fidgets. He walked past the sleeping figure, stopped and turned. Slowly he exhaled.

The man was Oriental, with a yellowish cast to his skin and wrinkles around his eyes. His straight black hair was streaked with gray. He was twenty or more years older than Jerry.

Rick judged the man's height to be similar to his own, about six feet three. That was much taller than the average Oriental. His build was also similar to Rick's, slim with broad shoulders.

To make more certain, Rick also studied the man's hands, which were clasped across his abdomen. The skin was yellowish, with curly black hairs along the wrists. The fingertip was missing from the scarred smallest finger on the man's left hand. Beneath the wrinkled black business suit there was a bulge to the left of the man's heart. A weapon? Possibly.

The man stirred in his sleep and mumbled something. Rick turned and immediately left the car.

He'd seen enough.

He walked back to his own car and climbed to his berth. The three old men were still drinking, smoking, and occasionally giggling.

From his travel bag he drew out the black box that contained his 9-mm pistol. He placed the heavy weapon in his waistband and inside his shirt. Then he lay on his back and stared up at the compartment's rounded ceiling.

He concentrated his thoughts on what he'd seen back in the chair car. The man could certainly be his brother, with tinted skin and the addition of wrinkles to make him look older.

In the dim rays from the overhead light, Rick examined the little finger on his left hand. It was scarred and the tip was missing, identical to the finger he'd seen back in the chair car.

He was too overwrought to sleep. Throughout the rest of the night, he lay on his side and gazed out the open compartment doorway at every person who passed by in the nearby corridor. No one stopped. A few glanced in at the compartment but weren't unduly interested in what they saw. He watched for the tall Oriental to come by.

Nearly everyone who passed was male and Oriental. Some were Chinese. Some were Mongolians, with high cheekbones and small noses. One or two were dressed as horsemen, with rough riding boots, fur hats, and long overcoats.

At midmorning, the train arrived at the rail station in Ulan Bator, the capital of Mongolia. The temperature outside was chilly.

The station was so small that hundreds of passengers waiting for trains stood outdoors in clusters along the tracks. Most were youthful Mongolian soldiers in olive-drab uniforms with red epaulets.

Rick scanned the crowds for the tall man but didn't see him.

He watched over an hour at the bus parking lot. Finally an aged and creaky bus arrived that matched the description Ginny had written in his coded instructions: *Bl. Bus Eng. Frt. USSR. $5.* It was the only blue bus, and its engine was in the front. The small, chrome Cyrillic lettering on its flank indicated it was manufactured in the Soviet Union.

Rick was the first person to board. The driver accepted his $5 bill without comment. Rick sat in the back so he could see everyone else who came aboard.

Soon the old bus was filled with the lively chatter of dozens of men and women who stowed fat handbags in the metal racks above the seats. They weren't Oriental. It soon dawned on Rick that they were Russian tourists.

Those who sat in front continued to talk in loud, cheerful voices. But those who sat near Rick didn't talk aloud. First they looked at him suspiciously. Then they whispered.

After that, they carefully kept from making eye contact with him. They made it obvious that he was the kind of foreigner they didn't trust.

The last person to board was the tour guide. She was a young Mongolian woman in a beautiful native costume. She wore a round, bowllike cap embroidered in red and yellow, a heavy matching vest, and knee-high boots made of padded red canvaslike cloth.

As the bus began to move, Rick glanced out the rear window to see if they were being followed. Apparently not.

The only other vehicles he saw on the streets and highways were trucks and buses. No taxis and very few cars.

Soon they left the city and its blocks of drab, Soviet-style apartment buildings. After that the road was unpaved and dusty, with many ruts. A huge cloud of yellow-brown dust rolled along behind the bus.

Using a balky hand microphone, the tour guide spoke Russian to the tourists in a high, thin voice.

After her monologue, she answered a few questions. She put the mike on a hook and walked back through the bus, smiling and making what appeared to be little jokes with the passengers. Then she sat in the seat beside Rick's, the only unoccupied one on the bus.

She knew he was not part of the group. She smiled and spoke to him in English.

"Passport please? Visa?"

After inspecting the documents, she returned them. Then she asked another question.

"You will go with us to Rhododendron?"

Remembering the coded word *Rho* in his instructions, he nodded.

"Do you know what Rhododendron is?" she asked.

He knew what it was, but by playing dumb he might get more info out of her.

"Afraid not."

She smiled warmly. "A resort in the high desert country. It is named for the purple flower that grows in the crevices on our slopes."

"Are they going?" Rick gestured at the Russians, all of whom were doing their best to show no interest in his conversation with the guide.

"Oh, yes. They are on holiday from Irkutsk in Siberia. They will stay five days."

During the second hour, the bus climbed slowly to a high desert plateau. Its expanses of dry rolling hills and mountains were on the eastern fringes of the Gobi Desert.

The temperature inside the bus grew cold. Rick put on the thickly padded jacket he'd bought in Beijing. The guide donned an overcoat embroidered with the figures of racing Mongolian ponies.

The Russian men wore thin white shirts open at the throat and summer-weight dark trousers. The women wore thin housedresses of various hues and thick black stockings. None of them seemed concerned about the lack of heat in the bus.

The Russian men drank vodka from bottles. Although he couldn't read the labels, Rick recognized the red-and-gold Stolichnaya trademark. A few of the women sipped vodka, but most drank steaming tea from small thermos jugs wrapped in many layers of red plastic.

On the outskirts of Rhododendron, Rick heard the sound of another engine. Glancing through the now-dusty rear window, he saw that the bus was being followed by a military vehicle containing soldiers.

The resort was on a grassy plain surrounded by low hills dotted with growths of stunted fir trees. The main building was a smallish two-story hotel constructed of reinforced concrete. Nearby were rows of wooden huts, painted in bright colors—red, blue, and orange.

In front of the huts was a single row of a dozen round white structures, which the tour guide called yurts.

The word *yurt* was in Rick's instructions. To avoid confusion, Ginny hadn't abbreviated it.

The yurts were native structures made of heavy layers of compressed white wool. They were circular, with conical roofs and red wooden doors decorated with Oriental symbols in gold paint.

As he stepped from the bus, Rick noticed that the military vehicle was parked nearby. It was a large Jeep-like truck with oversized tires for travel on the open desert. Its four soldiers were armed with heavy machine pistols.

As the soldiers got out, Rick noted with relief that they were Mongolians, short and stocky, similar to the Russian passengers from the bus.

Without being obvious about it, Rick gazed slowly around the compound and then at each of the huts and white yurts. Here and there were small clusters of people, gazing at the new arrivals. None of the men resembled the tall man he'd seen on the train. So far, so good.

During the bus ride, Rick had reached a significant decision. It involved much risk. But it had to be done.

He would try to put through a call from Mongolia to Agnes's unlisted phone machine in New Jersey. If he was lucky, she might have info to confirm that Jerry was on his trail.

He soon discovered that the resort had one phone. It wasn't in the hotel. It was in the biggest yurt, a more elaborate one that served as a meeting place and snack shop.

He was told by the yurt's elderly manager that his phone call would require a minimum of two hours to put through.

The old Mongolian had deep creases in his skin, which was as black as the polished surfaces of the yurt's stove.

"More . . . likely . . ."—he spoke in carefully composed English, with many pauses—"the call . . . will require five . . . to six hours."

With a grim smile, he added that the call would take at least twelve hours if placed in Ulan Bator, where demand for phone service was much greater. No matter where it was made, it would be rerouted via Moscow.

The need for a Moscow connection made Rick nervous. But he decided to go through with the call anyway. If he got through, that in itself might indicate Moscow still didn't know that Dr. Sierra was withholding information.

The phone was new and looked unused. It was attached to a shiny green metal box with a coin slot, but the manager said Rick could pay the $26 in Mongolian tugriks or in dollars.

Before attempting the call, the manager served snacks to all the passengers from the bus. Included were strong tea, large bottles of a cherry-flavored Russian soft drink, and small pieces of fresh black bread topped with white goat cheese and slices of boiled tongue.

Finally the old man went to the phone. He talked long and earnestly. Then he hung up.

"Four . . . hours," he said with a shrug. "Probably . . .

longer." Then he lowered his voice to a whisper. "Follow
. . . me. Bring your . . . suitcase."

Quietly, the two of them left the large yurt and went to a
smaller one nearby. After they entered, the old man switched
on an overhead electric bulb and carefully locked the door.

He placed his forefinger against his closed lips, cautioning
Rick to speak in whispers.

"You have . . . it?" he asked. "The . . . print maker?"

Rick wasn't surprised to find that the old man was his
Mongolian contact. But what the hell was he talking about?

"What gives?"

The old man didn't understand. He scowled and pointed
at Rick's travel bag. "Print maker. Show . . . me."

Rick unzipped the bag but shielded it so the old man
couldn't look in. He explored its contents with his fingers
but kept his hand in the bag.

"Animal," whispered the old man.

"Oh, sure."

Rick drew out the wooden saber-toothed tiger he'd been
given by the Chinese man on the Great Wall.

The old Mongolian bowed deeply. Then he unlocked a
large wooden chest and lifted out a small metal box. From it
he took a color photograph, a black ink pad and several
pieces of pink tissue paper.

Rick noticed that it was a photo of his brother Jerry. The
old man put it back in the box. Then he set to work with the
other objects, spreading them atop a small table.

He pressed the left front paw of the tiger on the ink pad.
Then he pressed the paw onto one of the pink tissues. He
had to try several times before he got a good impression.

He took a piece of green tissue from the box. With a
small magnifying glass, he compared the fresh print with
the old one on the green paper.

When he finished, he put all the objects, including the
wooden tiger, into the metal box, which he then replaced in
the larger box. He murmured something in Mongolian.
Then he turned back to Rick and awarded him a deep bow.

"It is . . . all correct," he whispered. "You are the . . . tall
foreigner and the print is . . . authentic. Please follow . . . me."

They returned to the large yurt, which was now deserted because the Russian tourists had gone to their individual yurts and huts.

The old man sat on a hand-carved wooden bench beside a carved table. He offered Rick more tea and bread and had some himself. Then he picked up a Mongolian newspaper and began to read.

Several minutes passed.

Rick stood up. He walked slowly back and forth between the poles that supported the yurt's conical roof. Something was wrong. According to his instructions, he was supposed to receive a letter of credit in exchange for the wooden tiger. He was then supposed to take the document to the International Bank of Mongolia in Ulan Bator. There he would receive a cashier's check for the equivalent of $5.2 million.

The old Mongolian looked up from his newspaper.

"Four . . . hours," he said. "Or . . . longer."

"No, not that," said Rick. "Where's my letter of credit?"

The old man raised his forefinger, warning Rick to keep his voice down.

"After . . . we do . . . phone. . . ." he whispered. "Patience . . . please."

"Patience hell!" Rick said in a louder tone. "I want the goddamn letter *now*!"

The old man rose quickly from the bench. There was fear in his eyes.

"Please," he begged. "Silence."

He motioned for Rick to follow him. Again they left the large yurt and entered the smaller one.

The old man took out the metal box. He opened it. His wrinkled dark fingers removed the green tissue that was marked with the paw print.

He handed it to Rick. The tissue was about four inches square. In addition to the black paw print, it contained a sum written in delicate brush strokes in black ink. The sum was $5.2 million.

Rick gave him an angry look and an angrier demand for an explanation.

"What the hell's this? I can't cash this!"

The old man grew extremely flustered and fearful. He signaled for silence. He urged Rick to be seated. Then he put his mouth close to Rick's ear and began a whispered explanation.

The original plan had been changed. The letter of credit and cashier's check could not be obtained in Ulan Bator. It would be necessary for Rick to take the green tissue to Taipei.

There, if he met certain authenticating procedures, he would receive a cashier's check for $5.2 million. It would be issued by a bank in California.

Rick didn't like it. It was a total contradiction of his instructions. It was true that he'd been given the code words *Tai, Tao, Temp. Sky*, referring to Taipei and the Taoist Temple of the Sky. But he was supposed to take a cashier's check to the temple, not a piece of green tissue. The Mongolian check was to be replaced by one that could be cashed anywhere in the world on receipt of an international cable.

"Please . . . ," whispered the old man fearfully. "Please do . . . not . . . kill me!"

"Why should I?"

The old Mongolian hung his head. "Because of the unexpected change. And because of this."

Very slowly and carefully, he placed his dark-skinned hand inside the front of Rick's open jacket. Very lightly, he touched the part of Rick's shirt that covered the 9-mm pistol.

"Can you . . . not . . . use it?" he asked.

Before Rick could answer, they were interrupted by the nearby sound of a tremendously loud bell.

The old man reacted as if he'd been shot. He leaped back. Then the bewilderment vanished from his face, and he grinned sheepishly.

Again they heard the loud ringing.

"Your call!" cried the old man with great joy and relief. "We must . . . hurry!" He put the little box back in the big box and locked it.

Then they rushed back to the large yurt. The old man

took the phone off the hook and spoke a few words in Mongolian.

"Yes," he added in English. "Mr. Minton . . . is here. He . . . is . . . ready."

He handed the phone to Rick. The connection was loud and clear. He heard what he hoped was Agnes's phone ringing on the other side of the world.

Her answering machine buzzed briefly and then clicked. Then he heard Agnes's recorded voice. She spoke very slowly, and at first her words made no sense.

"Milky Way, Snickers, and Three Musketeers. The man from the bathroom follows. Baby Ruth, Raisinettes, and Milk Duds, from your sweetest of the sweet."

The machine clicked off. End of message.

Rick slowly replaced the phone on the green metal box.

The old man gave him a puzzled look. "Mr. Minton, . . . you listened. You did . . . not . . . talk. Is everything fine . . . and all right?"

Rick didn't reply until he made sure he understood the key words in Agnes's message: "The man from the bathroom follows."

It was a reference to how Jerry had hidden in the hotel bathroom in Nevada. Shortly after that he had shot and killed the TimTomTon agent, Elijah.

The word *follows* confirmed his suspicions about the tall Oriental on the train. Now he was certain Jerry had trailed him to the Orient.

"Everything's fine," Rick said. "When does the bus leave?"

"Soon. . . . Patience . . . please."

The next two hours dragged. Rick spent the time walking around the compound and looking for the tall Oriental.

He watched a dozen Russians playing an enthusiastic game of volleyball over a net suspended between two yurts. Although the temperature was in the low 30s, the men were shirtless, and the women wore bikinis that barely covered their chunky rears.

At five in the evening, the bus departed from Rhododendron. Its passengers were a different group of Russians.

They were tired and subdued because it was the end of their vacation.

At the Ulan Bator rail station, Rick boarded a smaller bus for the trip to the airport. It had only three other passengers. Two were young soldiers and the third was a Mongolian officer with gold pilot's wings on the breast of his olive drab uniform.

The bus took them far from the city to a part of the desert that was low and flat. The airport was larger than Rick expected.

By the time they arrived, it was night, and the airport was ablaze with lights on the runways, hangars, and other buildings.

Armed guards stopped the bus at the airport entrance. A uniformed officer came aboard and checked the papers of the passengers. He examined Rick's passport and visa with great care but said nothing.

As he got out of the bus, Rick became aware that it was a military airport. Suddenly he felt very tired and tense. He sensed that there was danger here. And he felt that Ginny had let him down.

Her instructions had failed to mention that it would be a busy military installation with extreme security. Solders and military vehicles were on the move wherever he looked.

The aircraft being serviced included a few old propjet airliners and many Soviet fighter planes. The parked MiG jets were armed with rockets and dispersed between high mounds of earth and stones to deflect possible enemy bombs. Everything looked combat ready.

From his billfold, Rick drew the piece of paper containing his reminder code for Ginny's instructions. He saw that he hadn't forgotten anything. He was to pay for his airline ticket with the American Express Gold Card.

But use of the card was still risky. He counted the green bills in his billfold and decided he had enough cash left for his ticket.

The ticket office was in a reinforced concrete building with few furnishings. After he bought his ticket, he stepped through a side doorway marked with a sign that said *Pectopah*.

He found himself in a medium-sized yurt that was a combination waiting room and restaurant with a few tables. Only one other person was present, a man eating at a table topped with a blue cloth. The man was a tall Oriental. He sat with his back to Rick.

Rick felt his heart begin to pump furiously. The man wore a soiled black business suit and carried his left shoulder lower than his right.

He was the man from the train.

Jerry?

Undoubtedly.

A Mongolian waiter wearing boots and an embroidered vest entered quietly from the kitchen. He placed a pottery teapot and cup in front of the tall man, who did not look up from his dinner plate.

The waiter left the room.

Rick touched the pistol in his waistband but decided he couldn't use it. Firing it would attract attention and trouble. He needed an alternative. Could he kill his brother some other way? Of course not. Back in Nevada, Jerry had made the same decision and spared his brother's life. Rick would do the same.

A glance around the room showed him a possible weapon. A shelf contained a display of native artwork, including a carved wooden tray and the bronze figure of a Mongolian pony in a dramatic leap over a cliff.

Stepping to the shelf, Rick discovered that the tray and pony were fastened down with metal staples. But the large green shamrock displayed beside them wasn't attached. What a shamrock was doing this far from Ireland didn't matter. More important was its weight when he picked it up. It was solid and heavy, consisting of three large iron horseshoes welded together.

As he walked toward the table, Rick's soles crushed grit against the concrete floor. The noise was loud and distracting, but the tall man continued to eat with a robust appetite.

With both hands, Rick lifted the shamrock high in the air and brought it down as hard as he dared.

It struck the straight black hair at the crown of the man's head. The smashing sound was like a baseball being driven out of Dodger Stadium.

It was a blow enormous enough to kill. But Rick hoped it would only be enough to disable the man for a few days or a week.

Without a word, the man feel sideways. As he dropped to the floor, his arm flopped around loosely and knocked his dinner plate off the table.

Rick caught it before it hit the floor. Thin slices of boiled tongue and cucumbers flew through the air and landed soundlessly on the back of his brother's black trousers.

Rick placed the plate and shamrock on the table.

He went over to his travel bag and picked it up. He did not look back at the silent figure on the floor.

He went outside into the night and walked toward the tarmac where the propjet airliners were parked.

REO: No. 88
To: Rawhide, White House
From: Chicken Little
Subject: *Hollow Victory*

Consider what will happen in Nicaragua if the contras—backed by millions in U.S. aid—grow so large and strong that they are victorious.

Sandinistas by the tens of thousands will withdraw to the hills and wage guerrilla warfare on the new rulers. The conflict will be a hundred times worse than the present skirmishes/battles.

The U.S. president will not be remembered as the man who stopped the spread of communism in Nicaragua.

He will be remembered as the president responsible for that nation's greatest bloodbath.

This is why Sandinista squads are in the U.S. now, plotting your assassination.

☆ ☆ 29 ☆ ☆

This was it. The green island of Taiwan, the final and most important stop on his journey.

This was the Taiwan Connection—the Temple of the Sky where it was going to be win or lose, do or die.

And, Jesus H. Christ, who would have expected it to be such a catastrophe?

The scarred stub of his little finger turned out to be the key that won Rick ascendancy to heaven and an invitation to have his prick cut off.

From downtown Taipei, Rick drove his rented Chrysler out into the lush green countryside. He left his pistol in the car because his instructions told him the temple's security would include metal detectors. He put his glasses in his pocket so his resemblance to Jerry would be more accurate.

He parked near the Bridge of Twelve Slants.

A sign in both English and Chinese explained why the wooden foot bridge was built in twelve zigzag sections: Designed to Foil Dragons Who, According to Old Legend, Can Travel Only in Straight Lines.

Constructed of timbers and ropes floating on placid green water, the bridge crossed a small lake. On the other side, Rick entered an Oriental garden and followed a gravel pathway to the Temple of the Sky monastery.

His information about the Temple was sketchy. The monks who ran it weren't a strict Taoist sect. They were supposed to be some kind of splinter sect.

The Temple of the Sky was Chinese in design but didn't

resemble its name. Instead of being a tall pagoda reaching toward the clear blue sky, it was an enormous, rectangular red brick building, broader than a football field.

It was three and a half stories high with a red tile roof and tall front pillars painted a glistening blood red. Its immense eaves were gracefully upturned and covered entirely with shining gold leaf.

As he climbed the wide tile stairway to the arched main entrance, Rick was temporarily blinded by a flash of sunlight reflected from the gold leaf overhead.

When he opened his eyes, he found his way blocked by a man who stood before him with upraised arms.

The man was a Chinese monk with a totally hairless head. He wasn't very tall and had small hands. His age was indeterminate; he could have been thirty, forty, or fifty. He wore a long saffron robe with a high round collar. Slowly, he lowered his arms. Then he spread them wide so Rick couldn't pass through the narrow entry.

He spoke in Chinese. Rick didn't understand and shook his head.

The monk spoke a single word in English: "Water."

It was the word Rick had been told about. But he didn't expect it this soon.

He hesitated, trying to remember the complicated reply he was supposed to make. Ginny had given him the abbreviations in an exact sequence. It was the longest of all the codes—twenty-two words—and it was some kind of goddamned Oriental philosophy.

During the flight to Taipei, he'd rehearsed the words in his mind a hundred times. And every time he'd screwed up the sequence somewhere along the line.

The monk glared at him and spoke again, impatiently: "Water."

"Of course," said Rick. "The mind must emulate the effortless action of flowing water which unresistingly accepts the lowest level, but wears away the hardest substance."

It was a miracle. He hadn't loused up one word.

"The wisdom of the water," said the monk, very solemnly. "Put out your hands, palms up."

Rick did so.

The monk brought his own hands together. He clapped them loudly. Then he turned them palms down and extended them toward Rick's larger hands.

"The wisdom of the hand," said the monk.

He continued the ritual by crossing his wrists so his left hand would touch Rick's left hand.

Then Rick saw what all the mumbo jumbo was about. The tip was missing from the little finger on the monk's left hand.

So it made sense after all. Jerry had very likely contacted these people in the past and had been accepted because of his scarred finger.

The monk touched Rick's scarred finger with his own.

He nodded. "It is good. You have the wisdom of the water and the wisdom of the hand. Come with me."

Rick followed him through a narrow doorway, which, undoubtedly as a security measure, permitted only one person to enter at a time. The doorway was outlined with gold wire, which might have been a metal detector.

They walked into a gigantic entry hall. From its high domed ceiling hung a massive chandelier that was larger than Rick's rented Chrysler.

The chandelier's dangling crystals cast thousands of glittering patterns of light onto the golden walls and ceiling. The surfaces were covered entirely with large ornate murals of dragons, peacocks, tigers, swans, and Chinese religious men in elegant robes.

All the figures were layered with gold leaf. The room was filled with so much golden light and so many dazzling reflections that it could be shot at f-8 or f-11, creating a photo with spectacular depth of focus. Rick cursed. Once again, as in China and Mongolia, he found himself in a photo wonderland . . . with no camera.

The monk gave him a brief but stern lecture about his language.

"Sir, this is a Palace of Heaven. If you do not watch your tongue, it will be removed."

After the entry room they passed through two chambers

that were even larger. The walls were decorated in rectangular and circular patterns of gold and gleaming blood red. The furnishings included heavy wooden altars, thrones, and long tables, all enhanced with gold leaf.

Wherever Rick looked were examples of wealth and affluence—Chinese sculptures of mythical animals, paintings of serene gardens with waterfalls, and statues of oriental holy men.

They continued on, passing a third chamber, which they did not enter. The monk paused before its pair of huge closed doors. They were solid wood, enameled a gleaming red.

He cupped his ear with his hand.

"Listen," he said.

At first, Rick heard nothing.

"Stop breathing," commanded the monk.

Rick held his breath. Then heard a faint sound beyond the doors. It cycled, becoming louder, then fainter. It was like the droning of ten thousand bees.

The monk led him to an elevator. As they stepped in, Rick noticed the wall panel had ten buttons, indicating the temple had six floors below ground level and four above.

They ascended to the top of the building. Leaving the elevator, they walked out onto the roof to what appeared to be a small penthouse with upturned Chinese eaves of gold leaf and red.

The monk took a heavy brass rod from a wall holder and struck it against a thick brass plate on the structure's unusually narrow door. From inside came the distant voice of a man.

The monk replied in Chinese, speaking many words. When he finished, he spoke in English to Rick: "The Master of Heaven awaits you. I have told him you understand the wisdom of the water and wisdom of the hand."

He opened the door and told Rick to enter alone. Then he stepped back.

"I shall await you here."

The doorway was so narrow that Rick had to turn sideways to enter. It was outlined in a band of gold, probably another metal detector.

He walked along an equally narrow passageway into a room. It was quite small and lit so poorly that at first he couldn't see its single occupant.

Somewhere in the room, a male voice grunted.

Rick turned toward the sound and went a few steps to his left. He saw a Chinese man seated at a desk illuminated by a dim lamp.

As his eyes became accustomed to the darkness, Rick saw that the philosophy of this room was entirely different from the showy chambers below. Instead of great wealth, this cubicle was an example of poverty and thrift.

The rug on the floor was thin and worn. The man sat at an ancient rolltop desk with a wooden crate substituting for its missing fourth leg. Nearby were wooden filing cabinets with surfaces of scratched and faded varnish.

The middle-aged man at the desk did not in any way resemble a Master of Heaven. He looked like a rather ordinary Chinese bookkeeper. Atop his shaved head he wore a sunshade of semitransparent green plastic patched with white adhesive tape. His clothing consisted of wrinkled black trousers and a white cotton shirt with the collar unbuttoned.

Atop the desk was a single piece of modern office equipment—an IBM PC with rows of green numerals on its screen.

When the Master of Heaven finally greeted him, Rick was momentarily baffled by the language he chose. It was Spanish, the last thing he expected to hear on this side of the world.

"Como lo pasa, Señor Minton. Quien no sabe, no vale."

The Master of Heaven indicated that he wished to conduct the entire conversation in Spanish, with the exception of some phrases in Chinese.

Under his breath, Rick cursed his instructions, which hadn't prepared him for anything like this. Jesus H. Christ, was it possible that Jerry, whose code name was Minton, could now speak Chinese, as well as Spanish?

As their conversation continued, Rick discovered with further dismay that the Master of Heaven was fluent in Central American Spanish, including the Nicaraguan idiom. It was years since Rick had used some of those phrases and he was bound to be rusty.

The master sensed his confusion and repeated part of his words: "Quien no sabe, no vale." It was a proverb, "Who knows nothing is worth nothing."

From somewhere deep in his memory, Rick pulled out a schoolboy phrase that he'd heard many times in Managua.

"Sabe mas calle. Who knows most says least."

The Master of Heaven nodded, and Rick felt a little better. His proverb had been appropriate. It not only matched the master's in philosophy but, more important, might give Rick a chance to keep silent at times and look wise if the master touched on unfamiliar topics.

The Master of Heaven picked up a small black-and-white photo and studied it. His dark eyes also studied Rick's face. Then he turned the photo toward Rick, who realized it was the picture the man had snapped of him atop the Great Wall.

"I have heard much about you," said the Master of Heaven. "I am glad that we meet at last."

Almost immediately his tone changed from cordial to unpleasant. "You are a day late. Explain."

"Si." Rick spoke very quickly to cover his confusion. "May I sit?"

"No, you may not. No one sits in the presence of the Master of Heaven."

"Compa," said Rick, "may I show you something important?"

"You may not. Proceed quickly with the necessary explanation. Why are you more than twenty-four hours late?"

Rick felt overmatched. It was clear that the Master of Heaven wasn't going to fall for delaying tactics or doubletalk.

Opening his billfold, Rick drew out the small square of green tissue he'd been given in Mongolia.

But the Master of Heaven refused to accept it.

"The explanation," he said sternly.

Rick noticed the corner of another piece of paper protruding from his billfold. It was the receipt from CAAC, the China airline, and he was desperate enough to take a chance on it. He whipped it out and extended it toward the master.

"The explanation," he said.

Instead of accepting it, the Master of Heaven drew away from it, rolling back his chair.

"You must learn," he said coldly, "that no one contacts the Master of Heaven, even indirectly. Place it on the desk."

Rick put the white receipt on top of a heavy black ledger that was on the desk.

The master glanced at the paper. Then he looked up again at Rick. He said a few words in musical Chinese that Rick had no way of understanding. Rick kept silent. The Master of Heaven repeated the Chinese phrases, his words rising and falling like music from a harp.

Rick said nothing.

His failure to reply in Chinese caused great displeasure to flash in the Master of Heaven's small eyes.

Rick decided to try Spanish again. "I apologize. I have not spoken Chinese for many months. I must brush up."

"You must indeed, Señor Minton. Give me the other piece of paper.

Rick put the green tissue on the ledger.

The Master of Heaven folded his arms across the chest of his white cotton shirt. He gazed for a moment at the two slips of paper. Then he slowly passed his open palm over them, as if ridding them of contamination acquired from Rick.

Rick noticed then that the smallest fingertip was missing from the master's hand.

Finally, the Master of Heaven picked up the airline receipt and began to read it, giving Rick a chance to organize his thoughts.

His coded instructions had left out vital data. They didn't mention that his brother Jerry had never met the Master of Heaven during his visits to Taiwan. Nor had they set a specific day for Rick's meeting with the Master of Heaven.

Rick had no idea what had gone wrong. Was more data

missing because of the damage to Ginny's computer analyzer back in Arizona?

One part of the confusion might work in his favor. If Jerry and the Master of Heaven hadn't met previously, the master would be less apt to suspect that Rick was a substitute.

The Master of Heaven finished reading the airline receipt. He placed it back on the ledger.

His words in Spanish became more stern. "I note that you did not come via Pam Am. You came later via CAAC. And this is supposed to explain why you were tardy?"

"Correct. I had more delays in China and Mongolia."

"I accept that, Señor Minton." The master rolled back his chair and stood up. "I have traveled to many parts of the modern world and learned many languages. In airline travel it is indeed true that one time delay causes another . . . and then another . . ."

He picked up the green tissue and put it away in a drawer without reading it. He placed the white receipt on another part of the desk a goodly distance away from the ledger.

"I am very distressed"—his voice grew angry—"by this loathsome piece of paper!"

Lifting the ledger, he held it above his head with both hands.

"Very distressed, Señor Minton!"

Rick watched in amazement as the Master of Heaven angrily slammed the heavy ledger down on the airline receipt. He raised the ledger high and struck the receipt three times. Each blow rocked the desk and reverberated around the small office like a cannon blast.

For the next minute or so, Rick listened in silence as the master scolded him in Spanish as a teacher would when lecturing a hopelessly dishonest schoolboy. His crime had been his decision to fly on CAAC, thus putting money in the pockets of Chinese Communists.

The Master of Heaven's hatred for the leaders of Red China was so intense that each time he spoke the work "comunista" he raised a small porcelain cup to his lips and spat in it.

He called the Communists butchers, vipers, swine, and vermin. He reminded Rick that a generation ago all the decent people of China had fled to Taiwan to escape the Communist death squads.

His voice rose with rage: "And you—you stupid man—handed them our money! How much, Señor Minton, did you waste on your ticket?"

"Eight hundred and sixty-five dollars."

The figure sent the Master of Heaven to new heights of anger and disapproval. He mentioned that tens of thousands of loyal Chinese on Taiwan and throughout the world had labored for years and made great personal sacrifices to raise funds to fight Communism on mainland China.

He explained that the Temple of the Sky was the main conduit through which such funds were collected and dispensed. He emphasized that he and the one hundred Lords of the Temple had taken vows of poverty and lived on minimum rations in order to save every possible penny for their cause.

Suddenly he paused, and his anger became more controlled.

"You are familiar with the term *el miembro viril*?" he asked.

"Yes."

"Are you aware of the punishment I could give you for putting eight hundred and sixty-five dollars into the pocket of our enemies?"

"No."

As the master explained what he meant, Rick couldn't believe what he heard. The Master of Heaven had the power to invoke the wisdom of loss.

It wasn't *castrametacion*. It was worse than castration. It meant removal of the *pene* or *el miembro viril*, but not the *testiculos*. They would take his prick but not his balls.

Speaking in university Spanish as if he were a surgeon and a psychiatrist combined, the Master of Heaven described one of the advantages of the wisdom of loss. The energy of desire without a physical outlet could be channeled into art, music, mathematics, philosophy, or even higher goals of wisdom for the good of mankind.

The master stopped talking. He granted Rick a long moment of silence to contemplate what his future would be like without *el miembro viril*.

Then he added a few more words. He emphasized that although Rick would escape the wisdom of loss this time, it was still a possibility.

"We cannot forgive errors of thrift," he warned. "Our thrift cannot be desecrated. You must be very careful to carry out the rest of your financial assignment without wasting one additional dollar."

The Master of Heaven condemned Rick one more time for his folly in choosing the CAAC airline. Then he took off on an entirely different tangent.

"Señor Minton," he began. "Are you not part of the Sandinista apparatus in Nicaragua?"

"Yes. "

"And you are all dedicated Communists, are you not?"

"Yes."

"Do you find it strange that we dedicated anti-Communists on Taiwan are willing to give money to Communists in your country?"

He didn't wait for Rick's reply. Instead he launched into a complicated explanation of why the Taiwanese were willing to work—but only temporarily—with the Nicaragua Communists.

This was because the Taiwanese possessed the wisdom of the willow, which bends in the wind and thus does not break. They were willing to bend in the direction of the Sandinistas because their brand of communism was different from that of the leaders of Red China.

"Currently," he added, "the wisdom of the willow is our chosen direction. But we can unbend the willow whenever it becomes necessary."

The Master of Heaven opened the desk drawer and brought out the green tissue. He placed it on the desk and smoothed it with his fingers.

"If this paper is authentic," he added. "then we will turn over to you our largest sum ever. You, in turn, will deliver it to the man you know by his Nicaraguan name as Dr. Sierra.

We know that his hatred of the American president is equal to our own . . . and that he has the skills to eliminate this man from the face of the earth.''

Turning to a shelf behind the desk, the Master of Heaven brought down a very old and heavy black microscope. He plugged its cord into an electric outlet atop the desk.

"The world believes," he said, "that the American president has merely signed agreements to send millions in weapons and arms technology to Red China. What the world doesn't know is that this betrayer president has *already* sent—by secret means—billions, not mere millions, in weaponry to Red China. . . ." Sadly he shook his hairless head. "Once this man was our devoted and beloved friend. But after he rose to the presidency he changed his policies and became Taiwan's enemy. . . ."

Clamping the green tissue carefully between two clear glass slides, the Master of Heaven put it under the microscope. He looked through the eyepiece and moved the tissue slowly back and forth under the microscope's small spotlight.

The process continued for many minutes.

At last the Master of Heaven lifted his head. He swiveled his chair around and tinkered with the combination dial on an ancient safe. He opened the door and brought out a red-and-gold silk pillow on which rested a stack of large green papers.

He put the pillow on the desk. Bowing his head, he placed his hands together in prayer. He murmured several words in musical Chinese.

Then he glanced sharply at Rick and gave him a command in Spanish. "Say the prayer as I say it."

He repeated the Chinese phrase. Rick did his best to repeat it, slurring the syllables to conceal the fact that he was faking it.

The Master of Heaven gave him another sharp glance of disapproval, and Rick had the gut feeling that he'd screwed up. Now the master was bound to be suspicious and would order a more thorough identification check, including probably a finger print comparison that he would fail.

For a long time, their eyes locked. Then the Master of

Heaven pushed the red-and-gold pillow across the desk toward Rick.

He commanded Rick to pick up the green papers.

Rick discovered that the top sheet wasn't the cashier's check he expected. It was a large rectangle of crisp, expensive-looking paper, measuring about thirteen by eleven inches.

Examining it, he discovered it was a bearer bond for $1 million issued by the government of the United States of America. It resembled U.S. currency. It contained many lines of printing, large and small letters, plus intricate scrolls and financial designs in black and green ink. Embedded in the paper were tiny red and blue threads.

Rick examined the other six sheets and felt his stomach twist.

Goddamn! Each was a bearer bond. Five were for $1 million each. Two were for $100,000 each.

The seven bonds added up to the correct total—$5.2 million.

☆ ☆ **30** ☆ ☆

The Master of Heaven commanded Rick to place the seven bearer bonds back on the red-and-gold pillow.

Then he spread seven U.S. government forms out on his desk and told Rick to sign each one.

Rick signed his brother's alias, James K. Minton, seven times. He wrote it the way he'd practiced it during his flight to Taiwan, repeatedly copying the computerized signature specimen provided by Ginny.

"Come with me," said the Master of Heaven.

He put a small gold paperweight atop the bonds. Carrying

the pillow with great reverence on his outspread palms, he led the way outside to the roof.

The other monk was there, waiting.

The master spoke to him in English. "Escort us to the lords in the Chamber of Chants."

As they walked to the elevator, Rick had another decision to make.

He still feared that the Master of Heaven knew he was a phony and was waiting for the right moment to have him seized.

Should he grab the bonds and make a run for it? Or should he pretend to cooperate with them until a better opportunity to escape came along?

He decided to wait.

As they descended in the elevator, the Master of Heaven explained that it would be necessary for all the lords of the Temple to bless the seven bonds. Lord was the highest rank a monk could attain.

"For reasons of safety," he added. "The blessing will give these fragile pieces of paper our protection and the strength of a thousand dragons."

He explained that extra precautions were required because the bearer bonds were in such large amounts.

"In the past," he said, "the precautions weren't needed because the amounts were smaller. That was why you were permitted to accept them in our Temple of the South, instead of coming here."

As they stepped from the elevator and walked slowly toward the Chamber of Chants, Rick noticed there was an absence of outside doors in the Temple.

The only exit from the huge building was through the narrow front entrance. If he was forced to grab the bonds and make a run for it, they would know exactly where to intercept him.

They halted near the closed entrance to the Chamber of Chants. Rick waited with the other monk while the Master of Heaven, still carrying the pillow with great reverence, entered a small antechamber.

When he returned, the pillow and seven bearer bonds were missing.

Rick pretended that nothing was different. But he knew he'd made a stupid mistake. He should have grabbed the bonds while he had the chance.

The Master of Heaven now wore a long saffron robe identical to the other monk's. There were no special markings on it to indicate his rank.

He gave a command to the other man. "Lord Pai, determine if we may enter."

Lord Pai placed his ear against the crack between the two heavy, red enameled doors. He listened. Rick held his breath. He heard the faint sound of ten thousand droning bees coming from behind the doors. It was slightly louder than when he'd heard it before. They waited nearly five minutes until the droning stopped.

Then Lord Pai opened the doors and they entered.

The Chamber of Chants was very large, and its walls and ceiling were bare, without furnishings or decorations. It was illuminated by many large candles placed on the floor in heavy gilded holders set out in even rows.

Smoke from the candles filled the chamber like a heavy black mist. Beside each candle sat a motionless lord in a saffron robe. Each sat on the bare floor, holding a large open book across his folded legs.

The head of each man was clean-shaven. Each man stared at the head of the man in front of him.

Rick estimated that there were a hundred lords and a hundred large smoky candles. Each lord sat without moving.

All the heads turned slowly in unison and watched another lord walk slowly toward them. He was old and stooped.

The old lord held the red-and-gold pillow at the level of his wrinkled chin. On it was a thin stack of green papers and the gold paperweight.

Rick was too far away to tell if the sheets were the bearer bonds.

The old lord walked to the first row and knelt. He handed

the pillow to the first seated Lord. As he did so, all the lords began to chant.

It was the strangest sound Rick had ever heard. It seemed to be the word *yum* sung very low and repeated at regular intervals. The rhythm was slow.

The low *yum* . . . *yum* . . . *yum* filled the chamber with a sound that became powerfully resonant as it reverberated off the bare walls, floor, and bare ceiling.

The first lord passed his hand slowly back and forth above the green papers, blessing them. Then he handed the pillow to the next lord who did the same.

When that row of ten men finished the ritual, the pillow was passed to the lords in the next row.

Rick moved a few steps closer. With his handkerchief, he cleaned the lenses of his glasses. Then he put them back on.

Now his vision was better, and he was more certain of the phenomenon he was seeing through the heavy layers of smoke. The tip was missing from the small finger of each hand that was passed back and forth above the pillows. Each of the one hundred lords lacked the same fingertip.

Finally the last lord in the last row performed his part in the ritual. The old Lord took the pillow to the Master of Heaven.

The master placed it reverently on the floor in front of the seated lords. The lords continued to chant. At regular intervals, they turned the pages of their large religious books, but they didn't seem to be reading.

Rick noticed that the black smoke had a slight movement. It drifted toward the side of the room where there was a large rectangular shadow on the wall. He wondered if the shadow could be a ventilation opening of some kind. The smoke from the candles had to leave the chamber somehow, or the air would become suffocating.

As the powerful chanting went on and on, Rick grew more and more uneasy. He felt sweat collecting on his shirt, around the collar, and under his arms.

The Master of Heaven walked slowly over to Rick and beckoned for him to follow. They went through an open doorway into a long narrow room illuminated by overhead chandeliers.

This room was almost as bare and unfurnished as the adjacent Chamber of Chants. The master went to the longest wall, inserted a key into a lock, and turned it.

On silent hinges, he swung back a pair of immense cabinet doors. Each was dark mahogany, about four feet high and a dozen feet in length. Carved deeply into the front of the doors were intricate Oriental symbols mingled with the figures of holy men.

Behind the doors was an immense cabinet. The Master of Heaven touched a switch, and the cabinet filled with light.

"The wisdom of the hand," said the Master of Heaven with great reverence. "It dates back three centuries."

Fastened to the main wall of the cabinet were row after row of very small glass display cases. Each sealed case was about two inches high and an inch wide.

Each case contained a small gold object which glittered in the bright light. Rick glanced from case to case. He tried not to show disbelief. Each small case contained a fingertip. Each was covered completely with glittering gold leaf. Each fingertip had been cleanly severed. Each contained an intact fingernail.

Below each case was a small gold nameplate. Each was engraved with Oriental character, presumably the name of the lord who had made the sacrifice.

In the center of the display was a saber. It had a curved blade of gleaming sharp steel and a gold hilt. It was very likely the instrument used in the wisdom of the hand ceremony.

Rick hoped his face was as impassive as the Master of Heaven's. He wasn't supposed to be surprised by this, because his brother would have gone through the amputation ceremony some time previously, perhaps at the Temple of the South.

The Master of Heaven escorted Rick along the entire length of the cabinet They passed hundreds of the very small cases, all in perfect rows.

"By Western standards of culture," said the Master of

Heaven, "this display is bizarre and medieval. By our standards, however, this gallery of art represents the highest cultural and religious achievement of man for the past three centuries."

He explained that because of his devotion and sacrifice each lord would win ascendancy not just to heaven—but to the pinnacle of heaven where each would reign as emperor over his own infinite domain.

"Mr. Minton," he said, "you, too, will win ascendancy. Not to the pinnacle, of course. But higher than any foreigner will ever rise."

As they approached the far end of the cabinet, Rick noticed a smaller and newer section of the gallery, which was segregated from the rest by a black border. It contained six small glass cases with gold nameplates.

"You are here." The Master of Heaven pointed to a golden fingertip that was slightly longer and thicker than the other five.

Rick nodded. Because of his height and the size of his hand, Jerry's tip logically would be larger than the others.

"And here," said the Master of Heaven, "is the sacred offering of the only woman ever accepted into our temple in the three centuries of our history."

He pointed to the smallest gold tip.

"Your associate," he said. "She joined us two decades ago and has contributed many secrets to our Temple. Here she is known as Lady Lamma. You, of course, know her as Mrs. Remington."

The Master of Heaven turned away from the cabinet, giving Rick a chance to keep his face composed.

Jesus H. Christ and Mother of God. Aunt Louise. Never in his wildest nightmare would he have made the connection.

"When you see her again," said the Master of Heaven "give Lady Lamma my warmest regards."

Rick didn't trust himself to speak in a normal tone. He nodded.

The Master of Heaven went to the doorway and glanced into the Chamber of Chants. Then he returned and spoke.

"The chant nears its end. Soon you must leave us."

A small red light began to blink on a carved mahogany box inside the cabinet.

The Master of Heaven went to the box and opened a door on its side, revealing a white phone. He put it to his ear and listened. He replied in Chinese that rose and fell musically. The conversation was brief. After replacing the phone, the Master of Heaven turned and gazed at Rick. His face was still impassive, except for a corner of his mouth. It drew sharply downward as if by reflex.

"You are an imposter," he said without emotion. "I have just spoken with Dr. Sierra."

He took a single slow step away from Rick. His dark eyes glistened.

"For this, you will suffer the Wisdom of Loss." The Master of Heaven's hand moved slowly. He touched a switch on the cabinet wall. Immediately a series of loud bells began to clang in the Chamber of Chants and elsewhere in the temple.

Rick imitated the master's slow, deliberate movements and hoped that by doing so he would avoid making a rash mistake.

He walked to the center of the cabinet and took down the saber. Then he walked past the Master of Heaven, who did nothing to stop him. Rick walked out into the larger chamber where the chanting of the lords continued without a break in the rhythm.

Holding the saber down at his side, Rick walked slowly across the floor to the red-and-gold pillow. He stooped and picked up the seven green pieces of paper.

They looked like the bearer bonds. He jammed them into the deep right front pocket of his trousers.

The clanging of the bells became louder as the heavy doors of the chamber swung open. Five men came in. They weren't monks or Lords.

Although the haze of black smoke had grown thicker, Rick could see that they were Chinese guards, wearing dark blue uniforms and black boots. Each carried a heavy steel saber.

The Master of Heaven spoke to the guards in an unhurried, normal tone of voice. He seemed very sure that Rick could not escape. First he spoke in Chinese, then in English so Rick would understand.

"Take him alive. For the ceremony of loss."

Rick broke into a run. The five young guards didn't run. They walked toward him. Each step they took was slow and unhurried, as if they hoped he would dash for the building's single exit where they could capture him at their leisure.

Holding the saber upright, Rick ran past the seated lords. They did not stop chanting, nor did they look at him.

Rick sprinted toward the chamber's rear wall. As he approached, he saw that the large shadow on it wasn't the ventilation window he'd anticipated. It was a large tapestry, dark with age, with mythical animals woven into its designs. Its dimensions were about five by seven feet.

Rick stopped and stared at it. Black smoke from the candles were passing through the tapestry, as if being sucked from the other side.

Another valuable second passed before he saw that the tapestry was full of small holes through which the smoke passed. He slashed at the tapestry with the saber. The cloth was so ancient it fell apart like tissue, revealing that it concealed the mouth of a large ventilation pipe.

The candles were too far away to provide much light. He entered the dark pipe and immediately struck his head against hard wood. His probing fingers told him that the pipe was constructed of many lengths of smooth bamboo bound together with rough reeds. The wide mouth of the pipe narrowed immediately to a vertical opening that was about two feet in diameter.

More lengths of bamboo formed a pipe that led straight up. It was wide enough for him to enter. He pushed his head and shoulders in and stood up.

The pipe was full of smoke that made him cough. But he had no choice. He had to climb up into the smoke because the guards were now close behind him, slashing at the tapestry with their sabers.

As he climbed, something gave way. The force of his

knees against the sides of the pipe broke some of the ancient reed bindings.

Lengths of bamboo fell with a clatter away from the pipe, creating a new opening. He broke through into better light and found himself in a tall, narrow, chamber of red brick.

Overhead, about three stories up, a patch of dim daylight revealed that the rest of the bamboo pipe continued vertically, fastened to the side of the brick wall.

He needed both hands to climb. He stuck the saber, hilt first, into his collar and down the back of his shirt. Then he leaped onto the outside of the bamboo sections and began to climb. The lumpy reed bindings provided good hand and foot holds.

He glanced up to see how much farther he must climb. Sharp pain warned him not to tilt his head back again, because the tip of the saber had jabbed his skull. He felt the warmth of blood on his neck.

He climbed quickly into brighter daylight. When he reached the top, he found himself directly under a grill made of lengths of bamboo. The sharp saber slashed quickly through the thin tubes of bamboo.

After climbing out, he found himself on the roof near the Master of Heaven's penthouse. He picked up several pieces of the grill and ran to the mahogany elevator door.

He got there just before the elevator did and heard voices behind the door. He forced two pieces of slender bamboo into the twin door handles, which resembled coiled dragons, and prayed that the door would stay jammed for a minute or two.

He ran past the penthouse, hoping to find a stairway. There didn't seem to be any.

Glancing from side to side, he ran to the rear wall of the penthouse, failing to see a rope clothesline until it caught him hard across the throat. Three saffron robes hung from it, drying in the breeze.

Turning, he ran to the edge of the roof and looked down. There was no way to climb down the glass-slick side of the three and a half story brick wall.

Farther on were two old cypress trees, which grew against

the building. But the tops of their gnarled branches were too far down to do him any good.

As he ran back to the clothesline, he heard splintering sounds. He saw two sabers slashing the elevator door from within.

He cut down the clothesline with two strokes and realized the rope wasn't long enough. He tied one end of it to the base of the clothesline pole. By the time he knotted together the long sleeves of the three saffron robes, the elevator door fell open, slashed from its hinges. As he tied the robes to the short piece of clothesline, two guards stepped out onto the roof. Three more followed.

The five men looked at Rick and raised their sabers triumphantly. They started walking toward him, talking loudly among themselves.

They were in no hurry. They saw that the short rope and three tied-together robes couldn't possibly reach the ground.

Rick threw his saber off the roof.

Clutching the sleeve of the one of the robes, he followed the saber into the air. His leap carried him toward the two cypress trees. But they were too far away. And too low.

An ugly picture flashed before his eyes. He saw himself lying far below, his brains splashed on the pavement.

The clothesline and robes jerked tight, then slipped, but supported his weight. He swung like a pendulum, kicking the side of the temple to give himself more acceleration.

Again he swung. And again.

At any moment, he expected to fall, cut loose by a saber or because a knot broke. Back and forth. Back and forth. Looking up, he saw two round Chinese faces at the roof's edge, staring down at him. They were following orders.

The Master of Heaven had ordered Rick to be taken alive. That explained why they hadn't slashed the rope.

He kicked the building with all his strength, swung as far as the rope would allow, and let go.

He flew as far as he could, but the trees were beyond his reach.

At the last moment, his outstretched foot found the wall, and he propelled himself a little farther. As he fell, his fingertips brushed a thick horizontal branch, but he couldn't hold on.

He plunged farther and caught another horizontal branch with both hands. He held on with a death grip. Thank God for the resiliency of old and noble red cypress. It bent but didn't break.

The gnarled and twisted bough was at least twenty feet long and as thick as his upper arm. It didn't break. It lowered his hundred and seventy-five pounds to the pavement as smoothly as an elevator. He landed so gently that his knees didn't bend.

He picked up the saber. He ran beside the temple along a gravel path. When he reached the shady tropical garden, he saw guards emerging one at a time through the temple's front doorway. Like the guards on the roof, they carried sabers. They were young and ran fast. By the time Rick left the garden, the guards were entering it.

He ran onto the floating Bridge of Twelve Slants. For a few moments he halted, slashing its thick rope connections with his saber. The two severed sections of the bridge began to separate.

He grasped the handrail of the biggest section. Then he planted both feet against the smaller section and gave it a mighty shove.

It floated away.

He swung his legs back onto the larger section and began running.

As he left the bridge, he looked back and saw six or seven guards standing together on the smaller section. All they had to do was swim a dozen feet, and they could renew the chase. But they didn't. Shouting and gesturing, they left the bridge and ran back into the garden.

The engine of the big black '69 Chrysler started with one twist of the key. He drove one block.

At the intersection of two dirt roads, he met five early model Hondas racing toward him single file. Each was a tiny old classic in mint condition. Each was a dark blue hatchback, driven by a blue-uniformed guard from the temple.

The Master of Heaven knew all there was to know about religion. But he didn't know shit about how to train his young guards in methods of pursuit.

Back in his TimTomTon training class in Montana, Teodoro had given Rick a good lesson on rental cars: "Always rent the heaviest and fastest."

Rick drove the Chrysler directly toward the first little Honda in the row of five. He aimed for a head-on collision.

The young driver swung his car to the right. It was exactly what Rick hoped for.

He aimed the left side of the Chrysler's bumper at the Honda's left front wheel, turning it into an instant pretzel.

He hit the second car in the same place and knocked its left front wheel off.

The third driver almost avoided contact. The Chrysler's bumper caved in his door and shoved the steering wheel through the windshield.

The fourth Honda made a panic stop. The Chrysler's bumper slashed its left front fender. An arrow of twisted steel pierced the little tire, exploding it.

The fifth driver managed to get his Honda turned completely around. Before he could head back toward the temple, the Chrysler crushed his gas tank, and the car erupted in flames.

Rick drove at moderate speed into the outskirts of Taipei. He abandoned the Chrysler among the cars in a hotel parking lot.

Then he caught a cab and told the driver to head for the waterfront at the nearby port city of Keelung.

REO (Rawhide's Eyes Only)
Alert Memo No. CL-20
To: Rawhide, White House
From: Saddlebag One
Subject: *Ginny*

I am pleased to inform you that work is nearly completed on the new fortresses at the original Stirrup location in California.

Chicken Little is back at work in Santa Barbara and seems happier than she has ever been.

You will recall that we decided on the code name Chicken Little because she was but a tender child of thirteen when we began our association.

Now that she is a young woman of seventeen, she would like her code name changed to *Ginny*.

I have no objection to the change and trust you will not object either. Let me add that she has become an uncommonly beautiful young woman.

I was delighted at our recent staff meeting when you paid a wry tribute to her by saying: "Let's hope history never finds out that America's oldest president has the world's youngest adviser—a chick!"

She continues to perform her R&D duties with the greatest energy. One of her recent efforts is a compilation, extremely detailed and complex, of all the terrorist organizations worldwide that seek to assassinate the president of the United States.

At this time, her research indicates that the greatest such danger is being mounted by the Sandinista Communist government in Nicaragua. Their excuse is the millions of dollars in public and secret arms assistance you have arranged for their enemy, the Nicaraguan contras.

One of the Sandinista terror squads in America is headed by a brilliant man I have mentioned before in these memorandums. One of his code names is Dr. Sierra. His credentials for political murder are to be feared far more than those of the assassins who work for Libya's strongman, Qaddafi.

There is one bright spot in the Dr. Sierra picture—a youngish man named Richard D. Moore, a.k.a. Rick Moore, a.k.a. Richard D. Mohr. With scarcely any professional training, he appears to have become a valuable and trusted operative for TimTomTon.

Moore is currently in Asia where—from all reports received via satellite—he appears to be close to gaining a victory that will seriously impede Dr. Sierra's assassination plans.

Arms control advisory: Ginny has prepared a new report on Gorbachev. I am including it in this memorandum as my way of giving it the highest priority.

Following are her exact words: "Gorbachev's proposed timetable for the elimination of all nuclear weapons by the end of the century should be taken seriously.

"Not because those plans are a blueprint. More important, they are evidence that the Soviet Union may at last be ready for genuine major concessions in arms-control negotiations."

REO: No. 94
To: Rawhide, White House
From: Ginny
Subject: *Bombing*

I no longer oppose the plans to bomb military targets in Libya.

My conscience is troubled—as I know yours has been—but I feel the time is right for this step.

America is the only nation strong enough to confront terrorism head-on. And you are the only world leader willing to assume the risk.

Very likely, evidence will surface indicating that Libya is but a minor player in terrorist attacks. Syria and Iran are the major terrorists—but you cannot take the risk of bombing them.

Although the other Western nations will publicly condemn the bombing, in secret they will favor it.

☆ ☆ 31 ☆ ☆

He'd come full circle. He was back in Eldorado Park where it had all started two months ago.

Once again Rick was deep in his observation foxhole, with an earthen roof over his head. It was the safest place he could think of.

He sat in total darkness, waiting. He'd crept into the park a few hours before dawn. Because of the fog and moonless black night, he was certain he'd slipped in unseen. It was one of the peculiar wet fogs that oozed into the park occasionally in late spring. It was a heavy layer only five feet thick. Its surface was flat as a rug.

The branches of the catalpa, eugenia, and cherry plum trees looked like floating ghosts because the fog had swallowed their trunks. The fog was also peculiar in another way. At times during the night it smelled very slightly of smoke. In a fog this thick and moist, sound traveled well. So far Rick had heard only tiny, familiar, faint noises: the dripping of dew from the platter-sized leaves of the nearest catalpa, about one drop every five minutes; and the rustling of feathers, probably a brown fantail dove roosting on a twig and uneasy because of the foggy dampness.

He could be wrong, of course, but he doubted that any security men would be in the park in this kind of fog and darkness at four thirty in the morning. Throughout his long wait, he hadn't heard one sound to indicate the presence of another person.

But the absence of such sounds didn't mean anything. Well-trained security people could move around in the park without being heard.

Before he'd left for China, Ginny told him the two houses of her aunts were being converted into security fortresses. She'd lost her argument with Saddlebag One, meaning that for the first time TimTomTon security people by the dozens would be stationed in the pair of houses and surrounding areas, including part of the park.

There was also Dr. Sierra and his people to consider. Dr. Sierra would be aware that after returning from Taiwan, Rick would eventually need to contact Ginny for instructions regarding the bearer bonds.

And he might guess that Rick would follow his *modus operandi* and try to make the contact with Ginny in his favorite waiting place—the park a half mile from the president's ranch.

Dr. Sierra knew the park well. Two months ago the son of a bitch had lurked unseen in the foliage like a professional naturalist before blinding Rick with the white powder.

Was Dr. Sierra here now? Was he lurking out there again somewhere, forming an elaborate plan to nail Rick with the bearer bonds?

If Dr. Sierra reappeared, Rick would have a surprise for him this time. In his trouser pocket were two small glass vials containing a white powder he'd purchased during his airline stopover in Seattle.

The white powder was silver nitrate crystals used in photo developing. It wasn't the same stuff Dr. Sierra had used to damage his eyes. But it was caustic enough to cause blindness if he was lucky enough to get a lot of it into Dr. Sierra's eyes.

In the same pocket with the vials were the seven folded bearer bonds. They made a prominent bulge.

As he waited through the long dark hours, pondering what to do with the bonds, he'd kept his nervousness at bay by thinking about Ginny. It was possible that the security people wouldn't let her jog anymore. If so, he'd have to figure out some other way to contact her.

Moving his feet and legs to keep them from going to sleep, he found it impossible to believe that he was actually here again, and that he'd made it back all those thousands of miles without being intercepted.

Nor could he believe that he'd actually managed to bring the seven bonds back. Almost as hard to believe was the fact that the bonds were as negotiable as cash.

Although he had no expertise on the legal delicacies of bond language, he was convinced now that the bonds were genuine. Since they were made out simply to "Bearer," with no name written in, each could be cashed or banked by whomever had possession.

The bonds were a monstrous responsibility. All during his return trip by Chinese cargo ship and plane, he'd been tempted to shred them and flush the pieces down a toilet, to make sure that son-of-a-bitching Dr. Sierra never laid hands on them.

Suddenly he made the hard decision about the bonds that he'd been postponing since his arrival in the foxhole. He pulled the seven pieces of paper from his trouser pocket. One at a time he unfolded them, working by touch in the darkness. He opened each sheet very slowly so the thick, heavy paper wouldn't make noisy crinkling sounds. Then, an inch or so at a time he tore each bond in two, lengthwise. The process took a long time.

He put seven halves back into his pocket with the small glass vials. He put the other seven torn halves into a plastic trash bag and tied it with twine. Carrying the bag and his small metal spade, he left the foxhole. He groped his way through the fog until he came to the alder tree that was about ten feet away.

As soundlessly as possible, he dug a hole in the soft earth beside the alder tree. When the hole was deeper than his spade, he dropped the trash bag in. He filled in the hole. Then he covered it with decaying alder leaves. On top of the leaves he placed a heavy rock to keep foxes and other curious animals from digging the package up. On rare occasions, mountain lions and small bears wandered into this part of the park from their habitats higher up in the nearby San Rafael Wilderness.

As he returned to his foxhole, he noticed again that there was the smell of smoke in the fog, as if wood were burning not too far away.

The green glowing hands of his watch told him it was approaching five fifteen. Dawn was close.

He was aware that his problem was far from solved. The buried halves could be found by anyone willing to mount a major search. And until he got rid of the seven remaining pieces of paper in his pocket, he would continue to feel as if he were on the verge of causing a big screw-up.

Where in the hell should he hide the other seven halves? Or would it be smarter to give them to Ginny if and when she showed up? If she came, it probably wouldn't be for another two hours.

The hands on his watch seemed paralyzed. He wasn't sure he could last until seven thirty in this god-awful position without getting a cramp in his leg.

As the gray light of dawn descended into the park, he saw that the fog was finally dispersing and visibility was returning. Small birds and rodents were starting to stir, thinking of food. A clumsy, oval-shaped sow bug crawled past the foxhole's front port.

The sky was too heavily overcast for the rising sun to break through. But now there was enough light for Rick to see a fox emerging an inch at a time from his den.

Seeing the fox brightened Rick's mood. He slipped a small notebook from his shirt pocket and began jotting down observations with his ballpoint pen.

Judging by the amount of different-sized scat on the dirt apron in front of the den, a whole new fox family lived there. They'd moved in during Rick's two-month absence, taking over the large den abandoned by a previous family.

When the fox emerged, Rick saw that he was a handsome young male. His ears were rusty red and so were the longer hairs of the ruff around his neck. His back was grizzled silver-gray on top, with more red on his sides and on his long bushy tail. His throat and belly were white.

The fox trotted beside the sluggish creek. Then he went up and over a small grassy slope and disappeared. A few moments later, he barked.

It was a communication bark, not very loud, but his mate heard it and came quickly from the den.

She went over the slope to where the male had gone. She also disappeared from Rick's view.

Rick jotted down notes on the pair for Dr. Porterfield, the naturalist and zoology professor at U.C. Santa Barbara. Some day, when his life straightened out, he'd try to get back his old nature photography job with the prof.

In a few minutes, both foxes reappeared. The vixen carried a struggling gray mouse in her mouth. She went into the den.

The male didn't move as quickly as his mate because he had a bigger burden. He was half-carrying and half-dragging a small but weighty dead animal. What looked like the animal's broken leg protruded from the fox's mouth. As the fox came closer, Rick saw that he was mistaken. It wasn't a dead animal. It was some kind of heavy leathery thing with a strap and buckle.

Suddenly the fox was startled by a sound only his sensitive ears could hear. He dropped his burden in the grass and scampered away. Unlike his mate, he didn't go into the den. He hid behind a juniper bush where he could stand guard and keep invaders away from the den entrance. Ears up, the alert fox stayed on duty for several minutes. Then he went back over the slope.

Soon he reappeared. Between his jaws was a broken and quivering brown dove, which he carried into the den.

Rick jotted down more notes. The fact that the fox was no longer on guard was encouraging. If his sensitive ears and nose picked up no danger signs, then very likely no TimTomTon or Dr. Sierra people were in the park at this time.

Rick crawled out the rear tunnel from his foxhole and stood up. He restored the circulation in his legs by walking quietly back and forth.

He was curious about the object the male fox had dropped in the deep grass. But not curious enough to disturb the fox family by walking over their den to look at it.

At last it was seven twenty. If Ginny was on the same jogging schedule as before, she'd be here in a few minutes.

He waited.

Then he heard her faint footsteps. She was still a long

way off, on the other side of the knoll where the path ran almost straight.

He knew how she disliked being interrupted during her run. He decided to wait until she finished. Crawling back into his foxhole, he jotted down the time: *7:24 A.M.*

As Ginny's running shoes came closer, he felt his heart jump. Was it less than a week since he'd last seen her? God, it seemed so much longer.

When her shoes went tap-tap on the earth above his head, he looked up through his porthole and admired her thighs.

Oh, Jesus, she was more beautiful than ever. She wore pale pink shorts. Very short. And her legs were perfect. How could I have ever thought, even for a moment, that such an angelic creature would betray me?

Then she was gone.

Sighing, he picked up his notebook and completed his notes for the professor. He wrote, *sct. rd. myro.* referring to the fresh scat outside the den. It was flecked with bits of red because the foxes had been eating cherry plums from the myrobalan trees.

A few minutes later, Rick heard Ginny scream.

He pulled the pistol from his wasteband. He scrambled from his hole and ran. Never before had he heard anybody scream in such a terrified way.

As he ran across the top of the fox's den, he kicked something half-hidden in the grass. It landed just ahead, giving him a second look at it. It was a brown leather shoe, and there was something strange about it.

He found Ginny a couple of hundred yards away on the bridlepath near the tallest alders.

Her head was bowed. She covered her face with her hands and wept hysterically, reacting to the shock of what she'd discovered.

Then Rick saw the dead man, lying on his back. At first, all he saw were his shiny black shoes, sticking out from under the myrobalan tree. Then he saw part of the man's dark blue business suit. Stepping closer, he looked down at the victim's face and clean-shaven bald head.

There was a deep depression in the side of the head. It

was the size of a small avocado. A lot of blood had oozed out, but now the flow had stopped.

With the greatest shock, Rick realized he'd met this man only a few days previously.

The man was Chinese.

He was from the Temple of the Sky

He was the Master of Heaven.

☆ ☆   **32**   ☆ ☆

They stood together on the footpath. Rick held Ginny tight in his arms and tried to calm her. Very gently, he stroked her mass of shining yellow hair and spoke to her softly.

"Easy, Ginny. Easy. . . ."

At first, failing to recognize him, she fought wildly, striking his chest with her small fists. Her eyes were wide with panic, staring but unfocused, showing more white than brown. Gradually her hysterics diminished. But she continued to breathe in fits and starts because she was still in shock from her discovery.

He put the pistol in his pocket, shoving it down among the jumbled pieces of the bonds.

Tightening his embrace, he kept her face turned away so she couldn't see the bloody figure under the cherry plum tree. It took longer to calm her than he expected. He continued to speak soothingly, saying the same words over and over again.

"Easy, Ginny, . . . relax, Ginny, . . . everything's OK, Ginny, . . ."

A swarm of unanswered questions about the dead man filled his head. Action needed to be taken at once. But he forced himself to wait patiently until she regained control of herself.

As he stroked her hair, his gaze swept over the green landscape far and near, searching for anything that might explain why the Master of Heaven was here . . . and who had killed him.

A movement behind trees some distance away caught his eye. It was something large, gray, and indistinct. It kept moving slowly up, then slowly down.

It emerged partly from the trees, and he saw that it was a grayish white horse, grazing in the tall grass beside the bridle path.

With a start, Rick realized it was the president's horse. He'd seen that handsome animal once before. That was the morning many months ago when the president and his equestrian friends had ridden into the park from his nearby ranch.

In the distance far beyond the horse, a thin spire of smoke rose high in the overcast sky. It was wood smoke, brown and gray, rising straight because there was no wind.

The smoke was on the president's mountain top ranch. Very likely it was the source of what he'd smelled in the fog during the night.

Ginny's shoulders began to shake less violently. He eased the pressure of his embrace. He wanted to tell her how strangely wonderful it was to hold her close again, even under these terrible circumstances, and to touch her hair and cheek. But this wasn't the time. And the feeling was impossible to put into words.

She jiggled her arms and shoulders a little as if seeking release. It was a good sign.

He responded by opening his arms and freeing her.

She took a small step back, swaying uncertainly. He put his hands on her shoulders and held her steady.

Slowly she lifted her face and looked at him. Her soft pink mouth trembled, but the hysteria was gone from her eyes.

"Can you walk?" he asked.

For a long moment, she didn't reply.

Then she said very distinctly: "Yes."

Before they moved away from the motionless figure on the ground, Rick let his gaze traverse the entire green landscape around them, again near and far, hunting for something that might explain what had happened. Still grazing contently, the horse was the only thing in view that was out of place.

There were no signs of any security people. If TimTomTon or Dr. Sierra had put men into this section of the park, they were skillfully hidden.

He pointed out the horse and the smoke to Ginny.

Then they turned away, walking with small steps. He kept his arm tightly around her waist, steadying her.

When they reached the narrowest part of the algae-streaked creek, she was able to step across without difficulty. They walked up the green slope and down the other side, passing the shoelike object that he'd kicked while running to help her.

"OK if we sit?" he asked.

She nodded.

They sat together in the soft grass that covered the top of his observation foxhole. He chose that particular spot because it was low and surrounded by trees and slopes that gave them partial concealment.

He held her hands. They were so cold that he brought them together, covering them with his own to warm them. There were a dozen things they needed to talk about, all very urgent. But he didn't rush her.

She sat with eyes downcast. Finally she raised her head, and their eyes met.

Hers were dark and deeply troubled. But also so alert now and full of awareness that he knew she was in complete control of herself.

When she spoke, her voice was firm.

"Rick, I apologize for going to pieces. But seeing him so suddenly like that was so different from that other time—"

"Very different," he said.

He knew exactly what she meant. When the bomb exploded that night in Arizona, it was so dark that the dead man and his torn-up dog were hardly visible.

But this morning, death was too visible. And Ginny was totally unprepared for its abrupt appearance.

Once again he was impressed with how quickly her mind recovered its clarity and efficiency after a numbing experience. Only minutes after the bomb nearly blew her to bits, she'd worked out the whole complicated strategy for his China trip.

He told her the dead man was the Master of Heaven, the man he'd met in Taiwan.

Within her large brown eyes he could almost see the electricity switch on at full voltage. She asked questions that revealed how swiftly she'd grasped the most crucial elements of what had happened this morning.

"Did you bring back his millions from the Orient?"

"Yes."

"And he followed you to get them back?"

"Yes."

"And you were forced to kill him?"

"No! Of course not!"

He stared at her. He was stunned by her last question. And then he quickly realized that she was absolutely right about how his involvement would appear to any police or federal investigator. He would look guilty as hell.

Ginny extricated her hands from his, and he wondered if it meant something. Did she have doubts about him? She immediately sensed his concern. She covered his hands partly with her own and rubbed his fingers affectionately.

"Rick, I know you didn't kill him. And I can never thank you enough for being with me a few minutes ago." She gave him a small shy smile, revealing part of her silvery braces. "You surprised me, Rick. I didn't think you could do that."

"Do what?"

"Be so gentle. I thought you were too macho."

Reaching to the top of his head, she plucked a dry leaf from his curly black hair. It was small and yellow. She put it in the breast pocket of her white blouse.

Then she blushed bright pink, as if disconcerted by her small act of boldness in touching his hair and turning the leaf into a keepsake.

She laughed, and her confidence returned. "You were very nice, Rick. Do you know what I liked the best?"

"No."

"The way you kept calling me Ginny—"

Abruptly her tone changed, as if she feared she'd bared too much of her inner feelings. She turned from a shy, blushing teenager into a woman executive, asking more questions, analyzing and making decisions.

"Where are the bonds now?"

Patting the bulge in his pants pocket, he explained how he'd torn each bond in two and buried the seven other pieces under the nearby alder tree.

"A good temporary solution," she said. "Now we have to decide what to do with the rest. And we mustn't delay."

Very quickly, speaking in short sentences, she devised a plan. Their first priority was to steal extra time. They would do that by moving the Master of Heaven's body farther away from the bridle path, thus postponing its discovery for an indefinite period.

"I'll help you," she said.

"Are you sure you want to?"

"Of course. I'm perfectly fine now."

"They stood up.

Almost immediately, Rick pushed her back down into the grass.

"Someone's over there," he whispered.

He crawled to the alder tree and stood up behind its trunk, moving carefully so he couldn't be seen.

In the far distance, he saw a man putting a bridle on the president's horse. He looked like a ranch hand, wearing jeans, a blue denim shirt, and a yellowish cowboy hat. Then he noticed a second horse. It was being led toward the president's horse by a second ranch hand.

Rick slowly released his breath. He watched both men mount the horses. They rode toward the president's ranch, and away from the trees where the body lay.

They passed through an open gate. One rider dismounted and padlocked the gate. Both then rode away, crossing the buffer strip, riding uphill into dense dark green growths of scrub oak where they disappeared.

Surrounded by a high barbed-wire fence, the buffer strip was county property. It was a quarter of a mile wide and designed to keep people from getting close to the president's ranch.

Rick noticed that there was no more smoke rising over the ranch. He told Ginny what he'd seen and helped her to her feet. They started up the slope.

But then Rick stopped. "Do you think we can get away with it? Won't the cops notice that the body's been moved?"

She'd thought of that, too. "Eventually, yes. And that will be our second felony."

"What's our first?"

"Not notifying the authorities until we're good and ready."

"Christ!" He gave her a sharp look. "Aren't we sticking our necks out?"

"Yes. And I think I know what else you're thinking."

"What?"

"That maybe *I'm* the one. Maybe I killed the Master of Heaven. And that's why I'm willing to commit more felonies."

He laughed and shook his head. "Never in a thousand years."

"But I could be," she insisted. "This is no ordinary murder. I know it has something to do with TimTomTon and probably Dr. Sierra." She explained that it was because of TimTomTon's involvement that she was willing to commit a limited number of felonies.

"Much of what TimTomTon does is illegal," she said. "We have to fight illegalities with illegalities. It's a terrible choice. But at least ours will be different."

"How?"

"Because as soon as we're able we'll tell the proper authorities exactly what we've done."

As they climbed the slope above the foxes' den, Rick stooped and picked up the shoelike thing that was half-hidden in the grass.

Turning it over, he saw that it was a woman's brown shoe attached to an artificial foot. One of the buckles was open.

"Look at this," he said.

When Ginny saw it, she gasped with surprise and sudden concern. "Put it down," she said. "Be careful. There may be fingerprints."

But her concern went far beyond fingerprints. After Rick placed it back in the grass, they got down on their knees and examined it more thoroughly.

The shoe was a brown leather wedgie. The reddish brown stains around its thick heel very likely were dried blood.

"My God," said Rick. "That's why the fox picked it up. He could smell it. Blood."

"This is awful," said Ginny. "This changes everything."

"Why?"

She looked at him disbelievingly. "You don't know?" He said nothing. He waited to be told. "This is Aunt Pam's," Ginny said. "She hardly ever limps. Did you know she's crippled?"

He shook his head.

He listened intently as Ginny explained that her Aunt Pam had worn the artificial foot for many years. She'd lost her foot in a traffic accident caused by Louise's carelessness. Pam had several of the appliances, alternating them from time to time to keep her scarred skin from chafing too much.

"Leaving the foot here is dumb," said Rick. "I don't think Pam did it."

"Of course not. She isn't capable of it."

"The damn thing was planted here," he said. "And I think I know who had a reason."

Ginny waited expectantly.

"Louise," he said.

Ginny's reaction surprised him. She rejected the idea completely.

"Not Louise. She's a liar and all that. She fights with Pam all the time. But she wouldn't kill a man and make it look like Pam did it. That's absolutely out of the question."

Rick answered quietly. "Ginny, you're wrong."

He decided not to give her his explanation then. She

agreed that they should take care of the man's body first and talk about theories and motivations after the task was done.

They left the artificial foot partly hidden in the grass. Then they walked up and over the slope and along the path.

When they reached the body, Rick glanced at his watch. It was only seven forty-five. Twenty minutes had passed since Ginny made the ugly discovery.

Rick didn't waste any more time. He told Ginny he wanted to do it himself. Bending over the Master of Heaven, he grasped the wrists tightly and raised both arms. The skin was cold and the body was stiffening, indicating the master had been dead for hours.

"Could it have been an accident?" Ginny asked. "Couldn't he have been riding the horse in the dark and hit his head on a branch?"

"Hell, no!"

He was disturbed by her stubbornness. She was trying to fight off the obvious, refusing to accept the signs that pointed directly to the involvement of her family.

Walking backward, he dragged the body on its back past the trunk of the myrobalan tree and then into a low growth of bristly, tough green junipers.

For a moment he looked down at the body. One Oriental eye was open, the other was closed. The injury in the temple area was deep, and the blood was dark.

The rounded depression looked like it would match the rounded heel of Aunt Pam's wedgie.

There didn't seem to be any other injuries. The Master of Heaven had been struck once with great force, and Louise was big enough and strong enough to generate that much force.

He remembered the first time he'd met Louise and felt her hot anger. She'd struck him a vicious blow with her yellow hat. It was a lightweight hat, but she turned it into a weapon that slashed his face. Were Louise to swing something as heavy as Pam's artificial foot, she could easily crack a man's skull.

A lot of blood had poured out and was beginning to dry. It had dripped down the side of the master's face, onto the collar of his blue dress shirt, and then to the shoulder of his dark blue business suit.

Rick stepped away, and the juniper branches jumped back into their original position, concealing the body completely.

"Leave it like that," said Ginny. "The less we do, the less we'll have to explain."

On the way back to his observation foxhole, they didn't talk. When they were shielded again by trees and low slopes, he decided to give her the straight facts about Louise. He told her everything he'd learned about Louise back in the Temple of the Sky on Taiwan.

At first Ginny was dead set against accepting his facts. But as he went on, he could see her attitude begin to change.

"Do you remember," he asked, "the code name you gave me back in Arizona? Lamma?"

"Yes."

"Didn't you say Lamma was an important contact of Dr. Sierra's? And that I might run across Lamma's trail somewhere in the Orient?"

"Yes."

"You were right. I did."

"And?"

"Louise is Lamma."

A moment passed. Then Ginny's face fell with sadness and disappointment. She apologized for being so stubborn and not believing him sooner.

"I guess proof isn't necessary," she added, "but is there any?"

"Yes. On the wall. In the Temple of the Sky."

He raised his stunted and scarred little finger. He explained how he'd seen Louise's sacrifice displayed in gold leaf on the wall of honor in the temple.

"They call her Lady Lamma," he said. "The Master of Heaven told me with the greatest pride that for twenty years Lady Lamma had supplied him with valuable secrets. Do you know what they were?"

"Perhaps. I can see how I've been wrong . . . and Auntie Pam was right."

"In what way?"

Ginny explained that Pam had always doubted Louise's story that her fifth husband, the navy admiral, had died from a sudden heart attack.

Pam had always insisted it was suicide. She also insisted that Ginny could learn the truth about Louise by checking the Pentagon's secret files by computer.

"Auntie Pam kept pestering me," Ginny said. "So I checked. I found out that the navy had investigated the admiral's suicide. But I came up empty on Louise. The important details were missing. Page after page of testimony had been deleted from the files."

"Do you know why?"

"I can guess. To hide Louise's deception. Pam told me the admiral was on the U.S. ambassador's staff in Taipei and read all the high-level diplomatic advisories from the White House. I'll bet that for many years, the Temple of the Sky paid Louise for those secrets. When the admiral found out, the disgrace was too much . . . and he killed himself."

"Can you prove it?"

"No. But what you've told me about Louise ties in directly with Pam's ideas. And that's why I think I know who deleted those pages of testimony. A Pentagon deputy named McLaughlin who had access to the files. And he was later promoted to a high position in the White House."

"And he's still there?"

"Yes."

Ginny's eyes became shadowed with distress and disillusionment.

"Now he calls himself Saddlebag One."

REO: No. 96
To: Rawhide, White House
From: Ginny
Subject: *Trap*

I have read the deleted last paragraph of the secret Gorbachev letter in which he proposes a minisummit meeting in London or Reykjavík.

It is hasty and ill-conceived. I suspect that Gorbachev is setting a trap for you because he was so badly burned by the KGB's sloppy handling of Daniloff.

Gorbachev is in trouble in the Kremlin and needs to burn you back.

If you must meet him in October, use your Great Communicator finesse to avoid a head-on collision about Star Wars.

☆ ☆ **33** ☆ ☆

The morning regulars were coming into the park—silver-haired men and women out walking poodles and spaniels, a variety of semiathletic joggers, brisk walkers, and the arthritic woman painter who always arrived on the dot of eight to set up her easel near the pond.

Rick put the seven torn strips of bonds into the hollow artificial foot. He tucked one of the small vials of silver nitrate crystals in among the paper strips. He buckled the two straps tightly so the paper strips and vial couldn't fall out.

Then he and Ginny began walking to a part of the park where he knew they would have complete privacy. En route, Rick stopped near a sloping bank of the creek where high grass had overgrown a long-abandoned fox den. He parted a thick growth of green strands, found the small opening, and shoved the artificial foot and its wedgie in as far as his arm could reach.

As he left, the wiry grass sprang back in place, covering his footprints as well as the den entrance.

"How long can you stay?" Rick asked.

"An hour or less. I told Auntie Pam I was worried about my rabbits and I was going to look for them."

They walked rapidly to one of the park's storage sheds about three fourths of a mile from his observation foxhole. It was a small green building, windowless and very old. Its tightly nailed redwood siding and peaked roof had withstood years of attempted invasions by rain, wind, termites, and rodents.

Rick opened the combination lock, and they went inside. He clicked on the overhead bulb and closed the door.

Little had changed inside since his last visit two months ago. The air was musty. Extra lengths of white plastic pipe were stacked along the wall where he'd stored them after installing the new sprinkler system near the park's tree farm. His shovel, crowbar, hammer, and other tools were on the workbench.

On the dusty redwood shelf above the tools were some of Rick's personal belongings, untouched by other park workers who occasionally used the shed. Included were his miniature battery radio, a pair of gray park employee coveralls hanging on a nail, his defunct, old Pentax camera, a pair of rusty binoculars, an unopened and expired roll of Kodachrome 35-mm film, and one of the small spiral notebooks containing his wildlife notes for Professor Porterfield.

He and Ginny had a score of subjects to discuss and a limited amount of time to make their plans. Before they got started, Rick cleared away a clutter of old newspapers and spider webs so they could sit on one of the weathered old park benches stored in the shed.

"Can you tell me one thing right off?" he asked. "Which one is your mother—Pam or Louise?"

"Auntie Pam, of course."

During the next few minutes, she gave him facts about her family and a dozen other subjects. She spoke quickly but still managed to be amazingly thorough. She tied a bunch of seemingly unrelated subjects tightly together. From them emerged a single picture putting each into a reasonable perspective.

With her Pilot-M supercomputer, she had researched—

sometimes only in seconds—data bank files in such far-apart locations as the Santa Barbara County Courthouse, Warner Brothers Studios in Burbank, an abortion clinic in Los Angeles, the Temple of the Sky in Taiwan, KGB and R&R centers one thousand miles from Moscow, Sandinista headquarters in Managua, TimTomTon and CIA subcenters in Montana, the First International Bank of Ulan Bator in Mongolia, Nancy Reagan's petty cash fund in the White House, and the helicopter dispatch center on the president's ranch.

In swift succession, she gave Rick information that was substantiated by other facts:

1. The president would spend the weekend at the ranch. If the fog lifted, he would come by copter tonight; if the weather was bad, he and his party would arrive in a group of nine Ford Broncos.

2. The fire in the ranch's stables had severely damaged the building. Several horses had panicked and run away. Cause of the fire was believed to be spontaneous combustion in bales of hay.

3. Messages between the ranch and the White House during the night noted that because of the fire, security around the ranch would be substantially increased during the president's visit. The usual reports on subversives and political activists were being investigated.

4. Pickets would start a Stop Making Nukes demonstration at noon in front of the ranch's main green gate. A Libyan death squad was rumored to have arrived in Southern California, but the report could not be confirmed.

"What about Dr. Sierra?" Rick asked.

"The same alert as usual," said Ginny. "TimTomTon messaged that whenever the president is at the ranch, Dr. Sierra and his Nicaraguans must be presumed to be somewhere in the Southern California area."

"Something's fishy." Rick got up from the bench and stretched his arms. He was more than just nervous. His whole body felt tense and muscle-bound.

"All night long," he said, "there was no security in the

park, even though the president is coming. How do you explain that?''

"I can't. I know that last night Louise got some of the security people ordered away from her house because the new superelectronic system is finally almost complete. But that doesn't explain their absence from the park as well. Unless . . . '' After a moment's pause, she came up with an answer that made sense. ''The maggot in TimTomTon. Of course!''

"Saddlebag One?''

"Why not? Someone high up told TimTomTon to cut back the security for the night. That gave Louise the freedom to kill the master from Taiwan. And can you guess why she killed him?''

"Sure. He must've been all worked up. By losing the bonds, he had a terrible loss of face back home. To an Oriental that's worse than death. So he insisted that Louise help get them back. He probably threatened to mouth off about her being Lady Lamma—''

Rick noticed that it was nearly time for the 8:15 A.M. news. He switched on his miniature radio. As they waited for the news to start, Ginny remembered that she'd forgotten to give him a message from Agnes.

"Hold it a sec,'' he said. ''Listen—''

The fire on the ranch was the big local news, even though the damage to the stables was less than originally estimated. The heavy fog had kept the fire from spreading. Most of the horses had been rounded up. Only one was injured from jumping a barbed-wire fence.

The announcer emphasized that the fire wouldn't change the president's plans. ''The White House said he's eager to inspect the fire damage. The president knows that the biggest danger to his mountain top ranch is from forest fires. He remembers that the big wildfire of 1955 nearly destroyed the ranch when it blackened 80,000 acres from Gaviota to San Marcos Pass.'' The radio went on to other news and Rick switched it off.

"What about Agnes?'' he asked.

"Oh, yes. I got an advisory last night from TimTomTon. It said you notified her to meet you in Santa Barbara today."

"What? Impossible!"

"But it was properly coded."

"That's crazy. It must've been a fake. I sent Agnes a message from Seattle, but nothing since."

"Anyway, she's on her way," said Ginny. "She's due this morning."

For a long interval, they sat together in silence, contemplating this new complication. Was the coming of Agnes something devious cooked up by TimTomTon? Or was the trip simply Agnes's own idea?"

There were no easy answers. A lot was happening, or was about to happen. Instead of reaching solutions, he and Ginny seemed to be getting more confused. Their progress was nil.

Rick took the binoculars down from the shelf and told Ginny he'd be back in a few minutes. He left the shed and walked to the nearby knoll where he sometimes ate his lunch. It was overgrown with jacarandas, cedars, and sycamores but high enough to let him observe the comings and goings of the park's wildlife.

With the powerful 7/50 binoculars, he slowly scanned the park, turning until he'd made a complete circle. He concentrated the longest on the wooded area where the Master of Heaven lay.

He saw nothing out of the ordinary. There were a few of the park regulars nearby, feeding a tame doe, but no police and no other security activity.

He returned to the shed and locked the door. Ginny was still seated on the bench, deep in thought. Then she looked up at him. She was getting restless.

"Rick, how much longer can we stay here?"

"The rest of the morning, if we have to. But we better not. We've got to get you home."

"Not right away, Rick. Not until we figure out the best thing to do for you."

"Why *me*? What about *you*?"

"You," she said. "Because of your trip to China, and the bonds, you're suspect no.1 . . . or have you forgotten?"

"Hell no. But what about Pam?"

"She's safe for the time being. Unless they find her foot."

Ginny drew in her breath nervously and sighed. "All we're doing is guessing. I can send advice to the top man in the White House, but when it comes to police work I'm lost. . . ."

They talked over their plans again, came up with some new ideas, but reached no workable conclusions.

"I think Louise is the key," said Rick. "We have to get to her as soon as possible."

"It's too risky."

"We've got to," he said doggedly. "But first you've got to tell me more about Louise and what her lies have done to you and Pam . . . everything, OK? From the beginning."

Ginny filled him in on the most significant aspects. She tried to keep her voice steady and emotionless, but from time to time bitterness and frustration about Louise crept in.

Louise's private detective had destroyed the original courthouse records of Ginny's birth. But Ginny's computer had located a backup official file, stating that her parents were Reginald Carlos Colombia and Pamela Astrid Johnssen.

Warner Brothers Studio's payroll records stated that the real name of the late actor-director Reggie Ronson was Reginald C. Columbia. For many years he was Ronald Reagan's double and stand-in.

The studio's records also stated that Auntie Pam had small roles in several motion pictures. Under the name of Pamela Astrid, she'd had parts in two Ronald Reagan films but wasn't listed in the credits.

Louise could never bear children because the clinic in L.A. botched her abortion. She'd never wanted children anyway. But when Ginny was born, Louise became obsessed with jealousy that worsened each year. She flew into rages and mounted a bewilderingly complex campaign of lies in an effort to prove she was the child's mother and gain custody.

Down through the years, Ginny carefully refrained from telling either of her aunts that she knew Pam was her mother. Her rapport with Pam was already a loving mother-daughter relationship. If Louise even suspected that Ginny knew the truth, her jealousy would have kept the two households in a continual uproar.

Ginny's search through Louise's bank, IRA, Savings, and CD accounts revealed many mysterious deposits listed under the name of L.L. Remington, instead of Louise E. Remington.

Because Rick had turned up the name Lady Lamma, Ginny knew now that the L.L. accounts were the fortune in secret payments that Louise had received for twenty years from the Master of Heaven.

'Will that evidence hold up in court?'' he asked.

"Yes. It's all documented.''

He put his binoculars on the dusty shelf. Then he turned back to her.

"In that case, Ginny, I think we made a big mistake this morning.''

She rubbed her nose very hard. "I was afraid you'd say that.''

"We blew it. We should've gone to the sheriff's office immediately. Once they get the evidence about Louise, the law will be on our side, not Louise's.''

"And it's my fault,'' she said with deep down remorse.

"No. We both blew it.''

Rising suddenly from the bench, she turned her back and refused to look at him.

"Rick, I can't stand it when I make a mistake.'' Her voice, almost a whisper, was filled with guilt. "A terrible feeling comes over me . . . and sometimes I go all to pieces. . . .''

He put his hands lightly on her shoulders and turned her around. But she hung her head and wouldn't look at him.

"Everybody makes mistakes, Ginny.''

"I know. But I'm different. I absolutely can't let myself make mistakes. Sometimes I think I'm more mixed up than Louise.''

"Never, Ginny.''

Placing a finger under her chin, he tilted up her face so he could look into her brown eyes. They were bright with tears that were very close to overflowing.

"Ginny," he said with hesitation. "I love you"

The words had an immediate emotional effect on her.

"Oh, Rick!" She blinked rapidly and tried to escape from his gaze. But he kept his finger firmly under her chin.

"Ginny, do you know when I knew for sure?"

The tears overflowed her lashes and ran shining down her cheeks.

"This morning, Ginny. When you kept this . . ." He touched the yellow leaf stem that stuck up from the curved breast pocket of her white blouse. She placed her small hand against his. Then she pressed his hand firmly against her pocket. Coming from her, it was an incredible signal. He felt the firm swelling of her breast and her heart knocking madly behind it.

For a moment, neither moved.

Then she pulled his hand away and began to cry. He'd seen her cry the night her special portable computer had broken. She cried her eyes out with frustration and failure.

But these tears were different. When he tried to put his arms around her, she shook him off.

"Ginny, please. Can't I—"

"No! Don't touch me again—ever!"

She seemed to be choked up with guilt and misery deep inside where he couldn't reach her. Her withdrawal from him was so total it frightened him.

The mature, confident woman was gone. So was the teenager. She wept like a child of eight or nine, fragile and defenseless, unable to understand what was wrong, unable to help herself in any way.

He waited and waited, his mind a blank. It was as if her confusion gripped him, too, erasing his ability to say or do anything that would comfort her.

At last she began to breathe somewhat normally.

Minutes passed.

Then she spoke in a dead voice. "Rick, I cannot love you. It would be an even bigger mistake." She tried to swallow. "It's this fear I have. This terrible, terrible—and absolutely unreasonable fear of making a mistake. . . ."

She stood with her face to the wall. She was so rigid that he could see a tendon outlined starkly against the skin of her throat.

If he hadn't been so wrapped up in Ginny, he would have paid attention sooner to the approaching sounds outside the shed. They were light footsteps.

Suddenly the shed's old redwood door was splintered by a heavy boot.

The door flew inward and hung crookedly on its top hinge. A tall man stood in the opening. He wore gray park employee coveralls with the words El Dorado printed in blue on one side of his chest.

He also wore a gray baseball cap that partly concealed the bandage wrapped around his curly haired head.

"I've been standing here listening to you two," he said. "God, what a lot of loving shit!"

Jerry.

His brother Jerry was back, with a set to his jaw and fury in his eyes. Rick saw that Jerry was unarmed. Not that it made any difference. He had to be dealt with at once— knocked down and stomped if necessary to keep him from harming Ginny.

Then Rick saw the man standing beside Jerry and realized attack was out of the question. The second man held a heavy M76 submachine pistol. He also wore gray park employee coveralls. The hands that held the M76 were sinewy and powerful. They were the hands of Teodoro.

Teodoro, the maggot.

The maggot in TimTomTon. His former chief instructor.

REO: No. 115
To: Rawhide, White House
From: Ginny
Subject: *Imperfect people*

The most troubling aspect of the *Challenger* disaster

is the lack of warning from the five computers on board.

This tells us that SDI (Star Wars) will not work because "imperfect people cannot create perfect machines."

Computers will be a major part of any Star Wars plan to track and destroy hundreds of attacking warheads.

REO: No. 116
To: Rawhide, White House
From: Ginny
Subject: *Model-T Shuttle*

The *Challenger*'s failure is proof that the shuttle concept is a Model-T Ford in space.

NASA is staffed by oldtimers who still don't realize that work should have been pushed a decade ago on jet-propelled aircraft to fly in space.

Rocket power is obsolete. It costs $5,000 per pound to put a cargo in orbit via shuttle.

By jet propulsion, the cost per pound would eventually be reduced to $15.

☆ ☆ **34** ☆ ☆

He anticipated that they would raise hell, move mountains, and kill as many people as necessary to get the bearer bonds back.

He anticipated that they wouldn't tell him where they were holding Ginny.

But Rick never guessed they would threaten to kill his mother.

Imprisoned in a dark horse stall that stank of old horse manure, he thought he was hallucinating when they first mentioned killing his mother. His mother?

Impossible.

But that's what Teodoro told him only minutes after their arrival at the stables.

"Give us the bonds," said Teodoro, the maggot. "Or we kill your mother."

Absolutely *impossible*. There was no way they could kill her. *She had been dead for many years.*

His mother, Dr. Janine DuBois Mohr, had been killed five years ago in Sacramento by a hit-and-run driver. It happened on the day she was to receive another pediatrician association award for her work with mentally handicapped children.

"I'll give you five minutes," said Teodoro. "When I come back, I want the bonds . . . or your mother's going to be dead."

The minutes had passed. and now the goddamned maggot was coming back. Rick heard Teodoro's boots striking the thick planks of the floor. There was also another sound. A rhythmic squeaking that accompanied Teodoro's footsteps.

Suddenly a switch snapped, and an overhead light came on. It was blindingly bright because Rick had been in total darkness for more than an hour.

"Believe it or not," said Teodoro. "This is your mother."

Shielding his eyes with his hand, Rick peered through the open doorway of the horse stall.

Two people were out there. Teodoro was standing. The other person was sitting. Teodoro leaned forward. He pushed something, and Rick heard the rhythmic squeaking again. It sounded like a tiny field mouse.

Now Rick could make out the details. Teodoro pushed a metal wheelchair closer to the doorway. One of its wheels needed oil. An old woman was slumped sideways in the wheelchair.

"Believe it or not," said Teodoro loudly. "Look her over . . . and then, by God, you start talking!"

Rick got up from the wooden stool. Teodoro made no move to stop him as he walked into the doorway. Rick crouched beside the wheelchair and looked closely at the woman's thin, wrinkled face. Her eyes were closed. This tired, wasted woman wasn't his mother. This woman was at least seventy years old.

If his mother were alive, she would be much younger and still a beauty. His mother had suffered many mental and physical hardships during her years in Managua. But despite everything, she never lost the attractiveness and proud bearing inherited from her French family.

"Goddamn you!" shouted Teodoro. "She's real! Touch her!"

Rick remained motionless, staring at the thin cheeks and brow. Then he looked down at the frail fingers and saw the wedding band.

"Touch her!" commanded Teodoro.

His heavy hand slammed Rick's shoulder, knocking him against the wheelchair. Rick lifted the woman's hand and examined the ring. The gold was worn, but the entwined rosebuds and leaves were still visible. This was the ring his mother had pawned many times in order to buy food for her small boys in Managua.

Again he looked at the thin face, especially the brow. He closed his eyes and remembered the fine sculptured line of his mother's brow.

He opened his eyes. The brow line was the same, little affected by whatever had aged and weathered the rest of her face.

"It's her all right." Teodoro's powerful hand seized the collar of the woman's faded blue chenille robe and jerked her upright.

"Wake up, Mama! Look at your son!" He shook her again. Her eyelids fluttered open, then closed. "Wake up, damn you!"

He started to shake her again, but Rick seized his wrist.

"Stop that, you bastard!"

The woman's eyes opened again. They closed, then stayed open.

Rick let go of Teodoro's wrist. He looked into the woman's eyes.

They were dark brown, the same color as his own eyes, and the same color as the eyes of his brother Jerry.

She looked at him without recognition. Her eyes were dead. There was no intelligence in them, no awareness of anything.

"She had a stroke," said Teodoro. "She is ruined. *Que peña!*"

Now that he had looked into her eyes, Rick knew the truth. *This woman—this frail, hollow thing—was his mother, Janine.*

In some improbable way, and for some extraordinary reason, she had been kept alive for five years.

Rick got to his feet and faced Teodoro.

"Bastard! You did this to her!"

He swung his fist. His rage was so great that it increased his strength, his speed, and his reach. Teodoro leaned back but couldn't escape. Rick's fist struck his swarthy Latino cheek like a pile driver.

The impact echoed through the stables. Teodoro stumbled backward against the plank wall and then fell heavily to the floor. He immediately scrambled to his feet and lunged at Rick, fists raised.

"Stop! Imbeciles!" The angry shout came from Jerry, who stepped into the circle of light shining down from the bulb. He aimed the submachine at Rick, who realized that his brother had been there all the time, standing guard in the darkness.

"Rick, stop!" ordered Jerry, "or I blow you away!"

Rick lowered his fists. Teodoro did the same.

Jerry came closer to Rick but not close enough so Rick could snatch the weapon. Rick noticed that his brother no longer wore the cap. The back of his curly-haired head was bandaged, covering the injury Rick had given him in Mongolia.

"There's no time for this!" Jerry said. "Give us the bonds!"

"Never!"

Teodoro interrupted. "I'll handle this!"

He struck without warning, the way Rick had done moments before. His first heavy blow slammed the side of Rick's neck. The second landed higher, on the side of his jaw.

Rick fell to the floor. The first blow from Teodoro's oversized fist had done all the damage. Nerves had been struck, sending shock waves to his brain. The left side of his body felt paralyzed.

"Now we're even," Teodoro said. "And now, you son of a bitch, you *will listen!*"

Teodoro made a speech. It began with threats, included references to Janine and Ginny, and then added more threats. He spoke mostly in English, using a few ugly Spanish words to emphasize the threats.

He spoke of *matarife*, slaughterman. He referred to *matanza* and *matar*, implying there would be a massacre and that human beings would be killed deliberately.

He presented his version, bizarre but perhaps true, about what had happened to Janine. The Sandinistas' plot to assassinate the president had started with her fake death five years before. It was arranged by Dr. Sierra.

Janine hadn't been killed in the hit-and-run traffic accident. Another woman of similar age and build had been killed and substituted for her. Janine's immigration and citizenship records had been altered so the substitution couldn't be detected.

Janine had been taken back to Managua, imprisoned, and forced to work for the Sandinistas as a children's doctor. The following year, her son Jerry began indoctrination sessions, which led to her being assigned a role in Dr. Sierra's assassination plan.

But Janine only pretended to accept the Sandinista philosophy. When she tried to escape, she was clubbed on the head.

Teodoro insisted that the blows weren't related to Janine's stroke. He made such a point of this that Rick knew he was lying.

"Stand up," Teodoro said.

He grabbed Rick's arm and pulled him up. Rick leaned against the rough wooden wall. His left arm was still numb from the blow to the nerves in his neck, but feeling was starting to return.

"We must have the bonds," Teodoro said. "There is little time. We will give you three more minutes to make your decision."

Teodoro brought his dark face so close that Rick could smell the tequila on his stale breath and see the large red veins in the yellowish whites of his eyes.

"If you do not make the correct decision," Teodoro said, "in three minutes we will kill your mother."

The threat didn't bother Jerry in the slightest.

"It will be but a small loss," Jerry said, "because she is no longer the mother we knew. *Que peña*. Still, I think you will want her to live."

Rick was put back in the horse stall. Its door was slammed shut and locked.

The light was extinguished. He heard his mother being pushed again in the wheelchair. Soon the sound of the squeaky wheel went away.

It was madness. It was madness of the worst kind because of its façade of logic. It was the worst kind because these were all intelligent men. For five years they had taken step after logical step on their way to an act of supreme madness.

And because they were intelligent and logical and experienced in this kind of madness, they were a force to be feared more than any other. Their power came from within the White House itself. And it had the backing of powerful forces within TimTomTon and doubtless related agencies.

If they could bring his mother back to life, they had the power to do anything.

The president would come to his ranch tonight and stay for the weekend.

These stables were on a hillside adjacent to the president's ranch.

This ranch, hidden behind a hilltop and thick growths of

scrub oak, was the perfect place from which to launch an attack on the president.

But something was missing. They needed something to complete their plans. The bonds, of course. And something else.

What would they buy with the $5.2 million? It must be something extremely vital to the assassination.

His mind wasn't functioning at all well. They had played tricks with his mind by taking Ginny away and replacing her with his mother. Now the three minutes were nearly up and his mind was blank. Was it actually happening? Was it up to him to make the decision that would save the president?

Did these people actually believe that a low-level park employee could summon enough expertise for such a decision?

It was a terrible choice. His mother or the president.

If he failed to produce the $5.2 million, his mother would be killed. But if he gave them the bonds, the president would be killed.

He heard their footsteps returning and the sound of the squeaky wheel. *He could not let them kill his mother.* Her brain damage might not be permanent. There was a chance surgeons or medications could restore her.

As for the president, that decision wasn't as immediate. It could be postponed for hours until his arrival tonight.

The overhead light snapped on. The stall door was unlocked. Two people stood out there waiting for his answer. They stood behind his mother in the wheelchair. Different people this time. A man and a woman.

The man was Dr. Sierra.

The woman was Louise.

They were unarmed. In the dimmer light behind them stood Teodoro and Jerry, both of whom held submachine pistols and were ready to open fire.

"Where are the bonds?" demanded Louise.

"First bring Ginny here," said Rick.

"No."

"No Ginny, no bonds," he said.

"You son of a bitch! How dare you bargain? You—"

Louise was interrupted by Dr. Sierra.

"Why not bring the girl? Anything to save time—"

Louise shot him a scathing glance. "Shut up! Remember your place!"

"Sorry." Dr. Sierra's manner was by no means submissive. But there was a certain amount of deference in his attitude toward Louise.

"Bring her!" commanded Louise. "Bring Gin here!"

Teodoro snapped to attention as if Louise were a colonel or a general.

He went away. But not very far. In a few moments, he returned with Ginny.

"Bring her closer!" ordered Louise.

Holding her by the elbow, Teodoro brought Ginny into the brighter light beside Louise and Dr. Sierra. Ginny's face was pale. Her eyes were frightened, but she was all right.

"She's fine, of course," said Louise. "What did you expect?"

Louise turned to Ginny. "Tell him."

"Give them the bonds," said Ginny. "Or they'll kill you—"

"Excellent!" Louise turned again to Dr. Sierra. "You may now inform the seller that final negotiations can start for the profile chip."

☆ ☆ 35 ☆ ☆

As part of the bargaining process, they didn't send Rick out immediately to dig up the bonds. That meant the sons of bitches weren't going to kill him right away. It also meant that Ginny and his mother had their time extended. They needed Ginny for her computer skills . . . and might not kill her.

But Rick knew that he and his mother soon would be of no further use. When the bloody sons of bitches got their hands on the $5.2 million, Rick would head the list of expendables, and Janine would be a close second.

It was getting more insane by the moment. Louise was holding prisoner her own niece, the girl she claimed was her daughter, and was threatening to harm her.

He did his best not to dwell futher on such thoughts. And to keep from doing something rash and stupid, like trying to grab his brother's weapon, he forced himself to concentrate on what the sons of bitches were saying.

For some reason, their first priority involved negotiating with the seller of the profile chip. His code name was Zamboni, and he looked Italian.

Zamboni was an elegantly dressed, middle-aged business man representing a semiconductor manufacturer in Silicon Valley. He claimed to be an independent agent, with no ties to any government. He was a tough, sarcastic negotiator who resisted every move Louise made.

"We'll pay $4 mill and no more," insisted Louise, "and don't forget that if we decide to use *Plan B*, our alternate, you don't get another nickel."

"You will pay the full $5.2 mill," Zamboni said politely, "because I happened to know your *Plan B* is shit."

As Rick watched the people at the negotiating table in the kitchen, he found it impossible to believe that the man they called Dr. Sierra was genuine. There was something distorted and alien about him. His physical appearance seemed genuine but nevertheless could be false. He looked exactly like the man Rick had seen on the Colorado River shuttle boat. He was in his mid-thirties and had an athletic build. His face was possibly Latino. It was slightly rounder and fuller than in the TimTomTon photos.

He was highly intelligent, but his personality was all wrong. He sat meekly at the negotiating table beside Louise and let her rant and rave for the lower price on the chip.

It made no sense. Dr. Sierra was supposed to be a superman. The man at the table was exactly the opposite. Dr. Sierra was supposed to be a neurosurgeon trained at the

University of Moscow. He was supposed to be a master of many languages, a jet pilot, an electrical engineer and an attorney who had practiced law before the highest courts in the USSR and Nicaragua.

He was supposed to be a great macho leader, a man of such power and charisma that he negotiated face to face with men like Gorbachev, Castro, and Qaddafi.

So who was this almost humble man with the downcast eyes who refused to negotiate for the chip? Who was this wimp who took orders from a woman? Could this be the great Dr. Sierra, the devil himself, the man with iceberg blue eyes who executed Nicaraguans by the thousands?

If this was the same man, something shattering had happened to him. Either that, or he never was a superman.

But as the bargaining continued, Rick slowly became convinced—against his better judgment—that the man was indeed Dr. Sierra and that he had been drastically demoted by Moscow.

The new number one wasn't Teodoro or Jerry or someone with high connections in Moscow and Managua. The new number one was Louise, and she was at the peak of her powers, physically and mentally. Except for her age and fashionable clothes, she was a carbon copy of Ginny, a golden blond with radiantly fair skin. She was gorgeous. She wore her wide-brimmed yellow hat with authority. The yellow knit dress emphasized the lines of her figure by clinging to her breasts and hips.

She reveled in her new power to make decisions and to command the others to carry them out. She regarded them as mediocre subordinates, her blue eyes flashing fire, ice, and arrogance as her gaze shifted from face to face.

She went out of her way to demean and discipline Dr. Sierra in front of the others. She noted sarcastically that he had been outwitted repeatedly by Rick, a mere amateur in international intelligence operations.

She emphasized that Dr. Sierra was in disgrace for his series of blunders, which climaxed with the loss of the pistol code cartridge and the $5.2 million.

Nevertheless, she needed him. It was clear that Dr. Sierra

had the engineering education and expertise that Louise lacked. In a quiet, submissive way, he asked involved, high-tech questions, which indicated the profile chip was a tiny silicon device with thousands of circuits and unique capabilities.

Five people sat around the bargaining table: Louise, Zamboni, Dr. Sierra, Ginny, and Rick. It was a shaky walnut table located in the rustic old kitchen where the stable hands cooked, ate, and did their laundry.

Also in the room were three others: Jerry, Teodoro, and a man Rick had never seen before. The pudgy stranger was almost as elegantly dressed as Zamboni. He stood off to the side by himself, chain-smoking cigarettes, listening and saying nothing.

Jerry and Teodoro stood on guard near the table, holding their ugly M76's waist high, fingers on the triggers. They looked worried and anxious. If anything went wrong, they seemed ready to open fire on any potential threat—whether it came from Louise, Zamboni, Dr. Sierra, the pudgy stranger, Ginny, or Rick.

Strewn across the scarred table was an assortment of papers: blueprints, computer printouts, pencil drawings, lists of specifications, and extremely long numerical projections.

Suddenly, Zamboni stood up and began stuffing papers from the table into his shiny black briefcase. He looked and sounded disgusted. "Forget this shit. I'm leaving."

"Sit down," said Louise. "You've got another hour."

"No, I've had it. You can go back to Plan B."

As they argued, Rick realized that Zamboni had a time problem. If the price couldn't be settled within the hour, the deal was off.

He was scheduled to leave for Europe later in the morning. He made it clear that his departure had priority over everything else.

Louise was stalling, hoping to get a better price as the deadline drew nearer.

Zamboni locked his briefcase and headed for the kitchen door. He didn't look back.

"All right," said Louise with what was probably sham regret. "You win. For now."

Zamboni returned and sat down. Louise ordered Teodoro and Jerry to take Rick back to El Dorado Park. They substituted pistols, which could be tucked in their coverall pockets, for the heavy submachine guns. They produced another pair of gray park coveralls, which Rick put on. They left the ranch in the vehicle that had brought Rick and Ginny there. It was a new Ford four-wheel-drive van pulling a badly weathered horse trailer.

In a few minutes they entered the park and transferred to an open-air minitruck. It was something created for their purpose, closely resembling the mint-green minis used for park maintenance work.

After a short drive, they parked near the alder tree and Rick began digging. The greenish black plastic trash bag was exactly where he told them it would be.

Teodoro brushed off the dirt and opened it. He gazed at the seven torn strips of bonds and began muttering a stream of obscenities in Spanish and English. His mildest description of Rick was *hijo de outa*, far stronger than son of a bitch.

Jerry's reaction was milder. He told Teodoro to calm down. "You better have the other pieces," he told Rick. "Where the hell are they?"

Rick shrugged. "Nearby."

As they walked toward the fox's den in the slope of the stream bank, he remembered how tightly he'd buckled the two straps on the artificial foot. He wondered if he'd be able to open them with one hand while extracting the foot from the narrow den.

The glass vial in the foot was the only weapon he had left. His pistol and the other vial of silver nitrate crystals had been seized by Teodoro shortly after he and Jerry captured Rick in the storage shed. It was Rick's pistol that Teodoro carried now in the pocket of his coveralls.

Rick knelt on the slope and spread apart the wiry grass that covered the den entrance.

"Hold it," said Jerry. "Right there!" Pushing Rick

aside, he extended his arm deep into the den. He found nothing.

"Feel around," said Rick. "It's in there—"

"Dumb ass hole," said Jerry. "Who you trying to con?" As he yanked his arm free, his anger was as great as Teodoro's had been at the alder tree. He called his brother a series of repulsive names in English and Spanish.

Then he kicked Rick viciously in the ribs. "When we get back, you're dead! I owe you for how you split my skull in Mongolia! I've still got headaches!"

He kicked Rick again and told him to make another search. Rick forced his arm into the narrow tunnel as far as he could reach. He found nothing.

Sweat broke out across his forehead and under his arms. Hoping to change his luck, he probed the tunnel with his other hand. Same result.

He knew these dumb bastards wouldn't accept what was probably the truth. From their perspective, and since they were unfamiliar with animal eccentricities, it was too far-fetched. But it was all he had to offer.

He explained how, earlier in the morning, he'd seen the fox carrying the artificial foot around in his mouth.

"There's blood on it. Enough to stir up his instincts and his curiosity. So he came back and got it—"

"Bull shit!" said Teodoro.

"Horseshit!" said Jerry. "You buried the stuff! Where is it?"

Rick stuck stubbornly to his story. They bought part of it because they knew Louise had left the foot in the park after using it as a weapon.

"But forget that other crap," said Jerry. "You've got two minutes. Then we blast you!"

They watched impatiently while Rick searched for the den's other exits. He found two on the other side of the slope.

Both were empty.

"Time's up!" said Jerry.

"So blast me," said Rick. "And then you'll be on your goddamn own!"

Teodoro and Jerry held a quick, nervous conference. It was obvious that Zamboni's deadline had them on a hot spot.

Rick took a spade from the maintenance truck and began digging up one of the den exits. The earth was soft and moist. Instead of objecting, Jerry reached for another spade. Working together, they dug up all three den exits. Then they dug into the main section of the den, opening up a hole about three feet across.

They turned up nothing except the small dried bones of rabbits and doves, bits of fur, and broken feathers.

That did it. The pressure got to Teodoro, and he blew up with frustration and anger. He pulled out the pistol and aimed at the center of Rick's chest. The black fury in his eyes showed he was close to losing control of himself.

But before he could pull the trigger, Jerry grabbed his arm. "No, Teo!" Jerry aimed Teodoro's arm and the gun at the ground. "Not here! Later!"

Teodoro struggled. Then he seemed to return to his senses.

He cursed Jerry for interfering, but his heart wasn't in it. He realized he'd nearly made a critical mistake. But he didn't blame himself. He cursed Rick for screwing up. He cursed Dr. Sierra for screwing up. And he cursed Louise and Zamboni for wasting time with their screwed-up negotiations.

His anger subsided as quickly as it came, replaced by more worry.

He checked the time. "Goddamn. The chip's in the toilet!" He ordered Jerry to keep digging and looking. "I got to go back," he said. "I got to face those bastards with what we've got. Christ!"

Picking up the folded trash bag, Teodoro ordered Rick to drive. He sat in the rear seat of the minitruck and kept his pistol shoved hard against Rick's backbone.

"Don't try any tricks," he warned. "No me importa un cacao! One false turn of the wheel and your spine is soup!"

They transferred back to the dark blue Ford four-wheel-drive van and trailer. Rick drove and Teodoro sat beside him, the pistol aimed at Rick's belly.

He drove up the steep, winding section of Refugio Road toward the president's mountaintop ranch. When they were within five hundred yards of the main green gate, behind which lay other ranches as well as the president's, he turned off on a small narrow side road.

This was the short, very steep entrance road to the Ellington Bar-L-E ranch, part of which ran beside the president's ranch. The Ellingtons were a wealthy Chicago family who vacationed at their ranch several times a year.

Rick drove the van and trailer into a small parking lot that was cut into the steep hillside beside the white wooden stables building. It was a big building. Like the Ellington ranch house, it was built on a shelf excavated into the side of the hill. Because of the hill's unusual steepness, large sections of both stucco buildings hung far out over the incline, supported by thick cantilever beams.

Teodoro ordered Rick to leave by the passenger door, so he could keep him covered with the pistol. As they walked around the van toward the stables, Teodoro stayed close behind. A brief movement beside the porch caught Rick's eye. It was something yellow that became stationary.

Teodoro hadn't noticed. As they went up the red brick steps to the porch, Rick halted.

"Move!" ordered Teodoro, jabbing him in the back with the pistol. He jabbed again, harder than necessary. While Teodoro was occupied, Rick got a better look at what was behind the corner of the porch. For a moment, he saw part of a woman's face. It promptly drew back out of sight. All he saw was an eye and a flash of yellow hair.

The hair was the same color as Ginny's, but it couldn't be her because of the blue eye.

Agnes?

Yes.

He and Teodoro walked across the porch. As they went inside, Rick wondered how he could get a message to her. It was possible that Agnes, through her TimTomTon connections, was up to the minute on everything. But was she sharp enough to contact the Santa Barbara sheriff's department instead of TimTomTon?

Followed by Teodoro, Rick went into the kitchen where the others were waiting. All except Zamboni. He was on his way out. But Zamboni was willing to return and see what was in the trash bag.

Teodoro dumped the torn strips of greenish bonds onto the table. Louise looked at them, and her face lost some of its color. She picked up an irregular strip and examined it closely. She picked up another piece and tried to fit the two ragged edges together.

They didn't fit.

While Teodoro explained what had happened, Louise listened in silence. She controlled herself remarkably well. Then she made a quick but precise decision.

"So be it." Her mouth was pinched with anger, but her words came forth clearly. "We switch over to Plan B,"

"I don't think so," said Zamboni.

He sat down at the table. He picked up each of the seven torn strips in turn and examined it with great care,

"The deal's on," he said. "Six of these are redeemable."

A mixture of reactions went around the table. Louise smiled and tried not to look surprised. Teodoro swore with great satisfaction. Ginny glanced at Rick and shook her head with dismay. Dr. Sierra's face was expressionless. The pudgy stranger lit a new cigar and grinned through the smoke. Zamboni was happy and confident.

Zamboni separated the torn papers into two section on the table. One group contained six of the greenish strips. They were quite wide. The other section contained a single narrow strip.

Zamboni picked up one of the wide pieces, held it up to the light and admired it.

"You people are lucky," he said. "*Firstly*, because I happen to be a bond broker as well as an attorney. *Secondly*, because the paper is genuine government issue. *Thirdly*, because six of the pieces are nearly two-thirds intact and contain the necessary data. They are redeemable at any major bank."

Zamboni picked up the narrowest strip. "This is a reject. But its matching piece is worth $1 million. Does anyone have it?"

Louise conferred with Teodoro. Then they both glared at Rick.

Zamboni conducted the rest of the negotiations with speed and efficiency. He was willing to accept the $4.2 million in redeemable strips, but only if Louise came up with the other million.

"I don't require cash," he said. "Something of comparable value will do, but I won't wait."

Zamboni tapped his Rolex and gave Louise thirty seconds to come up with an offer.

Louise's mind was quicker. She needed only fifteen seconds.

"You've heard of the ASD analyzer?" she asked.

"Christ, yes! The Pentagon has only a few—"

"Only two, Mr. Zamboni. An incredible, top-secret device."

"You've got one?"

"Yes, Mr. Zamboni."

Until then, Ginny had been an onlooker, listening to everything but taking no part in the negotiations.

Suddenly she was a full and violent participant. Her chair fell over with a bang as she jumped up and attacked her aunt.

"Louise, no! It's treason!"

She seized Louise's shoulders with both hands. She shook Louise so violently that the yellow hat sailed to the floor. The attack lasted only moments. Teodoro grabbed Ginny by the arm and pulled her away. Then he immobilized her in a bear hug.

When Rick started to move in, Teodoro yanked Ginny around and lifted one hand. In it was the pistol, which he jammed against Ginny's ribs.

Rick backed off.

"Call Eduardo!" Louise ordered.

Teodoro bellowed for one of his assistants. The kitchen door opened partway.

Eduardo stuck his head in. "Un momento!"

His head disappeared. But in a few moments, he came through the door, carrying a heavy leather saddle as well as a submachine pistol.

A woman was handcuffed to the saddle. When Rick saw who it was, he realized he and Ginny had lost another round. The woman was Agnes, and there was an ugly bruise on her cheek. Rick and Ginny exchanged glances. Her eyes were full of defeat.

It was the same kind of defeat he'd seen there earlier in the morning. That was when they were together in the storage shed and Ginny had realized what a mistake they'd made.

By hiding the body of the Master of Heaven, they'd made sure no investigators would be summoned to the park or surrounding areas.

Now—with even Agnes unable to notify the authorities— the mistake was getting worse by the minute.

REO: No. 128
To: Rawhide, White House
From: Ginny
Subject: *Iran Weapons*

I have tapped into a backup data bank at Iran's Mehrabad Airport. I discovered that—with your approval—the U.S. is secretly sending missiles and spare F–14 parts to Iran in exchange for Iran's aid in gaining release of our hostages in Lebanon.

You cannot keep this two-faced arrangement secret much longer. The Arabs inevitably will reveal it to the world.

The resulting international uproar will be a major political disaster because you have repeatedly stated that the U.S. will not negotiate in any way with terrorists or their governments, naming Iran in particular.

I strongly recommend that you *publicly* reveal this deal *before* the world press discovers it.

36

AUNT LOUISE

They claim I was part of the plot to assassinate the president.

Absolutely ridiculous.

I did everything I could to prevent it.

I was a double agent. I pretended to be working with them. But actually I was setting them up.

The worst thing was the way my own loving daughter turned against me. But I forgave her because she didn't understand.

But I'll never forgive my sister for what she did. The lying bitch.

Pam knew all along that I was trying to stop the assassination from the inside. But still she kept telling those terrible lies about me.

Pam was crazy with jealousy. She went off her head when she found out that Gin knew for years that *I* am her mother.

Pam couldn't take it. When she saw how much Gin loved me, she started telling lie after lie about me. And she even committed a murder.

I don't think she was in her right mind when she did it. That's why I wouldn't want to see her executed. I think she should be put away for many years, in an asylum or jail.

It was Pam who went into the park at midnight to meet the Master of Heaven from Taiwan. She struck him down with a tremendous blow on the head, using her artificial foot.

As for my daughter Gin, I suppose she had every right to get so upset when she thought I gave the ASD analyzer to Zamboni. She didn't understand that with all the others there—and watching—I had to look like I was cooperating with Zamboni.

I gave Zamboni the key to our house and the code card for the door to Gin's new lab. I even gave Zamboni a note to our captain of security, telling him to let Zamboni have the analyzer.

I admit I lied to Gin about the analyzer. I rarely lie. I have made a practice all my life of telling the truth whenever possible.

I only lie when it's badly needed, such as to save someone's life.

A good liar has to be a terrific judge of people. A good liar has to have a fantastic memory. Mine is like a giant filing cabinet. I file away every little thing I ever say about anybody or anything.

The trick is to keep every fact straight and never mess up. It is extremely difficult. Most people can't handle it. It takes a genius to do it. I am very proud to be that kind of a genius.

I am also very proud that my daughter Gin inherited some of my genius.

Everything I did to stop the assassination would've worked perfectly if Gin and that goddamn stupid Rick hadn't interfered.

Gin was too young to understand all the delicate moves I was making from the inside. But that goddamn Rick was old enough to know.

I confess I've grown to appreciate Rick. When he first came along, he was such a loser—divorced, kicked out of the military, no decent job, no future. But then he really improved himself and did some surprisingly good work for Saddlebag One.

The trouble with Rick was that he wanted Gin so badly. The blind fool. He knew—because of the way he raped me —that I could give him the kind of excitement Gin couldn't even dream of. Gin is so dumb about sex that she thinks mouths are only for kissing.

I know that Rick and I could be a real love match because he's so tall and athletic and macho. His new glasses make him look very professional, like a doctor or a young bank executive. I go all soft inside when he looks at me with his bedroom eyes with those long black lashes.

I have always known that because of my unique mind and related abilities I was destined to do something great for my country. That's why I seized the opportunity when it came along. Only a handful of people in history have ever been placed in a position where they might save the life of their president.

Lies—very necessary lies—helped me do it.

I told lies to the Ellingtons when I made the arrangements to lease their ranch while they were living back in Chicago.

I told lies to pudgy Saddlebag Two to help discredit that monster Dr. Sierra.

But I never lied to Saddlebag One. I didn't have to lie when I told him Americans were getting sick and tired of the president's excesses in Nicaragua.

I warned Saddlebag One that those excesses might cause certain people to try violent means to eliminate the president. I told Saddlebag One I loved everything the president did for America, but that I, too, was sick and tired of his continual harping about sending millions to Nicaragua.

Saddlebag One is a dear old man, but he's losing his wits. Half the time he doesn't even know what's going on in his own office in the White House.

He made a really dumb mistake when he sent his fat-faced assistant—Saddlebag Two—out to Santa Barbara to look into what was happening.

Saddlebag Two isn't as smart as he thinks he is, but he's a very clever man. He's been a maggot in the White House for years, sending the hottest top-secret Nicaragua data to people like Dr. Sierra and Teodoro.

Saddlebag Two has this unfortunately soft plump face that makes him look like a fat baby at the age of forty. But I've never underestimated him. I know how dangerous he is. I know how many lives were lost in Nicaragua because of him.

By lying to Saddlebag Two, I was able to work closely with him. I was extremely grateful for the way he analyzed Dr. Sierra's series of asinine mistakes and demoted him.

I wasn't surprised when Saddlebag Two put me in charge. I knew how impressed he was with the way I set up Plan B on the Ellington ranch.

I always knew we needed Plan B as a backup in case we couldn't get the profile chip. Plan B was a lot more complicated and took a lot more planning and work.

I used Teodoro and Eduardo because they were experts at getting past surveillance. They worked their way onto the president's ranch in the middle of the night and set the fire in his stables.

The president's ranch hands dashed in and got the panicky horses out. In all the confusion, Teodoro and Eduardo were able to break down fences and scatter most of the horses onto other ranches and into the park.

The key to Plan B was getting all those horses too exhausted to be ridden. Teodoro made sure the only horse that didn't run away was one of the president's favorites.

That particular horse was white and very visible. When the president rode him, he would be an easy target for the missile.

Of course, Plan B was the inferior plan because it would've used the missile's heat-seeking ability to zero in on the horse.

Fortunately, we didn't have to use the backup plan. That was because of the deal I was able to make with Zamboni for the profile chip.

The profile chip was a miracle of semiconductor artistry. It was very expensive but worth it. It cost us a total of $31 million. Dr. Sierra and his people in Managua raised the first $25.8 million and turned it over to Zamboni.

Those millions came from the money the president *himself* sent to Nicaragua. It was intercepted by the Sandinistas.

I raised the last—and most important—$5.2 million. And Zamboni was as good as his word.

He had the chip delivered to the ranch two hours after we finished the deal.

With the profile chip, we could zero in on the president whether he flew to the ranch by copter or came in the fog by car. The chip was equipped with a microscopic diagram of Reagan's profile. It was designed to zero in on only that profile, ignoring all other profiles of people in the president's entourage.

Of course, every move I made was designed to prevent the others from carrying out the assassination. By pretending to be part of the plot, and even directing the final stages, I had the inside information to keep it from happening.

Zamboni was smart enough to skip out before the final action started. He left us a VCR instruction tape to show Dr. Sierra and Teodoro the exact steps to follow to launch the missile.

The most disgusting part of the whole affair came while we watched the tape. I didn't know that Dr. Sierra had made arrangements with Zamboni to have his own special video put in as an introduction to the profile chip cassette.

I should've known Dr. Sierra couldn't be trusted. I should've been suspicious when he begged me to let everybody be herded into the kitchen to see the tape.

Teodoro, Eduardo, and Jerry stood guard with their weapons. In the rest of the audience were my sister, Pam, Gin, Agnes, Rick, Saddlebag Two, and even Rick's mother in her wheelchair.

Dr. Sierra's special tape was a color film he had made back when he was Somoza's executioner. General Somoza was the bloody strong man who ran Nicaragua for a dozen years.

The film was the most nauseating thing I had ever seen. It was in color, mostly red. Dr. Sierra was always in the picture, directing the machine gunners who shot down the lineups of peasants.

The film went on and on. The scenes were filmed at different times in different parts of the Nicaraguan countryside. There must have been thousands of bodies lying in the fields and in the green jungles.

After Somoza was deposed, Dr. Sierra did the same thing for the Sandinistas, directing their mass executions.

THE PRODIGY PLOT / 311

Most disgusting of all was watching the expression on Dr. Sierra's face as he went around giving the *coup de grace* to the wounded.

He used a pistol, and he shot mostly wounded mothers with children. He was continually reloading. It was so terrible I couldn't watch.

I found out later from Saddlebag Two that Dr. Sierra was paranoid about mothers with children. It was a delusion from his childhood when he claimed his mother abused him in the most revolting way.

Midway through the film, Dr. Sierra became stimulated from watching it. A change came over him. He became very authoritative again and began marching up and down, giving orders the way he did in the film.

He shouted: "Die!"

He shouted it only once. Then he drew his revolver and marched over to the wheelchair. Before anyone could stop him, he shot Rick's mother in the forehead. Then he made a quick turn and put the gun against my head. But he didn't pull the trigger because Saddlebag Two shot him in the heart.

I knew Saddlebag Two was clever. But I never thought a man that pudgy and soft could react so quickly.

He saved my life.

I suppose I should have felt indebted to him for that. And grateful. But I didn't. Because I knew then how terribly dangerous he was. And how difficult it would be to keep him from killing the president.

All during our ordeal, I tried to keep my daughter and my sister safe from those killers. I made sure that most of the time they were kept in the smelly horse stalls behind locked doors. Pam never appreciated that. She kept yelling hysterically about how I was holding her prisoner.

And her lies grew bigger and blacker. Like the way she insisted I kept those negotiations going with Zamboni only so I could steal that extra $1 million.

Absolutely wrong.

I negotiated with Zamboni exactly the way I handle my real estate transactions. Give a little here, take a little there.

I figured the missing torn strip of bearer bond would turn up eventually. And it could be cashed for $1 million.

I confess that at one time I thought I was entitled to keep the million as payment for how I handled the negotiations.

But later I decided the $1 million should go for a good cause, such as aiding the families of all those mothers Dr. Sierra had executed.

The $1 million never turned up. It was supposed to have been lost by Rick somewhere in El Dorado Park. But I think the smart-ass knew where it was all the time.

☆ ☆ 37 ☆ ☆

AUNT PAM

Almost all the dread warnings the Rosicrucian lady gave me about the baby came true.

Years before, when I met her while riding on that Hollywood bus, she predicted that I could never avoid the dark forces that threatened my baby's life.

What the Rosicrucian lady didn't tell me was that my sister would lead the dark forces.

God, what a bitch. What a murderer. What a monster. My very own sister.

The bitch really put it over on me. During those years of dread, when I worried so about the baby's fate, I never suspected that Louise was the one I should fear the most.

I always knew Louise had evil tendencies. But I thought all they amounted to was rigging some of her real estate deals and maybe selling her husband's navy secrets to the Chinese in Taiwan. I used to think Louise was on the borderline of being crazy because of all her lies.

I was right. And I was wrong.

Louise had to be crazy to think she could get away with killing the president.

But it took a very sane woman—a very smart woman—to devise the plan Louise came up with.

I don't care how close to being a genius she was. I always thought of her as my half-wit sister.

For years when I called her that, it was just sarcasm. And I suppose I was jealous because of all her money.

Later, it wasn't sarcasm or jealousy. It was the truth. Only a dedicated half-wit could misuse the fabulous brain God gave her the way Louise did.

The bitch kept me locked up for a night and a day in the Ellington stables. Most of the time I was in pitch-black darkness, sitting on the stinking floor. I don't think I'll ever get the smell of horse manure out of my hair.

I knew she had the baby locked up in another dark horse stall. But I didn't know where. There were twenty stalls in those stables, and the baby was somewhere in the far end of the building.

I just about went to pieces. The baby was in the worst danger of her life. And, like the Rosicrucian lady said, I couldn't do one damn thing to help her.

I screamed for help till I was hoarse. No one heard me. I heard Agnes screaming for help in another part of the stables.

But none of the authorities heard us because the Ellington ranch was so far off the road and so high on that hilltop. And, of course, it was shielded by all that thick scrub oak and other trees.

All our screaming did was make the Ellington horses nervous. Only six or seven were in the stalls, and from time to time Eduardo went around feeding and watering them. He was supposed to clean up the manure, but he didn't.

I have to admit that my half-wit sister was brilliant and cunning the way she set up the Ellington ranch through her real estate dealings.

For the last twenty years, she handled the sale or lease of many of the ranch properties along Refugio Road. She was called in as a consultant to help the owners conclude the deal when they sold the old Pico ranch to Ronald Reagan.

So it was easy as pie for Louise to take a lease on the Ellington ranch and use it for her headquarters overlooking the Reagan ranch.

The president named his place Rancho del Cielo because it was up in the clouds. The Ellington place was up just as high, at two thousand feet.

Part of the Ellington hilltop looked directly down on the president's place. The other section looked down on Refugio road.

Narrow and steep, Refugio is the only road leading to the president's ranch. It winds through heavy growths of tall sycamores, alders, catalpas, and brush.

From time to time, Louise and those sons of bitches moved the baby from her horse stall. They took her to the kitchen where they had the computer set up for the missile.

With Dr. Sierra dead and Zamboni on the run, they needed the baby's input to help arm the guidance system.

Every time they moved the baby, I held my breath. Her life was on the edge. At any moment, those half-wits might find some reason to shoot her.

I never thought Louise would kill the baby. Not her own niece, her own flesh and blood. I prayed that Louise would come to her senses and use that brilliant brain of hers to keep the baby from harm.

The very worst part was knowing that the baby would reach a point where she would absolutely refuse to cooperate. The baby has very high moral principles and can be damned stubborn. When that happened, one of those half-wits might fly off the handle and shoot her.

As the time approached for the president's arrival, I went through hell. I was close enough to the kitchen to hear some of their discussions. So I heard how glad they were early in the afternoon when the fog started to settle down on the mountaintop.

By nightfall, the fog was so heavy that the president couldn't possibly come by copter from Point Mugu. That meant he would be driven in on Refugio Road—and would be a much easier target.

Those half-wits—Saddlebag Two and Teodoro—were so happy about the fog that they had a little beer party while setting up the computer. I could hear the cans hiss as they popped the tops.

God, I was thirsty and could've used one. It was hell in that dark, stinking stall. I was so goddamn uncomfortable and worried that I cried. Not just a little. I cried a lot.

All they fed us were dry salami sandwiches and warm Pepsi in cans.

When I had to go to the bathroom, I was escorted by Eduardo or Jerry. Occasionally, I could hear them escort the others one at a time to the toilet—the baby, Agnes, and Rick. Agnes had finally been freed from the handcuffs that held her to that half-wit saddle.

I really got scared when I heard the baby get into a big argument with that fat-faced Saddlebag Two. It turned out that he knew plenty about chips and programming.

At one point he yelled at the baby and cursed her. That was really dumb because it just made her all the more stubborn.

I didn't understand hardly any of Saddlebag Two's mumbo-jumbo computer talk.

"Goddamn it no!" he exploded. "You saw how specific the video is on that! It has to be encrypted the other way to correct the error!"

I couldn't hear what the baby was saying. But it was a hell of an argument, and Saddlebag Two got really steamed.

Later I found out from the baby what it was all about.

She took a terrible chance. It could've cost her her life right then and there. While Saddlebag Two was watching, she punched in some kind of a number that would affect the missile. She also punched in something so obscure that only a wizard with the baby's kind of skills would see it.

Saddlebag Two was goddamned up on that stuff. He didn't know what the hell she was doing, but he punched in something that neutralized it.

So the baby, bless her, took another terrible chance. While

they were finishing up, she punched in an entirely different something or other.

Saddlebag Two didn't know what it was. But he was very nervous and blew sky high.

He screamed at the baby: "Bitch!"

Then he pulled out his handgun, the one he'd used to kill Dr. Sierra. He was so mad, he wanted to shoot the baby right on the spot. It was then that my sister did the only decent thing she ever did in her whole life.

I wish I could've been there to see it. The baby said Louise put her own handgun against the back of Saddlebag Two's head.

"She's *my* daughter," Louise said in that real icy way of hers. "Harm her, and you'll need a new head!"

Saddlebag Two put his gun away. But he was still plenty worked up and full of threats. He ordered the baby to get away from the keyboard. As a result, she didn't finish what she wanted so badly to punch in.

After the missile was set up and ready, another hour dragged by.

Everybody in the kitchen got antsy.

Louise was the only calm one. She kept telling the four others—Saddlebag Two, Teodoro, Jerry, and Eduardo—that they were wasting energy being so nervous.

"We got our money's worth," she told them. "Relax. We're on automatic . . ."

What she meant was that the $31 million missile was so sophisticated it would do everything by itself. After the final programming, not one button needed to be punched.

The missile was a comparatively small one, less than two feet long, giving it extreme maneuverability. It sat in its rack in the fog out on the porch, waiting for its target to arrive. As soon as the target was in the proper place on the road, the missle would fire itself.

The president and his entourage of vehicles were due between 7:10 and 7:15 P.M. The fog was so thick that the vehicles would come up the steep, winding road quite slowly.

In the past I'd driven Refugio Road many times. Usually

there's very little traffic. One rainy morning I happened to be up there when the president's entourage passed. It was interesting to see how the Secret Service handled everything.

I was ordered to drive off the road and stop. Only two other motorists were on the road, and they did the same.

Then these nine dark Ford Broncos came past, escorted by five sheriff's cars. They all drove faster than I ever dared to drive that narrow road. Each of the nine Broncos was new and shiny black. They were short, high-wheel vans with blackened windows. Because of those windows, I never saw the president or his wife. All nine vans shot past in just seconds.

According to the baby, Mr. Reagan and his wife always rode in separate Broncos. Theirs were armor-plated with bulletproof windows.

In those damn dark stables, nervous time went on forever. While we waited for the president, a lot was happening back in the other stalls that I didn't know about.

The baby told me later what happened. When Eduardo escorted her to the toilet, she managed to kick a tiny wadded-up note under the door to Rick's stall.

His stall was so dark he couldn't read the note. So he didn't know what the hell he was supposed to do.

Meanwhile, Agnes had figured out a way to escape from her stall. The walls were seven or eight feet high, too high to be climbed. But Agnes climbed one anyway. She took off her shoes and socks. Then she went up the wall the really hard way by clinging to the boards with her fingers and toes. She worked her fingernails and toenails into the cracks between the boards. She fell more than once. When she finally got to the top, most of her nails were broken and bleeding.

The air space between the top of the wall and the ceiling was too small for her to crawl through. It was so small that even a child couldn't squeeze through.

But Agnes was one hell of a tough and determined woman. She squeezed through anyway. She did it by taking some of her clothes off. She lost a lot of skin and bled terribly. Finally the blood lubricated her skin, and she made it through.

She climbed down into a stall that wasn't being used. Then she crept past the other stalls in the dark and went to where the ranch hands stored some of their tools. She took a hammer and screwdriver to Rick's stall and slipped them under the door.

By pulling nails out of the wall, he began to remove enough boards for an opening. He eased the nails out as slowly and quietly as he could. One nail took longer than all the others because it made little squeals like a stuck pig.

Although the president was due any minute, Rick was very patient with that goddamn nail. He had to stop for several minutes when Eduardo went to the storeroom for something.

After Rick escaped from the stall, he went toward the kitchen where there was light enough to read the baby's note. It made hardly any sense to him because he knew so little about computers. But he had to try.

Pretty soon, we could hear the engines of the nine Broncos as they came up the winding road below.

By that time, Louise, Saddlebag Two, Teodoro, and Jerry were out on the porch. It was so foggy out there that they had to stand very close to watch the missile's tiny lights come on in sequence.

If I had known that the baby was also out on the porch, I would have had a heart attack.

They left that half-wit Eduardo in the kitchen to stand guard over the computer. But at the last minute, he went out to the porch to watch for the big explosion down on the road.

A tiny blue light began blinking on the missile as it sensed the approach of the nine Broncos five hundred yards away.

A tiny yellow light came on as the missile selected which Bronco to hit.

A tiny red light came on as the the profile chip zeroed in on the president's head.

Simultaneously, the missile fired.

It went downhill with a whoosh, maneuvering repeatedly to avoid the trees. Its armor-piercing warhead came within inches of the president's Bronco.

But suddenly the missile changed course.

It went straight up. Then it made a big loop and headed back to the stables. It returned to its launching site and blew the porch to bits. It also blew that half of the building into fragments.

Back in my part of the stables, the noise was unbearable. I felt the walls around me shake and rattle as if flying to pieces. The door flew off, but somehow the rest of the stall stayed together.

What I didn't know, of course, was that before the missile took off Rick had plenty of time to finish the baby's computer code. He stood there as calm as could be, studied her note, and punched in the letters XXY.

But he goofed. Nothing happened.

That was because he was supposed to punch the letters in a second time. Finally the damn half-wit did it right. Even so, he had enough time left to follow the rest of the baby's instructions.

In all that fog, the others didn't see him slip out the doorway and onto the porch.

Before the missile started its return trip, he picked up the baby and threw her over the porch's low railing. Then he vaulted over himself.

The drop was about a dozen feet. It wasn't a bad fall because of the steep slant of the hill beneath the porch's cantilever supports. The damp earth was soft.

Like barrels, they rolled down the incline. They were a long way from the building when the missile came back and exploded.

As pieces of boards and other junk rained down, Rick tried desperately to find the baby to protect her.

Floundering in the fog, he grabbed onto something soft and feminine, and he all but puked when he discovered he'd grabbed Louise instead of the baby.

That goddamned lucky Louise.

As the baby went over the low railing, she deliberately bumped into Louise and knocked her over.

"I had to," the baby told me afterward. "She's my aunt—and I love her."

And, of course, she felt obligated to Louise for saving her life when Saddlebag Two wanted to kill her.

It only took Louise about two seconds to put the blame for the missile foul-up on Rick. She went into an insane rage. She groped around in the fog until she found her handgun on the side of the hill.

She shot Rick.

Very calmly, the baby stepped over to Louise and took the gun away from her.

She shot Louise.

☆ ☆ **38** ☆ ☆

AUNT PAM

I couldn't believe how neatly TimTomTon tidied up all the details.

No one outside official circles even knew an attempt had been made on the president's life.

The baby told me Saddlebag One was the brains behind the coverup.

I went along with all the drivel they handed out because they promised to keep the baby from ever being mentioned.

The TV, newspapers, and other media did a lot of digging on their own and came up with some really stupid stuff. But mostly they presented the wrong facts exactly as released by the press officers.

The heavy fog that hung around for the next two days

helped TimTomTon set up its cover stories. A defective butane storage tank had blown up on the Ellington ranch, destroying half the stables and killing three horses.

No other casualties had occurred because the Ellingtons were in Chicago. Their two hired hands had been away for an hour or so on errands in town.

Twisted pieces of blown butane tank were photographed by the press. TimTomTon did one hell of a job hauling away the Ellington's new butane tank and replacing it with the wreckage of an identical model.

Two days later, officials identified the body of a tramp found dead in El Dorado Park. There was no connection between his death and the explosion on the nearby ranch.

The tramp was identified as George Chung Hong, an alcoholic cook fired some months previously from a Chinese restaurant in Los Angeles. While lying drunk in the park, he'd been kicked in the head by a runaway horse.

A week after the explosion, the White House announced the death in Brazil of Cornelius J. Mark, one of the president's deputy secretaries. While en route to São Paulo for trade talks, he'd been killed in the crash of a small Lear jet. The baby told me that not one White House correspondent ever discovered that Cornelius J. Mark was also Saddlebag Two.

No mention was ever made of Teodoro, Jerry, or Eduardo. It was as if they never existed. Getting rid of their remains and those of Saddlebag Two was no problem. There wasn't enough left of the four of them to fill an empty cottage cheese carton.

Disposing of the body of Dr. Sierra required elaborate planning. He'd been dumped in the horse stall beside the one Agnes had been in. Neither of those stalls was damaged in the blast.

The baby told me that TimTomTon decided to send the Sandinista government a strong signal of protest. The signal arrived in Managua in the form of two identical wooden crates. One crate contained the embalmed body of Dr. Sierra. The other crate stank like rotting fish because it contained the tidbits that were once Saddlebag Two, Teodoro, Eduardo, and Jerry.

The body of Rick's mother was handled with care and reverence. The funeral was held in a small Catholic chapel in Los Angeles. The service was private, with only three people in attendance. The baby couldn't attend because she was ill. I couldn't attend because I was taking care of her. The three who knelt together in the chapel were Rick, Agnes, and Saddlebag One. Rick's side was heavily bandaged because of his wound.

Afterward, Saddlebag One gave Rick two letters from the president. Both were in the president's own handwriting.

One letter was addressed to Richard Donald Moore and expressed the president's gratitude for services of great value performed for his adopted country. No details were given.

The second letter was addressed to his mother, Janine DuBois Mohr, M.D. It expressed the president's gratitude for Dr. Mohr's years of devoted service to impoverished crippled children in her adopted country.

While Louise was still recovering from her chest wound, she was admitted to Desert Memorial Hospital in the small town of Elda, Nevada. It is a private hospital for the criminally insane, and she was admitted under the name of Clara L. Bennett

Louise's hospital bills are paid monthly by cashier's checks drawn on the Third Central Bank of Washington, D.C. Although no such bank is listed in the capital's phone book, the checks are valid. They are expected to continue for the duration of Mrs. Bennett's hospitalization. Her type of mental illness can require years of treatment.

She isn't criminally insane, of course. Her confinement has spared the government the embarrassment of a sensational murder trial, which might have revealed many other embarrassments.

I don't see Louise very often because my visits always end with her screaming lies and accusations at me. She's confined in a lovely large room decorated in various shades of yellow. The door is steel and so are the bars across the windows.

I have wondered a lot about why Louise wanted so badly to kill the president. During our brief meetings in her hospital room, she never talks about it directly.

But from other things she has said, I believe there were many reasons—financial, political, and most of all emotional. She never forgave Reggie Ronson for spurning her advances. She hated him with a terrible passion.

After Reggie died, the man who was so much like him became the object of her bitterness. And as that man rose ever higher in world stature, her hatred increased tremendously.

There was never any reason for Louise to be told about the actions taken by the California courts. I was made conservator of all her properties and assets. I am paid a substantial management fee for these duties.

Each month I receive a plain envelope containing a check from the Third Central Bank of Washington, D.C. It's hush money. I don't need it, but it's nice to have.

The baby and I live very well in Louise's house. But not ostentatiously. No servants or anything like that. Just a cleaning woman and a gardener who come around a couple of times weekly.

I can afford French champagne, but I prefer Coors. I could eat steak and lobster, but I'd rather have salads, barbecued ribs, and ground chuck because those are the baby's favorites.

Immediately after the disaster on the Ellington ranch, the baby went to work in her computer lab as usual. But I could tell she wasn't well.

When Rick came around to visit, she was polite but withdrawn. On two occasions, she refused to see him.

I knew what was wrong. When Rick came around for about the sixth time, I decided to tell him. By then he knew it was all over between him and the baby. I gave it to him straight. The baby was never the same after she shot Louise. She became deeply depressed. I've never been able to convince her that she did the right thing.

At times, the baby turns it all around again in her mind

and believes she's Louise's daughter. She thinks she inherited her genius IQ from Louise.

Worst of all, she sometimes believes she also inherited Louise's criminal tendencies.

After sending one more report to the president, the baby resigned from the White House advisory staff.

Saddlebag One spent a week in Santa Barbara but couldn't talk her into continuing.

It broke her heart when he took away her supercomputer, the Pilot-M. As payment for past services, he let her keep the rest of her lab equipment.

For a month after that, Saddlebag One maintained armed security officers on our property. Then he withdrew them, saying they were no longer needed.

The lying son of a bitch. Insecurity is part of the baby's troubles. She has every right to be in constant fear that someone—perhaps an enemy of the president—will punish her for the work she did for four and a half years.

That fear will be with her the rest of her life. And it's all Saddlebag One's fault. If he'd done his job right, we'd still be safe and secure . . . and happy.

I still wake up nights with the same nightmare. I go into the baby's room and find her strangled, a steel wire tight around her throat.

On his last visit, Rick made a comment about the baby that I've never forgotten. He compared her to the swallow-tail butterflies that he loves to photograph while doing his nature studies.

"So beautiful," he said. "And so fragile."

I've seen those yellow swallowtails. As they flit around in the sunlight, they're the biggest and loveliest butterflies in the park. But if you catch one, it turns to dust in your hand.

I never believed Rick would be anything but a loser. I'm glad I was wrong. He's studying law in Los Angeles. And so is Agnes. They live in an apartment near UCLA. There's no talk of marriage, but it might happen.

I hope it does. Agnes is exactly the kind of woman Rick needs. It took him a long time, but he knows now that Agnes is the woman the baby can never be. If he does become a lawyer, he'll be a hell of a lot different from some I've known.

He'll be honest.

How do I know? About three weeks after all the tragedies at the Ellington ranch, Rick went into El Dorado Park to relax by watching the foxes. He saw one of the biggest males climb a tree. Then he came over to my house and told me about it.

"You half-wit," I laughed. "That's pure B.S."

It wasn't.

He showed me a photo in one of his nature books. It was the damnedest sight. A half-wit fox was shinnying up a tree.

Then he showed me something else. My artificial foot. He'd found it high in one of the park's sycamores.

Still stuffed inside was the vial of powder he'd never used for revenge on Dr. Sierra. With it were the six worthless pieces of bearer bonds, plus the torn piece worth $1 million.

Rick could've cashed it at any bank. But he didn't. He turned it in to the government.

He and Agnes decided they didn't want to go through life hiding from half-wit TimTomTon agents.

REO: No. 136
The Honorable Ronald Reagan
White House
Washington, D.C. 20500

Dear Mr. President:

After long and careful study, I have decided to resign as presidential adviser.

Please accept this letter as my official resignation. Unlike a resignation I tendered some time ago, this decision is irrevocable.

There are many reasons. But one stands out like a monument above all others.

Put simply, it is *failure*.

I have spent four years and four months in

presidential service. I have researched and composed over a thousand advisories. Many of them you acted upon positively, and this was rewarding and fulfilling.

But overall my work has been a failure.

I have done nothing to make the world a safer place, which was my goal.

The world, in fact, is now *far less* safe than it was four years and four months ago. I foresee that this condition will worsen.

You have ignored my warnings about SDI (Star Wars). The majority of scientific thought worldwide agrees that SDI will fail because it cannot be made perfect.

If 100,000 nuclear warheads are launched at the United States and SDI destroys 99,999 of them, the one that gets through will destroy incalculable multitudes of Americans. Worldwide nuclear war will follow, a war no nation can win.

Ironically, the trillions to be spent on Star Wars cannot prevent atomic war from being started by *a single individual*. Weapon technology has become so sophisticated that one person—carrying a nuclear weapon in a backpack—can destroy New York City.

Because of how I failed you, I cannot escape being an unwilling participant in such horrors.

I can no longer carry this mental burden.

You must accept my resignation.

Sincerely,
Ginny I. Johnssen

REO: No. 137
The Honorable Ronald Reagan
White House
Washington, D.C. 20500

Dear Mr. President:

I am grateful for your speedy reply and flattered by your unwillingness to accept my resignation.

Your arguments are persuasive. I am pleased that you still consider me an important national resource.

I cannot, of course, meet you in person because I would succumb to your well-know charisma and powers of persuasion.

This second letter confirms the irrevocability of my resignation.

By the time this reaches you, I will have left my family and my dearest friend and gone away. I am confident that all the forces of the White House will not be able to find me. I anticipate that even the CIA and TimTomTon will not succeed for a very long time.

It was kind of you to offer your own thoughts as to how you, as president, may have caused my resignation.

The fact that you were (and are) a professional actor has had no negative influence on my decision.

I have learned this unexpected *truth*: It is your *acting ability* that has become one of America's strengths. The way you have played your presidential role has made our nation stronger. Through your artful public relations, America is more respected throughout much of the world.

After you were wounded in the 1981 assassination attempt—and also after your cancer surgery in 1985—your stature increased a hundredfold in the eyes of the American people. This was because your bravery, your steadfastness and low-key quips produced a picture of a man with unique strength of character.

Were you an actor pretending to be a hero? America thought otherwise...and said so in the polls.

You asked for my assessment of your place in history, based on microprogrammed, mainframe analysis of world leaders during the past 2,000 years.

I place you among the top American presidents.

But I must warn you that your place among them will plunge if you and your advisers continue to think along the following lines:

Killing peasants in Nicaragua and burning their farms, is anticommunism.

A multi-trillion-dollar debt will go away.

Reykjavik was a great success (although the summit meeting collapsed without any agreements).

Women are second-class citizens.

The exchange of Soviet spy Zakharov for U.S. reporter Daniloff wasn't a swap.

Two hundred and forty-nine American marines died gloriously in Lebanon for their country.

Bombing Libyan civilians is a better solution than diplomacy.

Arming Iran and Iraq will bring peace.

Lying about the secret Iran/contras weapons manipulations will obtain the release of our hostages.

You asked, very considerately, if family problems influenced my decision to resign.

The answer is yes. I am ashamed of my Aunt Louise and ashamed of my stupidity in not realizing sooner that she was a great danger to you. She professed to be my mother. She was not. My mother is her sister, Pamela Astrid Johnssen, who has documentary proof (birth certificate) that I am her daughter. I feel quite certain that you have known for a long time that my father was Reginald Carlos Colombia, better known as your stand-in and friend Reggie Ronson.

Undoubtedly you have guessed by now that—having never met my father—I have regarded you as a father figure, and such thoughts have comforted me during the four years and four months of our association.

I have avoided meeting you face to face because in my mind I picture my father as resembling you very very much but with a slightly darker complexion. Were you and I to meet, that illusion would be in jeopardy.

You asked, again very considerately, if the recent assassination attempt and homicides near your ranch influenced my decision to resign.

The answer is an emphatic yes.

Because of my involvement, I am certain that I am a magnet that attracts danger to you. The assassins tried to reach you through me.

The CIA's strength wanes and waxes according to whether the nation is at war or peace. Those changes do not affect an informal organization that functions separately from the CIA and its subsidiary TimTomTon. This separate organization has no name but is generally known as the Secret Team. It is perhaps the most powerful policy-making agency in the United States.

In some ways, the power of the Secret Team exceeds that of the president.

The Secret Team's membership includes a handful of top executives of the CIA and National Security Agency, TimTomTon, White House officials and Pentagon chiefs in and out of uniform. No one knows exactly who these men are. The team's personnel changes from year to year, but its goals never change.

The Secret Team is responsible for many acts of political terorism throughout the world. Seemingly such acts are *never* instigated by the U.S.

Because of my advisories opposing your Nicaragua directives and Star Wars, I have been targeted for elimination by the Secret Team. I have also been targeted by elements hidden inside TimTomTon who survived its recent personnel purges. My family and friends have also been targeted.

By going away now, I hope to prevent harm from coming to my mother and the others closest to me. If I survive, I intend to seek psychiatric care to banish the delusions and layers of guilt acquired during the past four years and four months.

Mr. President, you can help me find the path back to stability by purging all traces of me and my work from all government and civilian files. I would consider it a great personal favor if you also order the dismantling of my data processing laboratories and the fortresses encompassing them near Santa Barbara and in other locations.

Unfortunately, nothing can be done to dismantle my conscience and the Pandora's box therein.

Because I love you like a father, and fear for your safety, let me offer this final advisory:

Your ranch security is *still* abominable.

The Secret Service *gambles* with your life each time you travel to or from Rancho Del Cielo in your entourage of nine vehicles.

The chances are *1 in 9* that you can be killed or hurt by an assassin.

The odds against you are *far worse* than the odds NASA gambled with when it launched *Challenger* and killed seven astronauts.

> Sincerely,
> Ginny I. Johnssen

Santa Barbara (Calif.) News Press,
News Brief, page 32:

The body of a young woman was discovered Tuesday morning on the beach near Stearns Wharf in Santa Barbara. Sheriff's deputies were unable to identify the woman, strangled with a steel wire.

Tedd Thomey, a California journalist and political analyst, is the author of nine novels and eight biographies which have been published in many languages worldwide. His most acclaimed book, THE BIG LOVE (Warner Books, 1986), was written in collaboration with Florence Aadland, the mother of Errol Flynn's 15-year-old-mistress.